MW01516145

The Donor

Don Perry

PublishAmerica

Baltimore

ISBN: 1-4241-9838-0
PUBLISHED BY PUBLISHAMERICA, LLLP
www.publishamerica.com
Baltimore

Printed in the United States of America

Acknowledgments

I would like to thank my parents, Don and Drudy, for their life lessons and support, which helped make this book possible. Thank you, Alyson, Samantha and David for putting up with all the long nights working at the computer. Vivian, thank you for letting me bend your ear and a very special thank you to Karen Baldino for all the work she did in support of a friend.

1.

The sheets of rain persisted as the wipers furiously made their way back and forth in a futile attempt to keep the windshield clear. Thunder boomed and lightning flashed through the dark sky. This storm was a big one and wouldn't be letting up anytime soon. He eased his foot off the gas as visibility went from bad to worse. The road was a familiar one, traveled every day for the past five years on his way to and from work. It was so familiar in fact, that he joked to himself that he could drive this way with his eyes closed, but he wouldn't be trying that today.

The lights from the vehicle coming the other way were barely visible. Struggling to see the shoulder, he eased the car over a little farther to the right. A quick glance at the speedometer told him that even 25 mph was too fast for the driving conditions. He tried to crank up the wiper speed, hoping they weren't already at full speed. He was disappointed to find that they were. Grabbing the steering wheel, he pulled himself up closer to the dashboard hoping that the new vantage point would improve visibility.

As the two vehicles passed, a wave of water hit his windshield with a thud. Suddenly blinded, he instinctively turned the wheel to the right and hit the brakes. It took only a few seconds for the overburdened wipers to remove the additional water, but it seemed like forever. The car started to shake as the rumble strips suggested he had overcompensated. The rearview mirror showed only faint taillights, so he eased the vehicle back to the left and into the driving lane or at least where he thought it should be.

The 24-hour convenience store came into view as he rounded the corner. This wasn't one of those big stores with rows of gas pumps and a mini supermarket inside, but it was the only store on this 10-mile stretch of road, and that made it his favorite. Relieved that he would get a short respite from his drive, he pulled in, as he did every day, to get his morning breakfast, a cup of coffee and a package of five mini white powdered doughnuts.

The parking at the small island of four gas pumps provided some temporary shelter from the driving rain. The corrugated plastic roof kept off the worst of the elements but it had several pretty bad leaks. Leaving the car running, he grabbed his briefcase and put it over his head and made a quick dash across the 20 foot expanse that stretched from the islands roof to the front door. It didn't take long to get there but he was soaking wet as he opened the door and made his way inside.

"Pretty bad out there!" commented the attendant.

"Very bad," he replied, half heartedly wiping his feet on the mat. "It's so hard to see that I almost pulled over to wait until it let up. Is Chief off today?" he inquired of the new attendant.

"Chief?" asked the attendant, "Who's Chief?"

"He's the guy that's been here every morning for the past year. I don't know his real name. I just call him Chief, kind of like my nickname for him."

"Oh you mean Kamar! He quit. After what happened last week, he couldn't handle it anymore. Bad dreams, just kept coming and coming," the attendant explained

"The young girl was a friend of mine," he answered back. "You hear about things like that on the news or you read about them in the paper. You never, for one minute, think something like that will happen to you, let alone someone you know."

As he headed toward the coffee machine, he saw a set of headlights pull in. The lights disappeared from the storefront window as the vehicle headed towards the back and side of the store. Odd, he thought watching his cup begin to fill, why wouldn't they park near the pumps and take advantage of the protection offered by the roof on a day like today. With his coffee cup now full, it was time to get the second course of his two-course breakfast. As he was reaching for the doughnuts, the sound of the rain intensified as the door opened. Both he and the attendant turned to see who came in.

A man dressed in dark clothes wearing a stocking over his head stood in the doorway. "Give me everything in the cash register and be quick about it," he instructed the attendant raising his gun. "You, by the coffee machine, over here," the masked burglar instructed as he tilted his head towards the location he wanted him. "Come on, come on, hurry up!"

Everything was moving in slow motion now. The clock on the wall read 6:20 a.m. and right underneath, *You can't win if you don't play* scrolled across the mini electronic marquee. The attendant hurriedly emptied the register and handed over the contents.

"Please don't hurt me," he pleaded as the burglar took the money from him. "Get in the back room," the burglar instructed.

As both men headed to the back room, the assailant looked away from the attendant and directly into the eyes of the man holding his coffee—"Not you," he commanded, "You stay put." The attendant made his way quickly to the back room and was locked in.

His hand started shaking uncontrollably. He hardly noticed the hot coffee that was spilling on his hand as he watched the man walk towards him raising the gun. "Nothing personal," he said removing the stocking. The barrel closed to within inches of his forehead. "You just came too close." He saw the trigger finger tighten. Just as the gun went off, Brett sat up.

Sweating and shaken, he looked at the alarm clock—three thirty in the morning. He cupped his hands and rested his head in them for a minute, hoping and praying to discard and forget the images he had just seen.

This was the third time, in as many days, that Brett had this exact same dream. Each time they started he tried to wake himself with absolutely no success. The dream always started the same way. He was driving in a torrential rain storm, getting splashed by the other car, and getting coffee. But with this last dream, the ending had gone a little farther. In fact, now that he was thinking about it, each of the dreams had progressed just a little bit farther. Strange he thought, the exact same dream every time. The ending building upon itself, getting a little longer, more vivid, and more real as each dream passed.

Like running from a monster, you can never run at full speed, only slow motion. This dream was a monster that placed him in a paralysis from the moment it started. It was like he was separated from his body. He was able to observe the happenings around him, but unable to do anything to influence the circumstances.

He had been having disturbing dreams for a long time but had been able to deal with them, or at least he thought he had. This dream sequence was just so different.

The fear he felt was so real. Was he only dreaming or did he really smell the coffee he was holding in the convenience store. He turned on the nightstand light to take a quick look at his right wrist; it seemed to burn a little.

Grabbing his lower right arm with his left hand he moved his right hand directly under the lamp. He open and closed it, rotated his wrist, and examined it from as many angles as he could think of. With shocking disbelief, he stared at his hand and it did in fact have some, ever so light, pink blotches that weren't there when he went to bed.

His mind started to race. Was it true what he had heard—if you die in a dream you die in real life? If someone had asked him that question several weeks ago he would have said it was the most ludicrous hypothesis he had ever heard. But now he wasn't so sure. *What if I hadn't woken up? How come I feel like I'm in the dream and not just having one? What is this thing going on with my right hand?*

Brett was scared and knew that he was going to need some help to sort this out. He was tired, so very tired, and now more than ever, needed some answers. His father had suggested that he seek professional help a few years ago when the dreams started but he resisted. Sitting there on his bed the last of his resistance melted away. He knew a few things for sure; it was just a dream, getting back to sleep would not be easy, and as soon as 9:00 a.m. rolled around he was going to make that phone call.

A watched pot never boils, Brett thought, as he tried to get back to sleep. The clock continued its march toward dawn, one deliberate minute at a time. After tossing and turning for an hour he resolved himself to the fact that he would be starting his day much earlier than he had planned.

2.

It was 9:00 a.m. when the phone in Joyce Davenport's office rang. The receptionist that answered the phone very politely informed Brett that they were not accepting new patients. He could try back in a few months or she would be happy to refer him to another psychiatric specialist.

Holding his ground, he explained to the soft, faceless voice that Doctor Davenport had seen his father a few years ago when his mother had died from a short battle with an aggressive form of breast cancer. When she was treating his father, it was suggested that she would be happy to see him. Brett knew this explanation was a long a shot at getting in to see her but it was the best he could do. Two years had passed, she wouldn't remember and probably wouldn't care at this point. To his surprise the receptionist asked him to hold the line.

Connected to the hold button was the elevator music. *Typical*, he thought to himself. Not his type of music but it was better than wondering if you'd been hung up on. A few minutes passed when the music was replaced with the receptionist's voice. Gloria gave Brett some unexpected news, the doctor would squeeze him in, and that she did in fact remember his father. She then asked permission to collect some basic information. With Brett's consent, a few questions came his way and then she confirmed his appointment for 4:30 that afternoon.

Brett arrived at the office building at 4:00 sharp. His father had always told him when he was young to operate on Lombardi time. That meant you were never late for an appointment. If you weren't there 15 minutes early, you were late already.

Pushing the elevator call button, two of the four doors immediately swung open and offered their services. Going to the closest, he stepped in and pushed 9. Final destination—Suite 915.

"What am I doing here?" he asked the emergency phone. A ding signaling he had just passed the 8ᵗʰ floor was the only reply. "Psychiatry isn't real medicine; it's the very *inexact* science of the mind, more like voodoo than medicine." *Ding.* "All I probably need is a dog." He smirked as the doors swung open to let him out.

"Let's see—off the elevators—take a right—third door on the left," he recited as he walked. Then, all of a sudden there it was, etched on a large brass plate with black lettering—*Joyce Davenport, MD, PHD Psychiatric Medicine.*

"Mr. Allen?" the receptionist inquired as he entered what was evidently the waiting room.

"Yes," Brett answered.

"Hi, I'm Gloria Johnson, Doctor Davenport's assistant."

Brett reminded himself that he should never try to imagine what someone looks like from hearing their voice. He always did it, and he was always way off. When he first heard Gloria's voice, he pictured a woman, mid 30s, about 5'5," slender with brown hair and an attractive face. At least he had the attractive face correct. Ms. Johnson appeared to be in her mid 50s; slightly on the chunky side and to say she was 5' would be pushing it. She was impeccably dressed, not one hair out of place, and had the warmest, most welcoming smile he had ever seen.

"Hi, Gloria, thanks for getting me in today."

She smiled, asked him to have a seat, provided some paperwork to fill out, and offered to bring him bottled water, which he graciously accepted. Sitting back at her desk Ms. Johnson picked up the phone and announced that Brett had arrived. "OK, Doctor," she replied. "Mr. Allen, Joyce will be with you shortly."

"Thanks, Gloria, and please call me Brett."

"OK," she responded through bright white teeth.

About ten minutes had passed when Brett slid the completed forms on Gloria's desk. She thanked him with a smile and Brett returned to his seat. The waiting room was washed in soft colors and tastefully decorated. There were several plants, some hanging and some in floor pots. As he examined his surroundings, he wished he could decorate his own apartment as nice as the room he was in.

"Brett—Hi, Joyce Davenport, won't you come in?" she asked from her now open door.

"Hi, Joyce," Brett acknowledged rising from his comfortable seat. Starting to feel a little uncomfortable he wondered if coming here was the right thing to do. As he walked into her office, he wondered if his uneasiness showed in his demeanor. She remained at the doorway and smiled as Brett passed. She then closed the door behind him.

"Am I in the right place?" Brett asked, "There's no couch in here."

Joyce giggled in response "Yes, you're in the right place. I don't have a couch in here for two reasons. My back gets sore when I have to lean over too much and I've found more loose change in chairs than I ever have in a sofa."

A good sense of humor, he thought, as he chuckled, his apprehension waning.

"Please have a seat," she suggested, pointing to a plush high back chair.

Brett complimented her on the appearance of the office as she took the chair across from him. It was a nice office, very professional yet not business like. It could have been someone's living room, minus the sofa and television of course.

Joyce was an attractive woman whose appearance reminded Brett of someone you would see on the cover of a magazine; not one of those high fashion magazines; something more on the wholesome side, such as a parenting magazine or something similar. What surprised him the most was that she didn't look *clinical*. She was tall but not willowy with auburn hair that rested gently on her shoulders. Business casual was her preferred attire and it suited her well. His dad had told him that she was more of an Ivory girl. Brett was too young to have ever seen those commercials and didn't know exactly what that meant, but now having seen her he had a pretty good idea that it meant a naturally pretty woman. It was not like some movie stars you see in candid photographs whose appearance can be startling without all the makeup. As they were easing into conversation, it was apparent that they liked one another. They just seemed to click.

Brett began to explain his dreams and how they were affecting him as she listened intently. Joyce had an excellent memory and knew a little bit about his childhood from the conversations she had with his father. She asked him to talk about anything that happened prior to his mother's death that he considered to be traumatic. For Brett that would be an easy one. As he began, Joyce mixed Michael and Brett Allen's stories together and got a pretty good idea of what happened that day.

3.

Twelve years ago…

Brett knew this was going to be a great day; after all he was now officially a teenager. His gaze fixed on an empty beaker in his junior high science class while he daydreamed about being a big league baseball player. Mrs. Williamson's voice bounced its way in and out of recognition. "OK, children, 15 minutes left." *I don't need to learn this stuff,* he thought, *I'm never going to need it when I grow up.* Brett's gaze shifted back to his test paper. Twenty questions about photosynthesis sat on the desk staring back at him.

"It's a good thing these are multiple choice questions," he mumbled as he tapped his pencil, "Maybe I'll be able to pass this test and finish the year with a C. That would make Mom and Mrs. Williamson happy." He could still remember the talk he had with his mother when she saw the last report card.

"Brett, can you come down to the kitchen for a minute, honey?"

"Sure thing, Mom, I'll be right there." He took off his baseball glove and tossed it on the bed. On the way out of his bedroom, he took a quick glance at his favorite picture. His father and he were sitting right behind the first base dugout at Fenway Park watching the Red Sox win the final game of a three game series against the Yankees. A smile broke out on his face as he made his way down the stairs to the kitchen.

As he rounded the corner to enter the kitchen, his mother turned to greet him. She cast a warm smile his way and opened her arms for a hug. He quickly walked across the room, arms stretching and opening along the way. Most kids his age didn't really appreciate the hugs and kisses of their parents. They thought that type of affection was for babies, but he loved it.

"Mmmm, I love you, Brett," Donna Allen said to her son as she gave him a warm hug and rubbed his back.

"I love you too, Mom," he replied, responding to her hug with a gentle squeeze.

"Hey, guess what I have for you?" she asked playfully.

"A new baseball glove?" he replied, hoping it was the right answer.

"No," she said, shaking her head trying to control the urge to giggle. "What's the one thing you always ask me for when you get home from school?"

He took his head off his mother's shoulder and looked at her a little disappointedly, "That's an easy one mom, chocolate chip cookies."

"Right!" she said placing her hands on his shoulders releasing him from their hug, "but today I'm saying yes. Go grab a seat at the table and I'll get you some. Do you want a glass of milk with them?"

"Yes a glass of milk too, please!" he said taking his seat at the table.

Just as advertised the cookies arrived with a big glass of cold milk. Donna sat down next to her son. "We got your report card today. It looks like you're still having some trouble in Mrs. Williamson's science class. Your dad and I know it's a tough subject for you and that you've really tried hard to bring up your grade. We're thinking that it might help if you had a tutor."

"What's a tutor?" Brett asked in the middle of finishing his second cookie.

"A tutor is special kind of teacher that works with just one person. They can really help. I had a tutor in high school for math and science," his mother explained hoping the fact that she had needed a tutor would make it an easier concept for Brett to grasp. "Those were my really tough subjects in school and without my tutor's help, I don't think I would have ever passed those classes."

"How can I have another teacher?" he asked. "My schedule at school is already full."

Donna looked into her son's eyes with sadness "Well, this would have to be done after school or on the weekends, which means you'd have to miss baseball practices, and some of your games." Tears welled up in Brett's eyes as she went on. "We know how much your baseball means to you and we're so sorry. Your father and I are just trying to do what's best for you."

"Please, Mom, please... Don't take away my baseball. I'll study even harder than before," he pleaded. "I'll ask Mrs. Williamson or even Mary Strut—she's a girl in my class that's real smart—yeah I can ask Mary. I'll ask her tomorrow if she can help me during study hall. Please Mom—anything but a tutor."

"OK, Brett. If it doesn't interfere with her work, if she agrees and if you both get Mrs. Williamson's permission, then I think we might be able to pass on the tutor for now. But those grades have to get better. Let me check with Dad when he gets home and talk it over with him."

Brett sprang up of his chair and wrapped his arms around his mother's neck and kissed her on the cheek. "Thanks, Mom!" He moved back to his chair and went to work on finishing his cookies.

As he was turning to the second and final page of the exam he glanced up at Mrs. Williamson. She was sitting at her desk, already correcting the tests that were handed in, including Mary Struts. "Two minutes left," she informed the class.

Brett took a look at his last questions. His face went pale as he shifted uncomfortably in the chair—fill in the blanks. He wasn't prepared for this.

The Light Reactions occur in the _____.

The Dark Reactions take place in the _____

How could she have fill in the blanks when all her other tests were multiple choice. The clock on the wall seemed to be moving faster. Time was running out. He remembered Mary telling him to relax when taking a test but she couldn't possibly mean now. Then it came to him—the rhyme she taught him. "Grana's are light—Stroma's at night. Photosynthesis reactions help us feel just right." When he was repeating it with her the first time he thought it was dumb; after the fifth time, he knew it was. But it worked, he remembered. He quickly wrote his answer for question 19 and 20. Putting his pencil down with a sigh of relief, the bell rang.

Mrs. Williamson got up from her desk and headed toward him. "Well, Mr. Allen... how do we think we did today?"

"I'm not sure," Brett answered back as the other kids filed out of the room headed for their lockers and a quick 2-minute, between-classes chat with their friends. "It was a pretty hard test."

"Yes it was. I also know you've been working real hard. I'm sure you did just fine. I'll correct your paper a little later and track you down during lunch period to give you the good news." She winked and smiled reassuringly as she picked up his paper and headed back to her desk.

The cafeteria seemed more crowded today than usual. Brett wasn't very hungry. He was more interested in finding his science teacher to see if he had passed his test. His entire summer depended on it. A passing grade meant he

15

could play baseball and have a normal summer. If he missed one question too many, summer school would be in his immediate future.

Finally after what seemed like forever, Mrs. Williamson walked through the cafeteria door. On her way over to the teacher's table, she gave a quick glance around the room and saw Brett waiting for her. She smiled and raised her index finger signaling him that she'd be with him in just a second. She leaned over and whispered something to Mr. Franklin, the history teacher, then started over towards Brett.

"Let's sit down over there," suggested Mrs. Williamson. As they walked over to the lunch table, he was trying to see something in her face to make him feel better but there was nothing. Even though he was a brand new teenager it was still really hard to figure out what the news was going to be.

As he was sitting down at the end of the lunch table, he could feel his heart racing. His whole summer hinged on the news his science teacher was about to tell him. The moment of truth had finally arrived.

"Are you ready for Babe Ruth this year?" she asked as a smile widened on her face. Without waiting for an answer, she gave him the good news. "Congratulations, you passed." In the split second that followed, he felt as if the weight of the world had just been lifted from his shoulders. He was right; this was going to be a great day.

Michael Allen had just left the sporting goods store with his son's birthday present, a new baseball glove. A glance at his watch told him he only had about 15 minutes in order to be there when Brett got home from school. He had taken the afternoon off. Something that was easy to do as the President of the company. Leaving work early didn't happen very often, but when it came to his son's thirteenth birthday, he decided to invoke executive privilege.

While heading for the car he reached into his suit coat pocket, a last minute check to make sure he had the second piece of the two-part birthday present. There was nothing there. Stopping dead in his tracks, his hand dug a little deeper. He shook his head in relief as his fingers found the two box seat tickets for tonight's Red Sox-Oriels game. The limited edition Ford Blazer answered obediently with two quick beeps of the horn as the door locks moved to the open position. Michael was walking a little faster than usual, almost running but not quite. Opening the door, he tossed the glove in the passenger seat, started his "truck" and headed for home.

As he eased his truck into the garage, he hit the remote and watched as the door closed behind him. The Blazer was so much larger than the Taurus he used to drive. Judging just how much room he needed to keep it from coming down on his new toy was still tricky. Donna was standing there watching him at what they called the *side door*, which led from the garage to the laundry room then right into the kitchen.

Donna greeted him the same way she had since they were married fifteen years ago, with a broad smile and a sultry voice. "Well, hello, handsome, care to come in?"

"I don't know, I've heard you had a jealous husband," he replied closing the driver's side door making his way towards her. "What if he comes home early?"

"If he comes early this is what he'll get." She wrapped her arms around him and gave him a warm, tender kiss.

"Being home early could be habit forming," he said with a chuckle.

"Not just for you," she answered back quickly as they made their way to the kitchen. "What time does the game start tonight?"

"Seven thirty, so I'm guessing we have to be out of here no later than six. That should give us just enough time for an early dinner and a piece of cake."

"He's going to love it," Donna said obviously excited for their son. "Now go make yourself scarce, he'll be walking through the door any second."

The bus stopped with the familiar sound of squeaky brakes. Brett made his way to the door and jumped from the last step to the sidewalk. He was really anxious to get home and give his mom the news about his test. The original plan was to run the half block home to deliver the good news but he wasn't quite feeling up to par so of he decided to walk instead.

He lived in a really nice neighborhood. Both sides of the street were lined with colonial houses accompanied with spacious and well-maintained yards. Something one would expect to find in an affluent Boston suburb. As he passed the McLaughlin's house, he noticed Mr. McLaughlin wheeling the lawn mower into the garage. He took a deep breath and inhaled the aroma of freshly cut grass. As he got closer to his house, he could see the badminton net in the back yard. That would be the center field wall for the whiffle ball field his dad had set up for tomorrow's annual tournament. This year would be the rematch of last years one run victory over Josh and Bob, his friends from little league that boasted they were an unbeatable combination. In last year's slugfest, Brett hit one over the net in the bottom of the ninth to secure a 17-16 win for him and his dad. Both teams knew that this year's game was going to be another close one and everyone was looking forward to it.

As he reached the front door, he felt an awful burning sensation just below the bottom of his throat. Hunched over with a grimace on his face, he rubbed his chest. *This must be what my mom calls heartburn,* he thought. He took a couple of deep breaths which seemed to provide him some relief. Then as quickly as it came the pain was gone.

"I'm home, Mom," he managed, swinging open the door.

"I'm in the kitchen, honey. How was school today?" Donna asked while placing the last candle on the birthday cake.

"You'll never guess what happened," he quickly fired back on his way to the kitchen "I passed Mrs. Williamson's science class. She corrected my paper right away and told during lunch."

A muffled, deeper voice came from the kitchen. "That kind of news would seem to warrant something a little extra special for a brand-new teenager."

"Dad, is that you?" Brett yelled out unable to contain the surprise and excitement he felt.

"It sure is, son!" Michael replied leaving the confines of the laundry room. "I thought I'd come home a little early today. I figured that maybe we could break this in before dinner," he went on, taking the glove from behind his back.

It was just what Brett wanted, a deep pocket, Rawlings ball glove.

"Before you two boys get started, dinner will be right at five today."

"Sounds great," Michael replied. "OK, Brett, go out in the garage and get two old baseballs and the glove oil. I'll run upstairs, grab an old belt and meet you back here. OK?"

"OK, Dad," Brett replied, heading out to collect the items they needed.

Brett unzipped the ball bag and dug around inside until he found the can of glove oil, then got two balls out, zipped up the bag and headed back to their meeting place, the kitchen table.

"Do you feel ok, Brett? You look a little pale," she said as she walked over and put her hand on his forehead, "You don't feel warm."

"I'm OK, Mom, I don't feel sick or anything just a little tired," he offered trying to ease her concern. "I didn't eat any lunch today, so I'm sure I'll feel better after dinner."

"Do you want something to munch on before dinner?"

"No thanks, Mom. I'm not really all that hungry."

"OK, but if you change your mind, you just let me know," she replied. "I also want to tell you how proud we are for what you've done at school. Passing science this year is such a big accomplishment. It was a lot of hard work and you stuck your nose right in there and got it done."

"Mary was a big help, Mom. If it wasn't for her, I think I'd have summer school this year," he said humbly.

"I'm sure that's true but you also had to be willing to do the work, the reading, reviewing and the studying," Donna replied. "Have you thought about getting a thank you gift for your friend Mary?"

"Can you help with that?" he pleaded. "I don't know what to get for a girl."

Donna smiled. "Sure I can, why don't we go to the mall tomorrow before your whiffle ball game and pick something out."

"OK. Will we be home before eleven? Josh and Bob will be here at eleven thirty; our game starts at noon."

"We can be," Donna answered. "As long as we're moving by nine."

Michael reappeared in the kitchen. "Got it," he said as he handed the belt over to Brett. "Remember how to do it?"

"I think so," Brett responded as he pushed the cap on the glove oil to the open position. "I've got to work it into the leather until it looks a little dark and wet." His fingers worked the oil into the new glove. Can you turn the oven on to 350?" he inquired of his father, who responded with a smile fulfilling his son's request.

It only took about twenty minutes for the smell of leather to seep its way out of the oven. Brett jumped up from his chair and set the timer for 5 minutes. Michael got the soldering iron, plugged it in and put it on the table. *What is that for?* Brett wondered as he sat down across from his father. He wanted to ask but decided he'd wait and see.

The buzzer went off. Brett grabbed an oven mitt, turned off the oven and retrieved the glove. Bringing it back to the table he tested the metal belt buckle with a quick tap of his finger. Yup, it was hot alright. Quickly rubbing the test finger with his thumb the heat dissipated. He carefully removed the belt and placed the glove on the table. The glove was warm but bearable to the touch.

"Can I see that for a minute?" his father asked. He swung the glove to his side of the table not waiting for an answer and grabbed the soldering iron. Brett didn't have a good view of what was going on but thought his name was being etched on the back.

"There we go," his father said, satisfied with his handy work. He slid the glove back to Brett. The mystery of the soldering iron was solved. Burnt into the back of the glove was a single letter, T. Brett looked at it trying to figure out what it meant but he was stumped. Seeing the look on his son's face Michael decided to explain.

"The *T* stands for think. Before each pitch, think about what you're going to do with the ball if it's hit to you. Sometimes the only difference between a win and a loss is a mental mistake and you don't want to lose because your head wasn't in the game. You have to be in the game on every play whether you're in the field, the batters box, on the bases or in the dugout. That's the difference between a good player and a great one."

Brett slid his hand into the glove as he contemplated his dad's words. It was still a bit warm near the fingertips but definitely ready for use and the *T* was easily visible. Think, he said to himself, Think.

"How does it feel?" Michael asked.

"It's still a little warm but it's really soft," Brett responded punching his fist into the pocket. The whole glove baking thing amazed him. You take a new glove, stiff as a board and bake it. What comes out of the oven is a glove that's instantly broken in, easy to close with your hand, and soft. What usually takes several weeks happens in just about a half hour. "I think it's ready if you are."

Unplugging the soldering iron they headed back for the garage. Michael grabbed his glove from its resting place on the shelf and Brett hit the button to raise the door. "We'll be out front, Donna," Michael called back to his wife. Brett stopped near the driveway while his Dad walked about twenty feet away in the front yard. They started having a catch, easy throws at first, to get the muscles nice and loose.

Michael reflected on his baseball career as the ball lazily made its way back and forth. He was a high school All American at the second base position and went to Oklahoma State University on a full athletic scholarship. He had good range, a strong arm, and set a school record his junior year with a .645 batting average. Several major league teams were interested in him until, during the last regular season game that year, he sustained a career ending knee injury, turning a double play. He knew his son not only had the desire but the talent.

"High sky today," Michael yelled over to his son.

"High sky?" Brett repeated.

"Yup," Michael went on to explain, holding the ball he just caught from his son. "No clouds up there. When a fly ball is hit on a day like today it's really hard to judge it. There's no clouds to give you a background so your depth perception is thrown off, makes it harder to get a good jump on it and a lot harder to catch. On a day like today, it's good to take as many fly balls in practice as you can get." He tossed the ball back.

"High sky," Brett repeated. "Back up, Dad, I'll throw you a pop up."

Michael backed up as his son reached back and threw the ball just as high as he could. He started to run back as the ball went a little higher and farther than expected. Barely managing to avoid the maple tree Donna had just planted earlier this spring he made the catch.

As he turned he saw that Brett collapsed on the ground. "Brett!" he yelled. "Brett," he tried again with no response from his son's still body. Running over to him, he screamed for Donna to call 911.

4.

The ambulance sped its way towards Boston Children's Hospital. Michael was sitting next to his son watching helplessly as the paramedics used the radio to pass along vital signs and symptoms to the Emergency Room staff. Michael bowed his head in despair and did something he hadn't done in a very long time, he prayed.

Donna was following close behind in the Blazer, barely able to see through the shroud of tears. *What's happening to my son? How come it's taking so long to get there? Why weren't people pulling over right away, like they were supposed to? Can't we go any faster?*

The ambulance slowed to a stop at a crowded intersection and wiggled its way through as drivers did their best to create a passable lane. "Dad?" Brett whispered as his eyes opened ever so slightly. Michael reached over and took his son's hand; hopeful that Brett wouldn't see the same fear in his eyes that he saw in his son's.

"I'm right here, son," the quiver in his voice more noticeable than he wanted it to be.

Brett's eyes slowly surveyed his surroundings. "I'm scared."

"Everything is going to be alright, son," Michael replied as convincingly as he could muster.

The paramedic quickly jumped in, seizing the opportunity. "Brett, my name is Jim; can you tell me if anything hurts?"

Brett nodded his head and pointed to his chest.

"Does it hurt anywhere else?" Jim asked probing for more information.

Brett shook his head no as he drifted back into unconsciousness.

"Do you know what's wrong, Jim?" Michael asked after Jim finished relaying the information to the hospital.

"I'm not sure, he seems to have stabilized and that's a good sign. Just try and relax as best you can, were almost there."

Donna pulled in right behind the ambulance. Spotting a place to park, she whipped the truck in and hurriedly made her way to the ambulance.

A team of medical staff met the ambulance at the entrance. "Sir, go into the waiting room. We'll be with you just as soon as we can," instructed a woman from the team as Michael tried to follow them in. "Sir, please go the waiting room," she repeated anxiously as Michael stayed with the group. Finally he relented. Donna ran over joining him, tears streaming down her face as they watched the automatic doors close and their son disappear into the hospital. He pulled her as close as he could, her body heaving with each uncontrollable sob. *I have to be strong,* he thought. *I have to be strong for us all.*

Time passes very slowly in the waiting room. Minutes can seem like hours and hours like days. Michael started to make his way to the triage nurse for the second time but before he could get there she shook her head in that "no news" way, that only nurses can. He made his back to the bank of plastic chairs. Donna stared aimlessly out of the window watching the cars go by on the distant highway. In the reflection, she caught a glimpse of someone coming over to them.

"Mr. and Mrs. Allen, I'm Dr. Franklin, Chief Cardiologist for the hospital."

"How is he? Is he going to be OK?" Donna asked turning to address the doctor.

"What wrong with him, Doctor?" Michael quickly added.

"He's doing OK all things considered. We're still running some tests. Can you take a walk with me?"

Donna and Michael followed the doctor into a smaller room that offered more privacy and sat down on one of the sofas.

"I'm afraid the news I have for you isn't very good" Donna burst into tears as the doctor continued, "It seems that your son's heart muscle is deteriorating and were not sure what's causing it."

"What does that mean?" Michael asked.

"It means that right now, his left ventricle can't pump blood adequately out to the body. We're also a little concerned that the muscle degeneration will spread to the other chambers of his heart."

"Please tell me my son is going to be OK," Donna pleaded wiping the sniffle from her nose.

"Right now he's doing OK. His condition is critical but stable. We've moved him to ICU to keep a close eye on him. The results of the tissue samples indicate that, in all likelihood, he'll need a heart transplant."

"A heart transplant! For God sakes he's only thirteen years old!" Michael exclaimed in disbelief.

"I'm so sorry," a compassionate Dr. Franklin responded. "The erosion of the heart tissue is something we just can't, at least right now, explain. At its current rate of progression we have a window of about twelve to eighteen months."

Michael sat down on the couch next his wife. *This can't be happening*, he thought. *It just can't be happening.* "Twelve to eighteen months? Does that mean if he doesn't get a transplant by then, he'll die?"

"Even if we can determine what's attacking his heart tissue and can stop it, I'm afraid that there's already been enough damage that a transplant is probably our only option."

"Can we see him, Doctor?" Michael asked trying to control his emotions.

"Sure, I'll take you to his room," he offered, leading them out of the room. "Just so you're prepared, he'll be groggy, maybe even asleep and he's hooked up to quite a few monitoring devices."

Donna was on the verge of collapse as they got up to follow. With most of her strength drained she rested her head and most of her weight on Michael's shoulder as they made their way to the elevators.

The scene in Brett's room was just as the doctor described. A bank of machines had their outstretched, wiry fingers placed all over his body. It seemed like something from a science fiction movie. Each mechanical sentinel offered its own unique resonance, informing everyone, that they were standing guard over the little boy.

Brett was in fact asleep, as Dr. Franklin stepped aside and allowed the Allens to enter first. It was probably a blessing given the shape his parents were in. A nurse was making some notes in Brett's chart. She turned as they entered and saw the doctor give his familiar head bob that told her to leave the room.

"Mommy and Daddy are here, honey," Donna whispered as she massaged his forehead "We love you so much!"

At first Brett was unresponsive. Donna noticed a small tear escape from her son's closed eyes. "Mommy," he called out in an unsteady, whispered cry for help.

"I'm right here," her soft and trembling voice responded, hoping she could comfort her son but there was no response.

"It's probably better if we let him rest; he's pretty heavily medicated and will probably be in and out like this until tomorrow," Dr. Franklin interjected. "You're welcome to stay with him while he's here. The accommodations are pretty comfortable. We've found that it does wonders for both the children and parent's emotional state."

"We'd like to stay," Michael responded.

"Good. I'll make the arrangements and inform the staff. I'd also like to ask you both to be available for a meeting Monday morning at nine with myself and our transplant team. That will give us the remainder of the weekend to finish up our tests and have a better picture as to how we'll want to proceed. I have to attend to some other patients. I'll be back later to check on Brett."

Michael drove home to get some clothes and personal items for their weekend stay with Brett. Turning into the driveway, he saw Brett's glove sitting right there on the lawn; exactly where it was a few hours ago when tragedy struck. Life can change so fast he thought as he brought the vehicle to a slow stop. In the blink of eye they went from having a birthday celebration to needing a heart transplant. As he bended over to pick up the glove, the letter *T* reminded him there were some things he had to do.

Michael opened the front door. It just didn't feel the same walking into an empty house. Going up the stairs to Brett's room he didn't really feel like he was home. No "hello handsome" no "Dad, do you want to have a catch after supper?" There was nothing, nothing but unsettling silence.

A house is just a house, he thought. It's the people that you share it with that make it a home. Sitting down on Brett's bed, he placed the glove on his son's pillow and wept deeply. The phone rang. Collecting himself, thinking it might be Donna, he picked it up.

"Hello."

"Hi, Michael, it's your dad. Is my grandson running around there somewhere? I want to wish him a happy thirteenth birthday?" There was an uncomfortable silence. "Is everything OK?"

"Dad, Brett's in the hospital. He's pretty sick."

"In the hospital, what happened?"

Michael proceeded to describe the events of the day as best he could. His father listened, silent and attentive.

"I'm going to get the next flight out of Dulles and be there sometime tonight," George Allen replied after hearing the graveness of the situation.

"We'd love to see you, Dad, and I know Brett would too but it might be better if you could wait until we know a little more. We're going to be living at the hospital for at least the next couple of days anyway. I promise I'll call right after our meeting with the transplant team on Monday and certainly before that if there's any change."

"OK, Michael, if you think that's best. I'm going to make a few calls myself. You call me right away if you need *anything*. You have all my numbers, right?"

"Yeah, I've got them all. I've got to call Donna's parents and a few of Brett's friends that were supposed to come over tomorrow, and then head back to the Children's Hospital."

"OK, Mike. You go on and get back. I love you, son. Tell Donna and Brett I love them too."

"I love you too, Dad, and I'll be sure to tell them."

George Allen was a prominent Senator from Massachusetts that was well liked and highly respected in his home state and Washington. Having chaired several, high visibility committees, he became known as a no-nonsense, straight to the point, get it done Senator. He played the political game early in his career but that was behind him now.

As Senator Allen's influence and power increased, so did his views on political and social issues. He didn't beat around the bush and hated the way every issue somehow became a political football to get votes or be used as ammunition to prevent people from getting reelected.

When he said he was going to make a few calls that usually meant he was going to bring all his power and influence to bear on a problem, cut through the red tape, and get results. This time the situation was a personal one. If necessary, he would cash in what was left of his IOU's to get them what they needed. Senator Allen got his personal address book from the desk drawer and started "influencing."

On Monday morning, Michael and Donna met with transplant team promptly at 9:00 a.m. The team had decided to release Brett in the afternoon. He would of course be taking with him a slew of medications, instructions on what to take and when, along with a list of recommended activities he could safely partake in given his condition. The team explained what would be involved in the procedure, how to prepare and what they could expect as far as the recovery period was concerned. Much to their amazement Brett had already been added to UNOS (United Network for Organ Sharing) waiting list and was placed at the top of the hospital's transplant list. "Thanks, Dad," Michael whispered to himself.

* * *

"I was pretty fortunate," Brett went on. "They found a donor about a month later and I got a new heart. It was a hard road getting back to being a normal kid. I had to make a lot of adjustments. Probably the biggest one for me at the time was missing baseball."

"When you had to put baseball aside, what did you do to fill the void?" Joyce asked.

"I got really interested in science, almost obsessed. I never liked it in school and barely passed my classes. After I was somewhat over the worst part of my recovery, I couldn't get enough of it. I read everything I could get my hands on. Biology and chemistry text books from the library, science magazines, you name it. I asked my father to get me my very first chemistry set and was hooked. When I finally got back in school, those classes were really easy for me. Almost like an elementary school review."

"That's interesting," Joyce related with a touch of surprise. "It's not unusual for people, when they have to give something up, to compensate the loss with something else. Swap one vice for another if you will, but that doesn't seem to fit in your case. What did you do with your newly discovered interest?"

Brett paused for a second. "This is the really weird part. When I finally got back in school, I breezed through every single freshman class. My guidance counselor was amazed. He had me take the Scholastic Assessment Reasoning Test just to try and get his arms around how well I was doing. I scored 780 in math and 730 in verbal for a total SAT score of 1510 out of 1600. No one knew what do with me. A week or so later a person from Harvard arranged for me to take some special exams. The rest, as they say, is history. I finished my bachelor's in biology when I was sixteen, master's in molecular biochemistry at seventeen and topped it off with a PhD just before my 19th birthday. I still love baseball mind you, but my real passion is scientific research."

Joyce couldn't hide the astonishment she was feeling. "That is truly amazing!" She just kept looking at him, searching for something to say. That moment was very similar to that *uncomfortable silence* some people experience when they go out on a first date.

"Wasn't that tough on you, Brett?" she asked finally breaking out of her trancelike state, "I mean you left all of your friends and classmates behind and were thrust into an extremely challenging academic environment in the blink of an eye. Stressful circumstances to say the least."

"I didn't feel that way at all," Brett said a bit defensively. "It was like I hadn't eaten in a week and someone finally brought me a steak dinner. The only hunger I had was for knowledge; the more I immersed myself the less important everything else became. I tried to stay involved with my friends but I just couldn't stay interested in the things they wanted to do. All I wanted to do when I was with them was to hurry up and finish whatever it was we were doing so I could get home and do some more studying. I was much more interested in debating my biology professor than chasing girls and playing video games."

"Sounds like you withdrew a little from your surroundings, what kind of social activities did you take part in?" Joyce asked.

"I didn't withdraw at all," Brett rebutted. "My circle of friends changed, that was all. I was spending time with people that were a little older and had similar academic interests. I still went to see movies, occasional played video games, went to Sox games and even chased a few young ladies around campus." He chuckled casting a smile Joyce's way. "Never really caught any though. I would say my social life was fairly normal if you discount the age difference"

"When you put it that way, I'd have to say I agree," Joyce acknowledged returning Brett's smile. "I'm going to make an assumption that you're pursuing your passion and working in the scientific community. What exactly is it that you're doing?"

"I'm a research scientist at Nelson Pharmaceuticals," Brett replied.

"I'm familiar with them," Joyce interjected.

Brett continued, "Then you probably know they're the industry leader in the development and manufacturing of cancer treatment drugs and anti-rejection medications. I'm there working on developing a universal anti-rejection medication to help people who've received organ transplants, just like me. This new medication, once I get it figured out, will require just one injection at the time of transplant with a booster perhaps ten years later. It may in fact, not even require a booster.

"I won't bore you with too many details. I can tell you it will save people a ton of money and give them some freedom from the normal 'every twelve-hour' protocol. I'm pretty sure that once we're there, the research will have some bleed over into other diseases and help there as well since this medication will operate not *at* the biological level but *within* it. Let's not leave out the most important part….I'm having fun!"

Joyce really liked the fact that Brett was down to earth, not just in the way he carried himself but in his conversation. He was highly intelligent but spoke on the layman's level. He didn't try to impress people with his scientific jargon or use $500.00 dollar words to subtly let those around him know he was a smart guy. Maybe, she thought, he purposefully spoke and acted the way he did so people wouldn't know. Her quick summation; a very nice likeable guy, humble, sincere, and sharper than any tack she's ever had sit across from her.

"I'm no scientist," Joyce candidly admitted, "but it sounds as though this could revolutionize medicine as we know it today."

"Sure could," Brett agreed. "We're still a long way off, but every day we get a little closer."

"How many people do they have working on that project?" Joyce inquired truly interested.

"Just me right now, but I'm actively looking for an assistant," Brett stated. "All of Nelson's research teams are small. I guess they limit team size for security reasons."

"Security reasons?" Joyce echoed skeptically. "I'm not sure I understand."

"I'm not sure I do either," Brett confessed sharing her skepticism. "I can tell you that I had to take a polygraph and sign a bunch of proprietary mumbo jumbo, non disclosure agreements and the like. My thought about that, and I'm not a businessman, is that Nelson got into the pure research aspect of things to keep discoveries *in house.* This helps to seal in the information and not share it, which is common practice with university level research programs. Once a discovery is made, the drug development phase can begin under their proprietary umbrella. When they're certain the drug works, they announce it and get FDA approval. This gives them a few years before the generic versions hit the market. Assuming of course, that one of its two hundred research partners doesn't find it first."

"So they get top dollar for a few yew years before they have to lower prices to compete with the generics," Joyce added.

"If we're assuming my theory is correct then we've hit the nail on the head," Brett said sneaking a look at his watch. "So the two-person team would be a way, of sorts, to minimize the possibility of trade secrets leaking out."

"So they must only hire the absolute brightest minds to run these programs," Joyce said, a touch of adulation in her tone. "I noticed you were glancing at your watch. Do you have to be somewhere, Brett?"

"No," Brett answered, embarrassed he was caught. "I just didn't know how long our meeting was supposed to last. It's almost six-thirty."

"Six-thirty, I lost all track of time," Joyce confessed. "I usually have Gloria buzz me at the one hour mark. She asked to leave a little early to run some errands so I told her to head out after you got here. I'm a little surprised, usually after an hour people are gnawing at the door to get out."

"I'm sorry, Joyce," Brett said in an outburst of laughter. "I just love your sense of humor."

"Ditto," Joyce responded with a broad smile as she stood up signifying their time together had concluded.

"I'm going across the street to grab a bite to eat. Care to join me?" Brett offered getting up from his chair. "I know there's probably some sort of professional taboo about that kind of thing but I'm hungry and would enjoy the company."

"Yes there is," Joyce admitted, "that professional taboo, as you put it."

"I'll tell you what," Brett interrupted not allowing Joyce to continue, "I'm going to head over to that diner across the street. If you just happen to come in and I just happen to see you, then, at least from my vantage point, it eliminates that doctor/patient thing. Just think about it. OK?"

"I'm not real sure about that, Brett," Joyce said hesitantly slowly making her way to the door. "Let's at least agree that we'll meet here next week. In the meantime, I'd like you to keep a notepad next to your bed and when you have your dreams, regardless of their relevance to the ones we discussed, write down everything you can remember and bring your notes along. How's that sound?"

"That sounds OK to me. I actually started doing that about a year ago. For some strange reason I thought it might help," Brett admitted. "Something told me you'd be asking for something like that. I have the notebooks, but left them in the car. As far as next week goes," he continued. "Do you want me to call Gloria in the morning and get penciled in?"

Given the nature of his profession, Joyce wasn't surprised that Brett had documented his dreams.

"No need to call Gloria, we can schedule it now, assuming of course, that you already know your schedule," Joyce offered knowing her schedule was pretty open for the remainder of the week.

"My formal schedule is pretty much the same every day. In to work at six a.m. and out at three. I usually stay until about seven or so, but as far as Nelson is concerned, when three o'clock rolls around, I'm off the clock. So I'd say any day at 4:00 would work out just fine."

"If you really want to get to the bottom of this we can start tomorrow" Joyce said in an invitation/question combination. "It would also be very helpful, if you wouldn't mind, to let me have a look at those notes before our next meeting."

"Tomorrow is fine for me, same time?" Brett asked.

"Yes, same time," Joyce replied.

"OK, as far as the notes go, I'll be taking a look at them while I'm having dinner across the street," Brett stated suggestively watching Joyce, waiting for a response.

Joyce knew she would enjoy having dinner with Brett and felt as though she knew him a little based on the extensive conversations she had with Brett's father during his course of treatment. She remembered feeling very sad for the young Brett Allen as his father shared as best he could the emotional turmoil they experienced when Donna Allen passed away. Brett was an interesting person, easy to talk with, and his story was intriguing.

Joyce gently shook her head form side to side, weighing and deciding, as she struggled with what Brett called the *professional taboo* thing. She really wanted to get her hands on those notes and ignored Brett's suggested form of bribery. She actually thought it was both cute and clever.

"Well," Joyce began, her decision finally made. "I suppose that if I happen to see you there."

"Great!" Brett said, cutting her off with a charming smile. "I'm starved!"

Joyce returned his smile with a nervous one of her own. She had always kept a safe distance from her patients for obvious reasons and wasn't feeling real good about skirting the ethics issue. As Brett walked by her to leave, she told herself that in a compelling case like this maybe bending the rules a little was the right thing to do.

5.

Brett took a seat in one of those two-person booths next to the front window that provided him a good view of patrons as they came and went. He hadn't been sitting for more than a second when a waitress appeared, seemingly out of nowhere.

"Can I get you something to drink?" the waitress asked.

"I'd really love a glass of cranberry juice if you have any," Brett replied.

"Sorry," the waitress said, scrunching her nose and shaking her head. "We have orange and grape juice."

"Grape juice would be fine," Brett said settling for second best.

Writing the juice down on her order tablet she continued, "Our specials for today are pot roast with mashed potatoes and carrots $11.95, hot pastrami sandwich—$7.00 and New England chowder $4.95. I'll be right back with your drink." Then as quickly as she came, she was gone.

Brett began flipping through the pages of his journals and spotted Joyce entering the diner. He placed his notes on the seat beside him and waived his hand to get her attention. Joyce spotted him right away and made her way to the booth. Brett stood up to greet her and waited until she sat herself before retaking his seat.

"Fancy meeting you here," Joyce said a little playfully, trying to keep everything in line with their agreed-upon departure from the rules.

"Frank's Diner, of all the places to bump into you," he responded following her lead.

There was the waitress again. "Hello, Doctor Davenport," she said with a smile, placing Brett's drink in front of him. "Would you guys like a few minutes?"

"Hi, Maryanne," Joyce replied as if seeing an old friend.

"I'm ready to order if Dr. Davenport is," Brett said

"I'd like the clam chowder and a glass of iced tea please," Joyce said wiggling a bit to get comfortable.

"I'll have the clam chowder too, Maryanne. Thanks," Brett said, completing their order.

As she finished writing the order down, she offered them both a smile and told them as she was walking away that their order would be right out.

"So, Joyce, tell me," Brett inquired, "what do you like to do when your not working?"

"I really enjoy painting. Watercolors mostly, I find the oils too messy for my liking," Joyce replied.

Brett went on to explain how he had tried painting once. Mostly out of curiosity, more than anything else. He had seen some guy on one of the public television channels painting with a broad knife and a brush more suited to painting a house than a canvas. So he figured he'd give it a shot. They both laughed when Brett told her about his first master piece as a bunch of "crimson" and "burnt sienna" tossed mercilessly on an unsuspecting canvas that could only be described as a modern art masterpiece.

Their conversation was continuous and pleasant. It was only interrupted by the occasional need to take a spoonful of soup before it got to cold and Maryanne asking if everything was OK. It was Joyce this time that was caught sneaking a look at the clock and Brett couldn't resist.

"I noticed you were glancing at your watch. Do you have to be somewhere Joyce?" Brett recited with a grin.

Joyce had a quick wit and fired right back, "No. I just didn't know how long our dinner was supposed to last. It's almost eight-thirty."

"Now where have we heard that before?" was their joint response.

"You're right, it is getting late," Brett admitted, reaching for the notes sitting beside him.

"As promised," he said, handing them to her and signaling Maryanne to bring him the check. "Probably not a best seller," he added grimly.

Joyce smiled as she took his one year collection of notes. "Anything in here you want to warn me about before I start going through these?" she asked jokingly a little surprised by the four volume set.

"Nothing you need to worry about, but no-doze is highly recommended," he said in an attempt to prepare her for the boredom that awaited her.

Brett left a twenty on the table as they headed for the door. Walking Joyce to her car, he told her what a great time he had and how surprisingly easy it was to talk with her. Joyce responded in kind and reminded him of their appointment at 4:00 the next day.

Brett bid her a good night as he closed her door. She returned a warm smile through an open window as she backed out. Brett was feeling better. He watched as she pulled out onto the street and headed for home.

Driving home, he was thinking about what his father had told him about getting professional help. *Dad was right,* he said to himself, *this can really help me. And Joyce, well, she's an ivory girl for sure.*

Joyce pulled into her driveway ready to execute her plan. She'd make some hot tea, sit on the couch and review some of Brett's journals. She didn't really know what she was looking for but was hopeful they would at least offer some insight into what was going on in Brett's subconscious mind.

Joyce entered the house and put her purse and Brett's journals down on the deacon's bench in the entryway and started some water boiling for her tea. Changing into her summer pj's, she returned to the whistle of the tea pot. She opened the cabinets and collected a coffee mug, tea bag, and a jar of honey. A two-minute steep, a teaspoon of honey and a quick stir made for her perfect cup of tea.

With a tea cup in one hand and the journals in the other, she sat down and began to browse through the handwritten pages of Brett's dreams. She was grateful that Brett had neat, legible handwriting; it made her reading assignment a whole lot easier.

As she went to take her first sip of tea, she almost spit it out. It was ice cold. She looked at the clock on the end table and was equally surprised to see that it was 2:00 a.m. She had been reading for almost four hours. Rubbing the fatigue from her eyes, she set the last, mostly unread journal, atop the three finished ones, and headed off to bed, eager for her 4:00 p.m. appointment with Brett.

6.

As Dr. Joyce Davenport drifted off to sleep in her suburban Boston home, Frank Whickers' day was about to begin. Frank had lived in Chicago for a good part of his young adult life and had recently relocated back from a very long stay in France. He didn't really care that much for the city but he traveled quite a bit. So rather than fly through Chicago on his way to the east or west coast he decided it was better to live there. That way each coast was about the same distance away by air so physiologically one trip wasn't more burdensome than the other; now they were equally burdensome.

Frank had a terrific apartment. His two-bedroom, 1240 square foot, furnished apartment, ran him almost $4,000.00 per month. For most people it was too expensive but Frank wasn't most people. What he liked about his high rise apartment complex was its size, the view of Lake Michigan, and the amenities that came with it. Tower A and Tower B were joined by an arcade on the first and second levels to create what he called the "hub."

The hub was a great place, complete with dentists, a convenience store, and dry cleaners, banking services and a lot more. Frank didn't like to have to go far if needed something and the hub was the determining factor on where he decided to live.

It was a little after 1:00 a.m. when Frank's phone rang. He was in a deep sleep and fumbled with the receiver as he tried to cradle it between his right ear and pillow.

"Hello?" Frank said quizzically into the phone with a sleepy voice.

"Happy Anniversary," followed quickly by a dial tone was the response.

As he hung up the phone, Frank looked through sleepy eyes at his *girlfriend* lying next to him. She wasn't really his girlfriend, although that's how Frank introduced her when they were out together; it was more of a hired companion type of relationship. Frank had met Veronica about a year ago from a service recommended to him by an old friend and he really liked her.

To Veronica, Frank was one of those big shot business guys that spent quite a bit of time out of town, had a lot of money and wasn't bashful about paying her for her time. Frank really liked Veronica but wasn't sure if she liked him or not and didn't really care. All he knew was that when he wanted company, Veronica made herself available.

He quietly got up and made his way to the shower. Still half asleep, Frank brushed his teeth, as steam filled the bathroom. A foggy mist now covered what was once his reflection. Taking his index finger, he drew on the mirror. Two dots for eyes and a sad smile. Frank watched the eyes cry as the moisture that had built up began a slow journey downward towards the sink. Rinsing the last of the toothpaste from his mouth he wiped the mirror clean with his hand and stared back at himself. "This is our last one. Time to hang it up," he said.

Frank only took one assignment a year, not because there was a lack of interest, he was after all one of the best in the business. When he got a call it usually meant someone with a lot of money had a big problem that he was the only one that could take care of it.

He was thorough and invisible. So thorough that each job took about a month. There were some exceptions, but not many. Frank studied his targets, learned everything he could about them, their habits, where they ate dinner, who they hung around with, travel patterns, etc. He did as much homework as necessary to ensure that, when it came time to execute the contract, it would be quick and his exit strategy would be fool proof.

Frank left Veronica sleeping in the apartment and headed to the Greyhound Bus Station on West Harrison St. Driving down Lakeshore Drive, he glanced out of his window towards Lake Michigan. Huge body of water, he thought, still impressed with its size. If there was even a hint of salt air, you'd swear you were at the ocean. Thoughts of Veronica accompanied him on the drive. He had after all became a little fond of her and told himself that after this job was over he would holster his gun, so to speak and settle down. Forty-five years of age was staring him in the face and it was time to develop a real relationship, buy a house, and live that American dream thing. He didn't see himself settling down with Veronica but would sure like to find someone with her looks and personality. "Can you get that without paying for it?" He didn't know for sure, but thought it would be interesting and perhaps fun to try and find out.

Frank didn't have many business customers, and was a little surprised that he had gotten a call from a very old client. It had been a long time since he had done work for them. Frank gently eased his thoughts of Veronica to the side and did several walkthroughs in his head of the steps he would take once he got out of the car.

Parking his car at the bus station, he walked in and headed across the terminal towards the men's bathroom. The station was pretty empty; there was a couple at the doorway having a cigarette, a few people meandering around the terminal, and a military guy in his uniform trying to get some sleep on the hard plastic chairs before his connecting bus arrived.

As he entered the men's bathroom, he was overcome with that *smell*. It was a smell you couldn't really describe but recognized right away as the gas station or highway rest area bathroom smell. Entering the first stall, he got on his knees and reached behind the toilet. The back of the toilet was damp from sweating and felt clammy against his hand. Despite the moisture, a piece of duck tape held a key firmly in place. Frank pulled it free and removed the tape. He shook his hand violently to remove the moisture that transferred itself from the porcelain to his hand. "Whew," he disgustedly mumbled, not very happy to be this close to a very dirty, very public toilet.

The auto flush feature on the toilet was working and said it's customary *so long* as Frank left the stall and headed to the bank of sinks to wash his hands. He punched the aluminum square on the hand drier and it whined its way to full speed. "These things never dry your hands," Frank thought out loud, a little perturbed that paper towel dispensers were virtually extinct. With wet hands he left the men's room and headed for the luggage lockers.

"The day of the month is the locker number," he said to himself. Even though it was very early it was officially the 23rd. Glad to be in fresher surroundings, Frank went to locker number 23 and inserted the key. He turned it slowly and the door popped open revealing the nylon backpack inside. Grabbing the new addition to his luggage collection, he removed the key, put it in his pocket and closed the door.

As Frank was leaving the bus station, the guy in the military uniform got up and tried to place a call from his cell phone. The battery on the disposable phone was almost completely discharged. "Piece of junk," the uniformed man muttered. Unable to get reception after several attempts, he decided a call from the pay phone would probably be OK. He dialed a long distance number using the calling card from his wallet. "It's on," he said to the voice that answered, and hung up. On his way out he dropped what was left of a roll of duck tape into the trash receptacle.

Veronica was sound asleep when Frank got back, just like he thought she'd be. He stood there and watched her for a few minutes just to be sure. Satisfied, he went into the guestroom that served as his office, turned on the lights and locked the door behind him.

Inside the top right-side pocket of the backpack was large aspirin-like bottle. The bottle could have been on found on any store shelf except for the fact that it had no label. Replacing the common product label were 3 bar code stickers. Frank carefully removed each one and placed them on a piece of clean white paper, one beneath the other and placed it on his desk.

Moving to the closet, he opened the door revealing his private safe. He spun the dial a few times to the clear it and then turned the numbers right and left until the right combination was reached and the door opened. He grabbed the backpack and started transferring the rest of its contents to the safe. Stacks of one hundred dollar bills, wrapped in their familiar purple bands, moved from their temporary home to a permanent one, as Frank placed them neatly beside one another, doing some quick math along the way.

Once the $120,000 down payment was tucked safely away, Frank closed his closet door and powered up his PC and all the peripheral equipment, scanner, printer, web cam, the whole nine yards. After entering his password, he navigated his way to the folder on his hard drive, simply named, "NP." Inside the file was one icon named "install." He double clicked on it and the process began.

Frank placed the piece of paper on his scanner and scanned the neatly placed bar code stickers. This created a picture file which he saved to the desktop on his computer. The program he installed from the NP folder was now ready to go. Prompted to insert a file, he double clicked on the newly created file which inserted the bar code images into the program. He then hit the cipher button and watched the program go to work analyzing the file.

It only took a few minutes before Frank was reading the first of two decoded pages. The first page had a hotel name and location. The second contained specific assignment details that he'd read after he arrived at his destination. He printed the information, placed it in his top desk drawer and locked it. He then uninstalled the program, shut down his office and headed back towards the bedroom.

It was 4:00 a.m., Veronica usually left around 6:00 a.m. Frank debated on staying up but decided he'd crawl back into bed for a few hours and start planning his trip to New England after she left. Lying in bed, that Bee Gees song "Massachusetts" kept replaying in his head until he drifted off to sleep.

7.

Brett's time with Joyce Davenport yesterday had yielded dividends he never expected. He woke up feeling refreshed and hadn't had any dreams, at least not any that he could remember. After his last three nights, not being able to remember if you even had a dream was something to marvel over. It was 5:00 a.m. when Brett picked up the phone. He knew his father would be awake and wanted to tell him the news.

"Hey, Dad," Brett said cheerfully.

"Hi, Brett, you sound spunky this morning," Michael Allen responded.

"I went to see Dr. Davenport yesterday, and you were right, Dad, she is really good. So good in fact I'm going back again this afternoon. I have to admit, I had my doubts but not anymore."

"Are those dreams coming back again, Brett?" his father inquired.

"Yeah," Brett replied slowly, "these recent ones are a lot different than the ones I usually get; they're much more intense, more real. They even scare me a little bit."

"Well I can't think of anyone better to have on your side than Joyce Davenport." His father paused a little before continuing, "I'm really glad you went to see her, Brett, she helped me *so much* after we lost your mom."

"I know she did, Dad," Brett said in a comforting tone.

Brett could tell that his father was still struggling with the loss. Brett wasn't sure he if either of them would ever really be over it. The emotional wounds left by his mother's death were very deep indeed. He had heard it said somewhere that time heals all wounds. Bret wondered if the person that coined that phrase had ever experienced the loss of someone as loved and cherished as his mom.

"How are things going at the site?" Brett asked, allowing his spunk to regain momentum.

"Were doing good, just a little behind schedule but nothing we can't fix with a little extra effort," his dad answered. "I may have to sub out a small piece but I'm not sure yet. Don't worry, Brett, things will be a lot better with the traffic real soon now," he added with a chuckle.

Michael Allen's construction company had grown a lot over the last decade. Allen Construction was now second only to Conceptual Building and Construction.

Michael was a smart guy and knew that Senator George Allen had quite a bit to do with him getting the amount of work he did. Michael was grateful to his father for everything he had done for him but Michael wanted to give it a go on his own for once and be out from under his father's shadow. After the construction project was complete, Michael was going to sell his company and start over. No Allen name recognition, no influential hocus pocus from his father, just him. Sink or swim, he would do it on his own.

"Will I get a chance to see you over the weekend, Brett?" his father asked hopefully.

"I'm not sure, Dad. Some things at Nelson are starting to come together and, in all likelihood, will require me to be there this weekend. It's pretty exciting stuff and with just a little more nudging of the old test tube, we may have something worth celebrating.

Maybe we can grab a bite next week sometime. I'll get the Sox schedule and get us some box seats, first base side, for the next night game. Sound like a plan?" Brett asked, already knowing the answer.

"That's the best plan I've heard all week. Give me a ring as soon as you find out. If you need anything I'm just a phone call away."

"Keep that little yellow helmet on," Brett said jokingly. They heard each other laughing as they simultaneously hung up the phone.

Brett grabbed his briefcase and headed out the door. He was running behind schedule and knew if he hit the lights just right he could still get to work on time. Brett didn't like feeling rushed and often wondered how some people functioned, and did so comfortably, in the perpetually late mode.

Every traffic light just seemed to know that Brett was running late. At every intersection he had to stop. Worse yet was the tease. The tease was that nasty light that seemed to stay green forever, then just as you got close, would quickly switch to red, just in time to make you stop. It was especially frustrating when your car was the only one at the intersection. You can't even begin to figure out why the light changed in the first place.

Despite his frustrating experience, Brett managed to arrive at the Nelson Pharmaceutical Research facility right on time, 5:45 a.m. A little heavier than normal right foot was a big help in his punctual arrival.

Luther the security guard greeted him, as he had every morning for last year or so.

"Morning, Mr. Allen," Luther said more cheerfully than should have been allowed for that time of day.

"Morning, Luther," Brett replied, feeling a little uncomfortable being called mister by someone twice his age. "It's going to be a terrific day, you're shift ends in about a hour, are you going to get nine holes in before you head home?" Brett asked.

"Oh yeah," Luther replied, taking Brett's briefcase and giving the contents the once over. "I shot a 102 last Sunday. With just a little more practice and a lot more luck, I'll break 100 this year," he continued while frisking Brett with his metal detector wand.

"It's pretty early in the year, Luther, with the start you're having, you'll do it no problem," Brett said as Luther opened the gate and allowed him access to the facility.

"If I were a betting man, I'd say you'd break 100 by the end of next month," Brett said walking through the gate. "Keep your head down and follow through," Brett yelled back as the distance between them increased. Shooting Luther a quick wave, he turned his back to the gate and headed straight for the lab. It was a good five minute walk to reach his destination but it was a quick five minutes. Brett usually thought about his research, pending test results and the like, but on this particular morning he was thinking about getting back to see Dr. Davenport. Brett knew it was early in the process but was excited nonetheless at the seemingly instant success as a result of his visit with her the day before.

Brett arrived at the lab and placed his briefcase on the desk next to the telephone that displayed a white blinking light. *A message, how strange,* Bret thought. The phone in the lab was rarely used so Brett was more than a little apprehensive about retrieving the message. The last time he had a message in the labs voice mail, it was about his mother.

He picked up the receiver and listened to the automated voice tell him to enter his password. "Come on," he said putting the phone down. "What's the password?" he asked himself. A few quick seconds passed until he blurted out an "Of course," and grabbed the phone. This time when Brett was asked for the password he punched the correct numbers 733769—REDSOX if he was going to spell it out.

Gaining access to his voice mailbox, he pushed one to play his message— "Dr. Allen, this is Richard Nelson. I've heard we've made some pretty significant strides with your research program. I'm very excited to hear all about it. I'll be in our Connecticut facility tomorrow and would like to meet with you there at 11:00 a.m. When you get to the security desk tell them you have an appointment with me and I'll send my assistant down to meet you. She'll escort you to my office. I'm looking forward to meeting you and getting your progress report." There was a brief second of silence then the prerecorded prompting began once again; Press 2 to repeat the message, 3 to delete the message, 4 to—Brett hung up.

"Wow," Brett said rather loudly to an empty lab. He sat down in the chair and began to question what just happened. *Since when does the CEO of a company personally call one of his employees to schedule an appointment? Why does he want to meet with me personally? Why go over my research project and get a progress report? Could this be the beginning of a big promotion and pay raise? I wonder how long it'll take me to get to Connecticut.* It was the beeping of his wrist watch announcing it was now 6:00 a.m., which snapped him back to reality.

Brett let out a sigh and turned on his computer. He logged on to the network, retrieved the notes he had recorded so far this week and began his morning review. Brett knew he was close to a breakthrough. In six months, Brett thought, *Maybe I'll be able to get off these immunosuppressant drugs.* Brett spent the majority of the day alone reviewing lab results, charts, and statistical models.

The alarm Brett set on his computer went off at 3 o'clock. Picking up his brief case, he left the lab and headed to the security gate. The same security procedures applied to employees both arriving at the research center to those that were leaving. Brett's briefcase was given the once over and after the wand frisk cleared him, he headed for his car.

As Brett was turning onto the highway en route to Dr. Davenport's office, flight 491 from Chicago to Boston was landing at Logan International. Frank Whickers put his magazine down and listened to the flight attendant give the local time, temperature and the customary *thank you for flying with us*. Frank glanced out of the window, prepared to put his well-rehearsed Boston accent into action, as he watched the 727 maneuver its way toward the concourse.

8.

"Hello again, Gloria," Brett said with a smile as he entered Dr. Davenport's office a shade on the early side of 4 o'clock.

"Hello Mr.," Gloria stopped, catching herself, "I mean hello, Brett," she said, casting her patented smile. "I'll let Joyce know you're here."

"Great," Brett replied sitting down in the same place he had just the day before. "Thanks."

Brett grabbed the time magazine from the table. It was only 2 weeks out of date, not bad for a doctor's office he thought. Brett started at the back, flipping through the pages, looking only at the pictures while occasionally stopping to read their captions. After making his way through, he decided to reverse course. This time he started at the front of the magazine and flipped towards the back. Brett was pretty surprised to realize that it took a whole lot more effort to flip through a magazine from the front to the back than it did from back to front.

"Hi, Brett," Joyce called to him from her inner office door. "Come on in."

"Is it just me, or is it harder to flip through a magazine going from the front to the back?" Brett asked as he passed Joyce and took the liberty of seating himself.

"I'm not sure," Joyce responded going to her desk collecting his journals. Brett could see the smile she was trying to hide.

"Just curious," Brett replied while Joyce seated herself across from him. "It's good to see you again," he added.

"It's good to see you again too Brett. Listen, I had the chance to look over most of your journal entries and I've found some things that are pretty interesting." Joyce responded eager to share her thoughts and ask him some questions. "I made some notes and wanted to share them with you to see what you think. Then I'd like to ask you some questions about what I see, as some common thread items that seem to run through a lot of your dreams. Would that be OK?"

"I've got to tell you, Joyce, last night was the first night in a long time that I slept through until the alarm went off. I can't even remember when I've felt so good. Whatever it is you want to do is fine by me," Brett said in a grateful tone.

"First of all, I was surprised by the amount of detail you were able to provide. I've had several people record dreams for me in the past and none of them were able to come remotely close to that level. Secondly," Joyce continued, "with the exception of your most recent dream, the convenience store robbery, none seem to be recurring. You said these dreams started shortly after your mother died. I realize you didn't start keeping the journals until about a year later but I couldn't help notice that very few of your dreams included her."

"That's right," Brett said confirming Joyce's observations.

"Dreaming of loved ones that have passed away is part of the grieving process. This allows your subconscious mind to continue toward acceptance of their death and gradually come to terms with it," Joyce explained. "Sometimes we overestimate our ability to handle things. I'm not saying that's what happened in your situation but I am a little curious as to how you dealt with the loss of your mother."

"Well, we all knew it was coming," Brett began to answer with a slight crackle in his voice. "People think that if you know before it happens, it makes it easier. It doesn't.

"I watched my mother get eaten away a little bit at a time by a horrible disease. I can remember helping her out of her hospital bed and being surprised at how frail and light she was. She must have been able to tell I was a little stunned. She was barley able to stand but she stopped in the middle of the floor and with every ounce of strength she had, she reached her arms out and gave me a hug. She whispered that God had given me a tremendous blessing with a new heart and this gift for science. But nothing would ever compare to the blessing he gave her the day I was born. Then she told me that she would miss me most of all. That's when I lost it. But my mom was so strong and did what she had always done. She wiped the tears from eyes, smiled, and told me everything was going to be OK.

"The next day she passed away. I miss her so much ,"Brett admitted, trying to get his emotions under control. "I didn't really feel like doing anything for quite a while. My father and I did the best we could to comfort each other and we tried to get on with our lives but it was so hard. My father, as you know started coming to see you for help, while I opted for the road less traveled and found my version of therapy by absorbing myself with work."

"Work can be good temporary therapy. It keeps your mind focused on other things, but eventually you have to face whatever it is, head on," Joyce stated "Your mom was mentioned 3 times in your journals and someone named Nadia Petrova appears over twenty times. The significance is that Nadia isn't associated with any recurring dream. It's her name that's recurring. Each time her name is mentioned the dream is different, one time it's on a beach, the other in a theater, in a car, and so on. Can you tell me a little about Nadia and your relationship with her?" Joyce asked

"I would if I could," Brett said helplessly. "I don't know anyone named Nadia. I can tell you this though, and it's pretty strange. When this Nadia pops up in one of my dreams everything else goes into slow motion. My entire focus is on her. When the dream ends, more often than not I don't want it to, I actually feel as though I've lost something. I can't explain what it is that I've lost, I just feel it. You said twenty times?" Brett asked with a hint of disbelief in his voice.

"A little more than that," Joyce said, reassuring him that her observations were correct. "I would have said that your mysterious subconscious friend was a substitute for your mother but perhaps that would be premature. Everyone has coping skills, some conscious some subconscious. Everyone uses these in different ways, with varying degrees depending upon how a situation affects them personally. I can't see how this Nadia fits into the coping equation so let's get back to that a bit later."

"That doesn't sound very encouraging," Brett said, massaging his right temple, hoping to keep the initial throb of a new headache under control.

"Don't get discouraged, Brett," Joyce said, her smile returning as she continued. "That's just my version of professional mumbo jumbo and it simply means I need more time to figure it out."

"You've got me for as long as it takes, Joyce," Brett said, returning her smile and ensuring her of his commitment to see this thing through to the end.

"I had the chance to review your notes about the convenience store dreams that started Friday night. Pretty scary," Joyce admitted.

"That's for sure," Brett agreed, rubbing his temple again. "I've had bad dreams before, we all have, but this one is so very different."

"You made several notes in your journal commenting on the realism," Joyce pointed out. "For example, you said you could feel the car shake going over the rumble strips, smell the rain, feel the wave of water from a passing vehicle hit the car, and what really caught my attention was you noticed some slight discoloration, blotches I think you called them, on your right hand when you spilled coffee."

"That's right," Brett said shaking his head, confirming what he had written. "Here, see for yourself," he suggested stretching his right hand towards her. "It's a little harder to see now that it's a few days old but I think you can still make it out."

Joyce threw a skeptical glance his way as she reached for his hand. As she drew it toward her for a closer look, Brett noticed her lower lip begin to drop and her eyes squint ever so slightly. Sure enough, there were some spots that resembled the remnants of a first degree burn. Joyce released Brett's hand while doing her best to remain composed.

"It would have been so much better if it had been cranberry juice. I can't stand coffee and you'd think, since it is my dream, I would at least be drinking something I like," Brett said jokingly, hoping to ease the tension that was obvious on Joyce's face and, hide his concern for something he couldn't explain or begin to understand.

"Brett, have you ever heard of the *Stanford Hypnotic Susceptibility Scales?*"

"No, sure haven't, but I've got a pretty idea of what they are."

"What *they are* is a test. It requires you to try and complete twelve exercises," Joyce began to explain. "The last couple of exercises test your response to posthypnotic suggestions. A lot of people can perform the first few; only a few can do them all. The farther you get, the greater your chances of being hypnotized. I'm only suggesting this because some of the events occurring in your subconscious mind have somehow managed to manifest themselves in your conscious reality. The stigmata phenomenon is a very strained comparison but the only one I can think of."

Brett's mood switched from a little less playful to a lot more serious. "So you're saying that what's happening in my dreams, more specifically what we call the convenience store dream, is having a corresponding effect in the conscious or physical part of my life?"

"Yes," Joyce replied waiting for Brett to continue, but he remained silent.

"The only piece," she continued, "and correct me if I'm wrong, that's made that... *transition*, is the spilling of the coffee, right?

"Right?" Joyce asked again, looking for an answer. But there was no answer coming.

Brett was staring out the window, lost in a sea of disbelief. Everything he had studied and believed in was based on measurable facts and verifiable test data. Now, just like storm surge, the waves of doubt were crashing in on him. The resulting undertow grabbed his belief system and carried it off to the dark depths of an unfamiliar sea.

Confused and afraid, he was searching within himself and his vast amount of knowledge for anything that made sense, but found nothing. Somewhere, perhaps just beyond the pane of glass, his eyes were fixed upon was the helm, a little piece of reality that would guide him to the safe shelter that only the walls of certainty could provide.

"Brett, are you OK?" Joyce asked, leaning over towards him to get his attention.

"Sorry, Joyce," Brett said slowly returning to the conversation. "I'm just having a hard time believing all this stuff. I believe Newton's third law of motion, for every action there is an equal and opposite reaction. I also believe if you put water in a freezer that you'll have ice in a few hours. That's tangible stuff, not hocus pocus. I'm a scientist, not a guest of the psychic friend's network."

"Brett, I can't say I totally understand it either, which is why I'm suggesting that we at least explore the possibility of hypnosis. Maybe we'll be able to find the cause of these dreams, maybe not." Joyce went on, leaning back to a more comfortable position in her chair. "If we can identify the root, we should be able to treat it, perhaps even remove it."

"Remove it, as in no more dreams, or at least no more dreams that *transition*?" Brett asked.

"No promises, Brett, but that would be the plan," Joyce replied.

"I had a great night last night, Joyce. Good company for dinner, and slept straight through the night until my alarm went. I can't even remember the last time that happened and I don't know for sure if I even had a dream. My point is, if you think there's something that might be able to give me more nights like *that*, I'll do whatever it takes. Not to mention that fact, that this whole dream/reality relationship thing has me a little scared, have you ever encountered anything like this before?"

"Not exactly," Joyce admitted with a touch of reluctance. "I've treated patients that were suffering from recurrent bad dreams but none had any transitional manifestations. I did manage to help those patients get rid of those dreams. I'm pretty confident if we can get to the bottom of what's causing yours, we can get rid of them as well. No more recurrent convenience store dreams, no more transitions."

"OK, Joyce, let's give it a shot. Just curious, how long did it take for your other patients to be well enough to stop receiving treatment?"

"It varies," Joyce replied, "but if I had to associate time with recovery, I'd say about four to six months."

"I suppose that four months," Brett began, opting for the more optimistic time table, "isn't all that long in the big scheme of things. What, if anything, do I have to do to prepare?"

"I'm the one that has to prepare," Joyce responded. "There is very little you have do. I want to try and clear a two-hour block of time, twice a week for us to get to the bottom of this. It's a very aggressive plan; some of my colleagues might say a bit too aggressive." She paused a looked Brett squarely in the eyes. "What would you say Brett?"

"I'd say that I've gone from almost not being able to see you at all, to being your star patient in just about twenty-four hours. I don't know if I should be really grateful or really worried?" Brett asked trying to recover his sense of humor. "As far as I'm concerned, the sooner we can get to the bottom of this, the better."

"So do I," Joyce admitted. "Do you feel up to the Stanford exercises?"

Brett shook his head giving her the go-ahead. After a few minutes of preparation they got started. Joyce began slowly with easy suggestions, and was encouraged by how well he was doing but didn't want to get her hopes up; most people did fine until they got closer to the end. She also knew that a scientific mind wasn't the ideal type for hypnotism; it was a lot more reluctant accepting suggestion.

As each step passed from one suggestion to the next, Joyce's hopes grew. About an hour had passed until they were finished, Brett's score, a ten. Joyce was pleasantly surprised; he was an excellent candidate for hypnosis.

"So, Brett, what did you think?" Joyce asked, putting some finishing touches on her notes.

"Pretty interesting experience, overall it wasn't bad," Brett responded.

Joyce smiled. "I'd like to have Gloria call you tomorrow and work out an advance schedule for us to meet. I will have to move a few things around but that doesn't pose too big of a problem. Do you think you can hold to your schedule of being finished by 3:00 p.m. every day? I think it would make life a lot easier for both of us if we could start around 4:00 on a regular basis; it would also help give us some momentum to get to the bottom of this."

"Not a problem, Joyce. I can make 4 almost every day. I will probably have to call Gloria tomorrow to get the schedule. I have to meet Richard Nelson, the CEO of the company, in Connecticut tomorrow for a progress report. The meeting starts at 11:00 and I have no idea how long it will last. So I'll give her a call around 9:30 from my cell."

"I don't think that will give us enough time to finish our juggling act and be able to provide you with dates and times," Joyce told him. "I have to free up some time, move some patients around, etc. so why don't you try Gloria on your way back from the meeting. We might be prepared to give you some solid information by then. If you happen to be there all day and can't call until after 5:00, my service will take your call, get me the message and I'll call you back myself to let you know what we've come up with."

"Totally understand," Brett acknowledged. "I want you to know Joyce that I'm grateful for all your doing. I'll give Gloria a shout sometime tomorrow afternoon, if I can."

"Terrific," Joyce said as she got up and walked back to her desk. "I'd like to hold on to these," she stated tapping on his journals with her index finger. "They will help me devise some sort of road map that I think will give us a pretty good head start."

"Absolutely," Bret quickly agreed.

"OK then," she went on collecting the note books and heading for the door. "I want you to do your best to relax these next few days. I'm going to take theses home again tonight," she said, raising his journals. "I want to get started on this right away. "

"The sooner the better for me," Brett said, sharing her anxiousness to get started.

Joyce turned off the office lights and locked the doors behind them. They shared a quiet elevator ride down to the first floor. It wasn't an uncomfortable quiet that strangers share. There was no staring at the floor indicator above the door, or watching your shoes to avoid eye contact and a potential hello from a fellow passenger. It was quiet because both doctor and patient were busy trying to organize their thoughts and get mentally prepared for the journey they would soon be taking together.

Brett walked Joyce to the car just as he did the night before, but this time they were on the other side of the street. He stood by and watched her buckle up and put the key in the ignition. She grabbed the journals sitting on the passenger seat and held them up so he could see them and gave him a reassuring smile, telling him, without saying a word, that he had a staunch ally in whatever lied ahead. Brett replied with thumbs up and a smile to send her on her way. He decided to head for the *Dug Out*, a local sports bar with an outside café ten minutes from his apartment. He'd sit at an outside table, catch the last hour or so of sunshine, sip on a cranberry juice and read the sports section of the *Globe*.

9.

Frank Whickers collected his luggage, two medium sized suitcases, from baggage claim and headed to the main concourse. He heard the familiar mumbled announcements over the airport's PA system. It reminded him of the dentist. It didn't matter which dentist office you visited, they all smelled exactly the same, and every airport, no matter where it was, sounded exactly the same.

Frank liked airports. It wasn't that he was a big fan of flying; he just enjoyed watching people and airports, by far offered the best variety. Frank thought this was going to be a first for him. He hadn't seen anyone making that last minute dash to try and catch a plane just before it took off.

Just as Frank was going to chalk one up in the record books, there she was. A young lady, maybe 25, tearing around the corner en-route to the gate her airplane was sitting at while it made final preparations for take off. You could see the angst all over her face. She had one of those nice suitcases with the small wheels on the bottom. She was pulling that thing so fast that it bounced like dice thrown on a hard table. Her feet got a little tangled making the corner and she almost fell flat on her face.

Most people would have taken a moment to slow down, have a quick look around to see if anyone had noticed, live through an embarrassing moment and move on. Not this girl, she was in too much of a hurry to be embarrassed, let alone slow down. She just regained her balance and moved on. Maybe she assumed no one had seen her, or if she didn't make a big deal about it, no one would recognize what happened. Whatever reason she had for needing to be on that plane, it was obviously very important. Frank watched her disappear around the corner. Her suitcase going a little airborne in an effort keep up. He wished her a silent good luck and headed out of the airport to find a cab.

Cabs were not hard to find at the airport and one pulled up to greet Frank almost immediately. He tossed his luggage in the back seat and climbed in next to it.

"Cavanaugh Hotel, Dalton Street," Frank instructed the driver, who merely shook his head and got underway. It was pretty obvious that the driver knew his way around. Most cab drivers, unless they were newbie's, could get you to any major hotel within 10 miles of an airport. In less than 15 minutes, he was being let off in front of his destination.

"Good afternoon," Frank said walking up to the reservation desk.

"Good afternoon, sir, are you checking in?" the young lady on the other side of the counter asked.

"Yes I am. I have a reservation."

"Name please?" she asked, fingers poised at the computer terminal.

"Steve Wilkinson," Frank replied with his favorite alias as the receptionist started punching the keyboard with her fingers.

Her fingers took a momentary break, hovering over the keyboard "Is that k-e-n, or k-i-n, Mr. Wilkinson?"

"I-n," Frank said, providing his matching credit card as her fingers resumed their work. *She must be able to type 600 words a minute,* he thought.

"OK, Mr. Wilkinson, You're all set," she said taking an impression of his credit card. "You're in suite 1231. My system tells me you'll be with us for a week. Here is your key and your credit card" she said handing them across the counter. "Would you like me to have someone collect your luggage for you?"

"No thanks, Janice," Frank said, reading her name tag. "I'll take care of that."

"OK, just follow the hallway around to the left. The elevators will be right there, you can't miss them. Go to the 12th floor, then right off the elevators. Enjoy your stay with us Mr. Wilkinson," she said ending her instructional dialogue with a polite, well-practiced smile.

"Thank you, Janice, I will," Frank replied with a practiced smile of his own. Picking up his suitcases, he headed for the elevators.

Reaching the 12th floor, Frank, aka Mr. Steve Wilkinson, turned right just as Janice had told him. Reaching his door, he put down his bags and took the key card from his pant's pocket and looked it over. Following the diagramed instructions, he got the green light telling him he could now open the door and enter his room.

Noting spectacular, Frank thought as he tossed his luggage on the king size bed. He went about his rounds, as he always did when staying in a new hotel. He checked the TV and remote, they both worked. Moving the heavy window drapes aside, he glanced out to find he had a nice view of what the locals called the "Back Bay." Next was the shower.

Reaching the bathtub, he turned on the water, slid the middle lever to the left, and watched water shoot out of the shower head. Frank was pleasantly surprised with the temperature and water pressure. A hot steamy shower in the morning was a must, otherwise he never felt awake. Turning off the water, he noticed that the small refrigerator was nicely placed and well stocked with a variety of soft drinks and juices. Stretching out on the bed, Frank tested his sleeping positions, back, right side, and then left. *Very comfy,* he thought, letting a big long sigh escape. *This will do just fine.*

After staring at the ceiling for a few minutes, Frank decided it was time to get busy. First things first, he said unzipping his suitcase, placing the clothes neatly in the drawers. He always counted for some reason, 6 pairs of sock, 2 pairs of jeans, etc. until every piece of clothing was not only put away but accounted for.

Sitting at the desk in the corner of the room, Frank reached in to his sock and removed a rolled piece of paper. Removing the small red rubber band that held it in its rolled shape he began to smooth it out using the flat of his hand. He rubbed it smooth against the table until it laid flat on its own then started to read.

Name: Brett D. Allen   Age 25 Status: Single
Description: Height: 6' 0"   Weight: 200
Hair: Brown   Eyes: Blue
Distinguishing Features: Long scar middle of chest
(Heart Transplant Recipient)
Automobile: 2001 Ford Mustang
License: (MA) 4356 HK
Residence: SpruceTree Apartments   Phone: (R) 617-555-1212
Newton Street #232   (W) 781-555-0202
Brighton, MA 02135   (C) 617-555-7777
Occupation: Research Scientist
Nelson Pharmaceutical Research Facility
Crosby Drive

Bedford, MA 01730
T&E: Parking Garage 7th floor
2002 Honda Civic—Black—License# (MA) 1729 SA.
Key Location: Elevator entrance 7th floor—ash tray
Comb: 7622
Vehicle Exchange: Red Audi (Day 6 P.M.) Logan Extended Parking
Economy—License# MA 3772 FR.
Key Location: Driver Side Wheel Well
Completion date NLT: 1 Aug.

So there it was. *This guy is just a kid,* Frank thought as he picked up his paper. *If I had known that before, I'm not sure I would have taken this job. It's a good thing this is my last contract. I'm starting to get judgmental and in this business that's not good.*

Frank went to the refrigerator grabbed a can of soda and put the room key in his pocket. He had a little over thirty days to live up to his end of the agreement and knew that would be enough time. Frank was very good at what he did but he did have a few quirks. He liked to study his targets for weeks before he executed them, and he allowed the victims to see his face in their last minute of life. He thought he owed them at least that much. That quirk spawned from his fervent dislike of the cowboys he watched on TV as a kid that shot their adversaries in the back. At least in his mind, he had found a solution he could be comfortable with.

With a soda in one hand, a now folded piece of paper in the other, Frank headed for the parking garage, specifically the 7th floor, to get his T&E (transportation and equipment).

When he got there, he didn't have to look around very much to find the ashtray. The ashtray stood about 2 feet tall, its metal top filled with fine, almost white, sand and several old cigarette butts. He picked out the old smelly butts and threw them disgustingly to the floor. Now with a clear field he started digging around the bottom of the sand. The key brushed against the tips of his fingers as he swept over it the first time. He quickly moved his hand back "There you are," he said, pulling it from its sandy hiding place.

Shaking the key to get the sand off, he also hoped the smell of stale cigarettes would somehow come off as well. Walking around the parking garage's 7th floor in search of his black Honda Civic, he wondered what this young man had done to be in the unenviable position of having to meet him on a professional level.

Passing a cement column, Frank spotted a black Civic. After checking the plate, he found it was a match. When he opened the driver side door, it swung open revealing plush leather seats and an interior loaded with all the bells and whistles. The glove compartment held the cars remote and a local map. He connected the key with the remote and tested the ignition. The Civic responded right away and idled smoothly. Reaching up to the driver side visor, he got the parking stub and put it in his pocket. Frank checked everything from break lights to the rear window defogger and found everything to be in order.

He reached down on the floor and found the right lever and popped the trunk. Pulling the trunk open, he saw the only thing sitting there was a seemingly oversized road side assistance kit. He had to pull out his paper again to get the combination to the lock that held it closed. A quick look around the garage satisfied his need to know he was alone. Leaning over, he rolled each of the tumblers into their positions, 7-6-2-2, and the lock opened.

The road side assistance kit turned out to be a gun case in disguise. The compressed red foam held a broken down PSG-1 sniper rifle with a specially made silencer and a Model 18—9mm Glock, his favorite handgun, complete with silencer. Frank didn't even like the thought of having to use the long range weapon; it was strictly for contingency purposes. His preferred method and only one he had ever used, was close range, face to face at the final moment, and the Glock is ideal for that scenario.

OK, Frank thought closing up the kit and locking it, *everything is going just the way it should.* He shut the trunk and locked the car with his recently discovered remote. The Civics' horn echoed off the concrete as Frank made his way back to the elevators. Pausing for a second at the elevator door, he finished his soft drink and tossed the empty can in the ash tray.

Frank decided he'd take the stairs back to the lobby and get a little exercise.

Reentering the hotel from the main lobby he noticed than Janice had just finished checking in a new traveler. He watched her on his way to the counter, part of his people watching fascination, to see if she would deliver the same smile to Jane Doe as she had delivered to him.

He hadn't made it more than 5 steps when he started shaking his head. Janice had just pasted on her well versed smile and he of course picked it up. Frank continued watching as the new check-in walked away. I wonder, he thought, do all the service industries train their people to smile that way? Sure enough, just as quickly and rehearsed as that wonderful smile appeared, it disappeared. *Too bad,* Frank said, *I thought for a minute she really meant it.*

Janice had her back to the counter when Frank got there. She continued with her work unaware that someone was watching her.

"Hello, Janice," he said in a friendly tone. As she turned toward him, the smile came back and it almost made him laugh.

"Hello, Mr. Wilkinson, is there something I can do to help you?" she asked.

"Yes there is," Frank said putting the parking stub on the counter. "A very close friend of mine let me borrow a car while I was in town so I wouldn't have to spend a fortune on a rental. He left it in the garage for me and I was wondering if I could go ahead and pay the parking fee."

"That's not necessary," she said, her fingers dashing over the keyboard "We'll go ahead and validate the ticket you have then I can code your parking garage access key and put the information in your computer file." If you can give me the vehicle information, I can save you the trouble of having to fill out another form. I'll need the make/model and license plate number."

"Sure, it's a white Ford Taurus," Frank said pulling his wallet from his back pocket, finding an old, somewhat tattered piece of paper that had Veronica's phone number on it. "Here it is, Massachusetts license plate number 198 BRL," Frank said adding a smile of his own.

"You've got some great friends," Janice said in an envious tone.

"I have some great business friends," he said. "When they come to see me, I do the same for them."

"Here is your garage access key, just insert it into the green slot, the gates will work automatically," Janice said, handing the card to Frank.

"Thanks," Frank said, taking the card, putting it into his wallet.

"My pleasure, Mr. Wilkinson," Janice replied turning her back to him, resuming the work she had started prior to his interruption.

Frank turned around and headed back to the garage, his parking dilemma now solved. Why did they even ask those questions he wondered? No one ever checked. He could have said he had a Pink 69 Volkswagen with Hawaiian license plates sitting out front and no one would have raised an eyebrow. Just as well, he didn't need to be worrying about a curious receptionist and the less he had to worry about, the better.

Adjusting the seat and mirrors to his liking Frank eased the Civic out of the garage. When he swiped his access key in the green slot, the gate responded just as Janice said it would. Stopping at the first 7-Eleven he saw, Frank picked up a disposable lighter, pen, small (pocket sized) notebook, and a crossword puzzle book then continued on his way to Brighton. His twofold purpose was dinner and a look at Brett Allen's apartment complex.

Driving on Commonwealth Ave., a pretty dense area of Brighton, he spotted the Triad Restaurant and decided he'd stop in and give it a try. Frank instantly liked the place. It had nicely polished floors, tasteful frescoes and tapestries decorated what would have otherwise been bland walls, and cozy tables that had comfortable distances between them. He was surprised to see that the kitchen was open until midnight on the weekends and made a mental note of it.

Frank opted for a booth along the wall. He ordered his dinner, a glass of the house wine, and started to think about Brett Allen. Opening the notebook to its very first page, he drew a pyramid. At one side of the base, he wrote *apartment*. At the other he wrote *work*, and on the top he put a question mark. The question mark represented what would be the last piece of the triangle. Once he had the last piece he could put together a 3 pronged strategy that would be use to complete this assignment. Where did he go when he wasn't working, where did he spend his free time and who did he spend it with?

His wine was delivered to the table, which was followed shortly thereafter by his order of Garlic Shrimp. The main course was delivered in a sizzling clay pot that left no doubt that its contents were hot. Frank ate in relative silence, being one of only a few customers in the restaurant. Although it was slow right now, he knew that from Thursday to Sunday this place was packed. The food and atmosphere were fantastic and the prices were reasonable.

Refusing coffee or desert, Frank finished what was left of his wine and asked for the bill.

The waitress delivered a small leather case to his table, the receipt tucked nicely inside, with a thank you, and that "I'd really appreciate a nice tip on a slow night like tonight" smile. Frank decided to oblige her. Taking the bill, he figured out 25% of the total, placed the cash in the adjacent sleeve of the leather case, and made his way to the door.

With his hunger satisfied, Frank jumped into the Civic and got underway. Newton Street was only about 3 miles away so he knew the trip wouldn't be a long one. There was no direct route and Frank would have to take several side streets to reach his destination.

Frank was grateful for the last sliver of daylight as darkness quickly approached. After wiggling his way through town, Frank let out an audible sigh of relief when he turned off of Brook St. and onto Newton. The directional signal broadcasted Frank's intentions as the Spruce Tree Apartment Marquee came into view.

Frank drove through the parking lot guided at each turn by directional signs.

These miniature marquees were shaped like arrows and apartment numbers were etched in the flat 4-inch shaft with the sharpened point indicating the direction you should go if any of those apartments were your final destination. It took longer than expected to get in the two hundreds, but the first time going anywhere always seemed to take longer. Frank saw his final arrow 220-240, the pointed end indicating he needed to turn right.

This was a big apartment complex Frank thought to himself, turning on the headlights as dusk had final settled in around him. He noticed, as his headlights passed over the parking spaces, that there were apartment numbers, very largely painted in each one, reserving them for the tenants.

The walkway lights came on casting a blanket of yellow light over the patio stone pathways and well manicured grounds. The parking space reserved for the tenant of apartment 232 was empty. Frank suspected that would be the case, Brett was, after all, a young guy and probably out on a date or having a good time with his friends.

Frank turned the car around and followed the arrows guidance to leave the complex and head back to the hotel. He stopped at a trash dumpster that was surrounded on three sides by a stockade fence and got out of the car. Satisfied the information he needed was memorized, he grabbed the lighter he had bought, pulled the instruction sheet from his front pocket and lit it on fire. The paper turned from white to black as the flame quickly consumed it. Frank rubbed his foot across the ashen remains to break them up, tossed the lighter in the dumpster, and hopped back in the car.

10.

As Frank was entering the hotel parking lot, Brett pulled into his assigned parking space and headed into his apartment. Looking around it was easy to see that Brett made a better than average living. Despite having the decorating skills of your average 25-year-old male, his place was smartly laid out and very nicely decorated.

Any visitor would have mistaken his entire apartment for an upscale furniture store advertisement and rightfully so. When Brett moved in he knew full well that if he had to decorate the place, the theme would probably be labeled "The Early American Warehouse Look." With that thought in the forefront of his mind, the first thing he did was to meet with a design consultant. This also explained why his entire apartment was furnished with top of the line items, no skimping. His PC, stereo system and 50-inch plasma television were some of the few items that didn't bear a traditional brand name. Just for kicks Brett added a few fake plants so he could honestly say he decorated a little of it himself. Other than that, he was relieved that all he had to do was dust the place every now and again.

Brett went to the kitchen, poured him a glass of cranberry juice and walked over to his computer. Wiggling the mouse brought the 25-inch flat screen monitor to life and he went right to the internet to do some research. He was primarily interested on exploring the connection Joyce had made between stigmata and what she had called his transitional manifestations.

He typed the word stigmata and sent it out over the internet. What he got back was over 150,000 different links to explore. After going through several, he found the one he was looking for. It gave a definition of the phenomenon and some scientific information.

Brett read the information with the focus of someone studying for a final exam.

A stigmata is the spontaneous manifestation on a person's body of the wounds that resembles the crucified Christ. According to the article, people who suffer from this feel physical pain, and experience sadness and depression. Blood will pour out of the wounds for an unknown amount of time and then just disappear and heal. Brett took a sip of his drink and sat back in disbelief. There were hundreds of documented cases but what really threw him for a loop was that, in some cases, the blood coming from the wounds of someone experiencing the stigmata was of a different type.

Brett knew that the internet was filled with a ton of garbage but found himself having to believe this stigmata thing, especially after reading about the blood being different.

He was also interested to find out that some physiologists maintain that the wounds might be produced by imagination coupled with lively emotions. But he didn't have real lively emotions and if he had to rate his imagination he would grade himself a C, unless of course it was in the scientific arena, then his self given assessment jumped to an A.

Most of the research material he could find about dreams suggested they were some sort of psychic communiqué, or represented some deeply suppressed emotion or desire from early childhood. There were a million and one "interpret your dreams" services available to find out the real meaning of your early morning hour imaginings. Brett was a little frustrated that he couldn't find more detailed information that wasn't associated with a crystal ball or symbol interpretations.

Brett kept hearing Joyce's voice saying "over twenty times." The chances of that happening were beyond coincidence and he decided to see what he could find out about his frequent dream companion, Nadia. It was almost 10:00 p.m., late for Brett, but he intended to sleep in until 7:00 a.m. and go directly from his apartment to the meeting in Connecticut, so staying up later than usual wouldn't hurt too much.

Brett went to every place on the internet he could find that offered help looking for people. He typed in Nadia's name and got nothing back. You could, of course, pay with a credit card for a more powerful search engine but he opted to leave the credit card in his wallet. Was that a gimmick he wondered, suck you in with a few close calls. Then if you wanted to spend fifteen or twenty bucks, you could upgrade a notch to a more sophisticated search engine and increase your chances of getting a match.

Across town, Joyce Davenport was getting some research of her own done. She wasn't looking for clues on the internet; she was buried in his journals looking for patterns, similarities, key events, anything that could give her some clues about what was going on in Brett's mind.

Most of Brett's dreams, at least the ones he began recording a year ago, didn't seem to share a common thread. There was no sequence, no rhyme or reason for the topics of his dreams or how they appeared in the journal. It was more like a movie with all the scenes put together in a totally disjointed fashion that, on the surface made little sense. The thread Joyce was looking for was a thin one, but she knew it was there and was determined to find it.

Joyce wanted to start with this Nadia Petrova woman. Pouring over her notes from the night before she found that Nadia had appeared exactly 24 times in his dreams. She started writing down the dates when she thought she noticed something peculiar.

She stopped writing, staring at the paper on her desk, there was something important right here in front of her but she couldn't put her finger on it. Feeling her frustration building inside, she decided to take a break.

Joyce prided herself on her excellent memory and it bothered her immensely whenever it seemed to fail. She remembered being at a social function several weeks ago talking to a friend about an old acquaintance, Jan Roberts. Someone asked her if she remembered the name of Jan's ex fiancé. Instantly Joyce could see his face, she could see him seated at a banquet table next to Jan, but just couldn't get the name. The harder she tired to remember the more it eluded her. When she headed over to get a fresh martini, that's when it came to her, James Snyder. She recalled the relief that came over her, suddenly released from the burden of trying to remember. Joyce was hoping for similar results now, maybe a slight departure from her focus would bring this stealthy, hidden-in-the-shadows item to light.

She headed to the refrigerator looking for something to eat. Opening the door and surveying the contents, a blueberry yogurt became the snack of choice. Removing the yogurt, the expiration date stamped on the top caught her eye. Putting the unopened yogurt on the counter, she went to her desk and retrieved her paper.

A prolonged, barely audible "Yes" came from Joyce as the pattern with Nadia started to reveal itself. Joyce rifled through her appointment book, matching dates on her calendar to the dates that appeared in Brett's journal. Nadia didn't show up on any dates that were weekdays, only those that corresponded to the weekends. *Now that's peculiar,* Joyce said to herself trying to arrive at a logical explanation.

She knew there were recurring dreams; those with central themes and dreams that occurred at different times while containing recurring parts of other dreams.

There were also those that had a mixed bag of ingredients. What she had just discovered was something totally new and to the best of her knowledge never before observed, treated or documented?

Apparently there were dreams, separated at times by weeks that shared a common, very detailed focal point. These dreams apparently recurred not in content but rather around the focus, in this case Nadia. That in itself was interesting but not that far removed from documented case studies. What separated Brett's situation from the normal, and captured Joyce's full attention, was that these dreams occurred at specific and predictable intervals.

Suddenly energized from the excitement of her discovery, Joyce started reworking her upcoming patient schedule. Most of her patients had the same day and time slot for months so moving them would be delicate. Joyce carefully wrote down each patient's name, some details about their treatment, and possible rescheduling options. After her patient list was completed, she used the other side of the paper to list available times.

What happened next resembled a school children's game where a child is asked to draw a line from a word on the left side of the paper to its synonym on the right. The more you were able to match, the better your grade. Joyce wasn't getting a very good grade. Her paper had lines drawn, erased, redrawn, and erased again. Some were erased so often, you could almost see through the paper. It was obvious to Joyce that rescheduling her patient load was not going to be the answer. Tossing her pencil down on the desk she leaned back in the chair and remembered she had a yogurt sitting on the counter.

"This isn't supposed to be this difficult!" Joyce said to an empty kitchen, annoyed. There had to be an easier way she thought, there just had to be. Joyce grabbed a spoon from the silverware drawer and opened her yogurt, walked to the sofa, sat down on the sofa to contemplate her dilemma. *How can I maintain the quality of care with my current patients and be able to find the necessary time to help Brett,* she wondered, searching her mind for an answer. She had so much running through her mind that it was hard to concentrate. Joyce knew that Gloria would once again come to the rescue.

Joyce always believed that everyone had a special gift and Gloria's was organization. Once Gloria got busy on this, she would have several potential solutions before most people could come up with one.

Finishing her yogurt, Joyce went back to her desk and jotted down the name of her esteemed colleague, Dr. Joseph Kaufman who was an internationally recognized psychotherapist with several acclaimed articles published in the *American and International Journals of Psychotherapy*. She wanted to get his opinion as to the best way she should proceed. There were, at least to her knowledge, no previous cases to study that came close to Brett's situation, therefore there was no basic protocol to follow.

A deep yawn reminded her that it was time to at least attempt to get some sleep. She turned her desk lamp off, put her yogurt cup and spoon in the sink and checked the locks on the doors. Satisfied that she was safe and sound, Joyce turned out the lights on the first floor leaving the kitchen stove's light to serve its dual purpose as a downstairs night light as well as a guide to the stairway. Tomorrow would bring a new day and a fresh start.

11.

Oldies played on the radio as Brett cruised south on I-95 towards Groton Ct. to his meeting with Richard Nelson. Providence was about 15 minutes behind him so he figured he was a hair more than halfway. He was feeling exceptionally good this morning and turned up the radio when heard on his favorite Mo Town tunes.

Brett acquired his love for MoTown quite honestly and at an early age. As far back as he could remember, MoTown was king in his house. Brett remembered his father telling him during the long drive to their vacation cabin in Maine that, the so called, contemporary and rap music, people listened to today, was just plain garbage. There were some exceptions Michael Allen explained to his son, but not many.

Certain songs always took Brett back to a specific point in time. "Love Train" took him back to his college days. Being a slightly pimply and lanky young teenager at Harvard was in itself, unusual. The fact that he liked MoTown just made him seem that much more unusual. He was well known on campus for his exceptional academic talent but fame, even at school has a price. When his classmates discovered his musical taste, the teasing started. It wasn't done with cruelty but in good honest fun and Brett played right along. His older classmates accused him of being an old fart trapped in a young man's body and that someday not only would he grow up, but his musical choices would mature right along with his body and bring him into the here and now.

Brett got a big kick out of that, especially when one of his critics needed some academic assistance. He started thinking about the time Corey Jones approached him in the library while he was reviewing for a molecular biology exam and asked him for a little help. Knowing that he didn't really need to study he decided it was time for a little payback.

"I don't know if I can, Corey, the exam is only a week away and this is some pretty hard stuff." Brett remembered answering.

"Come on, Brett, you're the smartest kid on this entire campus and if I can't get your help, I might fail this thing," Corey pleaded. "Please, Brett," he continued, "everyone has their price; just tell me what yours is. I really need to pass this exam."

Brett met Corey that night in Corey's dorm room with his books and his warm up music, his MoTown's greatest hits CD.

"Before I can get in the mood to study I've got to listen to at least a half hour of this," Brett explained holding out the CD set.

They both got a good laugh of it and Brett enjoyed every minute of the pain he inflicted on Corey's ears.

An audible chuckle snapped Brett back to the present.

As he continued to move along the highway with his Black Honda shadow, Dr. Joyce Davenport was on the phone with her colleague Dr. Joseph Kaufman.

"Hi Joseph, Joyce Davenport, how are you?" she asked.

"Joyce, how nice to hear from you," he answered back with real sincerity. "Are you ready to join forces yet? I'd even consider vacating my parking place for a yes answer," he added jokingly.

Joyce returned a polite laugh. "You just wont give up will you?"

"Just think of how wonderful it would be if we joined together," Joe went on with his pitch "We would have better patient coverage; more time to enjoy the things we've worked so hard for, not to mention the immense benefit our patients would get."

"And what benefit might that be?" Joyce asked suspiciously.

"They would have two of the best mental health professionals in Massachusetts under one roof," he said with a smile in his voice.

"Flattery will get you everywhere," Joyce replied returning the smile through the telephone line.

"I know you didn't call to hear my unpersuasive, three-year-old argument," he admitted. "What is it that I can do for you, Joyce?"

"I need some advice regarding a patient I just started seeing," she replied.

"Of course, Joyce, I'd be glad to help in any way I can."

Joyce went on to explain Brett's situation while Dr. Kaufman listened intently. Joyce heard some verbal signs of interest when she mentioned the dream journal, Nadia, and the transitional manifestations.

"I think you're right, Joyce," Joseph Kaufman agreed. "I don't think we've seen anything like this before in the psychiatric community. When did you say these dreams started?"

"They started shortly after his mother died. As time went on they increased in both frequency and intensity, and as a result he started his journaling," Joyce replied.

"He was close to her?" Joe asked quizzically

"Very close," she confirmed.

"The last sequence of dreams resembles nightmare disorder but that usually occurs in young children and fades over time," Dr. Kaufman stated, "some parts could be post traumatic stress disorder but again all the pieces just don't seem to fit. This young lady he dreams about seems to have some sort of hold on his subconscious. I'd probably start there.

"During hypnosis, you could see if his subconscious will release what this woman symbolizes," he said, continuing his thought. "Once you have that information, it may unlock the key to treating him. After you get that information I'd move quickly, well, as quickly as your patient feels he can, to the robbery dream. If my suspicion is correct, it's post stress, but I could just as easily be wrong. Sounds to me you've got an extremely interesting and delicate case on your hands."

"It is interesting and delicate for sure," Joyce said in a concerned tone. "I've got to be careful here. Thanks, Joe, for you advice. It's been very helpful. Maybe we could grab a bite next week."

"You're welcome, Joyce, and getting a bite with you sometime soon would be a real treat, just let me know when you have some free time."

"I will, Joe, thanks again." As he hung up the phone Joyce looked at the clock, 8:30 a.m., Gloria would be here in about half an hour and then the juggling act would begin. Joyce didn't know how Gloria was going to get Brett Allen plugged in to her already full schedule but was confident she would.

* * *

A big green sign gave Brett the traditional one mile notice that his exit was coming up. He shut his radio off so he could concentrate. What he didn't hear before was the sound of air rushing through a cracked window and it's slightly annoying whistle. He pushed his window button and made it disappear.

68

"OK, let's see what we have here," Brett said to his empty car, beginning to analyze his upcoming meeting. "I know the who, what, when, and where. What I don't know is the why." He glanced over at and the directions that sat comfortably on the plush leather passenger seat.

Left off the exit, straight for three miles, entrance on the right, stared back at him in black magic marker.

"Left off the exit," he mumbled. Then he silently restated steps 2 and 3.

Brett had never been to the manufacturing facility so he was a little curious to see what it looked like. He had glanced at the pictures on the company web site last night but knew, as do most people, that a camera doesn't quite capture the fullness of the object in its lens.

He hadn't been traveling on the two-lane road more than a minute when he came around a lazy corner in the road and spotted it. There on the right side of the road just up ahead stood a convenience store.

His heart started to race as the visions from his dream were thrust to the forefront of his mind. He decided on a quick test and eased the car toward the right shoulder. Sure enough, the rumble strips were right where they were supposed to be. A quick and unexpected sweat broke out on his brow.

I'm just over reacting he thought as he took a few deep breaths. After all, nothing looked familiar. Brett quickly remembered that in his dream it was very early in the morning and raining so hard he could barely see. So the fact that the surroundings didn't look familiar shouldn't come as a surprise. Brett's heart was racing now. It was beating so hard he could hear it and would have sworn that if someone was in the car with him, they'd have heard it too.

He took his foot off the gas to slow the car ever so slightly. As he got closer, he could make out the gas pumps. "Tell me there's four," he half whispered, hoping the number would be anything but. As he edged, a closer clearer picture emerged and he saw a small island of four gas pumps complete with a protective roof.

What should I do? Brett wondered, shooting a quick glance to the digital clock on his car stereo system. It was almost 10:00 so he had plenty of time if he could muster the courage within the next 5 seconds to pull in.

Just as he was about to reach the point of no return, he decided to stop. Not having time to mess with the directional, he turned the wheel hard right and whipped into the parking lot. He came in so suddenly that the attendant looked out the see what was going on. Not being there for gas, he pulled into one of the two parking spaces at the side of the building. All Brett could do for the first few minutes was to sit there. He was starting to feel claustrophobic, like he was locked inside a small box unable to get out; the air too thick to breathe, his chest heavy with panic. "Get a hold of yourself and relax," he said.

He started to read the gas prices, then the cigarette sign that hung next to the outdoor payphone. He did anything he could to divert himself from having a full-fledged panic attack.

Taking a deep breath, he exhaled hard and decided it was time to get out of the car. His legs seemed to weigh a ton as Brett force himself out. He stood up and drew in a deep breath of fresh air and surveyed the entire area. He looked at the gas pumps again and noted the distance from them to the door. He replayed the dream in his mind as he tried to image the setting at daybreak, immersed in a torrential rain.

Knowing the only way to be sure was to go inside, Brett started for the door. I wonder if the door will be the same, he thought. Brett knew it didn't matter how many doors you may have walked through, you never found two that were the same. They all had a different feel, a different weight and they all opened differently. Some opened easily while other had sticking points. Some doors felt solid and strong, others hollow and weak. Even the door to his apartment was different than that of his neighbors. Although it was exactly the same as all the other doors in the complex in that it was manufactured by the same company and installed by the same builder, they still felt and opened differently.

It was obvious to Brett that he was overanalyzing everything. He was looking for anything about the place that wouldn't match up to the still vivid memories of the nightmares he carried with him. If he had succumbed to analyzing doors, it was pretty obvious that his search for differences wasn't going very well.

Other than Brett's obvious apprehensiveness, his entrance into the store, door included, was unremarkable. Taking quick stock of the interior, he saw some immediate similarities. The back room that held the scared attendant was right where it was supposed to be, and the counter was in the right place.

Brett walked over to where he thought the coffee machine would have been. When he was in the right spot he turned slowly, just as he had witnessed himself doing in the dreams. Glancing out of the window, the scene replayed itself again and again. The driving rain, the headlights making their way to the side of the building, and a dark clothed man standing in the doorway was replayed in his head. He was stuck there; trancelike, watching the events unfold, helpless to do anything about it. It took a conscious effort for Brett to break out of it.

He turned toward the counter, grabbed a roll of mints and put it on the counter.

"Anything else?" the attendant asked.

"No... no that's it," Brett replied, tossing a dollar bill on the counter, anxious to get out.

The attendant gave him back a quarter in change. "Thank You," Brett said on his way out. He stopped suddenly to ask a quick question. "Has the store been remodeled recently?"

"Yes," replied the attendant. "We were closed last year for a month to put in the new pumps. The pay at the pump kind and we redid the inside. Why do you ask?"

"Just curious," Brett said taking another visual survey of the store. "Have you worked here long?"

"Not really, I started working here about 6 months ago."

"So you weren't here when the store was remodeled," Brett stated flatly. "How did you know about it?"

"My father owns the store," the attendant responded, repositioning the *We Check ID When You Buy Tobacco Products* sign that stood next to the cash register. "It's been in our family for fifteen years now. My father and I decided it was time for me to learn the business, so here I am."

For Brett, everything was too coincidental. It all seemed to match just too well. Brett started to feel his panic returning but figured he'd ask one more question before heading out.

"What's the address of this place?" Brett asked.

"1599 Bridge Street," the attendant answered, a bit puzzled. He had given a lot of directions to patrons but giving out the address of the store was a first.

"Thanks," Brett said as he left the store.

Getting into his car, Brett wrote down the name of the store and the address in his palm pilot. He wasn't sure what he was going to do with the information but he wanted it just the same.

Deciding to take a few minutes before he got on his way he jotted down some more notes in his palm pilot. These were more observations and comparisons about his current surroundings and how they, at least from his vantage point, related back to his subconscious movie scenes. If this was really the place in his dreams, if it actually existed, what would that mean to Joyce and this thing she referred to as transitional manifestations? Could his dream be some sort of a prophetic message; a look into the future perhaps? If it was a glimpse ahead, does that mean something bad is going to happen? Is there anything I can do to change the outcome? The more he thought about it, the more he didn't know what to think.

He was anxious to share this experience with Joyce to see what she would make of it. For the first time in his life, he started to wonder if there was any substance to the whole psychic phenomenon thing and if his reluctance to explore it further was premature.

Brett looked at his watch and confirmed his suspicion that it was time to get moving. He didn't want to be late for his meeting with the CEO of the company. Brett took a right out of the convenience store and rolled down his window thinking the fresh air might do him some good. Brett had heard through the company grapevine that Richard Nelson was a ruthless, egocentric man. He made his way to the top by stepping on anyone or anything that got in his way. The water cooler rumor was that he'd have no compunction whatsoever about running over his own mother if she stood between him and the next rung on the so called ladder of success. Not many of the folks that Brett knew had actually met Richard Nelson but one thing was for sure, everyone was intimidated by him.

Thinking about his upcoming meeting was a welcomed distraction for what he had just been through. He knew he couldn't put it totally in the back of his mind but was pretty confident that he could manage to keep it at arms length. And for now at least, that would have to be good enough.

Brett saw the Nelson Pharmaceuticals sign just up ahead on the right. As he pulled into the entrance, he noticed the entire complex or at least what he could see of it, was surrounded by an 8 ft. galvanized chain link fence with 3 strands of barbed wire added to the top for additional security. Two very large parking lots on each side of the road sat amidst professionally landscaped and maintained grounds. There was a shuttle bus service from the parking lot to the front entrance that could be used by employees and visitors alike.

For those people visiting the facility for the first time, there were large, tastefully done signs that diagramed the buildings and explained how to use the shuttle bus service.

For those desiring transportation and not wanting to walk the quarter of a mile to the front gate, they could wait at the bus stop that sat next to each parking lot entrance. The shuttle bus made its rounds every fifteen minutes so regardless of your arrival time the wait wasn't going to be long. The closer you were able to park to the front gate the more apt you were to walk. As luck would have it, Brett found a spot near the front gate.

Grabbing his brief case, he headed out on foot for the entrance to the compound. Frank Whickers was making a note of the time as he watched from his Civic. "I knew you'd end up here," Frank whispered adjusting his binoculars to get him in clear focus.

Frank had followed Brett from Massachusetts and had a pretty good idea when he got off the highway that his destination would be here. Frank recognized the area. He had been here several years before.

Brett entered the small building at the front gate. Several computer monitors sat atop the long counter, with three security guards positioned behind them. Brett went to a terminal and typed in his name and entered it. The only thing else he had to enter was who he was here to see and what time his appointment was. All the other information filled in because he was an employee of the company.

When he entered Richard Nelson's name, it took several seconds before a message came back on the screen. Brett knew he was being stared at by the security people and it made him feel a bit uncomfortable. He thought for a second that he had done something that messed up the sophisticated computer system, and then screen finally came back and displayed, *Welcome Dr. Allen, Mr. Nelson is expecting you. Please proceed through security; a vehicle has been dispatched to pick you up,* on the monitor.

Wow, Brett thought, *when you're here to see the king, you get the royal treatment.* He walked over to the security guard closest to the entrance and placed his briefcase on the counter, where it was promptly searched. He then went through the metal wand frisking and was cleared to pass.

"Dr. Allen, please proceed to the pavilion marked VIP. You transportation will be here momentarily," the security guard told him.

"OK. Thank you," Brett replied offering a polite, somewhat disingenuous smile.

Interesting place, Brett thought, as he stood at the pickup point. As he glanced at the informational map of the complex with its numerous buildings and color coded shuttle bus system, he was reminded of the "T" in Boston.

His map studying was interrupted by an electric golf cart that pulled up next to him. He looked over to see a pretty young lady looking his way.

"Dr. Allen?" she asked.

"Yes I'm Dr. Allen, good morning."

"Good morning, I'm Elizabeth Cranston, Mr. Nelson's assistant. I'm here to escort you to his office," she said, pointing her hand to the empty seat next to her.

"Great," Brett said sitting down in the golf cart. "How far to the first tee?" he continued checking to see if Elizabeth had a sense of humor.

"Not far," she said pausing for a second. "You're up next. Please remember to repair your ball marks and replace your divots. Allow faster players to play through, and on par threes, please allow the group behind you to hit up. Have a great round!" She glanced over at Brett with a friendly, I gotcha kind of a smile to find that he was glancing back at her with a smile of his own.

It wasn't long before the cart drifted to a silent stop. Brett noticed it was a special parking place reserved for this gold cart and obviously for people meeting Mr. Nelson.

Getting out and heading to the main entrance she asked Brett to follow her. He happily obliged.

When he walked into the main hallway, he was taken by surprise. This entrance way was impressive. A slate blue tile floor that was so well polished you could just about see your reflection in perfect clarity. Sitting on a dais in the center of the entranceway was an information desk. Brett noted that anyone that wasn't seven feet tall would have to look up slightly to make eye contact with the person that sat there. The Nelson Pharmaceutical logo was laid smartly into the floor. Almost like accent tile, it was just enough but didn't reach the point of excessiveness.

There were large trees in bronze pots that sat slightly behind each side of the information desk that made it look somewhat cozy. Against each side wall were unenclosed waiting areas that consisted of a leather sofa, a set of leather chairs, a round all purpose cherry table, complete with phone and data port. The furniture sat on a wonderful white area rug that had to be a monumental task to keep clean. Plasma screens sat snuggly in the wall of each waiting area playing a series of computer generated slides that were silently telling the Nelson story. Very corporate and modern looking Brett thought.

Hallways ran to the right and left of the dais. Brett followed Elizabeth and the sound of her high heels across the main entrance toward the hallway on the right. Elizabeth waived to the woman seated at the information desk and started down the hallway with Brett in tow. The sound of Elizabeth's high heals went form a tap to a dull thud as they reached the carpeted floor.

"Mr. Nelson's office is number 38," Elizabeth said to Brett, who was now walking next to her. Brett glanced over at the office door they were passing which was the number 2. They had quite a way to go since there seemed to be an unusually large amount of space between each office door.

"This seems like quite the place," was Brett's response.

"Yes it is," she agreed. "This was renovated about twelve years ago. It used to be the research wing until that department was moved to Massachusetts. Now this is the place all the big shots come for conferences, meetings, and things like that. There's a lot for the VIPS to do, they can golf, go to the casinos or just relax. Between you and me, most of them spend all their free time at the casino. One thing is for sure, it was designed to impress visitors and it does just that."

"It must have cost a fortune," Brett said looking around, genuinely impressed.

"I'm sure it did," Elizabeth replied, as they made their way down the hallway, and past office door 28.

Brett was admiring the surroundings when he slowed down to read something that caught his eye. *In loving memory of Dr. Russell Craft and Cynthia Dobson July 1991* was written on a large brass placard. *Nelson Pharmaceutical Employees* was written underneath in much smaller print making it clear that this small memorial was donated by the workers. The date instantly got his attention; that was about the time his heart transplant surgery was performed. His pace slowed even more, after all he had just been through at the convenience store, another coincidence was something he didn't need.

"Elizabeth, do you happen to know anything about these people, Dr. Craft or Cynthia Dobson?" he asked as calmly as he could.

"No, I don't. Sorry, Dr. Allen," Elizabeth said apologetically continuing down the hallway. "We're almost there. Once we get to Mr. Nelson's waiting room, would you like me get you something, a coffee or juice maybe?"

"No thanks, I'm OK for now but I do appreciate the offer," he said picking up the pace.

Reaching their destination, Elizabeth opened the door and allowed Brett to enter first. Brett could hardly believe what he walked into. The waiting room, he guessed was as large as his entire apartment. This room was very plush, very impressive and very comfortable. He couldn't even imagine what Mr. Nelson's office looked like if this was the preview. Elizabeth sat down at her desk and buzzed into Mr. Nelson's office that she was back from her journey and had Dr. Allen sitting in the waiting room.

"It will be a few minutes, Dr. Allen, are you sure I can't get you anything?" Elizabeth asked again.

"No. Really, I'm OK for now. Thanks," Brett responded, looking for a magazine.

Elizabeth had seen this before and knew what Brett was looking for. She decided to offer her unsolicited assistance.

"You'll need to look in the magazine rack over there," she said with a smile, pointing out the cache of magazines on the floor next to the sofa.

"Thanks Elizabeth," he said walking over to have a look at what was available to read.

Just as I thought, he said to himself with a smirk, everything in here is current. Not knowing what Elizabeth meant by a few minutes, he grabbed several and took them back to the chair he was sitting in.

He started to flip through the magazines while his mind drifted back to the events of an already full day. Grabbing his brief case that sat on the floor next to him, he opened it and once again took out his palm pilot. He wrote down Dr. Craft and Cynthia Dobson names. He had a strange desire to find out who these people were and what happened to them. Brett put his palm pilot away and went back to his magazine collection. It was getting close to 11:00 a.m. so he knew it wouldn't be waiting much longer.

It was becoming increasingly evident that Brett was wrong about the time table as he went through his magazines yet again. The clock slowly crept past 11:30 on its way toward noon and he was starting to get frustrated. Letting out an aggravated sigh, he caught Elizabeth's attention.

"Elizabeth, is there a bathroom nearby that I can use?"

"Sure, Dr. Allen," she responded, opening her desk drawer to get the key. "Out of the office go left, second door on the left past the water cooler."

"Thanks," he said on his way out, taking the key from her. "I'll bring this right back."

As Brett closed the office door behind him, Mr. Nelson buzzed Elizabeth and asked her to send in Dr. Allen. When she told him he had just stepped out to use the restroom, it was obvious that he wasn't happy.

"Let me know as soon as he gets back, Elizabeth!" an exasperated Richard Nelson demanded.

"Yes, Mr. Nelson," Elizabeth replied already feeling sorry for Brett and the reception he would be receiving.

Brett turned the key and entered the men's room and was impressed by its regal appearance. Everything around here is top of the line, he thought, turning on the cold water and splashing his face. "I've got a lot more important things to do than sit around here all day," he complained to his reflection. "I could be in the lab getting something important done, not walking around the Taj Mahal." He turned the water off and started back to join Elizabeth, wondering how much longer he'd be sitting around.

"Dr. Allen is back; would you like me to send him in?" Elizabeth asked as Brett returned to the office.

"Yes, send him in," the annoyed voice responded.

"Here's your key," Brett said handing it to her. "Should I just go right in?"

"Yes, go ahead," she said with a sympathetic tone.

"Thanks," he said in acknowledgment walking over to the chair and picking up his briefcase.

When Richard Nelson had his office built, it was constructed and decorated one notch above top shelf, ostentatious to say the least. Its size alone was daunting. His office had a full bathroom, complete with Jacuzzi, a fully stocked bar, a separate utility room that held a queen size bed and a walk in closet, fully stocked with a variety of Armani suits and casual clothing. It was large enough to be a small apartment and when someone walked in, there was no mistaking this as a high-powered place of business.

"Dr. Allen, how nice of you to join me," Richard said sarcastically. His high back leather chair was turned so that he could enjoy the view of the Long Island Sound and keep his back to Brett. "Why don't you take a seat?"

"Good morning, Mr. Nelson," Brett said trying to decide which of the three chairs he was going to sit in.

"Take the seat closest to my desk," Richard continued without waiting for a response. "It's not easy running a billion-dollar company, Dr. Allen. I can't expect everyone to see the big picture as I do. What I do expect," Richard said turning to face Brett, "is that when I ask someone to be available for a meeting, I expect them to be available. Waiting isn't fun, it's required. So if you are ever asked to a meeting, I suggest you take care of any personal issues well in advance so that when you're called, you're ready."

Brett sat there in total shock as he listened. *This guy really thinks that the sun rises and sets on his schedule and the only thing bigger than his office is his head,* he thought.

"Have I made myself perfectly clear?" Richard asked, now finished with his verbal reprimand.

"You have," Brett replied, with a touch of sarcastic enthusiasm that visibly didn't sit well with Mr. Nelson.

"Very well then," Richard said switching gears and attitude as if what just transpired never happened at all. "Good morning."

This guy is wrapped way too tight, Brett thought. *I guess once he says what he has to say, he expects people to obey the law, the Nelson law, and ignorance was no excuse.* Some guys don't hold grudges but Brett had a sneaking suspicion that Nelson wasn't one of those guys. Nelson was the type of guy that gave you just one chance after he went over the ground rules. If you messed up after that, he'd not only hold a grudge, he'd get even.

"I have a 12:30 lunch appointment so let's make this quick shall we?" Richard said flatly and with seeming disinterest. "I understand that you've made some pretty remarkable progress in our organ rejection research program and I wanted your firsthand account of the project's current status along with your projected time line of any anticipated breakthroughs. I know it's difficult to predict with a great deal certainty the cause and effect relationship when conducting research so in the absence of a definitive answer, an educated guess will suffice."

Brett wasn't intimated by Richard Nelson and if he hadn't already experienced some pretty bizarre events, he may have been looking to give him an uncensored piece of his mind. The worst thing that could happen to him would be to get fired and then have to go to work for those Harvard folks that constantly harassed him to join their staff.

Brett had been told by a few of his colleagues that he should have been from England. The English are known for many things. What Brett's colleagues were referring to was the way the British can administer a severe tongue lashing in a soft spoken, polite manner, so polite in fact that the recipient almost wants to thank them when it's over. That's how Brett was when he was in a confrontational situation, calm and soft spoken, his words carefully selected and stated for maximum effect. Brett just didn't have the energy today to get into it with Mr. Nelson but he knew he would meet him again someday and then he'd let him have it, both barrels.

"Let me start by saying that my research project has exceeded expectations," Brett began with purposeful emphasis on his ownership of the project. He may not have had the spunk for a direct confrontation but it seemed he had just enough for something a little more indirect.

"When I started this endeavor," Brett continued, "it was apparent that great strides could be made in improving the quality of long-term care for transplant recipients. One could argue that my passion for this project stems from personal reasons and I suppose that would be a valid argument. Last year, there were over 25,000 transplant surgeries in the United States alone. There has been, as I'm sure you know, some great progress with organ cloning which, in my opinion, could be a viable solution to the donor shortage in about ten to fifteen years. Which means the number of transplants could rise as much as thirty percent on an annual basis."

"Thirty percent!" Richard Nelson exclaimed as he rudely interrupted. "That would help a lot of people and improve our bottom line for our immunosuppressant drugs."

Brett just sat there in total disgust with the owner and allowed his face to show it. Perhaps the only thing greater than his arrogance was lack of consideration for others, Brett thought while he stared at Mr. Nelson.

"Please continue, Dr. Allen."

Before continuing, Brett sat there for a very deliberate second never dropping his gaze in hopes Richard Nelson got that if looks could kill, you'd be a dead man feeling.

"The drug I'm developing is called Cytanepax. Cytanepax exists, or will soon exist, in its incomplete form in about six months and will require three additional additives prior to patient delivery. Those being lymphatic tissue, bone marrow from the organ recipient, and a small amount of tissue from the donated organ prior to transplant. Once these are added to the base, the different cell types are introduced to one another in a carefully controlled environment. What Cytanepax does is allow for these cells to get acquainted in a friendly manner. After a brief volatile period, the cells coexist and intermingle with one another." Brett paused for a second to let that set in. "To keep it very simple and understandable, the Cytanepax solution is administered to the patient and allows the immune system to recognize and accept the new organ as if it were the patient's very own. The result, no organ rejection and immunosuppressant drug dependence becomes a thing of the past."

"Very intriguing scenario," Mr. Nelson stated thoughtfully. "How do you manufacture enough of this drug to ensure its effectiveness?"

"That's a great question," Brett said, not the least bit surprised by the business nature of the question. "Once the three additives are introduced, it takes about 72 hours for the donor tissue to be accepted by the recipient's cells. We can then determine the genetic footprint and reproduce it in the laboratory. The base drug can be massed produced.

"The patient delivery version is very unique and patient specific. Based on my research, I would say that and transplant recipient would need to take Cytanepax along with the prescribed immunosuppressant drugs for about two years. After that, the immune system should have adequate donor tissue recognition to prevent rejection and all subsequent organ rejection treatment could be stopped."

"That's absolutely incredible," Richard Nelson said truly impressed.

"Yes, it is," Brett agreed. "I can also envision this drug being perfected to the point of needing one injection at the time of transplant and a booster shot, for lack of a better term, perhaps ten years later, so all anti-rejection medications will no longer be needed. It may in fact, not even require a booster.

This opens a lot of possibilities. Imagine if you will, taking tumor tissue and reversing the Cytanepax effect. It could lead to an entirely new family of drugs that attack only the cancerous tissues and retains this knowledge thereby preventing recurrences. For the first time in human history, we could have a cancer vaccine that really works. Obviously we're a long way from the drugs full potential but it is very promising."

"Well, Dr. Allen, this truly is excellent news. We could potentially see the end of some forms of cancer in my lifetime. Do you need additional resources so we can move this projected date of six months a little closer?" Nelson asked with a hint of urgency in his voice. "Nelson Pharmaceuticals would go down in history as the company that discovered the cure for cancer and you, Dr. Allen, would get a Nobel Prize."

"We're a long way off," Brett interrupted in hopes of bringing Richard Nelson back to earth. "I just want you to be clear that my hypothesis about the drugs potential in the fight against cancer in just that, a hypothesis. I also don't think additional resources are necessary right now but I appreciate your offer."

"Alright, Doctor," Mr. Nelson said, rising from behind his desk, signifying the end of their meeting had arrived. "If you need anything at all to help me get this drug out into the market a little faster, you just let me know. Have a good trip back to Massachusetts."

Brett rose from his chair, grabbed his briefcase and turned for the door. He was never offered a handshake or given a "thanks for the hard work." Although he never expected either, Brett gave Nelson the benefit of the doubt until he could, at least from his perspective, confirm that in addition to being a shrewd businessman, he was an ungrateful, social misfit. As Brett reached for the door, he realized that no one had said goodbye. Refusing to be like Nelson, Brett turned around and said goodbye. Without waiting for a reply, he turned and left the office. As far as Brett was concerned, he now had all the confirmation he needed.

The sound of the closing door drew Elizabeth's attention to Brett. "I take it, Dr. Allen, that your meeting is over. Are you ready to be escorted back to the main entrance?"

"Yes, Elizabeth, the meeting is over and I'm more than ready to head out of here," Brett replied.

"Janice, I'm taking Dr. Allen back to the main entrance," Elizabeth said to her counterpart sitting at the desk to her left as she got up from her chair.

Brett watched the two women work and like a well-rehearsed play, each knew their part and played it flawlessly. It took less than a few seconds before

Janice verbally confirmed she had Mr. Nelson's schedule displayed on her monitor. This let Elizabeth know that Janice was now ready to assume control of the office while she took care of their VIP visitor.

Pretty efficient set-up Brett thought. He'd gotten a much better understanding of big business since he arrived here this morning. He no longer thought of it as high powered negotiations, multi-million dollar contracts negotiated and signed through a heavy blanket of cigar smoke during the wee hours of the morning.

Big business, at least in Brett's current opinion, was nothing more than just plain schmoozing. The bigger the deal, the larger and more elaborate the schmooze. Brett imagined that Richard Nelson had a pretty hefty account at each of the two nearby Casinos. This would allow his visiting VIP's to get a fistful of chips, compliments of Nelson Pharmaceuticals, to help them get started with their wagering. Where there was legalized gambling, there were usually other illicit activities that one could partake of if so inclined with no fear of retribution. These activities were often prearranged and coordinated well in advance of a VIP's arrival and would once again be compliments of the company. Brett couldn't be 100% sure of his conclusion but if he was at one of the Casinos and had to make a wager on it, he knew the odds would be in his favor.

Elizabeth made her way to the door and held it open for Brett, an extended arm offering him first passage.

"I can show myself out, Elizabeth," Brett offered as he stepped out into the hallway.

"That's OK, Dr. Allen, it will be a pleasure to escort you back," she replied. "Besides, it's a beautiful day. You wouldn't want to keep me chained to my desk on a day like this would you?"

"Never let it be said that I've deprived anyone of fresh air and sunshine," Brett responded as he watched his escort close the door.

Walking down the hallway together, Brett's eyes were once again drawn to the brass placard that held the name of Dr. Craft and Cynthia Dobson. He didn't stop this time deciding he had already gotten all the information from it he could and keeping pace with the fast walking Elizabeth was a good idea.

"First class operation," Brett whispered under his breath, the tapping sound of Elizabeth's high heels signifying their return to the building's entranceway. She once again waived to the woman seated on the dais and led Brett to the golf cart. Brett sat down and placed his briefcase in his lap as Elizabeth pushed on the pedal and started back to the main gate.

Brett noticed the landscapers were out in full force. Just like ants he thought, each member of the colony assigned to his particular task. Some cutting grass, others trimming hedges, while other members of the team walked around with air blowers to keep the streets of this little community free from clippings. Whatever the task, they were all working hard for the good of the group, focused on getting the job done and getting it done right. Brett filled his nostrils with the smell of fresh cut grass. It was still his favorite smell despite the fact it reminded him of Mr. McLaughlin's yard and the terrible memories of twelve years ago.

"Well, Elizabeth, it looks like our journey is over. Thanks for all your help," he said as they approached the VIP pavilion.

"My pleasure, Dr. Allen, have a safe trip back to Massachusetts," Elizabeth replied as she brought the cart to a stop to let Brett out.

"I will. Thanks again," Brett said, stepping out of the cart, grateful to be on his way back. What a tremendous waste of time Brett thought. He thought about stopping at the convenience store on his way out and then to the lab when he got back to get some work done but since the day was already shot, Brett decided he'd go straight home to try and tie up some loose ends.

Once again, Brett made his way through security and left the building. He was surprised to see the shuttle bus there and decided he'd take the free ride back to and perhaps spare himself at least a few steps in the rising late June temperatures. A quick check of this watch told him that if all went well he'd be back in Massachusetts by 2:30 p.m. Leaving the shuttle, he began his walk to the car as his mind traveled back to the convenience store he had visited a few short hours ago. He mulled over the similarities he noticed and again started to compare them to his dream. With his thoughts occupied, he reached his car much quicker than expected.

Opening the door to get in, he was immediately attacked by the heat that had been building up all morning. He quickly tossed his briefcase in the passenger seat, got the car and the air conditioning started, and jumped back out closing the door. Brett stood next to the car and loosened his tie figuring it would be at least a couple of minutes before the temperature inside was at a comfortable level.

Frank Whickers' face broke out in a smile as observed the events through his binoculars. He knew exactly what was going on. It did happen to everyone on more than one occasion. Frank continued to observe from a distance and when he saw Brett get back into the car he eased it into drive. "OK young man, let's go home now," Frank said with a sneer.

12.

As Brett got on the highway and headed for home, Gloria Johnson was working on Joyce's schedule in an attempt to free up the time Joyce had asked for. Gloria had been given free reign to move patients around any way she saw fit. Joyce made it very clear that finding the time she needed to treat Brett Allen was of the utmost importance.

It took all of Joyce's professionalism to maintain a genuine interest in her other patients and not focus all of her efforts, as tempting as it was, on Brett. Not only did she like him, his case was unique and somewhat unexplored. This was her chance to help someone that was suffering from something other than your garden variety phobia. This was her opportunity to delve into the unknown, explore uncharted territory and rekindle the same level of interest and enthusiasm in psychiatric medicine that she had when she opened the doors of her office for the very first time.

After examining Joyce's calendar, Gloria concluded that the lightest patient load was on Monday's, Wednesday's and Friday's. Joyce purposely kept Monday and Friday light as she liked to ease in and out of the work week. On Wednesdays, Joyce saw four patients, dedicating most of the morning to charting. With the exception of Friday, which had no patients scheduled after 3:00 p.m., Monday and Wednesday had light mornings and heavy afternoons.

It was 12:45 Wednesday afternoon and Gloria planned to put her persuasive skills to the test with Charlie Duncan who should be walking through the door any minute now for his 1:00 p.m. appointment.

"How was your lunch, Dr. Davenport?" Gloria asked as Joyce came walking through the door.

"Lunch was great, Frank's has this new bacon cheeseburger thing they call the Bostonian and it's absolutely fabulous. My arteries are probably in total rebellion with my taste buds right now," Joyce added with a smile. "If I had more time to spend at the gym that burger could be become a regular part of my diet."

"Maybe I should try one," Gloria added in a way that suggested she was looking for a *Maybe you should* response from Joyce which unfortunately for Gloria came back as a smirk indicating a *They sure are good*, response.

Joyce knew what Gloria was trying to do and she would have none of it. When Frank's came out with their chocolate cheese cake last year, Joyce merely suggested that Gloria might want to try it. For the next 3 weeks all Joyce heard was how it was her fault that Gloria gained five pounds. It was all in jest of course and made for some lighthearted office fun but after the cheesecake fiasco, Joyce decided that Gloria would be on her own for any decisions that involved sustenance. Refusing to be a willing participant, Joyce continued to her office wearing a smirk and closed the door behind her.

As Joyce's door swung quietly to a close her one o'clock appointment, Charlie Duncan walked through the door and into the waiting room. Charlie was suffering from Trichotillomania, a disorder that is characterized by recurrent pulling out of one's hair from the head, eyebrows, eyelashes or other body parts; causing noticeable hair loss. He was wearing his usual attire, a long sleeve shirt and baseball cap. It was the end of June and quite warm and muggy already. It was certainly too muggy for the way Charlie was dressed and she wondered if he wore long sleeve shirts in the middle of the August when heat and humidity were at their peak.

"Hi, Charlie," Gloria said, welcoming him "Nice to see you again."

"Nice to see you too, Gloria," Charlie answered back. "It's really warm today," he stated with his heavy Boston accent. "It's so nice in here, it must be 80 degrees and 90 percent humidity out there," he stated, obviously very happy to be in an air-conditioned office.

"We try to keep it comfortable," Gloria said with a smile. "When it gets really hot, I don't even like to go outside of the building for lunch. I put something together at home and bring it with me."

"This is one of those modern professional office type buildings; don't you have a cafeteria in here?" Charlie asked.

"No, just a few vending machines, and until I become a big fan of candy bars and soda, I'll have to keep bringing my lunch with me."

"I guess if those were my choices, I'd be bringing a lunch too," Charlie said in total agreement. "Was today a bring-in-your-lunch-from-home day?"

"No, it needs to be a little bit warmer to keep me inside but once we hit the nineties you have to drag me kicking and screaming to get out of the AC," Gloria replied.

Charlie chuckled a little bit. "I couldn't agree with you more, Gloria. The only difference between you and me is our temperature threshold. For me, eighty is enough. I'm sure some of it has to do with being out of shape and a little on the heavy side."

"On the heavy side or not, eighty is plenty hot enough Charlie, besides you don't look to be too far on the heavy side," Gloria replied as kindly and honestly as she could.

"Twenty-five pounds on the heavy side," he admitted.

Gloria knew that most people who mentioned a specific number associated with their weight were usually kind to themselves. People who were thin might add a pound or two and those that were on the heavier side of the scale usually subtracted. Taking a little closer look at Charlie Duncan, Gloria guessed he was being kind to himself to the tune of about fifteen to twenty pounds.

"You carry it well pretty well, Charlie," was the only response that Gloria could come up with to gracefully back out of the conversation. "Dr. Davenport needs to make some adjustments to her Wednesday schedule and is soliciting volunteers. I was curious if you had any flexibility with your schedule and if you did, would you have an interest in helping her out?"

"As a matter of fact, I do have some flexibility Gloria and after all she's done for me, it would be really nice if I was able to help her. What do you need me to do?" Charlie replied with eagerness.

Gloria explained Dr. Davenport's situation as Charlie listened intently. Brett's name was never mentioned During Gloria's explanation; Brett's name had changed to *a patient that needed a lot of help right away.* Having been in a similar situation just a few short months ago, Charlie empathized with the *patient that needs a lot of help* and offered Gloria a couple of different options to reschedule his appointments.

Joyce opened her door and sent a smile Charlie's way. "Hi Charlie, come on in," Joyce offered.

As Charlie stood up and headed for Joyce's office, Gloria thanked him. On his way by Gloria's desk, Charlie gave her a quick, you're welcome, wink and watched her pencil him into his new time slot. From now on Mr. Duncan would make his weekly visit on Mondays from 11:00—11:45 a.m.

"One down and three to go," Gloria mumbled with exuberance looking over the remaining 3 names on her rescheduling target list. She contemplated waiting for each one to come in to the office but decided to call them ahead of time. If nothing else it would at least plant seeds that could be watered when they came in for their appointments later in the afternoon.

Gloria picked up the phone, skipped the 2:00 p.m. time slot occupied by Mr. Peterson and punched in Mrs. Johansson's number. After a long set of rings, it had to be at least ten, the answering machine picked up. It spoke to Gloria in a monotone computer type voice and had the usual leave your name and number message.

Gloria never understood why people didn't record their own messages. She had heard all the reasons at least once. People didn't like the way they sounded was the most common and perhaps her most favorite. Gloria was very surprised when she he heard herself for the first time, most people were. The hardest thing people had to come to terms with was how they really sound. Regardless of the reason, Gloria thought it was downright impersonal.

Hearing the tone, Gloria identified herself as the caller and stated the purpose of the call. Just as she was getting ready to hang up Mrs. Johansson picked up the phone.

"Hello....Hello. Are you still there," Gloria heard in her ear.

Gloria acknowledged that she was in fact still on the other end and the two exchanged pleasantries. Gloria began to explain the dilemma that Dr. Davenport found herself in and that this call was not to try and move her regularly scheduled appointment time.

She was calling to see if there were any patients that would be willing to consider another day and perhaps another time to see Dr. Davenport and that doing so was strictly voluntary.

Mrs. Johansson explained to Gloria that her regular Wednesday visits had to continue at their normal 3:00—3:45 p.m. time. She had gone to a lot of trouble, not to mention her family members that had to make adjustments, to ensure she could make her currently scheduled appointments and just couldn't manage to go through that rigmarole again.

Gloria said she understood and wasn't asking her to change her appointment. She also assured her that her appointment later today and all the ones scheduled on subsequent Wednesdays were all set and not to worry. She thanked Mrs. Johansson and told her she would see her in a few hours for her appointment and said goodbye. The phone rang just as Gloria was hanging up, happening so quickly that it actually startled her.

THE DONOR

"Dr. Davenport's office," Gloria answered quickly recovering.

"Good afternoon Gloria, Brett Allen, I was calling per Dr. Davenports suggestion in hopes of getting my appointment times. I'm in the car on my cell phone so excuse me if I sound like I'm in a fishbowl as I don't think I'm getting a very good signal," he stated

"Good Afternoon Brett," Gloria said responding in kind. "Dr. Davenport told me to expect your call. Thus far, the only firm appointment I can give you is Friday at 4:00 p.m. When you come in Friday I'll be able to tell give you the other days. You and the doctor discussed two sessions a week right?"

"Yes, two a week," Brett said confirming Gloria's question. "Is there a rough idea of when the second appointment will be?

"I'm trying to move some things around on Wednesday's," Gloria explained, "with the hope that we can get you in then. The jury's still out on that so I wouldn't take that day to the bank just yet. If I can firm it up later today or tomorrow, I'll call you at the lab if that's OK."

"It's more than OK, Gloria; I'd welcome a call at the lab," Brett admitted. "Sometimes I need a break. I get so caught up in my work by the time I look at the clock five or six hours have zipped by. Just let it ring, it will go into voice mail after ten rings. I can usually get to it by then if I'm expecting a call. If not just leave a message and I'll call you right back."

"OK Brett, I'll give you a call at the lab," Gloria replied

"There's just one more thing, Gloria, before I let you go. I'd like to leave a message for Dr. Davenport," Brett continued. "Could you please ask her to call me on my cell phone when she has some free time. I have some extremely intriguing information related to my treatment that I know she'll want to hear."

"I'll make sure she gets the message just as soon as she is unoccupied," Gloria reassured him, "and I'll probably be in touch sometime tomorrow. Have a good evening, Brett."

"You do the same, Gloria, and I'll look forward to hearing from you."

Removing his cell phone head set and putting it in his lap, Brett glanced at the dash board. The digital readout looking back told him it was 1:25. If traffic stayed the way it was, Brett knew he could actually make it to the lab by 3:00 at the latest. After the combination of events he had experienced, the convenience store and a less than pleasant meeting with Mr. Nelson, Brett decided he wouldn't be going in to work regardless of when he got back. Taking it easy for the rest of the day and starting fresh tomorrow had a much greater appeal. Besides, he wanted very much to talk with Joyce about his experience and for that he wanted total privacy.

Frank stayed a good distance behind Brett reflecting, with a little uneasiness, about the place they had just left. Frank didn't get bad feelings very often but returning to a location where he'd executed a double contract was a little unsettling, even for him.

Always one to rely on planning and execution, Frank never put much stock in that thing people called luck. His little inner voice had other ideas. It kept whispering to him that returning to the scene of a crime was not a good practice and if he wasn't careful his luck might just run out.

I've been in this line of work for a long time and if practice makes perfect, I'm the model of perfection. I don't make mistakes; every conceivable scenario is planned for, every action executed with precision timing and according to plan. That's why I'm the best there is. There's no such thing as luck in this business, Frank thought reassuring and dismissing his silent companion. *"Besides,"* Frank added as a final footnote, *that was over a decade ago.*

Hunger pangs crept into the forefront of Frank's mind and he wondered if the young man he was following was going to stop and eat lunch. Making his way to the middle lane, he thought about going back to the Triad for his evening meal. The food was good, the price was right, and his waitress was kind of cute. Frank decided if his new scientist friend went out for dinner he would tag along, eat in the same restaurant, and get some more information about Brett and his habits. If Brett didn't eat out, then the Triad would move from its current status as an option to a definite.

Gently easing his foot down on the gas pedal to keep pace with the mustang, Frank noticed he was now traveling a shade over seventy miles an hour. If he wanted to keep pace, it was obvious that getting eighty out of the Civic was going to be necessary. Spending fifteen minutes with a police officer going through the license and registration drill was not something he wanted to do. There would be too many questions and a lot more attention from law enforcement than he'd ever want or need. If Brett got away from him on their way back that was fine, reconnecting with him was the more desirable option and would be easy enough to do. Easing off the gas, he set the cruise control at seventy and considered doing something he had never done before while he was on the job, getting in touch with Veronica and flying her out for some weekend companionship. His little inner voice started cautioning him again so Frank cranked up the volume on the radio to silence his annoying caution signal and, somewhat to his surprise, successfully drowned it out.

Gloria turned her head away from the paperwork on her desk at the sound of Joyce's door opening. Charlie Duncan walked out of Dr. Davenport's office. It was 1:45 and Charlie Duncan's appointment had just concluded.

"See you Monday at 11:00," Charlie said with a smile as he made his way past Gloria's desk toward the door. "Have a good weekend," he added cheerfully.

"You too, Charlie, see you then," Gloria replied.

Grabbing the note she had taken earlier from Brett she got up and went into to Joyce's office and gave it to her.

"Thanks, Gloria," Joyce said while scanning the note. "I'll give him a call right now, I've got about 15 minutes before Mr. Peterson's appointment right?"

"Yes, that's right," Gloria confirmed as she left the office, closed the door behind her and returned to her desk.

Joyce situated herself comfortably in the chair and dialed Brett's cell phone and a few short rings later Brett picked up.

"Brett Allen," he answered.

"Hi, Brett, Joyce Davenport," she responded.

"That's quick turnaround, Joyce, I'm impressed," Brett stated honestly.

"I just got the message and since I'm between appointments I thought it would be a good time to hear about this new information you've come across," Joyce said with obvious interest.

"Well, something happened to me earlier today that I think you'll find very interesting. As you know, I went to Connecticut today for a meeting with Richard Nelson. The trip was uneventful until I got off the highway. I was on Bridge Street in a town called Gorton heading toward our facility there and as I came around a corner, it was right there."

"What was right there?" Joyce asked taking advantage of Brett's slight pause.

"The convenience store," Brett said flatly. "The one from my dream."

"The one from your dream, are you sure it was *that* one Brett?" Joyce asked, unable to conceal her skepticism.

"I didn't want to believe it myself," Brett admitted, "but when I was driving, the road seemed so familiar. I was focused so much on the store that the car drifted off the road a little and hit some of those rumble strips, just like in the dream. Granted it's a little hard to be exactly certain since the scenes in the dream were engulfed in darkness and a torrential downpour. That having been said, I still think that this was in fact the same place. I almost drove by but decided to stop and have a look inside; I guess the need to satisfy my curiosity was greater than my apprehension. When I got inside, everything was in the same place Joyce, well almost everything. The counter, the view from the inside of the store, the big window and the room where the attendant was locked in, were all exactly the same. Quite frankly, I'm a bit shaken by the whole thing. I was going to ask the guy behind the counter if they had any trouble there in the past but couldn't muster the courage. So what do you think?"

Joyce didn't know what to say. She knew Brett was, to say the least, very unsure about this, not so entirely, new chapter in his life and not prone to make statements that he couldn't substantiate with at least some semblance of facts.

"Brett, can you meet me later here at the office like around 5:30 or so? I'd like to talk more with you about this and think doing it in person would be best."

"How about this," Brett began with his counter offer, "let's meet at a place in Brighton called the Dug Out. It's on Main Street and has a great outside café. We can maybe get a little privacy and grab a bite to eat or just have a drink while we work through this thing, what do you say?"

"All right, but let's say 6:15. That will give me some extra time just in case the traffic is bad; are you going to be OK?" Joyce said accepting his offer.

"Yeah, I'll be OK; I'm just trying to figure this whole thing out. I don't know why this is happening to me but there has to be a reason. I'm pretty concerned about the situation and can't figure out if I'm intrigued, scared, or both. But I suspect that we'll get to the bottom of it. I don't want to keep you as I know you've got patients to see so I'll look forward to seeing you later. Who knows maybe this is a stepping stone for a new career, the Brett Allen predictions column in some tabloid. Do you think Jeanne Dixon should be nervous?" he said with a slight chuckle. "No don't answer that. I'll see you tonight and thanks for your help."

Joyce sat back after hanging up the phone, her mind going a hundred miles an hour. *What's going on here,* she asked herself as thoughts of her conversation with Brett kept replaying in her mind. Could he indeed be a genuine psychic as he jokingly suggested? No, Joyce said to herself and quickly dismissed the thought. One thing was for sure, she said to herself, there's a lot more to Brett Allen's situation than I originally thought and I'm going to get to the bottom of it.

Joyce began mentally reviewing her plan attack. Start with Nadia as Dr. Kaufman had suggested then move to the robbery dream. Picking up the pencil that was lying on the desk she started to jot down a few notes when her buzzer rang.

Gloria's voice came softly from the speaker, "Dr. Davenport, Mr. Peterson is here for his appointment."

"Thanks, Gloria, I'll be right there," Joyce responded as she hurriedly finished putting her thought down on her legal pad and placed them in her desk drawer.

"If this store is in fact the one in his dream, then there's a very good chance that this Nadia girl could be an actual person, which makes finding her significance to Brett even more important," she said on her way to her door. Grabbing the handle, a strange thought crossed her mind. *The thickness of this door separates those who are waiting to get better and those who are in the process of getting better. An even finer line exists between reality and perception. I wonder when it's all said and done which side of the line Brett will land on.* Opening the door, she quickly switched gears, greeted Mr. Peterson and got their 2:00 p.m. session underway.

13.

Brett pulled into the *Dug Out* just a hair on the shy side of 5:30 and noticed there were plenty of free tables at the outside café. This came as no surprise as most of the *in crowd* liked to start their evening off a little bit later in the day and the Red Sox were traveling to Seattle so he knew the patronage would be well below normal anyway. A perfect time to meet with Joyce he thought.

Brett chose a table that had good visibility from the road so Joyce wouldn't have any trouble seeing him. The sun sat just outside the rim of the patio umbrella and right in his eyes. Unfortunately for Brett, he left his sun glasses in the car and didn't really feel like going to get them. Nothing was more irritating and distracting than trying to talk with someone with sun in your eyes so Brett moved his chair a little to the left and found at least some temporary relief. If the situation didn't improve once Joyce arrived, they could always move to a table that enjoyed the shadowy protection offered by the building.

Brett really liked this place and knew a good number of the regulars and all of the staff.

When the Red Sox, Patriots or Celtics were being televised the place was transformed, from a quiet place to have a drink, into a bee hive of activity. There was one large room in the Dug Out affectionately called the *Stadium;* this was Brett's favorite place to take in a ball game. People would come as early as an hour before the first pitch just to have an opportunity to watch a game from there.

Brian Jones, the owner of the Dug Out and father of the Stadium knew someone in the Red Sox organization and got about twenty of the old Fenway Park seats, refinished them, set them up in a theater type seating arrangement and put in a huge, state of the art projection television. Brian was a stickler for detail and redecorated the Stadium based on the season. This was baseball season and the atmosphere was Red Sox. Banners, pictures of players and other memorabilia were smartly placed on the walls and anywhere else he could put them. When the stadium made its Dug Out debut, it was a smash hit.

Frank Whickers parked his car several spaces away from Brett in a spot that would allow him a quick exit regardless of how full the parking lot would become. To get inside, he would have to walk right past Brett's table. Brett glanced over, as most people do, to see who was passing by and Frank offered the obligatory head nod hello on his way by and Brett responded in kind.

Frank took quick stock of his new surroundings and made mental notes of the general layout, exit locations and couldn't help but be amazed at the amount of sports paraphernalia that adorned the place.

His first impression of the place was mixed. He liked the horseshoe shaped bar but wasn't fond of the old fashioned, bolted to the floor, bar stools that surrounded it. Counting the bar stools out of curiosity, Frank came up with something in the neighborhood of forty.

Frank did some quick math, figuring in the people who'd be squeezing in between the stools when the palace was busy and took a somewhat educated guess that as many as sixty to seventy people could encircle the horseshoe trying to get the attention of the bartenders. There seemed to be a lot of open space in the bar area so even with a crowd that size, one wouldn't get that closed in feeling.

A separate area had a nice, well finished hardwood floor that served as a resting place for a dozen or so tables. Seeing, what appeared to be, a one page laminated menu wedged between the salt and pepper shakers of each table, Frank assumed if you were hungrier than you were thirsty that would be the place to go.

This place is a lot bigger than it looks, he thought to himself as he started walking with a bit of urgency, for the man/woman symbols that announced the location of the rest rooms. The restrooms were located near the back, getting closer, a short hallway revealed itself to Frank's right and wanting thoroughly to be aware of his surroundings, he put his bathroom break on hold. Walking about five steps the hallway opened up and he got his first glimpse of the Stadium. It did two things to Frank that were very hard to do; it both impressed and surprised him. He was captivated by the layout and stood there for a few minutes taking everything in until his need to use the bathroom could wait no longer.

"Hi, Becky," Brett said with a smile greeting his favorite waitress.

"Hi, Brett, wow two days in a row. I had no idea you missed me that much," Becky replied.

"I've been counting the minutes," Brett said as his smile widened.

Becky burst out laughing. "Me too," she managed through a slightly embarrassed giggle.

"Let me guess, cranberry juice for starters?" as she began writing down order with waiting for a reply, "and since you didn't bring a paper today do you want me to get one from inside?"

"Yes to the cranberry juice and no thanks to the paper. Someone will be joining me in a few minutes so I don't think I'll have time to read it. I think we might need a menu too"

"Coming right up," Becky said lightheartedly.

Brett was admiring Becky's figure as she went to get his drink. It would sure be nice to take her to dinner sometime he thought, watching her disappear inside.

"What's the worst thing that can happen?" he mumbled trying to bolster the courage to ask. "I might as well ask her. Until I do, the answer is no anyway, so why not get confirmation."

Brett was very outgoing with everyone and a good conversationalist but when it came to asking girls out on dates, he was super shy and lacked confidence. Now that he had prepared himself for what he was sure would be the answer, he made a nervous, and for him a very courageous decision to give it a try just as soon as she came back. Staring at the door, he began fighting off the jitters welling up inside when he heard a familiar voice.

"Hi, Brett, traffic wasn't so bad after all," Joyce stated in a somewhat relieved voice.

Startled by the unexpected interruption to his courage building session, Brett jumped just a little bit at he sound of her voice.

"Sorry," she said apologetically, "I didn't mean to startle you."

Smiling, he glanced over at Joyce. "Don't be. Really I'm actually kind of grateful to be let off the hook."

"Off the hook?" Joyce asked inquisitively putting her purse on the table and sitting down.

"Yeah, off the hook. I need to ask someone a question and I'm a little nervous about it," he admitted. "So I'm a pretty relieved that you got here when you did so now I won't have to."

Joyce didn't dig any further figuring that if Brett wanted to tell her, the perfect chance had just passed and that was all the information she was about to get on the subject.

Becky arrived back at the table and Brett made the introductions. At first, Brett thought he detected a bit of jealousy in Becky's countenance but couldn't be sure. If there was, it was gone as quickly as it came. *If that was jealousy I just saw,* Brett thought, *maybe, just maybe, I have a chance with her after all.*

"Hi, Joyce," Becky said with her usual perkiness "Can I get you something from the bar?"

"Hi, Becky, I'd love a glass of white wine."

"White wine it is. I'll be right back."

Joyce thanked her and turned to ask Brett a question. What Joyce saw was unmistakable. It was the same look he had on his face when she got there, a daydreaming, contemplative look. Joyce didn't say anything, she just observed Brett as he watched Becky head into the building. Brett had feelings for this girl, no question about it. If she could get him to talk about it, she wouldn't be bashful about giving him some sound medical advice.

"She seems very nice, do you know her?" Joyce asked seizing the opportunity to open the discussion.

"Yes. I met her when she started working here about three months ago so I don't know her real well, but I certainly agree with you, she's *really* nice," Brett said confirming Joyce's observations.

"Can I ask you a personal question, Brett?"

"Sure go ahead," he replied.

"I've been meaning to ask if you had someone close to you. Someone other than your father that you can talk to and spend time with," Joyce asked.

"Not really. I've got a lot of friends but none I would say that I'm real close to," Brett admitted. "My work keeps me pretty busy and occupies the majority of my time. When I need to relax and get out I usually come here. So I guess my inner social circle, if I can describe it that way, is pretty non-existent. At times it can get a bit lonely"

"For what it's worth Brett I think it would be very good for you emotionally to start developing some of that inner social circle, as you call it. There's a very good chance it could help with these dreams you're having."

"You might be right but until I finish my work on this anti-rejection project,

I don't know how much time I could devote to developing something like that."

"Here we are… one glass of white wine," Becky said approaching their table. "Would you guys like to order something to eat?"

"I'm not sure," Brett said glancing at Joyce to see if she was hungry.

"I had a late lunch so I'm not real hungry," Joyce admitted.

"How about an order of chicken wings, Becky, we'll play around with those," Brett asked.

"Large or small?" Becky inquired.

"Let's go with the large. I'm hungry and I'll even try to convince Joyce to have a few," Brett responded.

"OK, it'll be about ten minutes," Becky informed him.

"Thanks, Becky."

"You're welcome Brett," she said on her way to a new investigate her newest café customer, Frank Whickers.

"Now we're getting somewhere," Frank muttered glancing over at Brett's table.

Frank could see them talking but wasn't quite close enough to hear what they were saying. He quickly made plans to follow Brett's dinner companion when she left and find out everything he could about her. Digging into his pants pocket he took out his little note pad and recorded some new entries.

Becky arrived at Franks table a took his order for a draft beer and the Dug Out special which was nothing more than a ¼ pound cheeseburger with their special sauce and curly fries. He also took Becky up on her offer for the *Boston Globe*.

"As I was saying, Brett," Joyce continued, "I think it would really help if you tried to develop that type of relationship with someone. It would provide, what I would say, is a well needed distraction from your work and give you some form of an outlet. Take Becky for instance, she seems like a nice girl. You two could probably have a lot of fun together if you went out some time. It may be just what the doctor ordered," she added finishing with a smile. Judging for the look on Brett's face she knew she had just struck the right chord.

"I guess you're right, I haven't been out on a date in such a long time I'm not sure I remember how to do it," he said adding a smile of his own. "Maybe I will ask her."

Becky put Frank's beer on his table and handed him the paper.

"Could you do me a favor" Frank asked.

"Sure, what can I do for you," Becky responded.

"Could you bring me a tall glass of ice water and when you bring the special out, I'd like to go ahead and pay. I'm on call right now and I just never know when this darn thing is going to ring," Frank said pointing to his cell phone.

"Being on call can't be much fun. So a tall glass of ice water and the bill when I bring you your food. Do you want me to bring the water out now?"

"No, that's OK, let's wait until the food is ready."

"OK, it shouldn't be much longer," Becky informed him as she started back to the bar.

"Back and forth, back and forth, back and forth," Frank mumbled. "Being a waitress is a pretty thankless job." Opening the *Boston Globe*, he began to get acquainted with the local news.

Brett began describing the events he experienced earlier in the day as Joyce listened intently not wanting to miss the slightest detail. It was a little unsettling for her to watch this young man, desperate to find answers, wrestle with the sub conscious in the conscious realm.

Brett was going over his visit to the store and suddenly paused. Becky was weaving her way through the loose maze of tables that made up the café. The tray she was carrying had a large order of chicken wings, a cheese burger and a glass of water.

"Here you go, guys, enjoy!" Becky said taking a quick look at their glasses to see if they might need more refreshments. Satisfied that Brett and his guest were OK, she brought her other customer his Dug Out special and water.

"I think I'm going to do it," Brett said flatly.

"Do what?" Joyce asked curiously

"Ask her out for dinner, maybe a movie, I don't know yet but I'm going to take your advice, Joyce."

"That's a great idea, Brett, and whatever you do, I'm sure you'll have a great time doing it."

Brett put a couple of wings on each plate and put one in front of each of them. Joyce started laughing when he split the huge pile of napkins and plopped a bunch down next to her plate. Brett smiled, "Messy but good," he said as he started to eat.

Brett, always conscious of his manners, didn't like to talk with food in his mouth. After finishing a few of the tasty wings and washing it down, he picked up the conversation right where he left off. Joyce continued eating, apparently a little hungrier than she thought, and managed to almost finish the entire plate before Brett finished his account of the day's events.

"You know based on some research I've done and what you've shared with me, I think we may have something here that goes beyond just having recurrent dreams. There are some-well documented and verifiable cases where people have been able see things that happened in the past or experience precognitive dreams that represent things that haven't yet happened." Joyce explained, "This in no way suggests that the events you've been dreaming about specifically involve you, in fact in most of the cases I've been able to look at, these kind of things are usually about events that don't involve the person experiencing the premonitions."

"Are you suggesting that I'm some sort of psychic medium?" Brett asked a little shocked at the implication.

"I'm not suggesting that you get a crystal ball or a deck of tarot cards, what I am saying is that you may, at least for the time being, be seeing things in your dreams that may be based in part, on actual events. Now whether these visions, for lack of a better term, are a look at the past or a glimpse into future, I'm not real sure but when meet on Friday and undergo hypnosis we might get uncover some clues."

"Wow, I've got to tell you, Joyce, your explanation comes as a real surprise. It actually scares me a little," Brett confessed. "If what you think is true shouldn't there be something I should be doing about it?"

"Let's not jump the gun," Joyce said firmly trying to calm him down, "After all, we don't really know what these dreams represent just yet and quite honestly, we may never know even *after* hypnosis. With all the benefits a successful session can bring, it's far from an exact science but at this point in time, it's our best hope. Just try and relax and keep your mind off it."

"That's a whole lot easier said than done," Brett said succinctly, "but I'll do my best."

"Look," Joyce offered. "Why not take that nice young lady to dinner tomorrow, it will be something far removed from your normal routine. You'll have a great time and at the very least, doing something new with someone new, will be a nice distraction"

"I'm going to head home now," Joyce announced beginning to rummage through her purse.

"I've got this, Joyce," Brett said right away knowing she was going to try and pay her fair share. "I insist."

"Well thank you," Joyce said putting her purse down. "I've got to take a quick run inside to use the ladies room so I'll say goodbye for now and see you on Friday."

"Thanks for coming, Joyce, see you Friday," Brett said as he stood to shake her hand. "I hope it works."

"Me too," Joyce responded in agreement, shook Brett's hand and left to go inside.

Seeing his cue, Frank rose from his chair and made his way to the car. Noticing a slight sensation of heartburn during his short walk, stopping at a store to get something for it moved right to the top of his things to do list after he found out where this girl lived. "I knew I shouldn't have eaten those curly fries," he said in a self scolding tone and shut the car door.

Brett was thinking about Joyce's most recent hypothesis and started to wonder why all this stuff was happening. The thought of hypnosis had him on edge a little bit too, what if it didn't work, worse yet what if it did!

Brett's occupation with his thoughts broke when he saw Joyce leaving. Exchanging a wave he watched her get in the car and pull out of the driveway followed rather nonchalantly by a black Honda Civic. Out of the corner of his eye, he saw someone coming toward him, it was Becky.

"How was everything, Brett?" she asked.

"Just great, Becky," he replied, the nervousness about asking her out quickly returning.

"Can I ask you something, Becky?" Brett managed, noticing a slight quiver in his tone that he hoped she wouldn't pick up on.

"Sure," she replied with slight anticipation.

"Remember when I said I was counting the minutes?" he continued not really waiting for an answer. "Well I sort of meant it." Noticing Becky's cheeks getting a little red from embarrassment he wondered if maybe he should have kept quiet. *Here it comes,* he thought as Becky started to answer.

"Remember when I said me too? I really meant it. I've been hoping for the longest time you'd say something like that to me."

A tinge of excitement ran through Brett as he managed a smile of relief.

"Are you free at all this week for dinner?" he asked with newly resurrected confidence.

"As a matter of fact I am, I'm off tomorrow," she said blissfully and began writing something down on her order pad. "Here, take this," she said handing it to Brett. "My phone number and address."

"Can I pick you up tomorrow around 7:00?" Brett offered.

"That's perfect," she said.

Seeing four new customers settling in, she had to get back to work. Placing the bill on the table, she quickly apologized and asked Brett to call her tomorrow sometime in the afternoon to which he eagerly agreed. He watched her for a few minutes and now wondered if, now that he had a date with her, a bigger tip was in order. Chuckling, he pulled twentyfive dollars from his wallet and put it under his glass. Feeling a little giddy, a chuckle managed to escape on his way to the car. Despite everything that had happened today he couldn't remember the last time he'd felt so good. He whispered a quick, thanks Joyce, as he negotiated his car out of the parking lot and headed home.

14.

Frank picked it up the phone as fast as he could to put an end to the earsplitting ring. Frank didn't hear anyone on the other end and a quick look at the clock told him it was his 4:00 a.m. wake up call. There was no doubt he was awake, a ring that loud probably woke up the whole floor he thought adjusting the volume to something a little more reasonable. These early morning shadows, as he called them, were the worst part of the job. If Frank had his druthers, sleeping until 10:00 every morning would soon become a habit he'd really enjoy.

Walking lazily into the shower Frank decided that he wasn't going to be standing very close to his razor this morning. A little scruff on his face wouldn't hurt. It was real early and he was real tired so any little thing at this hour that he could cut out of the normal routine was welcomed. Cranking on the hot water the bathroom rapidly filled with steam. Frank watched the mirror fog while he brushed his teeth and gave it a quick swipe with his hand before deciding to hit the switch and turn on the fan. *I guess well see if the maid washes the mirror,* he thought rinsing his mouth for the last time. He didn't care much for the stain like smear the mirror would have once it dried. If the maid didn't get it by the time he got back then he'd do it himself.

Stepping into the shower Frank turned so the hot water could run down his back. Slowly feeling the life returning to his body he thought about the woman he had followed the night before and wondered if he'd be able to learn any valuable information when he tailed her in, what he hoped would be, a few hours. He didn't relish the thought of sitting near her house at 5:30 and waiting until she started her day but that's what had to be done.

Frank grabbed a towel from the rack, stepped out the shower, and started drying off. Eyeballing the small coffee maker, he wrapped the towel around his waist and made a pot. These little hotel coffee machines boasted a four cup capability but even filled to the top the best you could get out of them was two, unless of course you were using teacups. Hitting the switch the sound of water gurgling water verified the machine had started the process of turning ground roasted beans into coffee.

Frank started to get dressed as the smell of fresh coffee started filling the room, the aroma reminding him of Veronica. Whenever she spent the night with Frank, she would always make a fresh pot of coffee before leaving in the morning. What he really appreciated is that she did it because she knew how much he enjoyed a cup when he first woke up and he never once, not even the first time, had to ask.

Grabbing a small paper cup from the stack near the coffee he poured himself a cup, which in reality, was more like a sip and went over to the desk nestled in the corner of the room. Sitting neatly on top of the desk was a roll of antacids, a new map, and a package of signal dots he had picked up from a KMart he had found on his way home from his address gathering mission.

Clearing an area on the desk, he opened the map and started pressing the folds out so it would lie nice and flat. He opened his notebook and started to pinpoint the places he had been. Neatly placing a blue dot on the location of the Dug Out he wrote the number one on it and made a cross-referencing entry in his notebook. Combing the map, he finally found the address of the woman he followed and placed a yellow dot over that location and wrote a question mark on it followed by a number one. Making sure there was sufficient space for notes, Frank left plenty of empty lines between entries.

Frank really liked using this system even though it was little outdated. This marked the beginning of filling in that top spot of his pyramid. This method allowed Frank to get a visual picture of things as they unfolded and was an extremely valuable planning tool. Blue represented places he had seen Brett, yellow represented potential items of interest that warranted looking into. When a *hot spot*, as Frank called them, surfaced then red was the color of choice. Hot spots were places Brett frequented. After a few weeks the map would make a gradual transformation from multiple colors to predominantly red. Once Frank reached that point, it was time to start putting together his action plan.

Frank folded the map and placed it the top drawer of his bureau. He wasn't worried about anyone seeing it, least of all a nosey chamber maid. Anyone other than Frank that happened to get a glimpse of it wouldn't have a clue what it depicted.

Due to the seemingly unusual amount of traffic, it took Frank a little over fifty minutes to get back from last night's excursion not counting his pit stop at KMart. Wanting to allow ample time to get there, Frank collected his keys preparing to leave. It was ten minutes before 5:00 a.m. and guessing there wouldn't be a whole lot of traffic, it shouldn't take him nearly that long to cover the fifteen miles. Stopping at the door, Frank patted himself down to make sure he had his room key. Deciding that his wallet was a pretty good spot to keep it, he took the card key from his pocket and slid it into his wallet amongst his credit card collection.

Frank walked to his car through the hollowness of the parking structure, its reinforced concrete columns separating one level from another. The thought of going around in circles, descending to the exit, wasn't all that appealing to him right now and he was grateful for his good fortune of finding a parking place on the first floor.

Stopping at the gate, Frank fumbled around trying to get his garage access key. It was proving to be a little more stubborn than Frank cared for and after a few unsuccessful attempts to remove it, he grabbed all the plastic from his wallet and tossed them in the passenger seat.

Grabbing the key card and sliding it into the slot, he looked at the automated, yellow wooden plank gate and waited for it to let him out. "I should have had another cup of coffee." His tone reflected his disappointment at how things were getting off to a rather rough start. Removing the card, he noticed he had put it in backwards. Putting it back in, magnetic strip first, the gate immediately responded. Pushing down hard on the gas pedal, half accidentally, half out of frustration, Frank squealed the tires as he drove past.

Coming to the stop sign that guarded motorists traveling on Dalton St from those leaving the hotel, he ran the directions through his mind and took one more look at the ones that he had written down. As he turned onto to Dalton Street, his trip to Norwood was underway, final destination Margaret Street.

Brett was up early too but not because he wanted to be. He had just finished having a couple of different dreams. The first one was really disjointed and odd. It was about Nadia and computer disks. He couldn't remember much about it because his dream about getting shot made an encore performance right after and clouded his recollection. He didn't need any help waking up; his dream took care of that. He was more than wide awake. Almost afraid, he peered down at his wrist. Sure enough, the pink blotches had returned.

Knowing there was really nothing he could do about it, he started thinking about Becky and their date later in the evening, hoping it would help him to focus on something else other than the dream. It did help but only a little bit. The elation Brett experienced after Becky agreed to their date was gone. In its place was a familiar and unwelcome apprehension that always followed his chilling vision. He decided going to work a little early was a good idea and would probably help. It was shortly after 5:00 a.m. when Brett left his apartment and set off for the research center.

Bracketed by Washington Street and David Terrace, Margaret Street wasn't very long. It seemed to be pretty nice residential neighborhood given its proximity to Boston, sprinkled with relatively new homes and decent sized property lots. It was getting close to seven when Frank finished his fifth crossword puzzle, helped a little bit by some of the answers found in the back of the book, when his mystery woman finally got in her car to leave.

Frank was good at tailing people and made sure he kept a safe distance away learning a valuable lesson early on in his illicit career. During one of his first engagements, he was following someone a little too closely when they suddenly pulled over and made a quick U turn taking him totally by surprise. Before he could recover, he lost them and had to start over the following morning.

He enjoyed the fact that most drivers were very contentious about using turn signals. It made it easier for him to stay in contact with them if his view became somewhat restricted from additional vehicles getting into the mix. Joyce fit into the most drivers' category very nicely using her signals well in advance to announce her planned change in direction.

Reaching the outskirts of Boston, Joyce turned into her office building parking lot; Frank opted to pull into the diner right across the street to see what she would do next.

As Joyce began the trek to her office and vanished inside the building, Frank left his car and crossed the street. Seeing the small signs that dotted some of the parking lot, he guessed she parked in a reserved spot. Reading the name under the Reserved For heading as he walked behind the car, he discovered that Dr. Joyce Davenport was the person he had been following.

Frank entered the building and examined the glass cased marquee that provided the names and office numbers of the occupants. He took out his notebook and wrote down her name and office number. As a footnote he wrote down the words psychiatric medicine and circled it.

Frank headed back to get his car and wanted to confirm, as best he could, that he did in fact, just witness Dr. Joyce Davenport drive to work. Crossing the street he went to the pay phone, supported by a crooked metal pole situated near the front of the diner and dialed 411.

"What town?" the emotionless voice inquired.

"Norwood."

"What listing?"

"Davenport, D-a-v-e-n-p-o-r-t, Joyce," Frank answered, quickly flipping a few pages back in his notebook finding what he needed, "on Margaret Street."

He could hear the key strikes of the operator entering in the information. "Sir, I'm sorry that's a non published number."

"Thank you." He didn't know one doctor that was foolish enough to have a publicly listed phone number. Now sure, or at least as sure as he could be, that it was Joyce Davenport he hung up the phone and drove back to the hotel, put another yellow dot on the map and took a nap. Along the way, Frank made another decision; he was going to call Veronica later in the afternoon and have her come to Boston for at least part of the weekend.

Brett was glad to be back in the lab. At least here, unlike his current personal dilemma, he could control the environment and what happened in it, with some degree of predictability. Not having any notes from yesterday to review, he did a quick reread of what he looked at two days ago and walked over to his tissue/culture incubator and removed a petri dish he had labeled *Cytanepax 22*. Removing a small sample from the dish, he prepared a slide for examination under his, research level, compound microscope.

The white blood cells from number forty three, Brett labeled his laboratory animals numerically, were attacking the liver tissue of number forty four. Although initially disappointed with what he saw, the white cells didn't appear as antagonistic in Cytanepax 22 as they were in Cytanepax 21.

Intently observing the cell activity, he started to take some notes for comparative reasons. Eight months ago, this same experiment resulted in the total destruction of the foreign tissue so definite progress was being made. Satisfied that his recorded version of the events was accurate and complete; he lifted the legal pad from the lab table and walked to his desk.

Everything in the lab was immaculate, everything but his desk. Once a month he would look at the army of yellow post it notes that seemed to be just everywhere. Some he threw away and the ones he wasn't sure about ended up being re-stuck somewhere else. All the important information regarding the research project was kept on the company's secure computer system and to Brett that's what mattered most.

After entering the information into the computer system, Brett took his handwritten notes and put them through the electronic eraser which did a surprisingly good job. He was then required to shred the pages in the paper shredder. Seemed a bit much to Brett but procedures were procedures. After doing it for so long it became second nature, even at home, to look for a shredder before tossing a piece of paper into the waste basket.

Brett was thirsty and wanted to have something cold to drink so he left the lab, the door automatically locking behind him and followed the corridors en route to the cafeteria. Before visiting the Connecticut facility, Brett liked the appearance of the research center, now he thought the entire center looked overly antiseptic and lacked character. A comparison he wouldn't have made a few days ago.

Brett had to pass the main entrance to get where he was going and happened to look out towards the security gate. He saw a few police officers and several people walking around carrying signs.

"Hey, Elaine, what's going on out there," Brett yelled over to the receptionist.

"Some animal rights group, Doctor Allen," Elaine answered back. "I guess everyone needs a cause to believe in," she added.

"Yeah, I guess you're right," Brett said moving closer so he could talk in a more civilized tone. "I wonder what would happen if one of them got cancer and needed treatment. Do you think they'd refuse if they knew the very discovery that would save their life was made, in larger part, using animal test subjects?"

Trying to image the scenario, Elaine gave her response "I really don't know. I wonder if that happened, and can only guess there's a pretty good chance it would to someone somewhere, if the reason they're out there protesting would be worth dying for."

Brett was impressed with Elaine's answer. "I wonder myself, Elaine; I wonder myself" he repeated. Brett said so long to Elaine resuming his trip to the cafeteria and began thinking about his mother, he really missed her.

A small bag of chocolate chip cookies and a can of grape soda shared Brett's left hand, now back from his trip, as he punched his code into the key pad with his right. Putting his snack and soft drink on his desk, he pulled up the test results he just entered from Cytanepax 22 and the results from Cytanepax 21 and put them side by side on the monitor. Reviewing the results of the two experiments trying to find just the right blend of ingredients and additives, he felt like he was developing a new cook book recipe, which in reality wasn't far from the truth.

When Brett was in the lab time just melted away. A good three hours had passed since he started the analysis of his last two experiments. His evaluation and comparative statistical study resulted in several promising hypotheses.

Getting up to put two new petri dishes in the sterilizer, the phone rang. Quickly sitting back down, Brett picked up the phone. "Dr. Allen," he answered.

"Good afternoon, Dr. Allen, I mean Brett. This is Gloria Johnson from Dr. Davenport's office. I hope I haven't gotten you at a bad time," she said half apologetically.

"No, not all, Gloria, are you calling to give me my schedule?" Brett asked, searching for a pencil.

"Yes I am, and also with a question," Gloria answered.

"Go ahead with the question, Gloria," Brett said. "I'm still looking for something to write with, there's never a pencil around when you need one."

"I know how that goes," Gloria fired back with genuine empathy. "Dr. Davenport has two people that, for various reasons, cancelled their Friday appointments and she was wondering if you could somehow make it in at 1:30."

Brett's first reaction was to say no then the memory of his dream that he'd managed to push just beneath the surface of his thoughts came flooding back. "Let me check and see if I can make, I'll have to get back to you on that one."

"OK," Gloria said. "You know you may not need a pencil after all. The times are all at 4:00 and the days are Tuesday and Friday."

"I can remember that easy enough, Tuesdays and Fridays at 4:00. I'll call you back in about an hour and let you know about tomorrow. Thanks, Gloria."

Brett didn't hang up the phone. He just pushed the button down for a few seconds and retrieved Becky's number from his wallet and started to dial. The hard part about asking her out was over. Not quite sure of what he was going to say he could feel his angst returning. It was nowhere near the level he had just had before asking her to dinner but it was there nonetheless. Becky's answering machine picked up, her recognizable, bubbly voice was providing instructions as to the information she needed if the caller expected to get a call back. Brett left his name, phone number of the lab and his cell number and asked her to call when she got in.

As Brett resumed the task of making his Petri dishes ready for the next experiment Frank was just getting off the phone with Veronica. He had just given her flight information for her trip to Boston on Saturday. She had agreed, as Frank knew she would, to join him for part of the weekend while he was on his business trip. Frank would be picking her up at Logan International at 10:30 a.m., and bringing her back for a return flight to Chicago Sunday morning at 11:45. It wasn't a long stay but Frank wanted to take the day off and felt, although early in his assignment, he deserved it.

The lab phone rang again and Brett closed the cage that held the laboratory rats 43 and 44 satisfied after a brief inspection that by the middle of next day they should both be able to tolerate another fine needle aspiration of more liver tissue.

"Grand Central station today," he thought picking up the phone. "Dr. Allen."

Brett recognized Becky's voice. "Hi, I'm looking for Brett Allen."

"Hi, Becky, this is Brett," he said trying to conceal a giggle.

"Doctor Allen," she said a little stunned with the information. She thought all doctors were pretentious and from what she knew of Brett, he was far from that. "I had no idea!"

"I'll tell you all about it tonight assuming of course you still want to have dinner with me," Brett said offering her a way out in case she had changed her mind.

"I'll be ready at 7:00, where are we going?" she asked.

"I thought we'd go to the restaurant at the top of the Prudential Building. I've never been there but hear the food is great and the view spectacular. Does that sound OK?"

"Sounds wonderful, Brett, see you at 7:00. I'm looking forward to it. Oh before I forget, what will you be wearing?" she inquired not wanting to be too mismatched.

"I'll be wearing some Dockers and probably a nice casual shirt; nothing too fancy, does that help?"

"Yes it does thanks; do you need directions on how to get here?"

"No, I already got directions on line so I think I'm all set. See you soon, Becky!"

Hanging up the phone after sharing a cordial goodbye, Brett was a little too excited to concentrate on his work. Brett couldn't remember ever being so distracted from his work since he started his professional career. Gathering his things to leave a little early, Brett stopped himself on the way to the door and got back on the phone. He'd almost forgotten to call Gloria back and tell her he would be able to make it tomorrow at 1:30.

Brett sat there for a second, his concentration in a mild state of chaos, and ran through his mind making sure he had done everything that was on his agenda for today. With the exception of picking up Becky later, he was pretty certain it was safe for him leave. Content that he wasn't overlooking anything he got up and left.

Frank pulled into the research center parking lot and looked for Brett's Mustang. As he drove slowly he made two complete trips around the entire lot and came up empty. Cursing under his breath he pulled out and headed for Brett's apartment hoping to reconnect with him there. He wasn't even sure if Brett had shown up for work since he was busy much earlier in the day with Joyce Davenport.

On his way, Frank thought it was time for a new crossword puzzle book. Sitting around and waiting was excruciatingly boring. Despite the fact he was well compensated for his time, he didn't enjoy it all that much. Now that he was on Newton Street, he began to prepare himself for what could be another pretty long wait. He couldn't figure out how cops could stomach those long arduous stakeouts, especially with what they were getting paid. Everyone has their own crosses to bear Frank thought weaving his way through the apartment complex. "There is mine," Frank muttered, spotting Brett's Mustang and settling in for what could be a very long wait.

Much to Frank's surprise, his cross to bear, at least this time was only a few hours long. Brett emerged from his apartment a little after 5:00. Frank noticed Brett looked a little snazzier than usual which raised his level of curiosity a notch.

The Boston traffic was starting to take its toll on Frank. He didn't travel much this time of day unless it was absolutely necessary, which usually meant he was on the job. Frank finally pulled over on Lincoln Street and watched Brett walk into one of the buildings. A few minutes later, Frank saw someone else he recognized walking with Brett to his car. "The waitress from the sports bar," Frank said adjusting his binoculars to get a better look. Frank was surprised at just how good she looked. He thought she was pretty when he saw her at the bar, now she was stunning. Her black shoulder cut hair bounced lightly as she accompanied her young suitor. The navy blue dress she was wearing was a little on the conservative side for Frank's liking but complemented her nicely just the same. "Very good taste, Enjoy it while you can young man," he advised coldly.

It wasn't long before Frank found himself standing outside of the Prudential Building. Brett and his date had gone in a few minutes before. It was about 7:20

p.m. and well past regular business hours and Frank wanted to know where they went. Asking several passers by using the "I'm a visitor to the city routine," he got his answer. It was time to head back to the hotel, update his map and go to bed. It had been a very long day.

15.

Brett sat up in his bed wondering if the alarm clock could somehow be wrong, its annoying wail declaring a new day had arrived. Although Brett didn't get to bed until almost 1:30 a.m. he felt just great, still riding the high from a terrific date with Becky.

They had a great dinner admiring the view, the food, each other and talked well into the night. He shared with her the story of his youth and how came to be a scientist. Telling the story of his mother's passing, he remembered the tears Becky successfully held back. He didn't however share with her his tormented nights spent locked into dreams he couldn't escape from. When he was asked about Joyce, he told her that she was a psychiatrist and family friend that helped them through the emotional turmoil of losing his mother.

Becky went through a similar rendition and loosely described herself as an average girl who hadn't yet decided what she wanted to do when she grew up. She said that by the time her twenty second birthday rolled around in October, she was hoping to have a better idea as to the direction she wanted to take with her future.

She was very quick witted and had some decent jokes that Brett hadn't heard before. He wasn't one to laugh politely out of respect for someone's feelings. If a joke was bad, he felt little compunction in saying so, as Becky found out with a few of her more off color jokes. She wasn't offended and found it refreshing that he was willing to speak his mind. Most of the guys she had dated in the past always tried to impress her, and the fact that Brett didn't seem to go out his way for her, impressed Becky even more.

111

Their date ended on a comical note and Brett laughed, sitting there on the bed thinking about it. On her way to the bathroom, she had somehow got her dress caught on the edge of a table causing a split that went nearly to her upper thigh. "I knew before the night was over," Becky's voice displaying some false agitation, "that you'd see a side of me that only my mother has seen before" They both started laughing so hard it brought tears to their eyes.

They sat in the car outside her apartment for a few minutes before saying goodnight and Becky told him with the greatest sincerity that she had a fabulous time and really hoped they could go out again soon. Brett agreed and told her he planed to be at the Dug Out Friday night and maybe they could plan something when he saw her. He wondered if his day tomorrow at the lab would be a productive one or if he would think about Becky all day.

"Hey, Luther," Brett said going through security the next morning. "How are you today?"

"I don't think I'm as good as you Dr. Allen," Luther said observantly. "What did you do last night that's put that bounce in your step?"

"I went out to dinner with a great lady," Brett said gleefully.

"If she's a good one, don't you let her get away," he advised moving the wand over Brett's torso. "Good ones these days are hard to find."

"I'll take that under serious advisement Luther," he acknowledged moving into the research center grounds.

"Hey, Doc!" Luther yelled "shot a 96 yesterday afternoon."

"I told you, Luther! It was just a matter of time," Brett yelled back turning to go inside.

Brett sat down at his desk and laughed again thinking about Becky's dress. He wanted to call her but felt that may be a little too pushy so he'd wait until he saw her at the Dug Out tonight. Meandering through his work, he again lost track of time. Hearing the alarm on his computer go off, he went over to see what reminder he had left. *Joyce Davenport 1:30* was displayed on the monitor. He had even forgotten about his appointment. "I knew I was going to be scatterbrained today," he said, collecting his things.

Joyce knew Brett would be in the waiting room in a few minutes and did a final rehash of how she would like the session to unfold. She was a little skeptical about how Brett would do despite the results of the Stanford Scales Joyce and knew her skepticism would, one way or another, soon be over.

It was 1:15 when Gloria buzzed in and told Joyce that Brett had just taken a seat in the waiting room. *He sure is consistent,* Joyce thought moving from behind her desk.

"Are you ready?" Joyce called out from her door waving him in.

"As ready as I'll ever be," Brett said getting up and going into the office. He wanted to tell her about last night but thought it would be better if he waited until after they had finished.

"Before we get started, Brett I'd like to ask your permission to record the session."

"If that's what you want to do, it's fine by me," Brett consented with an indifferent tone.

"All right then." Placing the tape recorder next to the chair he was sitting in, she got the session underway. I want you to relax, take slow deep breaths, and imagine yourself floating in the air. Brett did as he was asked making a few minor adjustments to his sitting position.

"I'm going to count backwards from 8," Joyce began. "As I do, you'll drift closer and closer to where you're going. Eight—You're feeling very relaxed and comfortable. Seven—You're moving slowly now towards a tunnel continuing to feel even more relaxed. Six—Passing slowly through the tunnel now going down deeper into your sub consciousness. Five—Moving a little faster now you see a small white light at the end and move towards it." Joyce noticed Brett's closed eyes were dancing in REM state.

"Four," she continued. "Still very relaxed, you're moving faster now and the light is getting brighter. Three—You're going even deeper into your subconscious, independent from your body now. You're feeling very good and totally unafraid. Two—The light has surrounded you now and feels comforting. You're moving into the dream of Nadia you had a few nights ago. One—You're inside your dream now and able to see everything with great detail." Joyce paused for a few seconds; Brett looked like he was taking a nap.

"Where are you?" Joyce asked.

"I'm in a laboratory watching my friend cutting some cardboard. He has to make it just right so the disk fits in," was Brett's drowsy reply.

"Is Nadia with you?"

"No, we'll be leaving soon to see her but have to finish this first."

Joyce was taken off guard by his response; expecting him to have emerged with Nadia. Not wanting to lose momentum, she went right to her next question.

"What is it that you have to finish?" Brett heard a dream-like voice ask.

"He has some stuff on the disk that he wants Nadia to have. I guess it's kind of a secret. The only way he can get it past the guards is if he takes the picture frame and cuts a square out of the backing so the disk fits inside. Once the frame's back together, he's going to put in it his briefcase. If the guards asks about it, he's going to tell them he wants to have a newer picture on his desk so he's going to swap the old for the new and smuggle it out that way."

"What's your friend's name?" Joyce asked amazed at how well the session was going. She also couldn't remember reading anything like this in his journals and made a mental note to double check.

"I've known him for a while but don't know his name. I think he's a little scared of something but he won't tell me what."

Joyce noticed a slight change to Brett's tonal qualities; it was as if she was talking with a young boy, not a grown man.

"Can you tell me what your friend put on the disk and what it is he's afraid of?"

"He won't tell," Brett said responding nicely to Joyce's inquiries as his face started showing mild signs of frustration. "He says I should ask Nadia about stuff like that."

"Are you talking with him right now?"

"We're not really talking, he just kind of thinks of things and I sort of hear him. I can see him but I'm not really there," Brett doing his best to give his interrogator an idea of what was going on. "Forget it, it's way too hard to explain."

"OK, Brett, let's forget that. Were going to go ahead and move forward in time," Joyce informed his subconscious mind. "You're going slowly through the tunnel again, drifting ever so slightly ahead toward the time when you meet with Nadia. Slowly coming to a stop, you can start to see to Nadia." A smile began to emerge from Brett's face that told Joyce they were right where they wanted to be.

"Yup, I can see her pretty good now, she's smiling," Brett confirmed from somewhere on the horizon of his subconscious. "He just gave her a big diamond ring and they are going to get married soon. He gave her the picture too but she doesn't know the disk is inside. He doesn't want her to worry so he won't tell her."

"Worry about what? What is it your friend doesn't want Nadia to worry about?"

"I don't know! It's a secret, I have to ask Nadia for crying out a loud," was his testy response.

"Brett, can you tell where Nadia lives?"

"Sure, she lives in an apartment, a pretty big one too. In Lexington," he replied shifting a little in the chair. "I think it's Mill Street or Mill Lane something like that."

"Lexington, Massachusetts?" she asked with a touch of surprise in her voice.

"Yup, she works there too, at the bank"

"You've seen Nadia in a lot in the dreams you've been having, can you tell me how long you've know her and why she's so special to you?"

"I've spent a lot of time with Nadia and my friend; we've done a lot of cool stuff together. I think she's my best friend, well either her or Josh. I've been her friend for almost twelve years. It doesn't seem that long, time flies."

"What about your friend, the one Nadia is going to marry, isn't he one of your best friends too?" Joyce asked

"Sort of, but it's different. He comes to me at night and tells me things and shows me stuff. He's more like the person that takes you through a museum and tells you what everything means."

"What kinds of things does he show you, other than the time you spend with Nadia?" Joyce asked, the session taking on a whole different focus than originally thought.

"Oh," he said slowly with a grin. "That's a secret too."

Not wanting to push, especially during the first session she decided to bring him back.

"Brett, I'm going to lead you out of your subconscious now. I'm going to count to five, as I do you will slowly leave the place you're at and gradually begin to wake up. When you hear the number five, you'll be wide awake a feel totally refreshed and won't remember anything you seen or anything you've said."

Joyce counted to five and as soon as she finished Brett's eyes opened.

"How are you feeling, Brett?" Joyce asked greeting his return with a warm smile.

"I feel just great, I'm ready whenever you are," he told her.

"We've already finished," Joyce informed him wearing a comforting smile.

"Wow that was easy. How'd I do?" Brett asked, genuinely curious.

"You did just fine Brett," she assured him.

"Did we find out anything about my mystery woman?" he asked probing for more detail.

Joyce went over the information Brett had revealed while he listened intently.

"This is all pretty confusing to me, Joyce," he admitted hoping for a little advice.

"That's not uncommon after the first session. As we progress, I'm hopeful things will get a little clearer. It's very important not to try and read things into this."

"That's going to be hard to do. I had that dream again the other day," he confessed stretching out his wrist so she could see it. "If this woman, who I think we can both agree appears to be real, holds some key that can help me shake this thing I want to find her."

"I wouldn't really recommend that, Brett, at least not until we try and get some more information. There's a chance it could do more harm than good," she cautioned.

Brett sat there, staring at the wall trying to let Joyce's statement sink in. *She might be right, but I'm the one that's had to live with this thing and if this girl can help me, I am going to find her and try to get to the bottom of it.* "You've always given me sound advice, Joyce, so you're thinking after a few more sessions we'll have a clearer picture?" he finally asked, having every intention of doing a little detective work of his own just as soon as he got home.

"Yes, I'm hopeful that's exactly what will happen," Joyce said reinforcing her position.

"All right, Joyce, so next Tuesday we'll run through the drill again. Before I go I wanted to thank you for the advice you gave me about developing that inner social circle. I took Becky to dinner last night and we had a great time." Brett went ahead and gave her the short version of events as Joyce looked on.

"I am *so* glad you had a great time, Brett. I really believe close personal relationships outside of your immediate family will go a long way in helping you through this and you never know where they can lead. I'm really glad you had a nice time. I'll see you next week," she said, leading him to door.

"See you then, have a good weekend Joyce," Brett said, bidding her farewell.

Closing the door as he left, Joyce headed immediately to her computer and pulled up Brett's chart and rewound the tape so she could listen to it again. She had some real concerns about the revelations that she uncovered and began to wonder if this was moving into the realm of hocus pocus as Brett put it. If it was, she wasn't sure if she could handle this one alone. Joyce listened to the tape and began evaluating the information she had gotten as well as her technique.

Listening to the tape, some obvious questions arose. Who was this tour guide that visits him at night and was this the catalyst for his dreams? What was on the disk and what was behind all the secrets? He had known her for twelve years, what was the significance of that?

Looking at Brett's chart, she got a possible answer to the last question. It was about twelve years ago when Brett had his heart transplant. *What in the world is going on here? That's too much of a coincidence. If I can't figure something out after the next session, I'm going to have to ask Joseph for help.* Joyce had just about all the excitement she could handle for one day. It was 3:30 p.m., her schedule was clear, so she decided to close up and give Gloria an earlier than usual start to the weekend. This would also give her an early start on reviewing Brett's journal to see if her suspicion about getting totally new information was true.

16.

Becky was tired and managed to roll out of bed about thirty minutes before Brett's expected 8:00 a.m. arrival. Brett had asked her last night is she would be willing to take a ride with him to Lexington; he had to run an errand and wanted to talk with her about something. She was used to sleeping in until at least 10:00 a.m. when she worked the weekends. Getting home at about 2:00 a.m., it usually gave her about seven hours of sleep once she got washed up, changed and into bed. Although she agreed, it was contingent upon a hot cup of coffee, one cream and two sugars, arriving with Brett when she picked him up.

She liked the fact that Brett stayed until closing telling her that since she agreed to go with him, it didn't seem fair she should be the only one operating on a short night's sleep. She also knew that he would have stayed anyway even if she had said no. Saying no to Brett wasn't something she even considered. She wanted to be with him. From the first moment she saw him, Becky hoped he would ask her out. Now that they seemed to have spawned the beginning, of what she hoped would be a long-lasting relationship, she didn't want to miss any chances to be with him and explore its full potential.

Brett pulled out of the coffee shop a few blocks from Becky's apartment. He looked at the yellow post it note securely fastened to his rear view mirror with 72 Oakland written on it. Brett was really surprised at the luck he had yesterday afternoon.

He had gotten home from his appointment with Joyce at 4:00 p.m. and called information right away giving Nadia's name and address. He wasn't looking for a phone number but an address and true to form the operator gave it to him—I have a Nadia Petrova on 72 Oakland, nothing on Mill Street. He went quickly on line and punched Lexington Banks into the search engine and got only two listings. Knowing his chances of actually talking to a human being were remote, he was prepared for the, *if you know your parties extension you can dial it now, to dial by name press 1 followed by the pound sign.* Following the automated instructions, he hit pay dirt with the last Bank he had tried. Nadia's extension was 209. He couldn't believe it; he had actually found the girl who had been swimming around inside of his dreams. It was a little unsettling and he experienced a slew of emotions. After saving the information on his computer, he headed to the Dug Out to read the paper, watch the ball game and more importantly see Becky.

Brett yawned bringing his Mustang to a gentle stop in front of Becky's apartment and tooted the horn. Removing the yellow post it note form his rear view mirror, he gave himself a quick once over making sure he looked OK. Becky must have been standing right at the door because before the echo died she was on her way across the street. As they headed off for Lexington, Brett guessed the ride should be about a half hour, hopefully enough time to give Becky the full story about his dreams and the reason for the trip.

Frank was awake and getting ready to start his day. A feeling of uneasiness slowly crept over him. Now, for some reason, he wasn't sure if bringing Veronica to Boston was such a good idea but it was well past the point of doing anything about. If Frank had known that Brett was on his way to meet a woman named Nadia, someone Frank had shadowed nearly twelve years ago, not only would he have left Veronica at the airport, he would have moved his timetable up from a few weeks to a much riskier few days.

Despite not being sure how well his story was going be received, Brett wanted to make sure Becky knew what was going on with him. If their relationship was ever going to go anywhere, he felt she had to know everything and let the chips fall where they may. And that's exactly the way he framed the introduction to his tale.

Becky sat motionless in the passenger seat looking intently at Brett as his story unfolded. At first she could hardly believe what she was hearing, she started thinking that if he was seeing a shrink there may be something really wrong with him. "What have I gotten myself into?" Becky said to herself, wondering if going on this trip with him was such a good idea after all.

All that changed when Brett got a little more into the details of his hypnosis, and how it had led him to Nadia in Lexington. Her skepticism was gradually replaced with awe. She had always thought that dreams held more significance than the average person gave them credit for and Brett was living proof. It sent a chill down her spine as she tried to imagine having to live Brett's life since his strange dreams had started. She wondered if he got scared every night before going to bed, or if needed sleeping pills to help gently ease his mind into the beginning of an evening slumber. "I know I'd need something," Becky admitted as she tossed the scenario around in her head.

"He didn't have to tell me any of this. He could have kept it from me and I wouldn't have known any better. Out of his desire to be open and honest with me, he took a big chance that I wouldn't stick around. I can trust this guy to tell me the truth even if he thinks I won't like it. There aren't many around like that. He risked our relationship because he wanted to truthful." Finishing her thoughts, Becky decided it was time to speak and her turn to be honest.

"You know, when you started telling me all this, I thought you might be some sort of a nut case, but after listening to whole thing I want you to know," Becky said reaching over to hold his hand, "that I think you're the most courageous and honest person I've met. I really like you, Brett, and as strange as this may sound seeing we've only had one official date, I hope our relationship will grow into something very special."

Brett squeezed her hand reassuringly and smiled. "My mother gave me some good advice before she died and I've tried to life my life by it. Brett honey, she said, if you always tell the truth you'll never have to remember what you've said." Looking over at Becky, he could see a smile on her face as well. "And just so you know," he continued, "I think our relationship is already showing signs of being very special." Leaning over, Becky gave him a quick peck on the cheek. Brett's smile widened as he made the turn onto Oakland Street relieved that all of that was now off his chest.

Brett saw Nadia's house and a car that he supposed was hers parked in the driveway. He decided they would park on the street and walk up to the front door. Brett remembered how his mother would always get suspicious when a car she didn't recognize pulled into their driveway, even just to turn around, and Brett wanted Nadia to skip that step. She'd be apprehensive enough when she answered the door. Brett looked at the dashboard—8:40 a.m.

"Maybe we should wait until 9:00 a.m.," Brett said soliciting Becky's opinion.

"I say we go ahead and get this over with Brett," she offered.

"OK, let's do it," Brett agreed as they got out of the car and walked up to the front door.

Pressing the bell, Brett didn't hear the familiar *Ding-Dong* and wondered if maybe he should knock. Standing at the door of someone's house waiting for them to answer, especially someone you didn't know, had a way of turning seconds into hours. Testing the screen door, Brett found it to be locked. There goes that idea, he thought reaching reluctantly to ring the bell again.

Pulling his hand back quickly as the door slowly opened, anxiety surged through Brett's entire body. Standing behind the security of a locked screen door was Nadia. She had emerged from the inner sanctum of her house and looked at them, without saying a word.

In an instant Nadia had been transformed from an apparition that occupied his dreams, to a flesh and blood reality. She was older than the images that had, over time, been seared into his slumbering mind but this was her alright. Becky glanced over at him and saw both surprise and recognition written across his face. She didn't know if she should feel scared or excited for him. Brett caught Becky's glance out of the corner of his eye and turned toward her to see her nodding her head, encouraging him to get started.

"Yes?" Nadia said in an apprehensive, what I can do for you manner.

"Ms. Petrova my name is Brett Allen, this is my girlfriend Becky. I was wondering if we could have a few minutes to chat with you," Brett said disappointed that his opening statement had gone nothing like the one he had rehearsed.

"Look!" Nadia began a little irritated. "Don't you people talk to one another?" Brett noticed a slight Russian accent. "I told your friends that were here last night that I'm not interested."

"Our friends?" Brett asked.

"You're Jehovah's Witnesses aren't you?" Nadia replied pointedly.

"No were not. Nothing like that," Brett said now on the defensive.

"Well whatever it is you're selling, religion, coupon books, or vacuum cleaners, I don't want any," Nadia said beginning to close the door.

"Wait! Please!" Brett pleaded. "We have or had a mutual friend; it's a little difficult to explain. All I know is on the day you were engaged, you were handed a picture and I think I'm supposed to find out why," he finished quickly trying to beat the slam of a closing door.

Nadia started slowly swinging the door open with a stunned looked on her face. "What do you mean, picture?" she asked now standing in the center of the doorway examining her visitors a little more closely.

"As I said, it's really hard to explain and I'm not real sure I understand it all either," Brett admitted. "I only know that on the day you were engaged, your fiancé gave you a picture and I'm supposed to ask you about it."

Nadia stood there for a few seconds bringing back the memory of that day before she uttered a word. "How do you know this?" she asked. "The day we were engaged and I was given the picture you speak of, we were alone."

"I'm in the dark myself about a lot of this, Ms. Petrova but if we could come inside, just for a few minutes, I'd like to try and explain," Brett said hoping that what he told Nadia would result in an invitation to go inside.

Nadia glanced at Brett, then at Becky, struggling to make a decision. She wondered how this stranger standing at her door could possibly know anything at all about her, let alone something that occurred in the privacy of her old apartment. Looking closely at Brett, Nadia guessed he was in his early twenties. The event he had just described probably took place when he was very young, she thought now deep in astonishment, maybe eleven or twelve.

"Please, *kotehok*, just a few minutes," Brett repeated his plea, startled by the unfamiliar word that just flowed from his mouth.

Nadia's knees nearly buckled. Kotehok, the Russian word for kitten, was something she hadn't heard in a very long time. It was the pet name her fiancé had given her shortly after they first met.

"There are only two people that have ever called me that," Nadia, now totally bewildered, said unlocking the screen door to let them in. "My Russell and now you!"

Nadia led them into her living room, her outstretched arm directing them to sit on the sofa. Visibly shaken, Nadia chose the matching love seat directly across from them. Charming house Becky thought, sitting next to Brett admiring the country décor.

"Please, can you tell me your names again?" Nadia asked through a quivering voice.

"My name is Brett and this is Becky, my girlfriend," Brett said, obliging her.

"Tell me how you know these things you have said Brett," she asked, her Russian accent and speech pattern clearly more predominant than a moment ago. "No one could know such things, but here you are telling me things that happened in my most private moments so I must believe you."

Brett told his story for Nadia as she sat forward in her chair attentive to his every word. The look on her face was one that even Brett couldn't describe. At times she looked sad, at other times he could see a joyous glint in her eye but it was the underlying common thread to Nadia's demeanor that he was having trouble figuring out.

Brett touched lightly on several of the dreams he had the best recollection of, pausing from time to time allowing Nadia to ask questions. Suddenly it hit him; Nadia had a fearful look about her, that's what it was. It wasn't a terrified look like the one you see actors wearing on a low budget B horror movie; it was more subtle and controlled than that but it was there alright.

"She's got to be petrified with the whole situation," Brett considered, knowing full well he himself wasn't feeling real great about it either. "How often does a total stranger show up at your door early on a Saturday morning," he continued, "and give you the 411 about some of your most personal experiences, especially those shared with only one other person."

Reliving those memories was clearly a painful experience for Nadia who was now sobbing openly. Becky got up and sat on the arm of the chair next to Nadia and put her arms around her, hoping to provide some comfort. Nadia responded graciously and patted Becky's hand to let her know she would be OK.

Brett began the last chapter of his explanation as he told Nadia about being out under hypnosis and the results of the session. "And that's how we ended up here Nadia," Brett said in conclusion.

Nadia collected herself, stood up and walked over to the fireplace. On the mantel was a picture of her and her fiancé Russell. Sitting back down, Nadia started to fill in some of the empty spots for Brett.

"Everything you have told me Brett is the way it happened. Russell was such a good man; he was my whole life, the man of my dreams. We met in a Polish deli in Boston, he was in town for a week, some science convention, or conference I can't remember which. He asked me to have dinner with him that night and I said yes. It was, as they say in the movies love at first sight. From that day on, we spent as much time together as we could. It was hard, I lived and worked here in Lexington and Russell was living and working in Connecticut. We talked on the phone every day and he would drive up to see me almost every weekend. The separation was harder on Russell than it was me. I had a lot of friends that lived nearby here and he really didn't know anyone in Connecticut other than the people at his work. I told him to get out once in a while and make some new friends, live a little bit, but he always said he wanted to work extra hard during the week to make sure he could spend the weekends with me."

"Most couples wouldn't have made it but our love was greater than the distance that separated us. We had this type of relationship for almost a year before he asked me to marry him. I said yes of course."

"I can remember like it was yesterday," Nadia went on. "It was the long 4th of July weekend when he gave me a beautiful diamond ring and the picture you speak of.

"When he gave me this picture," Nadia continued looking down at the picture in her lap, "he made me promise to keep it, no matter what happened. I asked him what he meant when he said that but he wouldn't tell me, he just made me promise, so I did. That was the best weekend of my life. Russell spent it with me and went back early Sunday night." Tears beginning to well up in Nadia's eyes. "Then on Monday morning," she continued, "Russell stopped on his way to work for a cup of coffee and was killed when someone robbed the store he was in. It's been twelve years since Russell has been gone. They say every cloud has a silver lining and I now think this is true. Russell's death was tragic, but from his death," Nadia said dabbing her nose with some tissue, "many gained new life."

"When you say many gained new life from Russell's death, what do you mean?" Brett asked his stomach now tied in a knot.

"He was an organ donor," Nadia told him, wiping the moisture from eyes. "Because of him many people were given a second chance at life. Some of the people that received his organs were just teenagers desperate for a miracle, and their miracle ended up being Russell Craft." Brett glanced over at Becky to find that she too had tears in her eyes, obviously touched from listening to Nadia.

He started running that name through the library of his mind. "Where do I know that name from?" he asked himself, perturbed that he couldn't put his finger on it. As hard as it was for him to believe, it seemed pretty clear to Brett that Russell Craft was acting as the facilitator for his dreams. The more Brett tired to reason it out logically the more inexplicable the entire scenario became. *An organ donor too,* he thought, *talk about your coincidences!*

Brett's well trained and disciplined mind was being tossed about like a row boat in thirty foot seas. His physical body was responding similarly as a feeling of nauseousness started to build. All that he knew and all he believed to be true was now in question. None of this made any sense but the facts were now indisputable. Brett took a few deep and deliberate breaths trying to get control of himself.

"Nadia, can you tell me what Russell did for work?" Brett asked not really sure he was prepared for the answer.

"Russell was a scientist and worked at that same big pharmaceutical company you work for now, Nelson Pharmaceuticals I think you said. Yes, that's the right name. I remember a few days after Russell was buried a couple of men from there came to visit me. They wanted to collect any work materials Russell might have brought here. Russell never brought any work home with him or at least not to my old apartment. If he needed to do extra work, he always stayed at his office. I guess they were pretty strict about not letting people take things home. Russell told me he felt like he was working at Fort Knox since the security was so tight. I didn't have anything in my apartment to give them so they just said thank you and left. Russell never talked with me very much about his work. I wouldn't have understood it anyway."

Brett's breathing got shallow and labored as his skin began to turn pale. For a second, he thought he might faint. Both Nadia and Becky noticed the instant change. Becky placed his head on her shoulder then put her arms around him, gently rubbing his back attempting to calm him down. Nadia darted off toward the kitchen to get Brett a cold glass of water.

Brett graciously accepted both the comfort Becky was providing and the glass of water that Nadia had returned with. "Sorry," he said sipping from the cold glass of water, "I'm having a hard time accepting all of this." For a second, Brett thought about telling Nadia about the nightmare at the store but decided against it.

"I too am having trouble, Brett," Nadia stated empathetically "There are so many things in this world we just don't know or understand. Russell has chosen you, Brett, as a bridge from wherever he is to where we are. I don't know how or why, but it *has* happened."

Brett was almost totally convinced that Russell Craft was the victim he had accompanied on several stormy trips to a convenience store. He also remembered that Russell Craft was also the name he had seen a few days ago on the memorial placard in Connecticut. Bret wasn't really sure he could deal with everything he had heard and the conclusions he had drawn. *I have to find out more about this guy and see what kind of confirming information I can find before I let my imagination get to far away from me,* he thought, surprised that he could think that clearly at a time like this.

"I'm feeling a little better now," Brett conveyed to his concerned onlookers, the color returning to his face. He took a deep breath, sat up and finished his glass of water. "Thanks."

"Are you sure you're OK?" Becky asked, her concern for Brett evident in every word.

"Yeah, I'm OK, really," he replied appreciatively and asked Nadia another question.

"You said Russell's organs had given a lot of people new hope. You wouldn't happen to know by any chance who some of the recipients were, would you?"

"No, I don't know any of the people by name; it was a long time ago. I do know that a little girl in Ohio got one of Russell's kidney's and a young man from the Boston area got Russell's heart, other than that I don't know who else was helped," Nadia replied.

Putting two and two together wasn't a hard equation for Brett. He surmised that he was the very person that now carried Russell Craft's heart just beneath the scar on his chest. There were already so many unanswered questions and this newest revelation just piled more onto the growing list. Sitting across from Nadia, he couldn't decide if he wasn't a whole lot better off before they arrived at her house.

Nadia could see Brett searching for a coaster to put his glass down. "Here, I'll take that for you," Nadia offered, "and you should probably take this," Nadia said exchanging the picture for Brett's glass and brought in into the kitchen.

Brett turned the picture over and slowly wiggled the backing off revealing the 3.5 inch floppy disk that had been resting there for over a decade. Removing the disk he placed it on the coffee table in front of him and took a quick look at Becky as if to say, see here it is. All Becky could do was to shake her head in amazement.

Nadia returned to see Brett putting her picture back together and the disk he had removed lying on the table. She was very curious to know what was on the disk that Russell obviously went to great lengths to hide. "What should I do?" Nadia thought, struggling with indecision. "Maybe I can open it on the lap top; no that won't work, I've only got a CD ROM drive in that thing." Unable to come up with a quick solution, she asked Brett the only question she could think of "Do you think the disk is still good?"

"I'm not real sure, Nadia. I guess we will know soon enough," Brett said grabbing the disk as he stood up, Becky following his lead. "We're going to head back now, Nadia; I really don't know what to say other than thanks."

"I don't know what is on that disk and why Russell wanted you to have it but I'm sure it's a good reason. I'm not sure if I'll sleep very well this evening after our little talk," Nadia admitted, "but I am very grateful we had it. Would you please call me if the disk works and let me know what you find?"

"Thanks, Nadia, if the disk is still good, I'll call you. I'll call you either way, then you won't have to sit around wondering. This is all so very bizarre," Brett said, shaking his head. "With the exception of Becky and meeting you, I'd like to think that about five minutes from now my alarm is going to ring and I'll wake up." His comment drew a strained smile from both women.

Nadia stood at the door watching her visitors walk back to their car still trying to comprehend the astonishing two-hour conversation they had just shared. She was relieved they were leaving and couldn't get her mind off that disk. The fact that Russell Craft was somehow communicating with Brett from beyond the grave scared her, it scared her a lot. Although she maintained her poise in front of her unexpected guests, Nadia was barely hanging on to her last nerve. Closing the door, Nadia retreated to the comfort of her living room. Picking up the phone, her hand shaking uncontrollably, she made a very necessary call.

"I feel like I'm starring in one of those Sci-Fi flicks," Brett told Becky trying to inject a little comedy, hoping it would make them both feel a little bit better.

"Oh, my, gosh, Brett, I remember you telling me about your transplant at dinner, do you think it's Russell Craft's heart you got?" Becky asked her question laced with concern and confusion.

"I can't even begin to think about that yet but it would sure seem so. I wouldn't think too many children from Boston, other than yours truly, had a heart transplant twelve years ago," he answered bewilderedly, having a very hard time coping with the enormity of it all.

"I can tell you one thing for sure, this entire experience has totally changed the way I think about things," Becky responded.

"Yeah, me too," Brett agreed. "It's probably going to be close to noon before we get back. Do you want to come over to my place or do you need to go home and get ready for work?"

"I've got to be there at 6:00," Becky said thinking about her choices. "Believe it or not, I'm a little hungry. What do think about stopping for something to eat then dropping me off at my apartment?"

"Alright, let's grab a bite to eat," Brett agreed even though he wasn't very hungry.

"Will I see you at the Dug Out tonight?" she asked, hoping he would drop by.

"Yes you will," he said with a smile. "I wouldn't miss it for the world."

"I get off at midnight tonight, so if you don't have any plans and aren't too tired, maybe I can take you up on your offer?"

"Offer?" Brett asked.

"Yes, the offer to come to your place. Maybe we can have a night cap and talk. After the day you've had, I thought you might enjoy some company," Becky answered.

Becky was right. He had already had a pretty rough day and it wasn't even half over yet and he didn't relish the idea of being alone. There were a lot of things going through his mind and he knew sleep, at least tonight, would prove to be elusive. Brett laid out the rest of his day's schedule as the pulled into a Mexican Restaurant. He would drop Becky off after lunch, go home and see if he could retrieve the information on the disk and then go to the Dug Out. The Red Sox were playing the Mariners and if it was a good game, it would probably help take his mind off things.

"I would really like that, Becky," Brett said emphatically. "Are you sure? It would mean a *really* long day for you and I couldn't vouch for the kind of company I'd be given all that's happened"

"I'll catch twenty winks after you drop me off," Becky replied eliminating his concern, "so I'll be fine, but if you think you'll be too tired, we can make it for another time."

"Trust me, Becky, I'll be wide awake. That's not a threat, it's a promise," his smirk struggling to a smile.

As Becky and Brett were placing their order for lunch, Frank was watching Veronica walk towards him. She had arrived at Logan late due to some mechanical problem with the airplane.

Now that's more like it, Frank thought, comparing Becky's blue conservative dress he'd seen a few nights ago to Veronica's stretch dress that left little to one's imagination. Veronica had a voluptuous figure and a face to go with it. Frank especially liked her long blond hair and crystal blue eyes. She was a looker alright as Frank watched all the men's heads turn for a better look.

He was watching one woman give her husband or boyfriend the business. She had already slapped him on the arm, catching him sneaking a quick look and apparently he was now getting the verbal version. Frank's grin widened watching them banter back and forth.

"Hi, Frank," Veronica said, greeting him with a kiss on the cheek. "Sorry I was late getting in. They had us switch planes; I guess there was some trouble with one of the wings. I'm glad all I needed was a carry-on. At least we won't have to worry about any lost luggage."

"You look fabulous," he said, taking her carry-on luggage.

"Thanks, Frank, you know I like to look my best for you. I must say this is a first for me."

"You've never been to Boston before?" he asked leading Veronica out of the terminal.

"I've been to Boston a few times. What I meant was joining you on a business trip," she explained.

"Well this is the first trip I've taken from Chicago since we met. Because of the specialized nature of my consulting work, I make out very well financially so I don't have to go out of town very often," he said with a touch of egotism.

"I don't normally travel at all for work, but for you, Frank, it's worth making an exception" she answered back in a sultry voice.

Frank knew she was pushing his buttons a little but didn't really care; it made him feel good just the same. He figured he would try and push a few of Veronica's buttons as well.

"To be totally honest, this is a first for me too. I've never had anyone join me while I was away on business," then he repeated her words, "for you though; it was worth making an exception."

Veronica looked at him and smiled. "Flattery will get you everywhere. Frank, would you mind if we stopped by the hotel before we do anything else? I'd like to freshen up."

"Sounds like a good plan to me," Frank said, opening the car door to let her in.

17.

Brett thought about Nadia and their conversation on his way back from dropping Becky off so she could catch her *twenty winks*. Opening the door to his apartment, Brett was greeted by a rush of cool air. Central air was a must especially on these muggy New England days when the humidity hung in the air like a thick morning fog.

Brett sat down at his computer and slowly put the disk into the drive. He directed his mouse to the A drive and clicked on it. The disk drive began its familiar grinding noise as it attempted to access the information. It took just a few seconds before the monitor displayed the contents. Brett saw four separate files on the disk, all of which he noticed were text documents. Brett found the titles intriguing; *Financial Impact Study*, *Formulas*, *Memorandum*, and *Nadia*.

Brett's curiosity was mixed with a deep apprehension. He wasn't really sure he could handle more puzzling revelations on a day that already had more than its fair share but knew that moving forward was his only option. Brett hoped that following the path he had started down would somehow unravel the mystery of this man Russell Craft and put a stop to his troubling nightmares. With the memory of spending an uncomfortable two hours with Nadia still very fresh in his mind Brett decided to open that document last. Here goes nothing he said to himself taking a deep breath to help him through his uneasiness as he clicked on the financial document and began to read.

To: Richard Nelson II—Director of Operations and Research, Nelson Pharmaceutical Corp.

From: Bob MacReynolds—CFO, Nelson Pharmaceutical Corp.
Date: 21 May 1991
Subject: Financial Impact Summary (Research Project C2765)
Richard,
Per your request I have concluded the Financial Impact Study pertinent to research project C2765 and have summarized my findings below. It is important to note that the figures below are exclusively representative of the C2756 project and does not take into account other potential FDA approved pharmaceutical products currently under consideration.

Summary
Upon FDA approval and subsequent announcement, the following two fiscal quarters would be robust. It is safe to assume, based on historical data and the significance, the C2765 product will have on a global scale that competitors will quickly analyze and develop a similar product. The resulting effect is an estimated loss of half the market share during the second year and the necessity for a more competitive pricing plan.

Since the C2765 product will render our current treatment line obsolete, the three year projection does not include revenues that would have otherwise been generated from that line.

Current Gross Profit (Annual)—Current Line   675.64 Million Actual

Projected Gross Profit (Initial 2 Quarter)—C2765 3.74   Billion Estimated

Projected Gross Profit (Quarter 3)—C2765   875.2   Million Estimated

Projected Gross Profit (Quarter 4)—C2765   32.45   Million Estimated

Current Stock Value   38.43 p/s   Actual

Projected Stock Value (First Year)—C2765   75.00 p/s Estimated

Projected Stock Value (Second Year)—C2765   42.00 p/s Estimated

Projected Stock Value (Third Year)—C2765   22.00 p/s Estimated

Conclusion
Staying with the current product line and allowing for the historical

5% increase per annum in revenues over five years, the estimated gross profit would be approximately 3.87 Billion. Over the same period, the resulting gross profit from the C2765 line would be roughly 4.78 Billion for a net gain of approximately 910 Million.

Assuming that we can maintain our market share with C2765 and have average earnings of 32.45 Million per annum for years six through ten, the total projected earnings over a ten year period would be in the neighborhood of 5.7 Billion. The current line over the same ten-year period is much more promising, even if pricing remains flat for the second five-year period.

The current line after five years should result in 3.87 Billion in gross profits. At flat line pricing years six through ten the profits would be in the 4.8 Billion dollar range or a ten-year total of 8.67 Billion.

Supporting Figures

Five Year Estimate Five Year Estimate (5% price increase per annum)

C2756	**Current Line**	Net Gain/Loss
4.78 Billion	3.87 Billion	(G) 910 Million

Ten Year Estimate Ten Year Estimate (Flat line pricing year's six through ten)

C2756	**Current Line**	Net Gain/Loss
5.7 Billion	8.67 Billion	(L) 2.37 Billion

If C2765 is approved and goes to market, the long term financial projections show a loss of 2.37 billion dollars in revenue over ten years. This loss could be substantially greater if you consider that all research and development in this area will no longer be necessary.

Respectfully,

Bob MacReynolds, Chief Financial Officer

Brett read the document again just to be sure he had a full understanding of what it said. "Apparently my good friend Mr. Nelson ," he said cynically, "hadn't made the jump to CEO yet."

Brett knew Bob MacReynolds retired a few years ago. He had gotten a generic company invitation to join the celebration but didn't go. He remembered that on that night he chose Fenway Park and his father over wasting his time paying homage to someone he didn't even know. The next day at work, a few people mentioned not seeing him there, implying that he wasn't playing politics very well, but Brett could have cared less. His grandfather could play all the politics necessary for one family; he was a scientist and had no desire in seeing his name move up on the organizational chart, especially if it meant massaging someone else's ego.

Although Brett was fully engrossed with the letter, the thought of the MacReynolds' retirement party reminded him that he told his father he would get some tickets for a Red Sox game. Reaching into the drawer of his computer desk, he grabbed a yellow sticky, made a note, and stuck it on the upper hand corner of the monitor. Now that he was thinking about when he called his father to let him know about the tickets, he would also ask him if he knew who his heart donor was. He couldn't believe that after all these years, he had never once asked him that question and that his parents, if they knew, never told him. Taking the sticky off, Brett scribbled the word donor underneath the already present ticket reminder and put it back on the monitor.

Brett glanced over the document for a third time. He didn't know what research project C2765 was, but he was going to try and find out come Monday. He knew for a couple of reasons it was of immense importance. Just the fact that it would generate billions of dollars in about six months was astonishing. Brett also concluded from MacReyonlds' last paragraph, stating all research and development would no longer be necessary, that it had to be some type of a cure.

"That figures," Brett thought, a touch of anger nibbling at him, "only a pompous idiot like Nelson would put the value of a company's financial report above the value of a human life. Seems obvious to me," he continued on, "this company has never been about helping humanity; it's *always* been about how much money they can make. I'll bet he's even run the numbers on Cytanepax," he mumbled, shaking his head from side to side.

The more he thought about it, the angrier he became. Finally, totally disgusted with what the document insinuated, he came to a decision. "I don't care if that jerk sues me or tries to put me in jail; I'm going to figure a way to get my research materials out of that place. Once I do that, I'll give my two weeks notice and say so long to Mr. Richard Nelson and head over to join my friends at Harvard."

In his mind's eye, Brett could see Richard Nelson and that condescending smirk he wore, then a cascade of images flooded his mind as Brett did a mental rerun of his appointment with Nelson. Brett was looking for anything that might suggest his project was getting similar scrutiny. After several detailed examinations of their meeting, all Bret could really remember was that Nelson seemed anxious to get Cytanepax out on the market which seemed to be in contradiction to what he had just read.

Brett couldn't remember anyone that could get under his skin the way Richard Nelson could. Having only met him once and feeling the way he did, confirmed for Brett that Nelson was truly in a class by himself. Brett closed the financial document and was actually grateful to Richard Nelson. The anger he felt was just the right motivator and far outweighed any apprehension or nervousness he had felt. Brett was now more determined than ever to press on toward the finish line. "Maybe there was an extra bonus at the end," Brett thought, "Like an opportunity to put the screws to Richard Nelson."

Brett opened the Memorandum file.

To: Richard Nelson II—Director of Operations and Research, Nelson Pharmaceutical Corp.

From: Richard Nelson—Chief Executive Officer and Chairman of the Board, Nelson Pharmaceutical Corp.

Date: 28 May 1991

Subject: Research Project C2765

Richard,

After reviewing the documentation you forwarded to me last week regarding Research Project C2765, a full board meeting was convened on Monday 27 May, 1991. The purpose of this meeting was to fully review the potential of C2765 and determine the best way for us, as a corporation, to proceed.

After careful consideration the board voted 7/5

Brett couldn't believe it was only a partial memo and wondered why it was on this disk. This research project, whatever it was, apparently made it to the upper most level of the company's decision makers. To Brett that seemed very unusual, but he wasn't the business savvy type so maybe it was the status quo, he just didn't know. "So," he said, "Daddy helped you get where you are today. I didn't think you could have made it on your own."

Opening the formulas document, Brett discovered several different sets of formulas along with some statistical analysis. To an average human being, the information stretched across the electronic page would have been about as understandable as hieroglyphics.

To Brett the sets of random numbers and letters held the key to curing one of the most devastating and undiscriminating diseases, other than the plague, that mankind has had to face—cancer. Brett was fascinated, amazed and excited by what he read and decided right away that he would take this information to Harvard. There, what Russell Craft started would be finished for the good of the human race, without regard to how it would impact the bottom line of someone's balance sheet. Brett also drew some parallels to his Cytanepax project and thought he might be able to move his project up by as much as six months. For Brett, both prospects were exhilarating. "Talk about finding a treasure," Brett said, now fully charged with adrenalin and enthusiasm. "This will change the world forever!"

Brett printed 2 copies of the document; one he would deliver to Harvard on Monday and the other he would put in his fire box along with his birth certificate, passport and other valuable documents. Determined that this treasure chest of information wouldn't get lost, he made two disk copies and also copied the files to his computer. "You're not going to stop it this time," Brett muttered defiantly to his mental image of Richard Nelson.

There was only one document left, the Nadia document. Brett closed the partial memo and opened it.

Kotehok,
That's what Russell called her, Brett remembered. It meant kitten.
I don't have a lot of time to get this ready. Forgive me for not telling you about this disk but I didn't want you to be in jeopardy. I knew it wouldn't take too long before your eyes would grow weary of this ugly metal frame and you'd want to replace it. I had to use it to get by the metal detector.

First of all, this disk is a copy of the original from Richard Nelson's secretary, Bridgette. About a month ago, she flew out of her office one day and was running down the hall and a disk fell out of her purse. You remember the hallway to my office. Well the thick carpeting muffled the sound of it hitting the floor and prevented her from noticing it had fallen. I have no idea where she was going in such a hurry. There was no way a disk was going to get by security so my guess was that she was bringing it to someone in the building. I stood at the door of the lab and watched Bridgette as she turned the corner. I saw the disk sitting on the floor so I went and picked it up. I don't know why, but I quickly brought it into the lab and put it in the computer so I could have a look at what was on it. Maybe I had some secret desire to have dirt on someone, especially Nelson. What I found are the documents on this disk. The project they are talking about (C2765) is my project, so I was of course very, very curious and decided to make a copy. I returned the disk to the hallway just in time. I could hear Bridgette take a deep sigh of relief as I was closing my door; she had probably gotten to where she was going, noticed it missing and came back to look for it.

Anyway, it's now the morning of July 3; my assistant Cynthia was killed just last Friday. She was shot in the same store I go to almost every morning for coffee and doughnuts. The police say she was shot during a robbery but I'm not so sure.

We had a meeting about a month ago with Nelson and a few other people we didn't know. Cynthia and I told everyone in the meeting that we were pretty close to a cure for cancer. Nelson already knew this so I don't know why he had to have a meeting. Maybe he was trying to show off in front of those people. I tired to access some computer files today and the computer told me those files don't exist. That's got me really worried since access to those files is highly restricted and I know they were there just yesterday. I hate to say it but I don't think they want to lose two and a half billion dollars even if C2765 has the same impact on cancer as penicillin had on infection.

We're shutting down early today as you know and don't have to be back until the 8th for work so I'm hoping you like the ring I plan on giving you in a few hours and we have a great long four day weekend. I have to prepare the frame to get this out of here.

Love you, Kotehok,

Russell

P.S. I have put some key formulas from my research project on the formulas document. Please take them to one of local universities so they can continue my work.

"I'll bet they got rid of them to prevent their work from being finished, Mom," he said looking up at the ceiling. "If they could have finished their work there may have been a cure for you. As far as I'm concerned, these people killed you too. The information on this disk doesn't really prove anything, other than the fact that Nelson Pharmaceuticals is like any other American corporation whose primary goal is making money."

When Brett started this crusade, he had hoped to meet a woman named Nadia, as the day progressed he got a whole lot more than he bargained for. Not only had he met his mystery woman, he found out, in all likelihood that he was the recipient of Russell Crafts' heart, who also just happened to be the tour guide of his subconscious journey through space and time. He also uncovered a document that could, with a little elbow grease, rid the planet of cancer. "Whew!" Brett said, leaning back in his chair. Despite being charged up from the adrenalin rush, his mind was well beyond being toasted around the edges. It was completely fried. He had experienced every emotion known to man, maybe even a few undiscovered ones and had just a few more things to finish up before he could give his mind a rest.

Picking up the phone, Brett called Nadia. He got her answering machine and left a message for her to call him and gave her his home phone number. He moved right into his next call, even though his heart wasn't really into it, and followed the prompts and pushed the numbed one so he could get the English version of the automated instructions rather than number two which would have provided them in Spanish. Following the automated directions, he was finally able to talk with someone about getting some tickets. Friday night's game seemed to be the best; it was the opening game of a three game series against the Yankees. Brett could get tickets two rows behind the Red Sox Dugout or directly behind home plate. Brett chose the 1st base side knowing that's what his father would have wanted also, gave the person his credit card information and asked them to send him the tickets in the mail.

Brett dialed his father's cell number, pulled the yellow sticky off the monitor and tossed toward the garbage can. "Swish," Brett thought as his discarded paper landed dead center in the small circular receptacle.

"Hi, Brett," his dad said, answering his cell phone.

"Hey, Dad, how are you?" Brett asked.

"Doing just fine, son, and how are you and how are things going with Dr. Davenport?" his father asked through a bit of static.

"Everything is going just fine, Dad. Hey I've got tickets to Friday's Yankees game. First base side two rows back. Is that good or what!" Brett said enthusiastically knowing his dad would be happy.

"Perfect seats for the perfect game. Nice work, son. Game starts at 7:05 right? I know we'll talk before then but let's say we meet in front of Gate B at 6:00, does that sound OK?" Michael Allen said excitedly, anxious to see his son and share an evening together.

"Gate B, six o'clock on Friday," Brett repeated confirming the date, time, and meeting point. "After paying a hundred and forty bucks for two tickets, I'll be a little on the light side until next payday. Can I count on you for a hot dog and a coke?" he asked his father through a slight giggle.

"If you keep getting the tickets, you can keep counting on me for the other half," Michael said waiting for the response.

"Hey, wait a second! What do mean the other half? There's no way I could eat that much," Brett complained softly and playfully at the unfairness of his father's statement.

"Have you checked concession prices lately?" Michael went on to make his point, "I think we'll break even, in fact you'll probably do a little better."

Brett chuckled at the price comparison his father had conjured up. "Hey, Dad, before I forget, I want to ask you about something that happened a long time ago."

"Sure, Brett," his father's voice answered back, a more serous tone substituting for the playful one of just a few seconds ago.

"Do you know, by any chance, who the organ donor was that gave me my heart?" Brett asked, surprised by the blandness in his tone.

Michael Allen felt like he was blindsided by a speeding truck. Brett had never brought up the past and had never before seemed interested let alone wanting to talk about his heart transplant. Michael suspected that Dr. Davenport had him talking about some of this stuff as part of his treatment.

"Yes, Brett, I know the name of your donor. Shortly after you got sick," Michael Allen began explaining, "your mother and I agreed to talk about it only if you brought it up. We felt it was best to handle it that way and since you've asked, I'll tell you. Can you answer a question for me first?"

"Of course I can, Dad."

"What got you interested in knowing more about your transplant? Not that curiosity isn't normal especially given the gravity of an event like that, but it's been twelve years, and until now you haven't asked one question," Michael's curiosity evident in his tone.

"You won't believe this, Dad; I met someone this morning," Brett began, intent on not worrying his father even if it meant withholding some information. "Somehow we got on the subject of organ transplants. To make a long story short, this woman was engaged to a guy named Russell. About twelve years ago this Russell after some sort of tragic event, ended up having his organs donated. She told me that although she didn't know the names of any of the recipients or who they were, she did remember that a young man from Boston ended up getting his heart. I kind of put two and two together and came up with me as being the young man from Boston."

"Well you've got the first name right, Brett. His name was Russell, Russell Craft," Michael said, filling in the blanks. "Your mother and I didn't get a lot of other information, but as you can imagine, were very grateful that through him your life was saved."

"I'm grateful too, Dad. Thanks for the name," Brett said obviously in a hurry to get off.

"I wish I could tell you more, Brett. It all happened so fast. I'm sure you remember that day. We got a call in the morning from the hospital telling us we had to get you over there right away to get you prepped for surgery. They had found a healthy heart that was a match and as you know, every minute is crucial with organ transplants. We never asked a lot of questions, we were just so happy that a heart had been found and because we didn't feel it was the right thing to do given the circumstances. We asked for the donor's name so that we could thank his family. We were only given the donor's name and told that the surviving family members, names, addresses and the like, preferred to remain anonymous," Michael explained and sadly restated, "so that's all I can tell you about it, Brett, sorry."

"That's OK, Dad. I had a pretty good idea it was him but just wanted to confirm it. You know how we scientists like confirming evidence," Brett said picking a little on his profession. "I'm going to find this woman again and tell her just how grateful I am, or do you think that's a bad idea?"

"I would think that would be OK," his father replied thoughtfully. "It seems like that popular phrase, it's a small world, has an entirely new meaning. What are the odds of you meeting someone that actually knew Russell Craft, let alone the girl he was going to marry? It's just incredible."

"Your right, Dad, it is incredible. In fact, that's the best way to sum up my day so far. Well, I've got to get going, places to go, people to meet, things to do, that sort of thing. I'm looking forward to Friday and giving you a chance to break even," Brett said with a detectable smile in his voice, "And thanks for the info, Dad."

"You're welcome; I can't wait until Friday either. I'm sure well be talking to each other early in the week. Take care Brett," Michael said hanging up still totally amazed by his son's story.

What a day, Brett thought, his chores for the day now complete. Still all keyed-up from the discoveries of the day, he started thinking about what he should do next. *Maybe I should start studying these formulas in a little greater detail. They're so rich with information it would take some time to fully understand them. On second thought, I could give my mind a rest, if I can that is, and pick this up fresh tomorrow with a clear head.* It was his second thought that Brett chose to go with. He decided to lie down on the couch and maybe, just maybe, he'd be able to catch a short nap. After a few minutes, he was surprised to find he was actually drifting off to sleep. He wasn't quite asleep and not really awake; he was kind of in between. Brett thought about the evening ahead of him as he traveled closer to reaching sleep. When he got to the Dug Out later, he would put aside his cranberry drink for something with a little more medicinal value; that something would probably be a seven and seven.

While Brett drifted off to sleep on his sofa, Veronica was just getting out of the shower in Frank's hotel room. She always showered right after spending intimate time with Frank; at least it made her feel clean on the outside. Frank was sitting on the bed wrapped in a towel, his short black hair still dripping just enough to be annoying. He was trying to decide if he should wear pants or shorts on this humid Boston afternoon when the phone rang. It startled Frank; he certainly wasn't expecting a call from anyone.

"Hello," Frank answered.

"Hello, is this Mr. Wilkinson, Mr. Steve Wilkinson?" the monotone voice inquired.

"Yes," Frank acknowledged hesitantly.

"I'm surprised we caught up with you; this is Jason from the clothing store you visited a few days ago. You asked us to call when our line of three piece suits went on sale. So I wanted to let you know that the sale will start tomorrow and end on Friday. Will you be able to make it in before our sale is over, Mr. Wilkinson?" his mystery caller inquired.

"Yes," Frank said deep in thought and continued almost in a whisper. "Yes I will be able to get there before the sale ends. Thanks so much for calling. I appreciate it."

Veronica was carefully drying her hair with a towel. After hearing Frank hang up the phone, she loudly asked a playful question, "Was that your other mistress, Frank?"

"No," Frank managed through a chuckle. "It was my client, that wanted to know if I could finish my work by next Friday."

"Well can you? I mean that's only six days from now and weren't you supposed to be working here for a little over a month?" she asked curiously.

"I told them that I could, so starting tomorrow I'll probably be on the job sixteen hours a day, but don't you worry your pretty little head off," Frank continued responding to her question as he walked around the corner to the bathroom area, "Tonight's our night," he said putting his arm around his towel-wrapped mistress. "Whatever you want to do, wherever you want to go, just

140

say the word," he offered. Kissing her on the cheek, Frank headed back to his dresser and pulled out a pair of pleated shorts and a white short sleeved shirt. "I wonder what the rush is," Frank thought as he tried to figure out why he got his unexpected phone call. "Something big must have happened if they need this guy out of the way that quick."

As Frank got dressed, he thought he had better take the PSG rifle out for a test drive to make sure the scope was sighted in and the silencer was working properly. After dropping Veronica off in the morning, for her return flight, he'd find a secluded area where he could do just that. If it turned out the rifle ended up being his only option, and at this point it seemed likely, he didn't want to take a chance that it was even a hair off.

18.

Joyce Davenport was scanning Brett's journals looking for anything he may have been recorded that even remotely resembled the information she had gotten from their recent trip into his subconciousness and had so far found nothing.

She believed as Brett did, that Nadia was, in all likelihood, a real person and not just a figment of his imagination. What she couldn't be sure about, as her eyes made their way across the pages, was whether she was looking at a form of recorded history or getting a glimpse of the future.

Her kitchen timer went off signaling that 5:00 p.m. had arrived. *Five already,* she thought struggling to break away from her reading. Joyce rubbed her tired eyes, put a book mark between the pages that were open and closed the journal. As she was walking into the kitchen to shut the timer off the debate with herself began. "I did promise myself," she said, turning off the timer, "but now that I know these things are probably factual, it puts them in an entirely different category." Then Joyce's thoughts shifted to last night.

When she had gotten home from work, she started digging around in the journals and before she knew it midnight had come and gone. It was 3:00 a.m. before she squeezed herself into bed between the tightly tucked sheets and made the promise to herself not to spend all day Saturday reading and rereading Brett's written account of his dreams.

Joyce stood there staring indecisively at the timer on her stove. Was keeping the promise she had made to herself really as important now, as she thought it was when she made it. After tossing the question around in her mind for a few minutes, she reached for the timer and added three hours and pushed the button to start it once again. "OK," she said compromising with herself, "at eight o'clock I'm calling it quits for real!"

Returning to her couch with a ham sandwich and a glass of iced tea, Joyce picked up the journal and opened it right where she had left off. As she continued her reading, she started to wonder about this woman named Nadia. When she first read through the journals, Joyce didn't see it but now as she was going over them again, she got the impression that Nadia was a little self serving. Maybe, despite the fact Nadia had accepted an engagement ring from Brett's mystical friend; she didn't seem at all interested in a marriage type relationship. Everything Joyce could ascertain from her reading pointed to a one-sided relationship with all the effort going into Nadia with little or no reciprocation on her part. "I could be wrong. I've got to take into consideration that although these are pretty detailed entries it's pretty difficult to make assumptions regarding her emotions," Joyce thought making a note so she'd remember to discuss it with Brett when she saw him again. "It's not unusual for the person having the dream to be the most active character while the other players assume a more passive and less substantial role. It's definitely something worth looking into." Finishing her thought Joyce resumed her reading.

* * *

Frank and Veronica had just finished a very enjoyable hour and a half Duck Boat Tour of Boston. A pretty novel idea Frank thought, taking people around the city streets and out into the bay in an old World War II amphibious landing craft, highlighting some of Boston's more famous landmarks while the tour guide provided an informative and often comical discourse about the cities history.

"That was by far the best and most unique tour I've ever taken." Veronica's voice reflected the genuineness of her declaration.

"I know what you mean," Frank said agreeing wholeheartedly, "It's just a little after 5:00 p.m., what do you say we get an early dinner preferably in a nice air-conditioned restaurant. I don't know about you but this heat is starting to get to me."

"Air conditioning anywhere would be a good thing. Since we're in Boston, why don't we find a nice Irish Pub somewhere and eat there," Veronica offered.

"That's a great idea," Frank said looking around for a cab. "We can leave the car here and get a cabbie to take us; they know where all the good spots are in town. Besides I don't want to waste our time together hunting the streets of Boston for an Irish Pub."

"I don't want to waste our time together either. It would be nice if I didn't have to go back tomorrow; this trip is almost over already," Veronica said, hoping Frank would suggest she stay another day. "I guess I won't have to wait an awfully long time to see you again if you'll be home at the end of week."

"I had no idea you'd miss me that much," Frank said half jokingly and half hoping she was being sincere. "I'd like for you to stay too but I'll be wrapped up in work as soon as you get on the plane back to Chicago. Next week will go by fast," Frank said, pausing to flag down a cab, "you'll see."

"I know it will, Frank," she replied sliding in across the back seat of the cab. "It's just that I've kind of grown a little fond of you."

"What did you say?" Franks asked unable to contain his surprise as managed his way into the cab.

"You heard me. Don't you think you should tell him where we're going?" Veronica asked pointing at the driver.

"We want to have dinner at a nice Irish pub and we're not from around here. Can you help us out?" Frank asked, his voice struggling its way through the thick protective glass that separated the front from the back seat.

The cabbie shook his head, "I know just the place," he said as the cab jumped forward and into the flow of traffic.

"Now what did you say just a second ago," Frank persisted.

"What I said," Veronica replied with a touch a reluctance, "was that I've grown fond of you."

Reaching into her purse, she found the small jewelry box and brought it out. "I got you a little something. Here," Veronica said offering it to Frank. Seeing him hesitate, she had to encourage him a little. "Go on, take it!"

Frank opened the box to reveal a very handsome yellow gold gentleman's ring set with two small stones, one diamond and one emerald. Frank wasn't ostentatious nor was what he was looking at. A big grin began to mix with the flabbergasted look he was wearing on his face as he removed the ring from its box. He was impressed not only with its great look but with it's weight. This was one heavy and obviously very expensive ring.

"Well," Veronica asked, anxious for an answer, "do you like it?"

"I love it," Frank said sliding it on to his left ring finger.

"The diamond and the emerald are our birth stones, yours is the diamond mine the emerald," she explained, knowing that Frank was smart but still a man, and as a man, he would definitely need help with things like birth stones.

"This fits nice, how did you get my ring size?"

Reaching into her purse, Joyce pulled out a piece of what looked like kite string and dangled it in front of Frank. "I got it with this one night while you were fast asleep. I knew if I asked, it would have spoiled the surprise, and since both ring fingers are almost exactly the same size, I had a good idea it would fit on whatever hand you chose to put it on," Veronica explained.

"Pretty clever," Frank said with a touch of admiration. "So you're fond of me and now I have a ring with our birth stones on it. I don't know, Veronica, are you trying to tell me something?"

"Maybe," Veronica replied mischievously. "I think it's something we should talk about. But it really should wait until you get back to Chicago. Like you said, Frank, next week will go by fast," she finished with a smile.

Frank could hardly believe what he was hearing. He couldn't deny the fact that he really liked Veronica and had thought, even hoped at times for a similar scenario to unfold. Just the fact that she was with him on his *business trip* spoke volumes. *She's a professional escort,* Frank thought returning her smile with one of his own. *If she wants a closer relationship she'd have to give up what she's doing and even if she did, could I really get beyond it? Let's not jump to conclusions here. I don't even know if that's what she's thinking.*

Veronica could see that wheels of Frank's mind were turning. She had a pretty good idea of what he was thinking and decided to do some preliminary damage control before taking it up again when Frank returned home to Chicago.

"I'm sure we both have some pretty serious questions we need to ask each other before this goes anywhere, that's if you want it to go anywhere. I know there's a lot we still don't know about each other, Frank, but I believe we have feelings for one another that go beyond our current arrangement, and in my heart, I think it's worth exploring."

Frank didn't like the way she used the term arrangement but he had to admit, an arrangement was exactly what they had.

"I think it's worth exploring too," Frank agreed, "and yes," he added with a smile, "talking about it when I get back is what I think we should do."

"And until you do get back, you'll have this gift to remind you of me," Veronica told him putting on her most flattering smile.

"I really don't know what to say other than thank you," Frank said responding more to Veronica's smile than her statement. "This is so totally unexpected. I really do like this," Frank said, emphatically admiring his new gift. "As corny as this sounds, I don't think I'll ever take it off."

"Here we are folks, O'Reilly's Irish Pub, one of the best in town," the cabbie's muffled voice informed them that they had arrived.

"Thanks," Frank said giving him a ten dollar bill. "Keep the change."

Brett's eyes slowly made their way open as he started to awake from his nap. He wasn't like some of the people he envied that could close their eyes for ten minutes and wake up feeling refreshed. He was at the opposite of side of the spectrum and his couple of hours of sleep made him feel even more tired than when he laid down. His neck was sore too. The arms of the sofa were plush and comfortable enough as a head rest but the angle wasn't quite right for sleeping.

Brett sat up and began rubbing the back of his neck. He was surprised he had been able to sleep at all. Looking back, Brett wondered if he would have been better off staying awake. Brett liked brushing his teeth when he woke up. It didn't matter if he was getting up from a full night's sleep or a nap, it was something he just had to do.

Rising groggily to his feet, he began shuffling his way to the bathroom figuring he'd be able to get a few things done while he was in there. Flipping on the light and taking one look in the mirror told him that he did indeed look as tired as he felt. Leaning over the sink, he gave his face the cold water treatment, splashing it several times before daring another look. It didn't help much; he was definitely more awake but the slight swelling around his eyes would need more time before returning to normal.

Brett slid aside the doors of the medicine cabinet and opened the bottle of Tylenol. He tapped out two tablets, then one more for good measure and popped them in his mouth. Cupping his hand under the faucet he grabbed a healthy swallow of water and washed them down. "That should take care of my sore neck," he said.

Halfway through brushing his teeth his mind drifted back to the formulas he had looked at. *Brilliant,* he thought working his toothbrush toward his back teeth. *I'm going to take a real close look at that documentation tomorrow.* Richard Nelson suddenly came to the forefront of his mind and Brett remembered what Russell Craft had written. "I must have been too caught up in those formulas to have missed the most obvious similarities in our research projects," Brett told himself. "Craft was close to a breakthrough and Nelson called him in. I'm pretty close and Nelson calls me in. It wasn't too long after Craft's visit that both he and his assistant were dead." Brett quickly spit out the remaining toothpaste, did a quick rinse and hurried over to his computer to look at those documents again.

"Sure enough," Brett said scanning the documents. "I've got to be reading more into this than what's there, I've just got to be," he repeated, trying to convince himself. "Hold on, hold on," he told his mind as it started to run away from him. "You can't think clearly when you panic."

Brett started to introduce his very scientific and analytical analysis to his entire day.

"OK, this all started with the dreams about Nadia then the horrible dream about the store, which led me to Joyce and ultimately hypnosis, after which we discovered Nadia, found the disk and learned about Russell Craft. I have Russell Craft's heart and he is the one, or at least I'm pretty sure is the one, that's somehow orchestrating my dreams. I have to assume there's something in my nightmare I've been missing that he wants me to know, which is why I keep having them.

"I have in my possession a couple of memos, his note to Nadia and some scientifically monumental information. The information is loaded with inexplicable coincidences and innuendos but doesn't really prove anything other than Craft was scared and wanted to make sure his work was preserved if something should happen. He makes sure the disk makes it out and puts it in a place where he assumed it would be found a lot sooner than it was or perhaps he planned on retrieving it after a certain period of time. His fears turn out to be a reality and he meets his demise while getting his morning cup of coffee."

As Brett slowly went through his first real analytical review of the day, he could feel it having a calming effect and that's exactly what he wanted and needed to happen.

"Morning cup of coffee," he repeated. "Of course," he said out loud now seeing the undeniable connection. Brett looked down at his right wrist. "Of course," he whispered once again. Brett finally knew exactly what he had to do. He called Dr. Davenport's office and left a message with her service to call him just as soon as she checked in.

Brett pulled into the Dug Out's parking lot a little bit later than he had planned. Looking for a place to park, he could see Becky negotiating her way around the outdoor tables mingling with the customers making sure they received good service. The outdoor café had a pretty good crowd which surprised him; he thought that the heat would have pushed people inside, but apparently not.

Over the traffic noise and somewhat quiet chatter of the patrons, Becky heard a car door shut and looked over to see who it was, as she had been doing since she started work. Glad to see that is was Brett, she threw a dazzling smile and a wave his way.

Contagious smile, Brett thought waving back.

Becky waived him over to an empty table and pulled out a chair for him. She was curious about the disk but thought it would be better to keep things light. If he wanted to talk about it, she thought he'll bring it up. "Hi there, you look great in shorts," she said complimenting him.

"So do you," Brett acknowledged sitting down. "How were your twenty winks?"

"Great," she answered. "Looks like I'm going to have a busy night," she said, sitting down in the chair beside him "Are you going to stay and watch the game tonight?" she asked, knowing that his answer would tell her if they were still on for a nightcap after she got off.

"Sure am," he said with a smile. "Are you working the café side of the house all night tonight?"

"Yes, I can't wait until the sun disappears and it starts to cool off. The trips inside sure help, that little bit of AC makes a big difference. Will you be at the bar or in the stadium?" Becky asked.

"I was thinking about the Stadium. The game doesn't start until 10:00 so I won't have to fight for a spot back there, at least not yet," he told her.

"Yeah, it's only seven so the game crowd won't get here until about 8:30, so that gives you almost an hour and a half head start. Cranberry juice?" Becky asked standing up knowing she had to get back to work.

"Tonight I'm going to start with a seven and seven," he said, surprising Becky.

"What?" Brett asked curiously seeing her smile reemerge.

Becky leaned over so she could whisper, "I don't want people around here to get the idea that I'm feeding you the hard stuff so I can take advantage of you later," adding a touch of fabricated concern to her tone.

Brett started laughing. "Too late, I already called Brian and told him to let the cat out of the bag."

"Well then, since everyone knows already, how about a double?" she said joining Brett in a good laugh before heading in to get his drink.

Brett was amazed at how Becky could get him to take his mind off things. "Cute and quick," he thought taking a quick look around to see if his game watching buddy, Mark Whalen had made his appearance yet. It was a little early so Brett wasn't surprised he didn't see him and thought he'd ask Becky when she got back if she had seen him inside.

Brett thought about tonight's game between the Mariners and Red Sox and hoped it would be a good game. West Coast games started late and Brett considered that a bonus, it should keep him well occupied until Becky got off at midnight.

"Here you are, sir. Be careful, this one's a little sweaty," Becky warned, referring to the moisture on the outside of the glass. "I brought you this" she informed him putting the newspaper on the table "and thought about bringing you some chicken wings but I wasn't sure if you'd already eaten."

"Thanks. I'm not real hungry but it was awfully nice of you to think of that. Did you happen to see Mark lurking around in there anywhere?"

"I haven't seen him yet, want me to send him your way when I do?" she asked.

"Yeah that'd be great. He's so much fun to watch a game with, really gets into it if you know what I mean," Brett said, stating something that every regular Dug Out patron knew.

"I know what you mean alright, he's almost as much fun to watch as the game itself," she said demonstrating Mark's version of an umpire's strike three—you're out, which got them both laughing again. "Got to run and take care of these low tipping customers, see you a little later." Watching Becky walk away, Brett was left alone to finish the remnants of his laughter.

Brett started to take a sip of his drink and almost dropped it. The outside of the glass was sweating so profusely from the heat and humidity that is was actually slippery. Using his napkin, he wiped the outside of the glass and his hand. Feeling the faint rumble of the cell phone in his pocket, he took it out and looked at the number. It wasn't a number he recognized or had entered into the phone's electronic directory but decided to answer it just the same.

"Hi, Brett, Joyce Davenport. Is everything OK?"

"Hi, Joyce, I'm holding my own but things could be better," Brett told her. "You're not going to believe who I ran into today."

"Who?" Joyce asked anxiously.

"Our lady friend from Lexington," Brett replied softly.

"You're kidding me," Joyce replied unable to contain her astonishment.

"No, I'm not. I drove up there this morning, not only did I find *her*, I also got a 3.5 inch floppy disk hidden behind a photograph."

"This is incredible, Brett," Joyce confessed. "All of the dreams you're having are about events that have happened in the past."

Brett went on to explain in as much detail as he could exactly what happened from the time he arrived at Nadia's house until he left for the Dug Out. He even gave her the short version of his analysis.

"Joyce, Joyce, are you still there?" he asked the mouthpiece of his cell phone.

"Yes, Brett, I'm here. I have never heard such an incredible story in my entire life and quite frankly if I wasn't as involved and knowledgeable about the situation, I'm not sure I would have believed it," she admitted.

"I know, I don't understand it very well but all the pieces seem to fit," Brett told her confidently "I think we need to look into my nightmare during our next session. I'm also 99.9 % convinced that Russell Craft was killed at the store I was in. I also want to bring the police in on this. I'm sure there is some type of confidentiality waiver I have to sign that will allow you to share information with them right?"

"Yes, there is a waiver that you'd have to sign. Can you hold on for a second Brett? I want to grab something."

"Sure," Brett said tossing a wink Becky's way as she made her way inside once again to fill an order.

"I'm back," Joyce announced. "You said this store was in Groton right?" she asked looking at her notes.

"Yes, It was on bridge street in Groton, Connecticut," he confirmed

"I've got some friends in the Boston Police Department. Let me see what I can find out, if anything, about that store. I'm also going to clear my schedule Monday and would like to see you just as soon as you can make it in," Joyce instructed.

Brett found Joyce's urgency laced request a little unsettling but he wanted to get to the bottom of this whole thing and put it behind him just as soon as he could, not to mention the fact that he was more than a little disturbed about the situational similarities between him and Russell Craft. Brett was certain about one thing; he had no intention of participating in a similar ending.

"I'll see what I can do, Joyce. I have all my personal days left so I should be able to do that. Do you want me to call Gloria when I know for sure?" he asked.

"No, just call my service and leave your name. I'm going to tell them to page me right away when you call. Then I'll call you and we can work out the details. I would also like your permission to consult with one of my colleagues who just so happens to be one of the very best in our profession."

"You have my permission to do whatever you think is necessary, Joyce," Brett said, giving his unconditional consent.

"OK, Brett. Listen, I want you to occupy yourself for the next few days with anything other than Russell Craft and your work. It will help you relax and might make our time together on Monday a lot more fruitful." Joyce knew that relaxing wouldn't make a bit of difference but she didn't want him to worry. "One more thing, Brett, do you want me to prescribe something that will help you sleep?"

"No, I don't need any sleeping pills, Joyce, thanks just the same. When I first got hit with all this new information, my mind was transformed into a kaleidoscope of uncertainty, disbelief and fear. Taking a more informed and scientific approach on how to handle this has really gone a long way in helping keep my wits about me. I have to admit that I'm a little scared but it pales in comparison to my fear of the unknown. So, the more facts I have and the more educated I become, the easier it is for me to deal with it. I don't know if that makes any sense but it seems, at least for the moment, to be holding me together."

"That makes perfect sense to me, Brett, so you hold on tightly to that mindset," Joyce said. "I'll plan on talking with you tomorrow and remember to try to relax and keep your mind off things."

"All right, Joyce, I'll talk with you then and look forward to seeing you on Monday. Take care," Brett said finishing the call.

Joyce hung up the phone trying to put her arms around everything she had just heard. Her mind was now riding a rollercoaster of its own as she tried to regroup and get off. The bad thing about rollercoasters is once the train starts there's just no stopping it until the compete circuit of twists and turns have been negotiated.

Dr. Joseph Kaufman heard the phone in his study, alerting him that there was someone calling his private line. Closing the French doors behind him, he sat at his desk and answered the way he always did when he got a call on that line. "Dr. Kaufman."

"Hi, Joe, it's Joyce Davenport, I hope I haven't disturbed you by calling at a bad time."

"No, Joyce, not at all. For you to be calling me here, it must be pretty darn important."

"Yes, Joe, it's pretty important. Do you remember the conversation we had a few days ago regarding my patient that was experiencing recurrent nightmares?"

"Yes, of course I do," he replied.

"Well," Joyce said preparing to share Brett's information. "I think I might need your help."

Joseph Kaufman brought his leather chair to a more upright position, his interest level now on full alert. Of all the people he knew that practiced psychiatric medicine, Joyce Davenport was the one that held his highest level of esteem. *If she's asking me for help,* he thought, *this has to be serious.*

"Please go on, Joyce, you've got my undivided attention."

"That is truly one of the most incredible case histories I've ever heard," he commented as Joyce finished. "What really adds to the level of intrigue is the heart transplant and apparent connection between that and his dreams. I can't really provide any significant course of action until I have the opportunity to digest this plethora of information. I do however agree with both you and your patient that you should look into the nightmare for possible clues."

"Well, that's where I'd like your help, Joe," Joyce told him. "His nightmares are very intense and lead to the transitional manifestations I mentioned earlier. I think this will require a deeper level of hypnosis than I'm accustomed to providing and was hoping you would be able to lead that session. You have so much more experience with deep hypnosis and I'm fearful that any mistakes could have a devastating effect to his well being."

"I would love to assist you Joyce. Do you know if your patient would feel uncomfortable if I was leading the session?"

"I doubt it Joe, he wants to get to the bottom of this just as much as I do. He's willing to do whatever it takes, so I don't see any problems in that regard," she explained.

"OK then, with respect to getting started, what time table are you on?" he asked opening his day timer.

"I'm calling Gloria after I get off the phone with you to clear my schedule for Monday," she told Joe, knowing that the super short notice may be a problem.

"Monday," he echoed in a calm, monotone voice. "What time?"

"I won't know the time until tomorrow," Joyce answered, encouraged by his question that there was at least a chance he could make it. "I know how short notice this is, Joe, I myself didn't get the information until about an hour ago."

"It is extremely short notice, but this is an extremely interesting case, so interesting in fact that I'm considering clearing my schedule for Monday as well. With all the cases I have experienced and all that I've reviewed over the years, I think this one is in a class by itself. We'll be going into totally new territory. You call me tomorrow and let me know when you want me at your office on Monday and I'll be there."

"Thanks, Joe. I'll call you and let you know just as soon as I can."

"Joyce, before you go, a thought just crossed my mind. Can we agree to meet you at your office early Monday, somewhere in the neighborhood of six o'clock? I'd like to look at your cases notes and go over the recorded information in his journal that focuses on the nightmares. I think after that, we'll be in a better position to determine some of the finer points as to how we should proceed and the results we hope to get."

"Agreed," Joyce said gratefully. "See you on Monday," she concluded.

19.

Becky woke up startled by the unfamiliarity of her surroundings. *Oh my gosh!* she thought shaking her head in disbelief. *I fell asleep on him last night and he must have moved me into his bedroom. This must be how little kids feel when they fall asleep in the car and wake up in a totally different place.*

She quickly got up and made the bed. Walking quietly into the living room, she saw Brett sound asleep on the couch, with two half-filled wine glasses sitting on the coffee table. She walked into the bathroom, squirted some toothpaste on her finger and did her best to clean her teeth and remove the pastiness from her mouth.

"I can't believe I feel asleep on him!" she said to herself disappointedly. "It must have been a combination of the early morning and working in the sweltering heat all day. I hope he doesn't think I wasn't enjoying his company."

Eight o'clock wasn't terribly early and if Becky didn't have to meet her mother at ten for their weekly mother-daughter trip the Outlet Stores in New Hampshire, she would have stayed right there until Brett woke up. Since that wasn't an option, she had another idea.

Slowly opening the front door and leaving it ever so slightly ajar, she walked down the cement steps and reached over to the nearby flower bed and picked a pretty red flower.

Closing the door softly behind her, she took a piece of paper from his printer and wrote him a short note. Placing the flower over the note, she left both on the kitchen counter, walked back into the living room, gave him a kiss on the cheek then headed home to get ready for her shopping trip.

Unlike Brett, Joyce was wide awake and had been busy in her office for over an hour already consolidating and organizing Brett's case notes. She didn't like leaving things until the last minute and wanted to be sure that everything was in perfect order before Joe Kaufman showed up tomorrow. Joyce put the finishing touches on her notes and double checked her cross reference entries to Brett's journals to ensure they were accurate and clearly marked for quick access. Satisfied with the finished product and deciding it wasn't too early, she spoke with Gloria on the phone and gave her instructions to clear her schedule for tomorrow.

Last but not least, it was time for her do a little shopping of her own. She wasn't interested in looking for clothes or a new pair of shoes, today she would be shopping for favors.

Joyce was going to call her friend Brian Miller at the Boston Police Department. Brian was a senior detective with the department and she had helped him on several occasions by serving as an expert witness with some of their cases.

Joyce had a good relationship with Brian that started out as strictly a business one and quickly developed into a friendship. It had been a little over six months since Joyce had contact with Brian so she was a little skeptical as to just how willing Brian would be to give her the information she was looking for but it was not going to stop her from trying.

Joyce turned to her computer and opened the program she used to keep names, addresses, birthdays and the like. When computers first came out, she wasn't very keen on using them, to her they just seemed way too complicated. It was Gloria's persistence in asking for a computer that prompted Joyce to finally relent and get her one.

The transition was not an easy one for Joyce and took some time. Gloria would always ask Joyce to *come over here and take a look at this* as she passed by her desk. Gloria's two motivating factors were that she wanted Joyce to realize that her investment was paying dividends and to maybe, just maybe, spark her interest in getting her own.

Over time, as Gloria constantly raved about how much time she was saving and the things her new computer was capable of doing, Joyce's position on the old pen and paper way of doing things began to soften. Now being computer savvy and fairly proud of it, Joyce wondered how she ever managed without one. With her shorthand skills and sophisticated voice recognition software her charting time was nearly cut in half.

Joyce punched in Brian's name and picked up the phone knowing full well that the odds of catching him on a Sunday were pretty slim.

"Detective O'Hara," the voice answered.

"Hello, Detective O'Hara, this is Joyce Davenport," she replied quizzically. "I was trying to reach Detective Miller and must have misdialed the number."

"No, Ms. Davenport you dialed the right number, but since his promotion to lieutenant he's moved into his own office. When he got the office, I got his desk." There was a slight pause. "Is this Dr. Joyce Davenport, the one who testified for us in the Savoy Theater child abuse case?"

"Yes, that's me," she answered.

"I never did get a chance to meet you but was in the courtroom during the trail. You were very impressive and didn't let that scum bag and his lawyers fool anyone with that insanity defense," the detective said with gratitude. "If you can hold on a second I'll go into his office and tell him you're on the line."

"That would be great, thank you, Detective."

The familiar click of the hold button was followed by a short span of silence before Brian Miller picked up the phone.

"Joyce," his greeting laced with enthusiasm, "It's so nice to hear from you, how you have been and how did you know I'd be here on a Sunday?"

"Hi, Brian, I'm doing well thanks for asking and as far finding you there today it was just plain luck. I understand you've managed, through your hard work, to get a promotion, congratulations!"

"Thanks, I'm not sure if it was hard work or not. When Bernie retired a few months ago, that left me holding seniority so I might have just been the default choice. My heart is really in case work and making the adjustment to more of a manager has proven to be a little harder for me than I thought. The pay raise sure makes it easier to stomach and even though I'm considered a quote, unquote, manager, I work two weekends every month. If it's important enough for my detectives to be here on weekends then I think I should be here too."

"I always knew you to be the lead by example type," she said in a complimentary fashion. "Bernie finally retired did he? Good for him. I didn't speak with him very much when I was over there but always enjoyed our conversations and admired his commitment to the police force and community," Joyce admitted.

"He's a great guy and we'll miss him around here," Brian responded. "By the way, if you would be willing, we may need your services again a little down the road."

"Absolutely, Brian, always glad to help when I can."

"So to what do I owe the privilege of this call?" Brian asked.

"Well, I'm actually in need of your help this time, Brian," Joyce answered.

"This is a switch, you asking me for help. I'm all yours, Joyce, fire away."

"I want to warn you up front, Brian, that this is going to sound a little strange," she warned, "and I'm not sure exactly how much help you'll be able to give me, if any at all."

"I don't think there's anything out there that can shock me, Joyce, and after all you've done for us, I'll do my best to help. I, or should I say *we*, owe you that much."

"This is more on the unusual side of things and it involves a murder."

"Really," Brian responded, intrigued. "Please go on."

"I was hoping that you could check with some of your friends in Connecticut and see if anything has taken place at a store located at 1599 Bridge Street in Groton, Connecticut?" Joyce asked.

"That's easy enough to do. You wouldn't happen to be in your office on this glorious Sunday morning would you?"

"I sure am," she admitted. "This is pretty urgent, Brian. Is there even the slightest chance you could look into it today?

Brian sighed, "Today, that's not asking for a lot, that's asking for a miracle. I don't even know if I can reach the right people today."

"Please, Brian, I can't even begin to tell you just how time sensitive this," she pleaded.

"Alright, alright….let me make a few calls, but I'm not going to make any promises. Can you at least tell me why this is so urgent that it can't wait until tomorrow?" Brian asked, wanting to tag some justification to her request.

"Well, based on what you find out, I might need one of your guys over here Monday morning," she said obliging him.

"One of *my* detectives? Come on, Joyce, what's going on here?" Brian demanded.

"I have been working with a patient that I've confirmed to be clairvoyant."

Brian cut her off. "Hold on a minute! You mean someone who's having visions; you're not serious are you?"

"Please, Brian, hear me out. I've tested and examined him and so far he's been right on the money with everything. I've never seen anything like it and if I hadn't verified it myself as being genuine, I wouldn't have believed it either. I more than understand your skepticism but you know me, Brian; we've worked together on more than a few cases. I burrow deep beneath the surface to reveal the facts and toss aside all the junk on the way."

"That's you alright, all facts and no time for BS," Brian agreed. "One thing is for sure; your request is almost as unusual as the reason for it. I'll get back to you within an hour and let you know if I'll be able to get the information today or if it's going to have to wait until Monday. Should I call you at the office?"

"Yes, I'll wait right here until I hear from you. Congratulations once again on your promotion, and Brian," she paused, "thanks."

Joyce hung up the phone and stared out her office window trying to figure out what to do if Brian called back confirming her suspicions. Trying to impose the *let's cross that bridge when we get there* school of thought in hopes of breaking away from Brett and onto something else but it didn't help much. She was in this all the way now, hook line and sinker.

Reviewing patient charts provided some distraction but not nearly enough. She watched the clock move past 9:00 a.m., then 9:15 and at 9:30, the phone rang.

"Joyce, it's Brian, you're in luck. I just had a long conversation and got a faxed report from a friend of mine with the Connecticut State Police. We had a pretty long conversation and your suspicions were right. There was not just one, but two homicides at that location twelve years ago, both still unsolved. Both of the victims were shot at close range during a robbery. Here's the kicker, the incidents happened a week apart, and both victims were employees of a big pharmaceutical company down there, Nelson Pharmaceuticals. There are a lot of other details involving these cases that indicate both were professional, execution style murders. The consensus amongst the investigators was the robbery was being used as a cover to throw off the investigation."

Joyce couldn't believe what she was hearing, quickly scribbling notes as a genuine fear for Brett rose within her.

Detective Miller continued, "The first case, involving a young woman, Cynthia Dobson, was thought to be just as it appeared, being in the wrong place at the wrong time. After a Dr. Richard Craft fell victim to the second homicide, it was determined, based on the circumstances surrounding both incidents, that both were connected and professionally done."

Dobson and Craft, those were precisely the names Brett mentioned, Joyce noted.

"I know I'm asking a lot, Brian, but can you share some of the details?" Joyce asked knowing full well that details surrounding criminal cases were not released to the public.

"You are asking a lot, Joyce. I'm guessing you want to know the information that wasn't released to public," Brian replied already sure that was exactly what Joyce was looking for.

"Yes, Brian, I am," Joyce responded.

"Hold on a second, Joyce, I want to close my door." Leaving the phone on his desk, Brian closed his office door and quickly returned. "After all the perps you've helped us with, Joyce, I think I owe you this one. This is strictly *off the record*, agreed?"

"Agreed," Joyce said now very grateful that she taught herself shorthand.

"They interviewed the guy who was working in the store after the first homicide involving the young lady and he described how the man came in locked him in the back room after emptying the cash register, all of $175.00 dollars, and then a few seconds later, he heard a muffled gun shot. This is exactly what happened with the second homicide, same MO. They didn't have any type of video surveillance then, so there were no tapes to review. He described the assailant as a tall Hispanic man wearing a ski mask. He thought he was Hispanic because of a strong accent."

Joyce could hear Brian turning pages of paper.

"I guess they installed a video surveillance system a few days later and the local police agreed to have a patrol car drive by the location early in the morning and again somewhere around closing time. All this was in place when the second murder took place.

"Excuse me," Brian muttered clearing his throat and taking a sip of coffee before continuing.

"When the second homicide took place, I guess it was raining like crazy, very dark and hard to see. At about 6:10 a.m., the local police got a call from someone reporting an accident. Apparently a driver had lost control of a vehicle and driven off the road. The department dispatched the patrol car that was assigned to drive by the store since it was already in the area. When the officer arrived at about 6:20, he found an empty vehicle and radioed in that there was in fact an abandoned car on the side of the road.

"After running a check on the plate, he found that the car was registered to a Phillip Jackson and that his address was only a short distance away. The officer drove slowly in the direction he assumed the owner of the vehicle would have taken if he had decided to brave the weather and walk back to his house. He didn't find anyone walking on the side of the road and was pretty close to the residence where the car was registered so he decided to drive over and talk to someone at the house. What he found when he arrived was a dark house and when he rang the bell, a freshly awakened Phillip Jackson answered the door. Apparently Mr. Jackson was finding out for the first time that his car was stolen sometime earlier that morning. The number that the call came in on, it was learned later, was from the pay phone located at a small strip mall only ¼ of a mile from the store."

"You said the attendant was locked in the back room, right? How could that happen?" Joyce asked as the pieces of Brett's dream were more and more becoming a documented reality.

"Probably a padlock, once you close the hasp, you can stick the padlock, assuming it's open of course, right in there to keep the door from being opened from the inside," Brian answered.

"Of course," Joyce responded feeling a little embarrassed about the question she had asked. "I guess the guy that called for help probably got the owner's name from the vehicle registration."

"Probably," Brian answered continuing, "It's the entire planning thing that has me impressed. He must have done his homework to pull this one off. The Jacksons were an elderly couple and I guess they *never* get up before 8:00 a.m. *Tonight Show* addicts so they were up, what would be considered for them, pretty late almost every night.

"So this guy must have monitored these two for some time, determined to his satisfaction that anything between say 1:00 and 7 a.m. was his window of opportunity. He must have also known there was an officer patrolling the area of the store and used the stolen car as a means to get the police occupied and out of the area, allowing him the time he needed to carry out the hit.

"Let's also not forget the weather. I have to assume this guy knew it was going to be awful so it added substance to the bogus call for help and gave him a safety zone of extra time since everyone had to travel at greatly reduced speeds."

"I agree with you," Joyce interjected. "This guy sure seemed to know what he was doing."

"For sure, and that's not the end of it," Brian said, alerting her to the fact their conversation wasn't quite finished, "He goes into the store at around 6:20 a.m., all geared up, stocking on his head, surgical gloves, gun in hand. Now keep in mind the store has just installed an alarm and video surveillance system. The alarm could have been activated from a push button switch. One switch was under the counter top the other on the back room where these workers were locked up.

"He enters the store while the clerk is stocking some of the shelves so he can get and keep an on eye on his hands; this prevented the button from getting pushed. The counter top was too high for the guy to reach up and try to push it with his knee without alerting the killer. While the assailant is leading him to the back room, he takes out a small can of black spray paint and sprays the lens on the camera. A few seconds later, the gun goes off and it's over. So it's my guess that this guy also had his eye on the store when they installed the systems. But that's just a guess.

"Other than the 63 seconds of grainy video tape, before the camera got a fresh coat of paint, they never found a shred of evidence. The guy that got locked in the back room pushed the alarm button just as soon as he was locked in. The officer that got the call to investigate the alarm was standing on the Jacksons' porch taking a statement. He got to the store at about 6:30. Probably about ten minutes too late. Nobody knows how, but the guy managed to hang on until they got him to the hospital. There was nothing the doctors could do and he died shortly after. When the worker was interviewed, he said the guy had a definite Boston accent and walked with a noticeable limp.

"The guy who was working there when the first homicide occurred had quit that very day, I probably would have too. The Connecticut State Police questioned him again and showed him the video but no similarities were found. I guess they interviewed a slew of people at the pharmaceutical company looking for clues but didn't find anything substantial. Both people were very well liked and highly thought of.

"So that's it in a nut shell, Joyce, everything about the two adds up to the same perpetrator, a very smart and calculating professional. There was nothing at all random about these cases. There was a lot of speculation that someone at their company was involved but as I said, they found zippo," Brian paused for a moment and concluded with a reminder. "*Off the record*. Now that you have your information, I have a question. How does all this stack up against your physic?" he asked curiously.

"I hate to say it, Brian, but it matches perfectly. I can't say I'm surprised but I was hoping he was wrong about this. He also has a computer disk that appears to be from the time frame these murders took place. I'm certain the information on it contains some new leads."

"How did this person get their hands on that?" Brian wanted to know.

Joyce went through a very brief explanation of the case history, hypnosis, and Brett's trip to Lexington. "You mean to tell me that while this guy was under he came up with all this information?" Brian asked, his rational thinking mind now stretched to its limit.

"Precisely," Joyce answered. "Brett is pretty scared and I'm scared for him. He's already told me he wants the police brought in and given all the information, so where do we go from here?"

"You said you wanted somewhere over there tomorrow?" Brian mentioned, "Do you have this information in your possession?"

"No, I don't have it," Joyce admitted. "Brett will be coming in tomorrow and I'm sure he'll want you to have it. So what do we do now, Brian?"

"Let me call my friend in Connecticut and see what he thinks about this whole thing. He's going to need some convincing just like I did, but I have enough information to do that. He'll probably want to send someone up our way to meet with this guy Brett and rather than me sending one of my guys over, I'd like to drop by myself. What time are you planning on having him at the office?"

"I don't know exactly what time he'll be here. When he calls me later today to confirm that he can get the day off from work, we're going to arrange a time. If I had to guess, I'd say we'll be looking at somewhere in the neighborhood of nine."

"Alright, I'm going to give you my cell number," Brian said alerting her to get a pen and paper ready. "Call me on that number after you talk with him and let me know. In the meantime, I'll give the boys in Connecticut a heads up."

"OK, I'll do just that," Joyce confirmed. After writing down the phone number and reading it back to make sure she had recorded it correctly, Joyce left the office and headed for home.

Frank walked Veronica to the screening area at Logan International Airport. Ever since 9/11, showing up well in advance of a departing flight was an absolute necessity. Frank should have been focused on Brett but found his mind occasionally drifting to seeing Veronica at the end of the week for their *conversation.*

Veronica and Frank saw a man in an airport security uniform approaching as they said their goodbyes. "Miss," the young stranger called out looking directly at Veronica. "My name is Jeremy Collins, airport security. You've been randomly selected for a manual security check; would you accompany me the screening area?" he asked pointing to a roped off area in the corner.

There's nothing random about this, Frank thought. *This kid wants to seem important and spend a little time with a good looking woman. Hmm, I bet he hasn't even had to shave yet,"* he thought, feeling a little jealousy which surprised him.

"OK, but all I have is this carry-on bag," Veronica informed the security guard in mild protest.

"This won't take us too long, miss, I promise," he replied, adding a smile.

"Over there?" Veronica asked looking down the terminal as she prepared to follow him.

"Yes, the roped off area," he answered.

Veronica and Frank started making their way over, when the security guard stopped and turned toward Frank. "Sir, I'm sorry, you'll have to wait here and once the check is complete, no further contact is permitted. If you'd like, I'll give you a minute or two to say your goodbyes but once her bag is checked, she'll have to move directly to the departure area."

"Well," she said, "I guess they're going to send me through the check area. I had a good time, Frank. Good luck with getting your work done on time and don't forget about the little chat we're going to have when you get home."

"Thanks for coming out to see me," Frank said gratefully, giving her a hug. "I'll be home as soon as I'm finished and don't worry, I won't forget," he said holding up his hand to show her his new ring. "I have this to remind me, not that I'll need a reminder," he added with a smile.

Veronica returned Frank's smile and headed toward the roped off area with her young escort to get her bag manually inspected.

"So is everything all set?" the young security guard asked placing her single piece of luggage on the table.

"Yes, I tested it again this morning...fully functional," Veronica responded.

"After you get through the gate, you'll see an emergency exit with only two of the letters illuminated the X and the T. Make your exit there; we have a car waiting for you," he explained looking through her bag.

"X and T," she repeated quietly.

"Thanks for your cooperation; sorry for the inconvenience," he said zipping up the bag. "You're cleared to board, have a nice flight."

Veronica turned around to find Frank and waved goodbye.

Making her way down the long wide corridor, Veronica saw her X T illuminated exit sign. Turning around, all she saw was a freshly waxed tile floor and a few strays meandering around. Satisfied that she wasn't followed, Veronica made her stealth exit.

Elias Flynn pushed the button and lowered the window revealing the inside of the Jeep Cherokee "Hop in, Jessie," he called out.

Elias Flynn was the most senior agent with the Justice Department, in charge of deep undercover operations and had recruited Jessica Pierce over a decade ago from the University of Wisconsin.

"Nice work, Jessie," Elias Flynn said moving over a little to make more room.

Jessie sighed with relief. "Thanks, I was beginning to think we'd never get there."

"Me too," he replied as Jessie closed the door.

"OK, Let's go," Elias instructed the driver and they pulled away leaving the airport behind.

The Justice Department had been interested in Frank Whickers for a long time but was never able to get enough substantial evidence to charge him with anything. No one could get close to him until they put the squeeze on his business associate, after a selectively targeted drug bust.

Frank met his friend Billy Smothers when he was interested in buying a small amount of cocaine. After doing some intense homework on Billy, Frank was sure he was a legitimate small time drug dealer and not a local narcotic's agent. Frank didn't buy a lot of cocaine and would probably have been classified as an occasional, if not experimental user. As Frank became more comfortable with Billy and the shadows he and Frank had mentioned from time to time, he was interested in using an escort service.

That was just the information Elias used to set up their counterfeit adult escort/dating service in hopes of penetrating his highly guarded inner sanctum. Once all the pieces were in place, Elias gave Billy a couple of business cards and instructed him to give one to Frank the next time they got together for a transaction. Billy knew he would never survive being locked up in a cage, and twenty years in the state penitentiary was all the persuasion he needed. About a month later, the call Elias had been had been waiting for came in and the operation got underway.

Elias chose Jessica Pierce, a.k.a. Veronica Taylor, because she was without question the best deep cover agent he had. She was extremely beautiful, very well educated and mentally tough. He also knew she was strong enough to handle the emotional aftermath this particular assignment would leave behind long after it was over.

Elias knew from reading Frank's dossier that in addition to the talent he employed to make a living, he was also considered an expert in counter surveillance and computer technology. This ruled out a lot of the standard surveillance techniques like phone taps, bugs in his apartment, or conventional tracking devices, all of which would undoubtedly be discovered and send Frank into permanent hibernation. Frank's knowledge of computers, computer forensics in particular, also ruled out the chance of getting any information from his computer system. All of that pointed to Jessica as their best and probably only hope.

"I hope this is over now," Jessica sighed. "I feel so filthy."

"Why don't you take a few weeks in the Caribbean to relax and enjoy yourself? The department will pick up the tab, you've more than earned it," Elias suggested.

"If it's all the same to you, Elias, I've got a lot invested in this investigation and I'd like to see it through," Jessica said flatly.

Elias couldn't begin to imagine how she was feeling. Considering all she had to endure he thought it best to let her decide. "Your call, Agent Pierce, totally your call."

Jessica pulled her lipstick holder out of her purse and handed it to Elias. "Whickers was pretty surprised to get such a nice gift. I want to see how surprised he is when we bring him in," Jessica said, managing a smile. Elias rotated the bottom of the lipstick holder to the right, illuminating a small red light no bigger than the point of a well sharpened pencil.

Looking over at her and shaking his head in approval, he put a call into the operations center.

"Campbell, this is agent Flynn, we're hot. The GPS transponder chip is in place and functional. Pull down the Boston area overlay and let's get this show on the road. We'll be there in thirty minutes."

Brett woke up grateful he had learned his lesson from the day before. After putting Becky in his bed, he laid down on the couch to sleep and instead of using the sofa's arms to rest his head on, he laid a small throw pillow flat on the cushions and just like magic, no sore neck.

Getting up from the couch, he noticed it was almost 10:00 a.m. and wondered if Becky was still sleeping. He grabbed the wine glasses and took a detour to the kitchen so he could put them in the sink. Seeing the red flower and piece of paper his suspicions were confirmed that it was a note from her.

Brett,

So sorry that I fell asleep on you last night and had to run out this morning before you got up. I thought about waking you before I left but you just looked so peaceful and cute. I couldn't bring myself to do it.

It must have been a combination of little sleep and the heat that did me in. I'm going shopping in New Hampshire with my mother today. If I didn't already have plans, I would have stayed and showed you what a good cook I am. =)

I should be home around five and I'm not working tonight. Maybe we can go to a movie, or just rent one and have a pizza delivered. If you want to get together, call me. If you can't for some reason, call me. Either way, please call me.

Can't wait to hear from you!
Becky

That was a nice note, Brett thought and decided to keep it for whatever sentimental value it may hold at a later time. Despite the fact that he didn't have a whole lot on his plate for the day, the late start somehow made him feel rushed. Brett jumped in the shower and started his accelerated routine to get ready for the new day.

Brett was running a towel through his hair while leaving a message with Dr. Brian Winslow, the chief researcher at Nelson Pharmaceuticals and technically Brett's supervisor even though Brett rarely saw him. Brett explained in his message that he needed a personal day on Monday and apologized for the short notice. He went on to inform Dr. Winslow that he would have very limited access to his cell phone and would return any messages just as soon as he possibly could.

Brett sat at his computer reviewing Russell Craft's formulas once again. He just couldn't get over how brilliant he was. Once you see things written down, you wonder why you couldn't have figured it out on your own. It was like people that played the lottery, sometimes they'd pick their own numbers, sometimes they elected to have the computer do it for them. Regardless of how they did it, once the numbers were drawn, those holding the losing tickets wondered more often than not, how they could have missed picking the now obvious sequence of winning numbers.

The sound of a ringing phone drew his attention away from his computer. "This would be Nadia or Joyce," Brett said.

"Good morning, Brett, it's Joyce. Are we all set for Monday?"

Brett answered joyfully. "Good morning to you, madam, and yes I'm all set for Monday."

Brett knew he'd probably have another late night with Becky and he didn't want to have to get up too early. "I was thinking about a 9:30 show time, is that OK?"

"That'll be great and let me tell you what you can expect to find when you get here. A friend of mine, who happens to be one the best psychologist in the country, will be joining us. I've also asked him, pending your approval, to lead the next session of hypnosis. He is far more experienced than I when it comes to deep hypnosis and I'd feel much more comfortable if he was leading you." Joyce paused for Brett to answer.

"I suppose that will be OK. We are going to have a session that looks into the nightmare, right?" Brett asked seeking confirmation.

"Yes, that's right and if, after meeting Dr. Kaufman you're not comfortable with him, just let me know and I'll assume the lead, OK?" Joyce said giving him the option.

"Fair enough, Joyce," Brett said preparing to say goodbye.

Joyce had spoken with Brett enough now to know that was his lead in to a so long so she quickly jumped right back in.

"There are just a couple of other things before you go, Brett. There will also be two police officers here, one from the Boston PD the other from the Connecticut State Police. I called a friend of mine that works in Boston's detective squad and shared some of the information you gave me yesterday."

"Really, what did they say?" Brian asked inquisitively.

"Well, he thought it was definitely worth looking into and called his counterparts in Connecticut. I believe they're very interested to meet and also have a look at the information on the disk." Joyce paused briefly before continuing, "You know something just came to mind, if this is going to be too big of a group, let me know now and I'll trim it back."

"The group's not too big. If you had a hundred people that you thought could help, I wouldn't consider that too many. I just want to get to the bottom of this and move on with my life. Is there anything I can do to prepare for this, maybe bring some tarot cards or something?" Brett could almost hear Joyce smiling over the phone.

He still has his sense of humor, she thought slightly surprised, *even through all this.*

"No, Brett, there's really nothing at all you need to do except bring a copy of that disk with you. Hey maybe once this is over, I'll sit down with you for a reading," Joyce informed him adding a touch of humor of her own. Right after saying it, she wasn't really sure it was appropriate and was relieved when she heard Brett laugh.

"I'll look for a deck but I have to warn you, my prices are a little on the steep side," Brett countered. "See you in the morning."

It took some time after leaving the airport, but Frank finally found a perfect spot to put the PSG-1 through its paces. He had been driving along the northern Massachusetts border and finally came across what appeared to be a sparsely populated area and followed a wood road that had eventually opened up into some nice open fields. The road itself was overgrown and deeply rutted and obviously got very little use other than the occasional tractor or ATV. Getting out the car, Frank and took a look at the underside of the car. He had bottomed out a few times and wanted to make sure that everything at least looked OK.

Frank did a quick survey of the field and spotted a few likely trees that looked to be an acceptable distance away. He chose a big red oak tree in the distance and started walking toward it counting the paces. The field grass was about ankle deep and left a slightly matted down path behind him.

"Two hundred twent- five, two hundred twenty-six," Frank said stopping at the big oak. Looking back at the car, he noticed he hadn't walked in a very straight line so his yardage measurement was at best a rough guess. It didn't really matter much. To Frank the difference between two hundred twenty and two hundred thirty yards wasn't very significant. If the scope was on at that range, he'd be all set.

Reaching into his pocket, Frank removed a small box of push pins he had picked up along the way and tacked two pieces of paper from his notebook, at eye level, to the tree. After drawing a dark circle in the middle of each piece, he made his way back to the car and opened the trunk. Moving the combination of the lock to the 7622, position he removed the lock, opened the container and quickly assembled the rifle, attaching the scope and silencer.

With the exception of a few chirping birds and the dull sound of what Frank guessed was a small single engine airplane, it was dead quiet. Looking through scope he scanned the perimeter of the field to make sure he was alone. Other than one big gray squirrel, Frank didn't see anything that looked out of the ordinary.

Frank leaned over the hood of the car to get a nice steady rest, brought his self made targets into the crosshairs and squeezed the trigger. The bullet sped on its way, leaving a dark hole, just outside the circle as it slammed into the tree. "Hmm, high and to the right," he whispered as he made a few minor adjustments.

"Tack 1," the Cessna pilot said into his headset using his call sign to confirm the last radio message.

"Make sure you're not too low or directly overhead as you make your pass, Tack 1," Elias reminded the pilot. "I don't want him getting suspicious."

"Tack 1," the pilot responded.

The operations center was similar to the ones used by the Army. It was highly mobile and easy to set up. A technological wonderland loaded with the most sophisticated electronic equipment in the world provided Elias fingertip access to every conceivable combination of information he could possibly want.

Elias and Jessica were looking at a large screen display of a topographical map; an amber flashing light represented Frank's position. Latitude and longitude coordinates were also displayed at the bottom center of the display and directly linked to Tack 1. From the display and associated coordinates, it was obvious that Frank had stopped at a secluded location and Elias, having a good idea why, wanted confirmation.

It didn't matter how many times Jessica was in a field operations center; she was always impressed. One particular technological set up provided real time information on a suspect's location from a chip no bigger than the eye of a needle. A technician could, with the push of a few buttons, enhance a positional overlay so fine you could see the shingles on a roof of a house. Elias had always preferred the standard overlay which resembled a street map you find in a typical atlas.

Frank looked up as the drone of the airplane's engine grew closer. Scanning the horizon, Frank finally spotted the small plane. It was quite a distance away and he doubted that whoever was flying around would be able to see him even if they happened to look in his direction. Even looking at the plane through his binoculars, he couldn't make out the slightest detail.

"Let me hurry up and finish this," he said, feeling a little exposed. "I need to get out of here."

He tossed the binoculars through the open drivers' side window and brought the crosshairs to rest on the middle of the circle. This time the bullet found the center. "Perfect," Frank said, observing the target through his scope. He moved the scope to the second target, squeezed the trigger and got the same result.

The speakers in the operations center came to life once again. "Cobra, this is Tack1. We've got what we came for and we are on our way back."

"Roger," Elias acknowledged. "Good work, Tack 1."

The pilot double keyed his mike, banked the plane east and headed back.

Frank was breaking down the rifle when he heard the sound of what he thought was an ATV. *Great,* he thought completing his task with a greater sense of urgency. Whatever it was, it was getting closer in a hurry.

Frank pulled out the 9mm, closed the trunk and got in the car. He wasn't taking any chances. He thought about picking up the brass but the rifle ejected the casings about ten meters which made it impossible for him to do.

Frank knew there was no quick way out. If he went too fast, he'd wind up leaving the whole bottom of the car in one of those deep ruts in the road. Getting stranded out in the boonies would not be good, it could lead to police involvement, total loss of the vehicle and a lot of questions he didn't want or need to answer.

The ATV was really close now. Frank couldn't actually see the vehicle itself, what he saw instead was the flickers of light from between the trees and thick foliage as the dark shadow made its way toward him. Frank took a deep breath knowing that in about ten seconds the driver would arrive right where he was parked.

Frank chambered a round, put the pistol in his left hand and held it between himself and the car door. "OK," Frank said to his approaching shadow. "Let's see what's on your mind."

The ATV came around the corner and made an abrupt, unexpected stop. Frank tried to see through the visor of the drivers' helmet to get a look at the person staring back at him. The sun was at just the right angle and converted the visor into a mirror so all Frank saw was a distorted reflection of the surroundings.

Both Frank and the driver sat motionless, trying to decide what to do next. Frank started the car hoping his intended departure would persuade whoever it was to move along and leave him alone. It didn't work. Getting off the ATV, the driver, probably only twenty feet away, got off and started to approach. Frank started to think about what he would have to do in the event eliminating his unwelcome visitor became necessary.

Removing the helmet, a young man, probably in his late teens, walked over to the driver's side.

"Hi there," the young boy said greeting Frank.

"Hello," Frank said, deciding it was time to employ his Boston accent, "do you ride back here a lot?"

"Yup, all the time," he told Frank. "You back here looking for deer?"

Frank nodded following the teenagers lead. Reaching over in the passenger seat, he grabbed his binoculars. "Yes as a matter of fact I am," he said holding them up so the boy could see them.

"Lots of people come here from the city to hunt. Don't you think it's a little early to be scouting?" he asked curiously.

"I suppose it is a little early but I've never been back here before. A friend of mine hunts here a lot and suggested I check it out," Frank explained, "I wish he would have warned me about the road," he added, rolling his eyes a little for effect.

"Yeah no kidding, I'm surprised you got here without dropping an axle; it looks like you don't have a whole lot of ground clearance. If you come back here again you might want to try River Run Road just on the other side," the young man suggested looking across the field. "It'll leave you with about a half mile walk to get in here but it's better than using that road."

"I'll do just that," Frank said. "Thanks."

"I'd talk to your friend again," the young man suggested putting his helmet back on. "If he sent you back here without mentioning River Run Road, he might not want you hunting back here after all."

"What a dirty dog. I am going to have a talk with him," Frank said, returning the boy's grin. "Thanks again."

"Do you want me to lead you out? I can probably help you avoid some of the bigger ruts," the boy asked.

"No, that's OK, but thanks for the offer," Frank replied. "I'll take it slow."

"No problem," he said getting back on his ATV. Waving at Frank, he started his vehicle and headed back the way the came.

When Frank was sure the kid was long gone, he got out of the car and put the 9mm back in its case, locked it up and started to slowly drive out. The plan was to go back to the hotel, review the information he already acquired and come up with a more aggressive plan to finish his assignment and get back to Chicago.

The operations technician watched the status bar on her computer terminal fill to solid green. "Sir, we've just finished downloading the information from Tack 1," the operations technician informed Elias Flynn.

"OK, let's see if we can find out what our friend Mr. Whickers is up to," Elias said.

Elias, Jessica and two other field agents, Andrew Campbell and Francine Kelly, huddled around the technician's terminal as the first of ten photographs was put on the screen. Tack 1's digital surveillance camera had an effective range of twenty miles and had incorporated within it state of the art imaging technology that would have put the Hubbell telescope to shame.

Elias was pleased with the team he had been able to put together. He personally hand picked each one for this assignment. The department tired to force some local agents on to his team because they lived in the area and it would save a little money. This was far too important for Elias to take agents he knew little or nothing about just because they lived in or near the area of operation. He had grown weary of the *let's make sure we stay cost effective* argument.

Elias argued successfully, before a three member panel of his superiors, that Frank Whickers background and extensive field experience more than justified any additional operational costs. Giving each panel member a classified copy of Frank's dossier was all the justification the panel needed. After several minutes of answering questions, Elias left the meeting with authorization to use whatever agent resources he deemed necessary and an approved supplemental budget

All of the technological advances made Elias wonder how they ever managed to do investigative work in the past. If this were the old days, they would have had to wait for Tack 1 to land, collect and process the film, then have the film scrutinized by a photo interpreter. What would have taken several hours, now took just minutes. Tack 1 had sent the digital images directly to the operations center using wireless technology, and computers were used to assist in analyzing the information.

The technician pulled up the first picture and made some minor adjustments.

"Move in on the suspect and let's enhance the image," Elias instructed.

Moving a small crosshair over Frank's body, the technician made a few keystrokes and the image was magnified. It was a little fuzzy when initially magnified but was quickly corrected. What they saw was Frank leaning on the hood of the car.

Elias moved over and put his finger on the screen. "Right here," he said.

Repeating his steps, the technician zeroed in on the area Elias had indicated with his finger.

"Hmm," Jessica chimed in, "looks like he's getting in some target practice."

"Enhance and analyze," Elias directed wanting to know what type of weapon it was.

Within seconds, the picture was enlarged and the information about the weapon was displayed on the screen.

Jessica read the heading aloud, "PSG-1, 7.62 semi auto sniper system." Jessica was impressed with his choice for a weapon. "That's top of the line hardware."

"Let's go into the briefing room and go over what we know so far," Elias said to his agents, wanting to make sure everyone present had the all the details fresh in their mind. He thanked the technician and entered the briefing room with Jessica and his two other field agents.

Elias told everyone to have a seat, opened Frank Whickers' dossier and began to read.

"Frank Whickers, a forty-eight-year-old CIA trained operative that disappeared from the radar screen almost fifteen years ago to pursue, what we believe to be, freelance work. We also think that when he broke away he left the country and set up operations somewhere in Europe.

"He surfaced in Chicago about a year and a half ago. When we discovered him, our friends in the CIA gave us their blessing to apprehend him and believe it or not, they've been very helpful this far. This is the first time he has been out of Chicago since we started keeping an eye on him. He's heavily trained in surveillance and counter surveillance techniques, computer/electronics technology, and considered a small arms expert. He was and still is considered to be one of the very best field operatives in the world and is currently operating under the alias of Steve Wilkinson.

"Because of his background we determined that any attempt to tap his phone line or get electronic surveillance into his residence would have been detected and alert him, so we opted for Operation Escort.

"As you know, Operation Escort evolved from information we got from a small time drug dealer Mr. Whickers used to support his occasional cocaine habit. We also used this newly turned informant to introduce him to our escort service.

"After a few months, we received a call from Mr. Whickers looking for an escort. One of our best deep cover agents," Frank purposely kept Jessica's name and association with the operation confidential, "went in and, after almost twelve long months, was able to earn his trust and lead him to develop an emotional attachment to her. Developing that attachment was our primary goal. This was one of the finest pieces of field work I've ever seen and the reason we're here in Boston.

"We know from the agent on scene that on June 23, he received a short phone call at approximately 1:00 a.m. central standard time after which he left his residence and proceeded to a bus station on West Harrison St. A review of the station surveillance tape shows him leaving the station with a small backpack, most likely an advanced payment.

"He left Chicago later that day and arrived here in Boston.

"A few days ago Mr. Whickers called our agent in Chicago and requested her presence for the weekend. After careful consideration and on the recommendation of the field agent it was determined that our new GPS transponder could be successfully planted in some sort of gentleman's ring. And as you can plainly see, it seems this new surveillance tool has worked out very nicely.

"So," Elias continued, "we can now track his movements and hopefully will be able to determine his engagement area before the contract is actually executed, which by the way will be sometime within the next five days. We need to catch him at his engagement point. The information we currently have has sufficient probative value to bring him on a weapons charge but we're after the one that he's working for. If we picked him up now, there is no way he'd divulge that information. If we can catch him in the act, we can drop the entire weight of the judicial system right on his shoulders, which should leave him wanting to cut a deal."

"Our current asset summary looks like this; we have our recon plane—call sign Tack 1 and our ultra quiet recon helicopter—call sign Tack 2. There are currently nine field agents assigned to this detail, not counting myself or the three of you. Of these nine, three have been introduced as hotel employees, one as a chamber maid, the other two will work the reservation desk during the afternoon and midnight shift. We've arranged it this way because were pretty certain that our suspect will be out most of the day. We picked up the hotel phone records and other than wake up calls, he has only had one outside phone call. The number unfortunately was to a disposable cell phone so there's virtually no way to track it.

"The remaining six field agents will be positioned within the suspect's normal travel boundaries, which we hope can be established by Tuesday. Remember he himself is on an accelerated schedule so he will have to limit his activities accordingly. Each agent will work as an independent unit, not in the normal tactical teams of two.

"We do have some tactical advantages on this. First and most importantly is we have the element of surprise. He has no idea we're here so let's be careful to keep it that way. Secondly, he's let his guard down. I'm sure that a level of overconfidence has played a part in that. Regardless of the reasons, he seems to have left a crack in his armor and we're going to take advantage of that.

"The one thing we don't know is the target. As information comes in to our tactical overlay system, it's very important that it gets analyzed and disseminated immediately. Mr. Whickers will be hanging close to his target, perhaps closer than he'd like so I want to be notified when he spends more than fifteen minutes at one location, no exceptions.

"Jessica, Francine, you get our six field agents in here at 1300 hours and brief them, also come up with a contingency plan should our GPS transponder fail for some reason. I'd like that plan in place by 1530 today. Andy, I'd like you to be the operational liaison between us and our folks in the field. Are they any questions?"

Seeing there were none, Elias concluded the meeting. "We're only going to get one shot at this, guys, so let's make it count."

Jessica walked over to Elias as the room emptied. "Any success on the call he got in his hotel room?" she asked in a whisper.

Elias shook his head slowly back and forth somewhat dejectedly. "Disposable cell," he mumbled in response as they walked out of a now empty room.

20.

Brett turned off his computer having had his fill of glancing at pages on the internet about physic phenomena. Nadia popped into Brett's mind and he was curious why he hadn't heard from her yet. He dialed her number and got the same result as yesterday, her answering machine.

Brett had a good three hours before Becky would be back from her shopping spree with her mother and despite all the things he had to think about, he found himself bored stiff. He really didn't feel like doing anything at all. Golf was on television but after a few minutes of watching that, Brett thought he'd run down to the local video store and pick up a few DVD's from the new release section. Hopefully, he would be able to rent at least one that Becky would like. Brett decided to cover all the bases and pick up a romantic chick flick type, an action adventure DVD, and a comedy and then head over to the Dug Out for a while and call Becky from there.

Frank wasn't quite as bored as he sat in his hotel room contemplating his best course of action. He was examining his map that was sprinkled with signal dots. Taking out his pen, he darkened Brett's typical route to work each morning thinking he might be able to catch him stopped at a traffic light early in the morning and pump a 50 caliber round through the driver side window. He also thought about the layout of the research facility and the potential of a much longer shot as he emerged from the security screening area and walked toward the main building. Frank had a lot of possibilities but not much time to explore each one, make a firm decision, come up with a plan and finally execute it.

Although he didn't relish the idea of using his long range weapon, he was somewhat relieved that his 4:00 a.m. mornings were now a thing of the past. He could research potential engagement areas on his timetable and not be tethered to anyone's schedule but his own.

Frank's stomach let out a dull roar telling him it was time to get some nourishment. The last time he had anything to eat was early in the morning. He and his companion Veronica had braved the hotel's complimentary continental breakfast before going to the airport. Both were surprised to find a better than expected selection of food that was actually palatable. He thought he'd head over to the Dug Out and see if Brett would make an appearance. It was still important for him to keep tabs on Brett until his work was finished and since he could potentially kill two birds with one stone, the Dug Out seemed liked the best choice. *No curly fries today, Frank,* he thought putting the roll of antacids in his pocket as a precautionary measure just in case the temptation proved too great to resist.

* * *

"Special Agent Flynn," the technician called out getting Elias's attention. "The suspect is nearing the fifteen-minute threshold."

Elias was viewing the bus station surveillance tapes from the 22nd and 23rd of June and quickly turned his attention to Trevor Taylor, the technician on duty.

"Where is he, TT?" Elias asked, using the nickname he had given him.

"Present location is 2639 Main St. in Brighton, sir," Trevor replied

"Bring up the agents' locations with respect to the suspect's. I want to know who can get there the quickest," Elias instructed.

All the field agents carried their own specially encrypted GPS locaters. This allowed the operations center to distinguish one agent from another. Agent locations were represented by small solid blue circles of light on the agent overlay screen.

"Switching to dual overlay mode," Trevor said banging away at the keyboard. Six blue lights were displayed on the overlay along with a number that represented each agent's unit designation. This overlay was electronically superimposed over Frank's current location to give Elias the information he requested.

"Looks like unit five," Trevor said.

"Andy, get unit five over to 2639 Main Street in Brighton," Elias told him via radio. "The suspect has just made his first stop since leaving the hotel."

"I'll get five over there right away," Andy radioed back.

"TT, can you pull up the location information for me?" Elisa asked.

"Sure thing, boss," Trevor said entering more information into the computer. It took a few seconds for the computer to search the database before giving up its answer. "That would be a local sports bar called the Dug Out."

Elias did a quick review of the information displayed. *Everything but the kitchen skink,* he thought. He was right, all the information one would ever need about the Dug Out was there. The date of establishment, liquor license number and date it was awarded, the date of the the last Department of Health inspection, the owners name—Brian Jones, lease agreement information, building permits, criminal activity summary which amounted to one drunk and disorderly arrest in the past seven years, etc.

"I just love the technology age, TT," Elias said thoughtfully still scanning the information.

"Andy," Elias called out over his radio, "pass along to unit five that the location is a sports bar, the name of the establishment is the Dug Out, the owner's name is Brian Jones," Elias said.

"Will do," Andy replied.

Frank could have walked into the Dug Out with his eyes closed and known he was in a bar. No matter how well a place like this was cleaned, the smell of stale smoke and spilt beer always lingered.

Frank looked down the bar and saw two middle-aged men sitting next to each other. In front of them were two half empty glasses of draft beer and several empty shot glasses. The pile of green bills and loose change that sat on the bar between them told Frank that they were planning on sticking around for a while.

The bartender emerged from the kitchen, walked through the waist high swinging doors that allowed him access behind the bar and walked over to where Frank was standing.

"What can I get for you?" he asked.

Frank took a quick survey of what was on tap and decided on a Bud Light.

"Hey, Paul, can we get a couple more shots down here?" one of the guys from down the bar yelled over.

"Hold on a minute, Louie," the bartender yelled back filling Frank's glass.

"Pretty slow today," Frank said as Paul brought his glass over.

"Only for about another hour," Paul said responding to Frank's observation. "Then the crew will be in to watch the ball game."

178

"Do you always get a big crowd for the games?" Frank asked.

"Always! That's a dollar seventy-five," Paul said, setting the glass of beer on the bar.

"Hey, Brett," Paul said as Frank was taking a five dollar bill out his wallet. "You're a little early today, the game doesn't start until 4:00."

"I know," Brett said looking down the bar increasing his volume. "I'm bored so I thought I might be able to sit in and listen to Louie and Pete share war stories."

Louie and Pete took a break from their heated dialogue and looked over at Brett.

"Come on over, doc, you can help me explain to my good friend Louie over here why the Sox are 4 games out of first place" Pete yelled over with a slight slur in his words.

"OK," Brett chuckled, "let me grab a drink from Paul and I'll be right there."

"Put it on my tab," Louie bellowed.

Brett looked at Paul, shrugging his shoulders. "How about a club soda?"

Paul smiled. "Sure, you better get down there. I think Pete's getting ready to chew Louie's head off. You know how they get after a few pops. I'll bring it down to you."

"OK," Brett said.

"There you go," Paul said putting Frank's change on the bar.

"Thanks," Frank said as he took a sip.

"How are you?" Brett said to Frank who had now turned to leave.

"I'm doing well thanks," Frank said and made his way outside to get a table.

Brett recognized the face but couldn't place it and quickly dismissed trying to figure out where he had seen him before. He had to go play referee for a couple of slightly tipsy acquaintances. *This will make the time go by and certainly take care of my boredom,* Brett thought walking their way.

Frank didn't like being face to face with his targets unless it was the moment of truth and this made the second time that Brett had seen him. *I better back off a little,* Frank thought, *I don't want this kid to start getting any ideas. I've got to decide on an engagement area and pick him up from there.*

Sitting down at the same table he was at the last time he had dinner here, Frank made a decision. "I'm going to finish this thing Thursday or Friday and get out of here," Frank told himself. Using his thumb to fiddle with the ring Veronica had given him, he started debating about just how much information he was going to share with her when he got back.

179

Brett sat with Louie and Pete and participated a little in their debate about how the Red Sox could improve their standings in the American League East. What started out as a pretty intelligent conversation slowly eroded, with each passing drink, to a battle of disjointed ideas and slurred words. Brett was grateful to have been able to kill some time with these guys and now that the alcohol was starting to get the better of them, he was relieved that it was almost time to try Becky.

Finishing his early dinner and having no great need to tail Brett, Frank paid his bill and left. According to the tactical plan, all field agents would remain at the target location for at least fifteen minutes after Frank's departure then radio in a report from their vehicles. They weren't taking any chances and didn't want Frank to have the slightest notion he was under surveillance. If Frank stopped again and it was necessary to investigate, another agent would be dispatched.

Frank was making his way back to the hotel and had found himself a car wash along the way. Frank parked the car in a stall and went to the change machine which eagerly inhaled his ten dollar bill and just like a slot machine spit out ten tokens into a metal tray.

After a cursory wash and vacuum, Frank got busy at wiping the car clean of any fingerprints. Using a towel he had taken from the hotel, he meticulously wiped the inside clean then did the same to the outside.

Back at the operations center, Elias knew exactly what Frank was up to. It was day six of Frank's operation and following standard procedure, it was time for him to switch vehicles and get an entirely new highway identity. Elias had gotten confirmation from Unit Two's drive by of the car wash as to Frank's activity. "You still do some things by book, Frank," he said as a smile came to his face.

The operation center used four portable air conditioning units that attached to the operations center from the outside. These units pumped cold air inside to keep it the temperature an equipment friendly 70 degrees. Andy had just returned to the operations center after taking a look at one of the units that wasn't working.

"Andy," Elias called out, seeing him walk in. "I want agent Williams to move from the reservation desk and into the security room at the hotel. Tell her to keep an eye on the parking garage video cameras. Frank is going to be switching vehicles. When he makes it back, I want to know what he's driving."

"Got it," Andy said picking up the phone and calling the hotel.

Frank wasn't real surprised when he pulled into the long-term parking area to find there was absolutely no security. It must have been OK if someone wanted to blow up a bunch of parked cars as long as they weren't *too* close to the airport and its large transient population. Judging by the condition of several vehicles Frank saw parked there, it wasn't much of a stretch to think the people who owned those cars would probably welcome a disaster just like that and have their insurance companies help replace their old, run down vehicle with something a little newer.

Scanning the vehicles in search of his red Audi, Frank caught a glimpse of the shuttle bus. Its handful of passengers would soon become a bus full before its twenty minute journey to the terminal was completed. As the people on the bus immigrated to the terminal, it would only be a matter of hours before being on their way to new destinations. Frank watched the bus for a few minutes and wished he was on it. It wasn't so much that he wanted to be back in Chicago, it was more him wanting the assignment to be over than anything else. Boston. Frank continued driving around the large parking lot hopeful that 4:45 was late enough for the prearranged afternoon switch.

Brett had snuck away from the dynamic duo at the bar so he could call Becky from a more private, less boisterous setting. When Brett got a hold of Becky he asked her how her shopping trip was and outlined the Pete and Louie scenario. Becky liked those guys but knew from experience that they were a little past their limit as far as drinks were concerned. If she showed up at the Dug Out, they'd have a very hard time getting away from them. Both Becky and Brett didn't want to spend a good part of the evening placating two inebriated gentleman so agreed it would be best if they met at Brett's apartment and that's exactly what they did.

Becky showed up at Brett's door with a large mushroom and onion pizza, under her arm a two-liter bottle of soda.

"Here, I'll take that," Brett said taking the pizza and soda from Becky. "So what are we having?"

"We are having a fine pizza dough, covered with a very special, hand made, tomato sauce, topped with a savory mozzarella cheese and just the right amount of mushrooms and onions," Becky said describing the contents of the box as Brett brought the stuff into the kitchen. "I went with the onions because I wanted to show you I was brave," she added getting herself a seat in the living room.

"Brave?" Brett asked, stumped for sure.

"Yes, I'm going to enjoy our pizza and not be afraid to talk with you afterwards," she explained moving into the kitchen with him. "Why don't you let me get this stuff here ready. Maybe you could go over to your clicker collection in the living room and put a move in for us."

Brett smiled. "I hope I can be as brave as you. Don't you want to know the movies I picked out?" Brett asked, a little surprised that Becky didn't seem to care which movie they watched.

"No, not really," she replied indifferently as a thin smile appeared on her lips. "I think we have similar tastes, besides I *really* like your taste in women so I'm sure whatever one you choose will be fine."

"OK," Brett called back to the kitchen still wearing his smile. "You really are brave aren't you?"

Becky brought two plates, pizza, and their drinks over to the coffee table and put them down where Brett suggested to with his finger. Becky apologized early into her first piece of pizza for falling asleep the night before.

Brett quickly put her at ease. "Don't think twice about it. I was on the verge of falling asleep myself, you just beat me to it that's all."

Becky was using a napkin to wipe the corner of her mouth. "You're just saying that to make me feel better."

"Is it working?" Brett asked

"You know what would *really* work?" Becky asked putting her pizza down and wiggling over next to Brett. "A nice hug."

Brett eagerly obliged her and had to admit, a hug made him feel a lot better too. The movies sat in the trays of the DVD player waiting expectantly for a request to provide the evenings entertainment but remained dormant as the night progressed. Brett and Becky were enjoying each other's company too much to spoil it with a distraction. Their conversation moved from a very casual, almost tentative discussion to a deeper, more intimate exchange.

For the first time, Becky talked about her father. Becky remembered watching him from her bedroom window late one snowy New England evening.

"On that night, it was snowing really hard so I couldn't see all that well," she began telling Brett. "My father was nothing more than a dark silhouette on a poorly lit street. As he walked along the snow-covered sidewalk, the combination of new and drifting snow filled his tracks almost as quickly as he made new ones. In his left hand was a suitcase packed with, what I guess he considered, the things he really needed. As he walked away, I noticed the end of his scarf was flapping in the stiff winter wind, almost like it was waving goodbye. I could hear my mother crying downstairs. I wasn't going to cry. I was going to be strong. I was going to go after my father and do whatever it took to stop him from leaving us. I grabbed my coat and ran outside despite my mother begging me not to but I was too late, he was gone. I started running down the sidewalk in the direction he had gone but Mother Nature had already erased the snowy pathway he had taken. So I just stood there at the intersection, in the middle of this blizzard, balling like crazy and trying to figure out what to do. That was almost four years ago and we haven't heard from him since."

Brett's heart was just breaking for Becky. He could see that she was holding off tears. "So what did you do?"

"I decided right then and there that no one was going to hurt me or my mom that way ever again," she said. "My father was, or is, a liar and a cheat. It got to where he couldn't tell the difference anymore between the truth and a lie. I don't even know if he really ever loved me. My mother told me shortly after he left that all men were the same and I believed her until now. Before I met you, I would go out on the same old dates. Guys trying to impress me by exaggerating or bending the truth a little or trying to impress me by the car they drove or their address. That's how it started for my mother and as soon as they went down that road, they were history. You're different; you're the genuine article, the real deal. I know now that no matter what happens, you will be honest with me. You even tell me when my jokes stink." She managed a giggle. "So that's the story of my dad and also clues you in a little on why I like you so much but I might have told you that already."

"I'm really sorry to hear that about your father, Becky. Regardless of the circumstances, it always hurts when you lose a parent and yes, you're right," he went on trying to add a touch of humor, "some of your jokes *are* bad."

"Hey!" Becky playfully protested and followed up with a Mark Whalen *You're out a here!* imitation that got them both laughing.

After sharing a good laugh, Brett told Becky all about the information he found on the disk and the conclusions he had arrived at. Brett then, very calmly and self assuredly explained the game plan for Monday morning and how he hoped it signified the entire mystery was nearing an end.

Despite Brett's composed demeanor, Becky could feel the tension and turmoil Brett held at bay just below the surface.

"Listen, Brett, I'm going to suggest something and I don't want you to get the wrong impression. I know that you're under a tremendous amount of stress; I mean who wouldn't be with everything that's happened" Becky said, laying the foundation for the suggestion to follow. "It's probably going to be pretty tough to get a good night's sleep," she continued looking at Brett who

183

was unsure where she was going with all of this, "and I'm not sure that you being alone, especially before such a big day tomorrow, is such a good idea. So if you have no objections I'd like to stay with you tonight but no hanky panky!" Becky insisted.

"I'd love it if you would stay tonight, Becky, and don't worry," Brett assured her with a smile, "I've got a pretty good headache going."

21.

Joseph Kaufman arrived at Joyce's office right at 6:00 a.m. Trying the door and finding it unlocked he left himself in. "Anybody home?" he called out so his voice carried through the waiting room and into Joyce's office.

Recognizing the voice, Joyce answered back, "Morning, Joe, come on back. I've got some fresh coffee and some danish if you're interested."

"Who could resist such an invitation?" Joe said entering her office and taking a seat. "You always knew how to make me feel welcomed. By the way, I like the way you've redecorated, the office looks really nice."

"I wish I could take the credit. Gloria is the one here that has the decorative touch," she admitted.

"Do you think you could loan her out to me for a day? I'd like to get some suggestions from her on how I could change the atmosphere over at my office," Joe asked.

"If you're really serious about it, I'm sure she wouldn't mind," Joyce told him trying to determine his level of sincerity.

"Dead serious, this place looks great!" Joe exclaimed. "I'd even consider tossing a cash token of my appreciation her way if she'd agree to do it."

"I'll be sure and mention it to her when she gets in," Joyce promised, handing him a cup of coffee and a blueberry pastry.

After exchanging pleasantries, Joyce explained the situation and informed Joe that some detectives would be joining them at around 9:00 a.m. Dr. Kaufman had some concerns about having police officers around but knew that if Joyce had them coming it was probably the right to do. After all he didn't really know all that much about Brett Allen or his case history. Joe didn't verbalize his mild objection and asked Joyce for the case notes and Brett's journal so he could start his review and evaluation. After a few minutes of reading, he passed along a compliment that Joyce didn't expect.

"Joyce," he said, "I really like the way this is organized and cross referenced. I'd like to use this over at my office if you don't mind?"

"Not at all, Joe," Joyce replied feeling very good at getting a nice review of her prep work from someone of his stature. "Be my guest," she added with a smile. "The licensing fee isn't that much."

That got a laugh from Joe as he went back to his review. Joyce knew there wouldn't be a whole lot of conversation until Joe finished going through her material so she decided got a jump start on reviewing patient records and charting.

"Good morning, Dr. Davenport, you're in early today," Gloria said walking in ready to start the new week.

"Morning, Gloria, come into the office and grab a Danish," Joyce offered. "I got them fresh this morning from the bakery."

"I am not real sure if I should have one. I…" Gloria paused in mid sentence when she walked in and saw Dr. Kaufman, "put on a few pounds over the weekend. Dr. Kaufman," Gloria said, addressing him directly, "this is an unexpected surprise. How nice to see you again."

"Nice to see you again too," he said, closing Brett's journal. "A little birdie told me you were responsible for this exquisite redecorating work. My compliments."

"I didn't really do the work, Dr. Kaufman. I came up with the color schemes and picked out the furniture I thought would best accentuate the look we were going for, our professionally pleasing look. Clean but not clinical and soothing to the senses."

"I think you're mistaken, Gloria," he reassured her, "about doing the work. It takes an artistic mind to come up with something like this," he said waving his hand around the room, "that's the real work, anyone can paint and move furniture around."

All Gloria could do was smile. She knew why this guy had a great practice; he was able to make people feel good about themselves and what they've accomplished.

Joyce responded to Joe's cue right on time. "Dr. Kaufman was hoping that I'd give you a morning off so you could take a run over to his office and maybe give him some ideas. You know how men are when it comes to decorating, everything has to be equally spaced, level, and represent some sort of geometric shape. It just gives me creeps."

Everyone burst out laughing, not so much because of what Joyce said, but because the way she somehow managed to contort her face, to illustrate what the creeps meant to her.

"Since you put it that way," Gloria said as she tried to calm down. "I don't see that I have any options."

"Terrific," bellowed Joe Kaufman. "Would it be OK to talk later and iron out the details?"

"I suppose that you'll have to do that with Dr. Davenport since she'll be giving me the morning or maybe even the whole day off," Gloria explained taking the opportunity to drop a hint. "Just one minor item before I go out to my desk. Dr. Kaufman, you're not here to try and steal my boss way from me are you?"

Joe looked Gloria straight in the eyes. "Heavens no....well, at least not today," then smiled and winked.

"Now there's an honest answer," Gloria said, returning to her desk. It was time for her to clear Joyce's schedule and get busy clearing her patient schedule for the day.

"Gloria, before you get busy," Joyce said over the intercom, "I wanted to remind you that at about 9:00 I'm expecting Brian Miller and a friend of his from Connecticut. Then Brett Allen will be in at 9:30. As they arrive, please send them all right in."

"OK, Dr. Davenport," Gloria responded.

"Well, Joyce," Joe began rising to close her door. "Let's discuss how were going to handle this."

With the door now closed, Joe started to explain to Joyce his thought about how best to proceed.

"I want to share some observations with you, go over the steps I'd like to follow, then solicit your ideas and opinions to make sure that you think I'm on the right track, does that make sense?"

"Yes it does," Joyce agreed.

"I think what has happened here, and I can't believe I'm saying this, is that Brett Allen has somehow acquired the memory of Russell Craft. I'm basing this assumption on the information we've discussed, what I've managed to get from his journals and the fact that Brett has Russell Craft's heart keeping him alive. There's a school of thought that suggests the heart is a great deal more than just a person's strongest muscle. Some believe it contains the essence of who we are as human beings and locked within its walls are our emotions, our hopes, our deepest desires.

"When Brett had his heart transplant, he went from a mediocre student at best to a genius and it was practically overnight. I consider this to be strong supportive evidence for my theory. And although he acquired Russell Craft's academic knowledge, the emotional piece didn't surface until Brett experienced the intense emotional trauma when his mother passed away. This again in my opinion is also strong supportive evidence and when you add your hypnotic session and the resulting events that occurred afterwards, I don't see any other theory that makes sense. Would you agree?"

"I totally agree, Joe. So far were on the same page."

"Good, I thought we might be. The nightmare is the challenge for us; it always starts around the same time and stays the same with the exception that with each passing dream the ending gets just a little longer and closer around the time the bullet enters the body. This could mean any number of things but I've concluded this to be a warning of sorts. You said Brett told you about a meeting that Russell Craft had with his boss based on his cancer research and the fact that, supposedly, he was close to a cure. Now you have this young scientist Brett, working for the same company who has confessed similar success in the organ transplant arena of research and by coincidence, he has a meeting with exactly the same person. All this adds up to something way beyond a coincidence. I think his dreams represent a timetable of sorts. With each passing dream, he sleeps juts a little longer and moves ever closer to the ultimate end. This premonition, for lack of a better term, is telling him that with each passing day, he draws nearer to the same tragic ending Russell Craft found one rainy day in Connecticut."

Joyce shifted uncomfortably in her chair and Joe picked up on it right away.

"Brett's case is truly remarkable," he said "and I doubt there will ever be another on like it, at least not in our lifetime. It's also quite unnerving to discover that his dreams are the fabric of a tightly woven quilt that represents both the past *and* the future."

"What are you thoughts with respect to putting him under?" Joyce asked anxious to hear what her colleague had in mind.

"With respect to hypnosis, I plan on taking him down to the deepest caverns of his subconsciousness. In some of his more recent dreams, the man responsible for the murder takes off his stocking mask and pulls the trigger. Brett wakes up at the sound of the gun shot but apparently can't see the face of the person holding the gun. I can only assume that the time between the two events is perhaps no greater than a few seconds. I want to take him right there and slow things way way down. In doing so, I believe we'll be able to get a look at the face of the gunman. If Russell Craft's essence is leading Brett's subconscious, and I find this likely, maybe getting a look at the person who killed him is the reason behind it all."

"So you think that Russell Craft has been leading Brett down an obscure subconscious roadway and the end of the road is locked somewhere inside his nightmare?" Joyce asked.

"I wish I could come to another conclusion Joyce, unfortunately I can't. Now the big question, based on what my analysis shows, do you still want me to proceed with your patient?"

"Yes, Joe, I think it's in the best interest of Brett if we go ahead and move forward. I don't think it's wise, at least at this point to share those observations with Brett."

"Alright, I just wanted to be sure," Joe said.

"You said that Brett may actually be able to get a look at the gunman's face. I was curious if people under deep hypnosis have ever been able to see and respond on both sides of the consciousness boundary. "

"If you're asking if people can mentally hover somewhere in between the two states and respond to stimulus in both arenas, the answer is yes. The information provided within such a session isn't as accurate but it has been done. What are you thinking?" Joe asked inquisitively.

"I'm thinking if we can get Brett to describe the man that shot Russell Craft then maybe a police sketch artist can give us an accurate portrayal of what this person looks like. Or do you think the likelihood of that happening is too remote?" Joyce asked.

"Actually, Joyce, I think it's a pretty good idea. You said Brett was very resilient. Do you think he'd be up for it?"

"He'll do just about anything to get this behind him," Joyce assured him, "and so would I."

Joe sighed and clasped his hands in front of him. "Well then, I'd like to suggest you contact your detective friend and see if we can get one of their artists over here, you never know what we might be able to come up with."

* * *

Brett woke up to the clanging of pots and pans in the kitchen and the unfamiliar smell of a freshly cooked breakfast. Becky had just finished washing the pan she had used to scramble the eggs and went in to wake Brett up.

"Good morning, sleepy head," she said sitting down on the bed next to him. "Rise and shine, breakfast is ready," she announced leaning over to give him a kiss on the cheek.

"Are you always this perky in the morning?" Brett asked groggily, struggling to sit up.

"Only when I've had a great night's sleep and last night, I slept really well. Hey not too bad in the fridge for a bachelor," she commented. "The eggs, bread, and cheese were fine but I had to dump the milk. So it's scrambled eggs with cheese, a couple pieces of toast, an instant cup of coffee for me and a glass of cranberry juice for you. It's not a five-star breakfast but it was the best I could do with what you had."

"Sure smells good," Brett said, getting out of bed. Adjusting his gym shorts to remove a sneaky overnight wedgie, he made his way to the bathroom. After brushing his teeth and giving himself the quick once over in the mirror, he joined Becky for breakfast.

"You were right about breakfast not being a five-star affair," he said finishing the last of his eggs "I'd give it a conservative six. It was terrific, thanks for making it."

"My pleasure," Becky said, picking up his empty plate and putting it in the dishwasher.

"You don't have a whole lot of time before your appointment so I'll head to my place and let you get ready. How about calling me when you're done, maybe we'll do a little shopping. What do you say? The inside of your refrigerator could definitely use a woman's touch."

All Brett could do was smile. He could tell that she really wanted to be close to him and was trying not to push things too fast. For some, Becky would have been moving a warp speed but Brett was comfortable with the pace of their relationship. He was also pleased that the foundation they were building upon was not solely focused on physical attraction but on trust and mutual respect and as far as Brett was concerned that was a wining combination.

"OK, I'll call you from my cell as soon as I leave Dr. Davenport's office. I have no idea of how long this is going to take though," Brett warned as he watched Becky collect her things so she could go home.

"Other than my hair appointment at 11:15 today, I don't have to be anywhere until Wednesday afternoon at five. So as long as you're done before then we should be OK." Becky gave him a big encouraging hug and a soft kiss before she left. "You're going to do great today, Brett!"

As Brett got in his car to go to Joyce's office for his meeting, Justice Department agents were having a meeting of their own. The operations center never slept and Elias rarely did when he was running an important operation. The operational team was assembled to review the data collected from the day before and hopefully try to predict with some degree of certainty what Frank's plans were.

"Good morning, everyone, if you'll take a quick look at the folders in front of you, you'll see Mr. Whickers had somewhat of a busy day yesterday. We are all aware that Frank took in a little target practice yesterday. From his positioning, the computer did some vector analysis and we know now that his target was approximately two hundred yards from the vehicle. So it's pretty evident that he's going to engage his target at long range. Just so you know, we have documented evidence that he has taken down targets at ranges in excess of 500 meters.

"Special Agent Cranston's report from the restaurant was inconclusive. According to the report, he didn't seem to be waiting for or following anyone. She asked the bartender a few questions and apparently this place is well known throughout Eastern Massachusetts and very highly patronized. At this point, we think he was just hungry, heard about the place and decided to check it out.

"Later that day, Frank switched vehicles at Logan Airport. He's now driving a red Audi. Massachusetts license plate number MA 3772 FR. The Civic he was driving is still in long term parking and we're keeping an eye on it. As a precautionary measure, we're not going to move on that vehicle and take the chance of tipping anyone off.

"Frank then went on a little Sunday evening drive that took him from the airport, through Brighton, where he had stopped earlier for a bite to eat, then up to Bedford, Mass, where he spent a total of fifty-seven minutes in the area of Route 62 and Crosby Drive."

Pushing a button on a small black remote control device, a topographical overlay appeared on the briefing room display screen. "Here is the topographical overlay of that area, now I'll superimpose the target overlay," he said pushing another button.

It was like watching a James Bond movie. Frank's amber dot moved slowly west on Route 62, Elias's narrative matching Frank's route, past the Interstate 3 overpass then turned north on the access road and got on Route 3 going south.

Elias froze the overlay. "Ladies and gentleman, may I present the Nelson Pharmaceutical Research Facility. You'll notice Frank drives around this

particular complex three times." Elias put Frank's historical data in motion once again and accelerated the display twenty times normal speed. "This is our best lead so far as to one possible engagement zone. As you can see in the topographical overlay, there are several wooded areas that could provide adequate cover and escape routes. We have a team there now masquerading as state workers on litter patrol to give us a ground level assessment of the best shooting areas based on parking lot locations and employee access points" Elias switched the display off. "So Frank's target in all likelihood is an employee of that company. There are over four thousand employees at that company and we should have the complete list in a few hours. One added note. On his way up to recon the pharmaceutical company he stopped at an Army surplus store and picked up a pair of jungle fatigues.

"So far today, Frank is still in the hotel. We're hopeful that today maybe we can start establishing some patterns and that once he leaves the hotel, we can get our chamber maid into his room and maybe catch a break."

"Tack 1 and 2 are on fifteen minute alert status. Please brief your field agents via secure radio and bring them up to speed. Andy, I want each of us here and our six field agents to have tactical battle dress available to them before the days over. OK, let's meet back here at 16:30 hours for our afternoon briefing."

Elias and Andy left the briefing room and Jessica could tell that Special Agent Francine Kelly was hanging around wanting to talk with Jessica.

"I really miss being out in the field," Francine confided in Jessica. This was Francine's first assignment as a Special Agent Supervisor (SAS). It was supposed to be a promotion but she didn't quite see it that way.

"Miss sitting in a car for hours on end?" Jessica's frigid, emotionless response caught Francine off guard.

"Actually, Jessica, I hated sitting for hours on end in a car, it's the detective work that I really miss. When I got this so-called promotion, I had no idea I'd be trading hours in a car for hours in this high tech tent."

Jessica knew she owed Francine an apology and gave her one. "Sorry, Francine. I don't know where that came from. A lot of agents struggle with the same thing when they make it to the SAS level. It's natural to feel somewhat disconnected, but our role here is important. Not only are you asked to mentor our younger agents, but we're called upon and expected to use our extensive field experience to assist in the analysis and decision making process.

"The success or failure of an operation depends in large part on the

decisions we make right here. We're not very deep into this operation yet and as we move along, you'll see what I mean. My point being that you have to be a little patient. We're very early into this operation and trust me when I tell you that you'll be plenty busy the next few days. After it's all said and done I think you'll agree that being in an air-conditioned tent, if you will, making tactical contributions is more desirable than baking in the hot sun."

"You're probably right, Jessica, thanks for sharing that with me. Oh, by the way, no apology necessary. If I wasn't being so self centered about what was going on, I would never have made the comment. I'm going to head back to the situation room and start reviewing the overlays and data we have in already," Francine said, hoping Jessica would join her.

"That's a good idea, Francine. You go ahead. I'll be there in just a few minutes. Maybe when I make it over there we can start looking into this pharmaceutical company and see what they're all about," Jessica said offering a little advice to help Francine along.

"I'll start digging into that right away. Great idea, Jessica."

Jessica managed a tired smile to send Francine on her way. This had been a grueling assignment for Jessica. She played her part as Veronica better than any Oscar winning actor ever could have. But unlike a Hollywood actor, there was no statue or large cheering crowd, no fanfare or big to do, that made you smile and feel good about your accomplishment. Instead, you were told from the shadowy recesses of a back office to go away for a while, relax and take your mind off of things. Shake off what you had to do for the good of the country and get back in the saddle. She was a hardened deep cover agent but this one left her feeling violated and dirty.

She thought about seeing the department's shrink to help her smooth out some of the rough spots before they grew into something she couldn't handle. Agents were told early on in their career that counselors were there to help and agents would not be looked down upon if they felt that seeking professional counseling was necessary. Nothing was farther from the truth.

If an agent had a really hard time dealing with the emotional scars from a deep cover operation and elected the counseling route, it usually meant the agent had enough and was looking for a way out. Everyone Jessica ever knew that went in for counseling came out of it with a desk. Once an agent was taken out of the field and given a desk, it was theirs until retirement.

There was no way Jessica could handle a desk, which put the department's psychiatric staff out of her reach. She'd deal with her problems alone and do so very willingly given the alternative of being strapped to a desk. Just the thought of having to show up at the same place day after day wondering if you'd forgotten your turn to bring in the doughnuts made her skin crawl. Jessica sighed as she got up from chair. "Let's go help Francine."

22.

Gloria was on the phone rescheduling the last of Joyce's appointments. She felt especially bad telling Charlie Duncan that the doctor needed to cancel his appointment. He was the most agreeable when she was trying to make some room in the doctor's schedule last week. Hearing the door start to open, Gloria glanced over and saw Detective Brian Miller and his counterpart from Connecticut, Detective Hank Beard, walk in to the waiting room. Smiling at them and raising her index finger she got the reaction she had hoped for, a pair of nodded acknowledgments as both men sat down on the waiting room couch.

Gloria continued looking at the two men on her couch until she got off the phone.

"Good Morning, Detective Miller."

"Hi Gloria, long time, no see. How long has it been, eight months maybe nine?" he asked.

"I'm not sure, but it has been a long time," Gloria agreed.

Brian took care of the introductions. "Gloria Johnson—Detective Hank Beard, Connecticut State Police. Hank—Gloria Johnson, Dr. Davenport's assistant."

Both exchanged the *nice to meet you's* and Gloria ushered them in to Joyce's office as she had requested.

It was Joyce's turn to lead off with the introductions and social pleasantries. Once everyone got briefly acquainted, Brian informed everyone that the sketch artist would be over somewhere between 10 and 10:15.

"I sure hope you're right about this guy, Joyce," Brian added.

Everyone was already briefed and knew why they were here. Joyce didn't have to waste time with any lengthy explanations and opted for a quick, down and dirty summary which included Brett's transplant, journals, and recent trips to Lexington, MA and Groton, CT. She also shared, for the benefit of her police visitors, the conclusions that she and Joe Kaufman had arrived at after analyzing and discussing the data.

Out in the waiting room, the door opened at precisely 9:15 as Brett walked in carrying a cheerful hello for Gloria. "Good morning, Gloria! Has the audience gathered and are they anxiously awaiting my appearance?"

"Good morning, Brett, yes your new fan club is fully assembled. Dr. Davenport wanted me to have you sign this waiver and release form."

"Sure thing," Brett said approaching the desk and signing on the dotted line.

"There you go, Gloria," Brett said, giving her back a signed form.

Gloria put her hand on the intercom button and smiled. "Shall I announce your arrival?"

"No need to bother, my dear, I'll just mosey on in if you don't mind."

Taking her hand off the intercom, she extended her arm towards Joyce's door. It reminded Brett of those television models directing your attention to the prizes on a game show. Brett winked a thank you on his way by Gloria's desk, gave a knock on the Joyce's door then walked in.

When Brett entered the room, everyone with the exception of Joyce was surprised by his appearance. Joe Kaufman and the detectives didn't expect to see a down to earth, clean-cut, and well dressed young man. They were leaning more toward something that fit into their tarot card reading, psychic-medium stereotype. Someone more aloof, perhaps eccentric, but certainly not the young man standing in front of them.

Brett went ahead and introduced himself before Joyce had the opportunity to, then sat down in the only chair that wasn't occupied. The office was plenty big enough for two or three people but five made the once spacious office feel tight and claustrophobic.

"Well, what do you say, shall we get this party started?" Brett suggested removing two disks from his portfolio.

"OK, Brett," Joyce said taking the lead. "Detectives Miller and Beard are going to hold off on any questions for right now and take the disk and some of your journal entries into the other office so they can examine the information. Dr. Kaufman and I will remain here and lead you through the hypnosis. Once the session is completed, the detectives will come back in and we'll see where the road leads us. OK?"

"OK by me," Brett answered, giving a disk to Joyce and Detective Beard. "I'm really hoping something significant can come of all this."

"So are we, Brett," Dr. Kaufman said, sharing Brett's cautious optimism.

"We'll go have a look at this. Just come and get us when you're ready," Detective Miller said getting up to leave.

"A pretty serious group," Brett said after the door closed behind the detectives. "They don't seem real happy to be here."

"They're just a little skeptical that's all," Joyce said. "No different really than the way I felt when I started exploring this with you. It took a lot of persuasion to get them here but I know, as you do, that when they actually see everything they'll have an entirely new perspective on the situation. Wouldn't you agree, Dr. Kaufman?"

"Most definitely," Joe quickly agreed. "I must confess," he went on, now addressing his comments to Brett, "that I too was initially unconvinced. It was only after Dr. Davenport's detailed account of your recent experiences and my review of your journals earlier this morning that made a believer out of me. One thing I can assure you of, Brett, is that in just a short while, both of the gentlemen that just left here will be believers too."

"I'd like to explain what we're going to try and get accomplished from our session. Then if you have any questions or concerns, I'd like to address those before we actually begin."

Dr. Kaufman succeeded in easing Joyce aside and moving into the lead role so subtlety that Brett almost missed it. *What a smooth transition of leadership,* Brett thought, a little impressed, as he listened to Dr. Kaufman explain deep hypnosis and the goal of session.

"I just have one question Dr. Kaufman, before we begin. I understand the goal is to get a look at the person who shot Russell Craft but what happens to me if I'm still down in the shadowy canyons of my mind when the bullet hits. Will I expire right here in this chair?"

Dr. Kaufman sat there for a minute and replied reassuringly, "We're not going to let it get that far. Under deep hypnosis, you will be able to control the tempo of everything that happens. It will seem like one of those instant replays during a football game except you will control the playback button, slowing down or speeding up the course of events as you see fit. So when we get to *that* point, we're going to slow it down until we can see his face. Once we do that, we're then going to back away and pull out of the situation before the trigger is ever pulled."

Brett's apprehension showed for the first time. Glancing a little uncertainly at a silent Joyce Davenport, he asked Dr. Kaufman another question. "Would I be correct, Doctor, if I were to say that you're basing that very comforting explanation on case history and not just an assumption?"

Without hesitation, Brett got his answer. "Yes, Brett, you would be correct in saying that."

Brett's exhale was as deliberate as it was audible. "OK then, I guess I'm as ready as I'm ever going to be. It's your show, Doctor."

"Very well then, Brett, let's get comfortable and begin."

Dr. Kaufman's tone changed to something Brett found unexpectedly soothing as he got the session underway.

Brett drifted slowly through the darkness and suddenly found himself floating on a thin cushion of air just above the surface of a storm driven sea. The wind howled through his ears as he watched the high rolling swells and dark purple clouds move hastily by. Distant peals of thunder and flashes of lightning added to the eeriness of his new surroundings. *This is what it must be like in a hurricane,* he thought searching for a way out only to find that the ominous undulating horizon had completely encircled him.

Amid the tempestuous sky Brett could see his life flashing before his eyes. Everywhere he looked the personification of his life replayed itself; each split second frame representing a significant event in his past. Brett could hear a barely audible, yet authoritative voice instructing the panorama to slow down.

As the scenes slowed Brett knew he was near the time of his heart transplant. The voice told him he would see the entrance to a cave if he looked over his left shoulder. Brett slowly turned his head and saw the entrance begin to appear. A black, barely visible smudge slowly expanded and transformed itself into what appeared to be a passageway.

The rolling sea was slowly forced back and around the mysterious opening, as if it were a solid object. With a gentle pull that originated from its center, Brett was starting to be drawn toward it.

"In your pocket are two red balls. These are your markers and represent your pathway back. Take one out and leave it here," the faint voice of his invisible companion instructed. Reassuring him that entering the tunnel was the next step and not to be afraid the voice encouraged him onward. As the dark circular void gradually engulfed him, Brett saw his surroundings change. He was now high above the earth, suspended in the tranquility of space. He saw the earth below him, no bigger than a plum.

"You're going to leave here now and move faster but you won't be afraid— there is nothing in your new world that can harm you. I want you to take the other red ball out of your pocket and drop it here. These balls are markers to your pathway back and you will remember where each one is."

Brett moved in slow motion and dropped the second red marker which drifted lazily in place. As soon as the marker left his hand Brett started moving faster and faster. It was like he was sitting atop the world's largest roller coaster and suddenly, out of nowhere, the car plunged its way down that first endless drop.

As quickly as his ride began, it had stopped. Brett was standing inside a very familiar convenience store.

"Are you at the store, Brett?" Dr Kaufman asked.

Brett answered in a half whisper. "Yes, I'm at the store," he whispered in reply. "It's raining really hard; I can hear it hitting the ground."

"I want you to remember, Brett, that nothing in here can hurt you; relax and control your breathing. If it gets too intense I want you to tell me and I'll bring you out," Joe Kaufman informed a deeply hypnotized Brett Allen.

"Nothing can hurt me," Brett repeated slowly.

Brett's head began to move from side to side and breathing quickened. "Tell me what's going on, Brett."

"He's here now, taking money from the cash register," Brett said nervously, "then he's going to lock the clerk in the backroom and come for me."

"Listen carefully, Brett," Joe said, "he can't hurt you; he is in your world, not his and you're in control of it. When he comes out of the room, I want you to slow everything way down, put things in slow motion. He is going to take his stocking cap off and I want you to look carefully at his face."

Brett responded lazily, "My world...in control."

Ten seconds of silence passed uncomfortably, then Brett's right hand started to shake. Joyce looked over at Joe and drew his attention to Brett's right wrist as it began to turn a blotchy pink. A grimace of pain was now evident on Brett's face. "My world....not his."

"Take a good look at him and remember his face. Stop everything in your world and he will stop as well. He will be immobile like a statue. When you come back, you will remember what he looks, you will remember."

"Get a good look...remember," Brett repeated.

Brett flinched as the gun went off and suddenly found himself speeding away from the store and into space following his red markers back the way he came. Everything around him blended together in undistinguishable colors and shapes as his speed increased.

Brett screamed unexpectedly and opened his eyes, startling everyone in the office. Joe immediately looked over at Joyce in total disbelief and she knew exactly why.

Brett exhaled heavily, his chin resting in his hands. "Whew that was so close." He was disoriented and looked around the room. It was obvious to everyone that Brett wasn't sure where he was.

Joyce quickly moved right in front of Brett, deep concern evident in her voice, "Brett, it's me, Joyce, are you alright?"

Brett looked right through her at first then his gaze softened as he started to become aware of his surroundings. "Joyce," he said through a strained smile, "where's the bathroom?" he asked trying to get to his feet. "I think I'm going to be sick."

Brett was hit with a spell of dizziness as soon as he stood up. Grabbing the arm of the chair, he managed to maintain his balance and quickly dropped to one knee. Joyce got up to help and noticed Brett's skin was pale and clammy looking, she thought he might faint.

Joe Kaufman hurried over to help Joyce steady Brett and get him into the bathroom at the back of the office.

"Can I get you anything?" Joyce asked feeling the weight of Brett's body pressing down on her shoulder.

"No, nothing. Thanks for the help," Brett said making his way into the bathroom. "Just give me a few minutes and I'll be fine."

Brett turned on the faucet and splashed his face with cold water. "I look awful," he thought, "and feel even worse." He walked over to the door and closed it. "If I'm going to be sick, I can at least try to retain a sliver of my dignity."

"What just happened?" Joyce asked in a slightly accusatory fashion. "I'm beginning to think this whole thing was a horrible idea!"

"That was the most incredible thing I have ever, ever seen," Joe admitted as they made it back to their chairs. "No one has ever brought themselves out of deep hypnosis, at least not until now."

Joyce was pretty amazed by what had happened and was obviously more concerned about Brett's well being than Joe. "Do you think we should have him checked out by a physician? It looks like he's in pretty bad shape."

"He does look pretty pale but I think any of us would if we had just gone through what he has. It's really hard to say," Joe responded thoughtfully. "We carefully guided Brett through several layers of his subconsciousness and brought him to the deepest most subterranean level known to our profession. Then, all of a sudden, he is thrust back to the present. No guide, no assistance, nothing. We can't dismiss the fact that it's entirely possible a part of his psyche or mental energy may have been trapped somewhere along the way. If you noticed his hand, you saw the transitional manifestation phenomena, very remarkable in its own right, manifested itself just before he came back, which leads me to believe that some of his energy may have been left right there at the store. My biggest concern is that a much stronger link may have just been established between his different realms of consciousness. What that means is he could start having cross over visions while he's awake. If that link *truly* exists, it could prove to be very dangerous."

"You mean he'll react to the vision's stimulus while let's say driving, and very likely have an accident perhaps killing himself or someone else!" Joyce said, stating her assumption.

"Yes," Joe said evenly.

Brett came out of the bathroom feeling a little better after having gotten sick a couple of times. His mother had always told him that if he felt sick, he should just let it out. There was no reason to make the misery last longer by trying to fight it off. Brett knew his mother was right but it didn't make any difference. Throwing up was one of the worst things for him and every time he felt sick to his stomach, he did everything humanly possible to stop it even if it meant adding hours to his discomfort. He fought it this time too but lost.

Returning to the group, Brett made a request. "Before you both start asking me a bunch of questions or bring in our police friends, I could really use a cold drink of water."

Joyce moved quickly to her desk and got Gloria on the intercom and looked sternly at Brett. "You stay put! Gloria, would you please bring us a bottled water?"

"Right Away, Doctor," Gloria replied into the intercom.

"Oh and in about five minutes, please ask Detectives Miller and Beard to join us," Joyce added.

Gloria came into the office with bottled water and had to consciously avoid staring at Brett. She had been with Joyce for a long time and had seen a lot of patients in every situation imaginable, but today was the grand prize winner. Walking over to Brett, she tried to act as normal as possible.

"Here you go, Brett, nice and cold," she said, handing him the bottle and returning to her desk in the outer office.

Brett took a small sip, hoping that drinking water wouldn't send him running back to the bathroom. Getting the green light from his stomach, he quickly polished off the rest of the bottle.

DON PERRY

"Are you sure you're feeling up to this?" Joyce asked.

Brett's answer didn't surprise either of the psychiatrists.

"I've come too far to turn back now, Joyce, and I don't think," Brett said looking at his blotchy pink wrist, "that I could handle another trip like the one Dr. Kaufman just sent me on. So regardless of how I feel, I don't have much of a choice."

"Alright," Joyce said hitting the intercom, "Gloria, please show the detectives in."

Officer's Miller and Beard had been out in the waiting room for about twenty minutes and were anxious to ask Brett some questions. When they came back into the office, there was a surprising change in their interest level just as Joyce and Joe said there would be.

Dr. Kaufman was chomping at the bit to ask Brett about his experience but Detective Beard beat him to the punch.

"Mr. Allen, we've only been able to complete a very preliminary review of your information and have compared that to the actual police report. From what we can determine, your characterization of events at the store in Groton matches the statement given to us by the only eye witness, the young man who was working there when this happened. If I didn't know better, I'd have to label you as the prime suspect."

Hank paused for a second collecting his thoughts before going on. "I just want to make sure I've got this straight; you've been seeing the events at the store in these dreams you've been having and then after you wake up, you write down everything you can remember in these notebooks."

"Yes, Detective," Brett answered, "you've got it right."

"I've got to tell you this is the strangest set of circumstances I've ever seen in my life. The contents of the disk have been emailed to my detectives in Connecticut; we're going to reopen this case. Detective Miller has agreed to assist us by checking out Nadia Petrova and anything else that arises up this way. Did you have any success during hypnosis?" Hank asked, looking to Dr. Kaufman for an answer.

"We haven't had a chance to discuss that yet," Dr. Kaufman answered. "Well, Brett, can you share with us what happened during the session?"

"Well, it was really bizarre. I was standing near the coffee machine, everything moving slowly just like you said it would. I was still scared. The guy came toward me, walking down the short aisle with that gun pointed at my head. When he reached over to pull his mask off with his other hand, I heard him say, 'Nothing personal.' I could barely understand what he said. It reminded me of listening to one of my father's cassette tapes that was on its way out. You could hear the words but they were coming out of the speakers ten times slower than normal, but I know that's what he said.

"Then it was like someone hit a switch. Things started to move forward a little faster. It was barely noticeable but I managed to pick it up and tried as hard as I could to slow things down again. It didn't work. Then suddenly, out of nowhere, something shoved me violently out of the way and sent me flying back through space and I guess I ended up right back here."

"Were you able to get a look at the assailant?" Dr. Kaufman asked, looking once again in amazement at the blotchy discoloration on his hand.

"Yes, I got a look at him," Brett answered. "Do you want me to give you a description or wait for the artist to get here?" he asked the police officers.

"Our sketch artist will be here any second," Detective Miller informed Brett. "I think we'll wait for her to get here then you'll only have to give the description once."

When the sketch artist arrived, she began to ask Brett a series of questions. She asked for the general facial structure, shape of the nose, positioning of the eyes, etc. At first, her sketch pad resembled nothing more than some squiggly lines. As the paper slowly began a transformation into a charcoal portrait, Brett was able to suggest some minor adjustments that turned it into a recognizable portrait.

"That's it, that's him," Brett exclaimed as the police artist turned her pad around for everyone to see. "No question about it.

"Wait, Wait a second. I've seen this guy before," Brett exclaimed. "He's a little older but definitely the same guy."

"Are you sure about that?" Detective Miller asked.

"Oh yeah, I saw him at the Dug Out, not once but twice. He was there when Dr. Davenport and I met to discuss the very reason we're all here right now. That was last Wednesday. Yesterday, he was standing at the bar. I got there around two in the afternoon and there he was. I actually said hello to him. He's following me. He's following me, isn't he?" Brett repeated, not wanting to believe it.

"No question about it, Mr. Allen," Detective Miller said a little too candidly. "He's following you alright, and I think everyone here in this room, including you, knows what that means."

"It means that I'm next on his list,." Brett looked at the two detectives "What can we do? Can you arrest him?"

"I'm afraid we don't have any substantial evidence that will hold up in court," Detective Beard answered. "So we've got to get some and get some quick. First we have to try and find out who this guy is. We can't flood the newspaper with this guy's picture and let him know we are on to him. It would either send him running or force his hand, and right now were not prepared for either scenario.

"How about some fingerprints?" Brett asked. "Look, I'm a regular at the Dug Out, a lot of people know me over there. If this guy is following me then he'll be there the next time I am, right? He won't be suspecting anything. After all, everyone that's seen him is dead now. I'll have a waitress collect his stuff, glass, mug, or whatever he uses and get it over to you guys so you can dust them and run his prints. How does that sound?"

"If we can get prints on this guy that would be huge and the sooner we can get them, the better," Miller said, impressed with Brett's plan.

"OK then, I'll go over there for a late lunch and just hang out until he gets there. I don't think it would be a good idea to have anyone from the police department hanging around, at least not yet. After I get the prints, who do I call, you, Detective Miller?"

"Sure, take this," he said handing him his card with a smile, "use my cell phone. I'll have an undercover unit there before you hang up. Hank, are you going to want to stay up here for a few days to see where this goes?"

"You bet I'm staying. Why don't I follow you back to your office and I'll make some last minute arrangements and delegate a few things for my officers to do in my absence? After I get that taken care of, I'll drive back to Connecticut, pick up some clothes, apologize to my wife and kids and then come back. Brett, we would like to take your journals with us. We haven't really had enough time to go over them in detail. I don't want to miss anything."

"Joyce," Brett asked as color slowly reappeared in his pale skin, "do we still need them?"

"Not right at the moment but maybe I can have Gloria make copies for you," Joyce said, looking at Detective Beard, "that way we can have them too, just in case."

Everyone in Joyce's office agreed that making copies of the journals was a good idea. Brian Miller and Hank Beard had also acquired a deep level of respect for Brett and his courageousness. Here was a young man, no more than a kid really, that knew someone was planning to kill him. It was just a matter of time as to when. A lot of people would have locked themselves up in their home or tried to run away and hide but he was going to stand where he was and fight it out to the finish. Brian really wanted to assign a few of his detectives to a protective surveillance detail so they could keep a safe eye on him. When he mentioned it, Brett refused, saying that any change to his environment might be picked up by this guy and send him scurrying back under the rock that he'd crawled out from under. No one in the room could argue with his logic.

"I'd like to make a recommendation," Brett said. "If this guy is following me then there's a real good chance he's somewhere outside waiting for me to leave, right? It would probably be better if I left first and you guys left maybe fifteen minutes after me.

"Shelia can pass as a civilian, but you two guys, well you just look like cops. Maybe I'm being overly cautious but if I can tell then this guy following me would probably spot you coming a mile away."

"He's right!" Hank said, a little embarrassed that he didn't think about that. He turned to Brett "You should have been a cop. In fact, if you ever think about tossing in the test tubes you be sure to get in touch with me! Why don't we all wait here for say twenty minutes after Brett leaves then each of us should leave alone at 5 minute intervals so no associations can be made."

Brett said his goodbye and agreed to come back tomorrow for his regularly scheduled 4:00 p.m. appointment. Detective Miller agreed to get in touch with Brett as soon as the fingerprints arrived at the police station. That would also give them the opportunity to discuss the next step in the investigation and what role, if any, Brett might be able to play. Brett also gave Dr. Kaufman the OK to join in on his appointment. Being a scientist, Brett knew how important it was for both psychiatrists to find out more specific details about what had happened while he was under. This would allow for not only a written account of what happened, it would also provide an analysis tool that would be used to improve upon current methods of hypnosis and help future patients.

Brett finally had most of the answers he had been searching for; now it was time to do something about and it he hoped he was up to the challenge.

23.

Becky was already sitting at a table when Brett got to the Dug Out and he quickly walked over to join her. He had given her a lot of the details about what had happened at Joyce's office when he had spoken to her over the phone.

"Is everything ready?" he asked a little under his breath.

"Yes, we're ready. Susan is waitressing and Paul is bartending today. They both think we're playing a practical joke on someone so they won't be anything other than their cheerful selves. When I get up with the tray in my hand, that's the signal for Susan to *go on break* and for me to take over. I've got silverware, plates, and a few glasses all cleaned up and put in a special spot just waiting for our mystery man."

Brett had a photocopy of Shelia's drawing and pulled it out of his pocket so Becky could get a look at him. Brett saw her eyes light up with recognition "You're right, he has been here before. He's a little older than what the picture suggests but it's him alright."

"If you happen to see him before I do," Brett said quietly, "come and tell me where he is so I know."

Brett was usually at the lab this time of day and was surprised by how busy it was. The outdoor café was probably three quarters full, the bar was more sparsely populated. This must be the Brighton lunch crowd he thought.

"I had no idea that these many people eat lunch here. Is it usually this busy during the day?"

"The days I'm working it is," Becky said. "The lunch crowd peaks at about

1:30, which I've never been able to figure out why, and tapers off at about 3:00. I think people come here from all over just to say they've eaten here."

"That's right, I keep forgetting that this is a pretty famous place. And before I say one more thing, I want to thank you, Becky, for helping me," Brett said with all the sincerity his heart could muster.

Becky reached over the table and put her hand over his. "Brett, I will *always* be here for you. I have to tell you I'm more than a little scared about what's going on."

"Me too, Becky," he confessed putting his other hand on top of hers, "but we've got to be stronger now than we've ever been before. I can't continue to live with these dreams or this goon trying to hunt me down. On the way over here, I think I spent more time looking in my rearview mirror than I did looking through the windshield. So if I want to have a life that means something and be able to focus on our relationship with all the attention it truly deserves, I have to get rid of this once and for all."

As crazy as it sounded even to her, she was sitting next to the man of her dreams. They hadn't even been seeing each other for a full week yet, but she knew deep down inside that she was right. He had just told her, in his own way, the he loved her and that thought caused tears to run down her cheeks.

Brett picked up a napkin to dry her face. "I'm sorry, Brett, I just can't bear the thought of something bad happening to you."

"Hey, Becky...look at me please," he asked, feeling awful that she was crying.

As she raised her eyes to his, it was if he was looking through the window of her heart. He saw love, hope and fear locked together in combat, each emotion trying to emerge as the victor and have the right to dominate her outlook.

"Nothing bad is going to happen. We've got a lot of good people helping us with this and we have the advantage. He doesn't know that we know."

Out of the blue Brett grabbed his stomach and curled over as if someone punched him.

"Brett, are you alright?" Becky asked startled by the suddenness of his attack.

"Wow that was strange" he said sitting up straight. "I just had an incredible wave of nauseousness sweep over me. It came over me really quickly and then it just vanished." Brett started to take a sip of water and slowly put his glass back down on the table "Uh oh, Becky, our mystery man is here. He just got out of the car and he's coming our way."

"Well, I guess I'd better get ready," Becky said, grabbing the serving tray and standing up, "Do I need to go into the bathroom and do something for my eyes or are they OK?"

"They're as beautiful as ever, just like you," Brett said with a wink trying to keep her mind from focusing too much on the task at hand. She just needed to be herself and everything would be fine.

Susan saw Becky start into the building and quickly followed suit, oblivious to the seriousness of the situation.

Frank sat down several tables away from Brett and was actually pretty surprised to see him there. He had spent a pretty good part of his day up in Bedford surveying the landscape looking for just the right spot to shoot from. He actually wanted to get into the woods and test the view from a couple of different spots that he had thought looked promising. His plans were thwarted by a later than expected arrival and a crew of state workers scurrying about the area on a trash collection detail.

Becky came out of building carrying a cranberry juice and newspaper and stopped over at Brett's table. "I'm ready" she whispered.

"Here is your newspaper and cranberry juice. If you're a good boy today, maybe we'll go out and get a treat later." Her tone was much more audible now.

"Young lady," Brett said playfully, "I will be on my very best behavior."

Frank watched Becky approach and felt a little sad for her. In just a few days from now, her new boyfriend would be no more than a memory, and whatever hopes she was holding onto with this guy would soon be erased in the blink of an eye.

"Good afternoon, welcome to the Dug Out. Would you like the run down on the specials?" Becky asked summoning all the energy and perkiness she could find.

"No need to go through all that. I'd like the Dug Out special and a draft beer," Frank said.

"Curly fries?" Becky asked

"Absolutely," Frank answered, placing his roll of antacids on the table with a smirk, "and if you have an extra newspaper, that would be terrific."

Becky returned a short time later with Frank's paper and draft beer. Now that she knew his little secret, just looking at him sent a chill up her spine. She could feel his eyes following her while she waited on some of the other customers. Becky disappeared inside and decided to wait there until the special was ready. She didn't want to be out there with that animal any longer than she had to be.

She called Susan over to tell her that the practical joke was a flop and she'd be sure to fill her in on Wednesday. "Special's up," Paul yelled over.

"I'll take this last one out, Susan, then you can have the reins back, OK?" Becky said as she walked over to pick up the tray of food.

"OK, I'll be out there in just a minute."

When Becky left the building, she was relieved to see that Frank had made pretty quick work of his beer. All she had to do now was get the glass and both she and Brett could get out of here and away from him.

"Here's your special, would you like another beer?" Becky asked, putting his food down in front him.

"Another beer would be nice," Frank responded. "They're dollar drafts until 6:00 right?"

"Yes, until 6:00 every weeknight but Friday. Brian likes a big crowd on Friday so he gives them away at fifty cents," Becky answered trying to be normal. "So cheap it's almost like stealing. Oh and Susan will be your waitress in about thirty seconds."

"Susan?" Frank asked.

"Yes, I was filling in for her. We were supposed to play a practical joke on one of her friends but he never showed. Do you see that handsome man over there?" she asked him pointing at Brett "That's my boyfriend and what he doesn't know is that in about ten minutes, we are going to be leaving here to go horseback riding. I've been dying to get him to go with me and today he finally has some free time."

"I hope he can ride," Frank said.

"I guess we'll find out," Becky said, grabbing his glass and smiling. "Enjoy your food."

Becky walked into the bathroom at the Dug Out and replayed the conversation she had just finished making sure she had covered all the bases if their mystery man got a little curious. Satisfied there were no holes in her story, she put his glass in her purse and went out to join Brett.

"Are you ready to go horseback riding?" Becky asked. "Come on now, you said you'd go as soon as you had some free time. No backing out on me this time."

Brett finally gave in. "OK, OK, horseback riding it is. Do you want to drive or shall I?" he asked, getting up from his chair.

"You drive," Becky insisted as they headed for the parking lot.

As soon as they turned the corner, Brett got on his cell phone and called Detective Miller to give him the good news. Miller was really surprised that he heard from Brett so soon and told him to drive over to the convenience store on Commonwealth Ave. and someone from his unit would be there waiting for him.

Both Brett and Becky were shot from their experience and didn't have much to say on their way to deliver the fingerprints. Pulling into the convenience store, Brett saw only one car in the parking lot. He took the glass from Becky's purse, careful not to touch it too much, and opened his door.

"I'll take that glass from you, Mr. Allen, and deliver it to Detective Miller," the voice told him.

A very startled Brett turned to see what looked and smelled like a homeless person and wasn't real sure what to do. "Who are you?" Brett demanded.

"Give me the glass now!" the undercover police officer demanded. "Detective Miller will be in touch with you."

Brett relinquished control of the glass and watched the detective shove it under his five-sizes-too-large shirt, and walk up the street until he was out of sight. Just like that, it was over. They just sat motionless in the car for a minute and felt the life literally drain out of them. The adrenaline hadn't failed them when they needed it most.

"We can't stay here," Brett said, feeling paranoid. "Is my place OK?"

All Becky could do was shake her head up and down. The torrent of emotions had finally overtaken her and she began to sob deeply. Brett did his best to console her as he guided his vehicle toward home just as fast as he could get it there.

Brett began to think about what had just happened. He wondered if things were ever actually the way they appeared to be. Five minutes from now, someone might stop that homeless person that had just left the car and offer to buy him lunch, or perhaps hand him some money thinking they're doing a good thing for someone less fortunate. What they couldn't possibly know was the truth. The truth was that the homeless person they were feeling sorry for was in reality a police officer that had just been given crucial evidence in a murder case. *Who would ever know that?* he thought.

"Becky, are you going to be OK?" he asked, doing his best to console her.

Becky was OK physically but emotionally had little left. "I'm not sure," her wavering voice declared. "I've never been through anything so terrifying in my life and it was so much more difficult than I thought. I just keep seeing those dark lifeless eyes of his. They just look like death and I know he's coming after you. I'm so scared."

"You were so good over there, Becky. Without you, we'd never have gotten those fingerprints and without those prints the chances of me coming out on the other side of this thing wouldn't be very good at all."

"What do we do now?" Becky asked.

"I'm not really sure, but maybe it's better if you stay away from me for a while, at least until they get this guy. I'd never be able to forgive myself if something happened to you."

"No, Brett, I don't think that's a good idea. I know for a fact that he's been hanging around for almost a week. If we all of a sudden stopped seeing each other, don't you think he'd notice? I don't want to take a chance of him running for cover. I want him caught too, just as much as you; I want the chance to get to know you, a chance to share your hopes and dreams, a chance to grow together. I want to be a part of your life, Brett, and that doesn't exclude now."

Brett didn't really know how to respond as he tried to digest everything she had just said in all of its spoken and unspoken fullness. One thing was for certain, she was scared but had no intention of running away to hide and letting him face this alone.

It wasn't long after the glass arrived at the police station that Detective Miller's phone was ringing with the results of the fingerprint run. The lab had been able to get three prints off the glass. One set belonged to Brett Allen, who had been fingerprinted as part of his pre-employment security check with Nelson Pharmaceuticals; the second set came back clean with no matches, so they knew Brett's girlfriend hadn't been in any real trouble.

Lieutenant Miller's presence was requested when they ran the third set.

"Alright I'm here, this better be good," an irritated Brian Miller warned.

"Take a look at this, Lieutenant," the young officer said pointing to the monitor.

Brian saw the Justice Department emblem sitting center screen with the words Access Denied S-4 Authorization Required—Please Log in IAW DOJ 233-12.342 Procedures superimposed over it.

"What's it mean?" the young police officer asked.

"It means trouble with a capital T," Lieutenant Miller said as he headed back to his office.

Trevor Taylor was busy running an analysis on the data from the most current overlay when and automated alert forced its way on his display screen. Making a few adjustments, he was comfortable that it wasn't an equipment problem and let his boss know.

"Special Agent Flynn," Trevor called out tweaking a few more settings. "We have an F3 alert situation."

"Very Funny, TT,' Elias answered back, half ignoring what he heard.

F3 situations were very uncommon and occurred when someone tried to access a classified file specifically tagged with the F3 designation. Under normal circumstances deep cover agents on assignment had their fingerprint reports adjusted to protect their cover and the integrity of the case they were working on. The F3 tag was placed on records when the government agency or department lost track of an agent that went rogue. When a fingerprint request matched an F3 record an alert was immediately sent to the special agent in control of the record for appropriate action. Because of skills possessed by these F3 tagged rogue agents, an alert usually meant that the agent had been killed.

"You better check out your gear, Trevor," Elias reminded him.

"I've already done that, sir. Tracing sequence has been initiated," Trevor replied insistently. "F3 identity tag also coming in." Trevor paused looking intently at the screen for a few seconds until the information was presented. "Sir, the tag belongs to Frank Whickers."

"Come on, TT," Elias said slowly walking over to Trevor's station careful not to spill his full cup of coffee. "This is no time for joking around."

Trevor was watching the timer in the bottom right-hand corner of the screen. "Estimating sixty seconds to trace completion, sir."

"You're not kidding, are you!" Elias said, inquisitively leaning in for a better look.

"No, sir," he replied, both of their eyes now glued to the status bar.

"There we go, sir. Boston Police Department, downtown headquarters," TT said.

"I'm heading over there," Elias said, the urgency he felt echoed in every word. "I want the phone number of the person running the investigation, and I want it in five minutes," Elias demanded walking out the door. On his way to Boston's police headquarters, Elias decided to call Jessica to tell her the bad news.

Jessica was in the situation room with Francine going over information on the pharmaceutical company, running overlay analysis and examining pictures of Frank's colorful tactical map that was delivered by Elias's planted chambermaid. It took Francine all of two minutes to figure out what it was. She had TT manually enter the locations that weren't already identified in the system and asked Andy to dispatch some agents to put some *eyes* on those areas.

"Looks like were starting to make some progress," Jessica said, shifting her gaze from the papers on the table to Francine, still feeling a little guilty about the way she had responded to her earlier in the day.

"Sure seems that way," Francine replied, obviously not nearly as concerned about what had happened in the morning as Jessica was. "I'm going to ask Trevor to run the new addresses for *any* possible similarities. If we can come up with any, I'm going to toss in the pharmaceutical wild card to see what happens. What do you think?"

Jessica smiled shaking her head in approval. "Sounds like I'm listening to a seasoned SAS making some good investigative decisions. I'd also…" her cell phone provided an unexpected interruption. "Pierce" she answered.

Francine gave Jessica Pierce a quick, I'm going to get started wave and left the situation room bound for Trevor Taylor's work station anxious to get him started on her plan for the new addresses.

"It's Elias," Jessica heard, returning Francine's wave. "We've got an F3 situation."

"We haven't had one of those in a very long time; who's the identity tag belong too?" Jessica wanted to know, already thinking about what part of the world it came in from and who she or Elias would have to mobilize to check it out.

"Frank Whickers," Elias said flatly. "The trace shows the point of origin as the Boston Police Department. I'm on my way there now. Frank would have never made such a drastic mistake to get himself fingerprinted. Ever since we've been keeping an eye on him, he hasn't been anywhere near a police officer or a police station for that matter, so this just doesn't add up. "

Jessica was just as baffled as Elias. Her first thought was one of their sister organizations, the CIA or FBI, was involved but this investigation had unprecedented cooperation and information share from both those entities so that was very unlikely. Besides, she reminded herself, they already knew everything there was to know about Frank Whickers including having his fingerprints. Elias was right, something wasn't adding up.

"Want me to meet you there?" Jessica asked hoping her twelve months of emotionally painful undercover work wasn't in vain.

"No, depending on what happened, I might need you right there…there's Taylor," Elias said getting the familiar beep of another call, "I'll call you right after I'm done there," he said, disconnecting her to take Trevor's call.

Brian Miller noticed the private line in his office ringing. The only person that had the number was his wife Ellen, and he thought it was a little early for the can you pick up some milk on the way home question. It was good she was calling now; he could tell her that they'd be having company for dinner. "Ellen" he said enthusiastically "I'm glad you called."

"Lieutenant Miller, this is Special Agent Elias Flynn from the Justice Department. I'm about twenty minutes away from your office and was hoping I could talk with you for a few minutes when I arrive."

"How did you get this number?" a surprised Brian Miller asked.

"That doesn't really matter, now does it, Lieutenant. I shouldn't need any more than fifteen minutes of your time," he said, reiterating his request in a different form.

"I suppose you're on your way over to discuss some prints we ran a little while ago. I must confess that I'm not the least bit surprised to hear from one of you government types. I am a little surprised however at just how quickly we heard from you. You'll be here in twenty minutes huh? What were you doing, waiting outside our backdoor?"

"Look, Lieutenant, I'd like to keep this friendly," Elias said with a hint of confrontation in his tone. "All I really need to know right now is if I'm going to get my fifteen minutes."

"No need to get testy, Agent Flynn. I'll be here, just ask for me at the sergeant's desk and I'll come down and get you," Brian said, happy that he ticked him off a little and really hoping that making him wait would help add just a little more to it.

Elias had underestimated Boston traffic and was about ten minutes later getting to the station than expected. Elias walked in the front door of the station, made a bee line for the sergeant's desk, identified himself and explained who he was there to see. The sergeant manning the desk asked him to sign in and have a seat on one of the hard wooden benches against the wall. Lieutenant Miller had called down before hand and told his good friend Sergeant Johansson that Agent Flynn was an unexpected guest that should have to wait at least a good half hour on those comfortable wooden benches before being sent up.

Elias wasn't all that unfamiliar with the drill either. In almost every case where he had to engage the local police department, the welcome mat wasn't exactly strewn across the floor in anticipation of his arrival.

Sergeant Johansson looked at his watch to make sure Elias had his full measure of time on the department's finest furniture before calling up to Lieutenant Miller who gave him the OK to bring the government agent to his office.

"Special Agent Flint," Johansson called over, "would you please follow Officer Young, he'll take you to Lieutenant Miller's office."

"It's Flynn, F-L-Y-N-N, and I'll be happy to have Officer Young escort me to the Lieutenants office," Elias said trying his best not to show his irritation.

"Monday's are just awful around here, Agent Flynn; sorry you had to wait so long," Johansson said through a disingenuous smile, "Most of the local creeps like to make sure we start off the week with a lot to do."

"Well, keep up the good work, Sergeant. I'm sure that knowing you're here on duty is a deterrent unto itself that keeps a lot of them at bay. So just try and imagine how much work you're saving your fellow officers," Elias said, dropping an insult directly into Johansson's lap on his way to the elevators.

Elias wasn't surprised when he got his first look at Brian Millers' office. It's steel desk and filing cabinet were vintage 70s. The phone system was in desperate need of an upgrade and the dusty one inch aluminum blinds offered some privacy when the chain was pulled just the right amount. The large, high back leather chair Miller was sitting on was totally out of character with the office motif. Elias figured that he brought it in on his own.

Brian looked at the man standing in his doorway but didn't get up "Agent Flynn I presume, please come on in and have a seat. Sorry about the wait, but with all these budget cuts, we've got to do a lot more with a whole lot less."

"I totally understand the budget thing," Elias said while slowly and purposely taking another look around the office. "Ever since 9/11 we've all had to pretty much put our dollars into man hours and judging from the looks of things around here, I'd say you're definitely in the same boat."

Oh, this guy's pretty good, Brian thought. *Very subtle with his insults and I doubt a heck of a lot gets by him.*

Brian wasn't going to let that comment go uncontested. "I understand where you coming from, Agent Flynn. You probably haven't been in a small city police department in awhile. We're not fancy, we don't have a really big need to impress anyone here, we don't give a whole lot of tours, come to think it, we're so busy doing police work we just can't seem to find the time to have our congressman over for afternoon tea so we can discuss how the budgets shaping up for next year. So, I'm not sure which *boat* you're in, but I can tell you, it's not even close to the one my team and I sail in every day. So please, Special Agent Flynn from the Justice Department, spare me your astute observations, have a seat, and tell me why you're here."

"Alright, Lieutenant," Elias said, taking a seat. "Let me get right to the heart of the matter and cut through all the crap. As you mentioned on the phone, you ran a set of fingerprints on an individual today that we are very interested in."

"We run a lot prints from here every day, Agent Flynn, can you be a little more specific?" Brian said cutting him off.

"Look, Lieutenant, I don't have time for games or a colorful exchange of witty banter. You know the set of prints I'm talking about, the set that required the S-4 authorization. You were probably called in by your technician when the display came up and asked what it meant. Do I need to go on?"

"No," Brian said. "I know the set of prints you're referring to; they're part of an investigation were running. Who's the guy?"

"Who said it was a guy and how did you manage to get the prints in the first place?" Elias countered.

Brian wasn't in the mood for this back and forth stuff and it was evident in his tone. "*You* said you wanted to cut through all the crap! If that was a true statement then you better start using a machete. I've dealt with you government types before and your truth leaves a lot to be desired. This is just amazing to me. I ask my guys to run a set a prints and what do I get back, a sexy government emblem and a bunch of gibberish telling me I can't get the identity of this person because I need some mysterious authorization. About five minutes after that I get a call, forty minutes later the troops from the ivory tower are here asking me about a set of fingerprints, why?"

"I can't tell you that, Lieutenant," Elias said.

"Of course not," Brian agreed in a boisterous tone. "Let me guess, it's classified and a matter of national security right?"

"Something like that," Elias answered back calmly. "There are some highly sensitive issues we're dealing with here. There are things at stake here that you know nothing about—big things. The prints you ran are on someone we've been interested in for over a decade and have been following for some time now. I wish I could give you specifics but I just can't. Look, Lieutenant, I didn't come over here to get anyone upset. I was hoping we could get some cooperation from your department, that's all."

"From my vantage point, Agent Flynn, it doesn't look like you want cooperation; it looks more like you want us out of the picture. I can tell you two things as you sit right here in front of me; one, I'm not suspending our investigation and two, if you expect any cooperation from me or my department, you're going to have to be a lot more forthcoming with information."

Elias had heard all this before. Local law enforcement never wanted to walk away from a case and when the government was involved; there was always friction and an element of mistrust. Elias really wanted to give Lieutenant Miller more information but just couldn't do it.

"I'm sorry you feel that way, Lieutenant. Unfortunately it looks like I'm going to have to go over your head," Elias said.

Brian started to scribble something down on a piece of paper. "Here you go," Brian said, ripping the paper from its glued binding and handing it to Elias.

"What's this?" Elias asked.

"The name and number of the mayor is on top, the commissioner's information is underneath. I'd let you call from here but you know how tight the budget is," Elias said, flipping him a quarter. "There's a phone on the first floor you can use."

"Lenny," Brian called out, "show this gentleman the way out."

"You have no idea of what you're dealing with, NO IDEA!" Elias said, taking his turn at raising his voice before he left Miller's office, "You're in *way* over your head, Lieutenant. Oh, and don't be surprised to see me here tomorrow. I'm really looking forward to seeing what your new, more cooperative attitude will look like."

"Not a chance," Brian said watching Elias and Lenny heading toward the stairwell. "Not a chance."

24.

The caller ID told Brett that Joyce was trying to reach him and he anxiously picked up the phone. Joyce's stomach had been tied in knots ever since Brett left her office that morning.

She was involved in a case that was so bizarre and foreign to her that she didn't really know how to proceed. It seemed that every decision she had made and every step she had taken with Brett now had life and death consequences. That really scared her. It was one thing to help people with phobias and other garden variety disorders but to actually have someone's mortality hanging on your every decision was a burden she never asked for and quite frankly never expected.

"Hi, Joyce," Brett answered.

"Hi, Brett, I just wanted to give you a quick call and see how you and Becky were doing. I assume you're home because you've already finished what you set out to do when you left the office this morning."

"Yes we got them alright," Brett said with the strain of the day apparent in his voice. "I have an entirely new respect for the police, especially the ones that work undercover. I mean all we had to do was get a glass and we were both on the edge of our stress threshold. I have no idea how an undercover narcotics officer can do the job, none whatsoever. Becky and I are still trying to settle down, and before I forget I wanted to thank you, Joyce."

"Thank me? What on earth for?" Joyce asked.

"For giving me a fighting chance," Brett replied without hesitation.

"Without the information you've uncovered, I'd be walking around not knowing there was bull's-eye tattooed to my back. Now that I know I can at least try and do something about it. Without you, we'd never have gotten Russell Craft's research material, which will put an end to cancer. That's just scratching the surface."

Brett's comments made Joyce feel a lot better and helped her to see the situation more logically than emotionally. He was right, if they hadn't been working together, none of the things he mentioned would have happened. Now at least Brett knew what was going on and had some help to get him through. As far as Joyce was concerned, the whole cancer thing had little meaning to her if Brett didn't make it out of this alive.

"I am supposed to be making you feel better, not the other way around," Joyce confessed.

"Speaking of feeling better," Brett said casually changing the subject, "something weird happened to me at the Dug Out this afternoon. I was sitting at the table with Becky and all of a sudden, out of the clear blue sky, I got super nauseous. When it started, it was like someone had punched me in the stomach. It didn't last very long, maybe five seconds then it was gone. It was the same kind of feeling that I had after the session this morning."

Thoughts of her conversation with Joe Kaufman and the link he mentioned came rushing back to her memory. "Brett, think very carefully. What happened right before and after you felt sick?"

"Hmm...right before and right after, let me think," Bret said thinking out loud for Joyce's benefit. "Well, I met Becky at the Dug Out and we sat at the table. Neither of us had had anything to eat and we were both drinking water. We were just talking and all of a sudden I felt sick. It passed very quickly. I took a small sip of water and then I saw the guy we got the fingerprints from, our convenience store gunman. I think that's everything."

"Alright, Brett, thanks. Do me a favor and grab a piece of paper. I want to give you my home number and personal pager number. If you need anything, someone to talk with, something to help you sleep or relax, I want you to call me. I don't care what time of the day or night. OK?"

Brett agreed. "OK, Joyce, go ahead. I've got some paper now."

"Good. I'll see you tomorrow at four, right?" Joyce asked wanting to reconfirm that he would be able to make it.

"I'll be there, Joyce."

Joyce knew right after Brett described the course of events at the Dug Out that the link Joe Kaufman had talked about existed. It was hard to believe that a piece of Brett's subconsciousness was actually locked in another plane of existence. Joyce reviewed the day's events in her head, interrupted for a short moment when Gloria said good-bye.

Looking at her notes she noticed she circled the words transitional manifestation with "bridge" written next to it. Then it started to come back to her. Brett had been thrust back from a deep hypnotic state shortly after the appearance of the burns on his wrist. When he came around, he was sick. Earlier today, he felt the same sickness and the only common denominator was the killer.

Joyce started to mentally search for the connection. The killer was the only person that physically existed in both places; he was at the store twelve years ago and now here with Brett in Boston so maybe he was the link that existed and not some strand of mental energy unwillingly deposited by Brett.

Maybe Brett really did leave a piece of mental energy there that was acting as a conduit between the two different levels of consciousness with the killer acting more like a switch. When he came around, the switch was turned on, but only briefly enough to alert Brett via a nauseous stomach that the two levels were coming together again.

Then, of course it could be Russell Craft reaching out from somewhere beyond, guiding, influencing, warning and protecting Brett. Then again, it could also be any combination of the three.

Frustrated, she grabbed her notes and headed for the elevators. She would be calling Joe Kaufman just as soon as she got home to discuss this with him and get his opinion.

Elias arrived back at the operations center still visibly upset from his visit with Brian Miller. Jessica had known Elias for a long time and hadn't seen him off kilter like this in a long time. She knew his visit to the police headquarters didn't go very well.

Elias walked over to Andy and handed him a piece of paper. "I know you don't need this," he said, "but I want to meet with Boston's police commissioner first thing in the morning or the mayor. Better yet, see if you can arrange it so I can speak with them both."

"Hey, Jessica, take a look at this," Francine said.

Jessica turned her attention to the Bus Station tapes she had already seen at least half a dozen times already. "Whatever it is Francine, you're going to have to point it out to me.

I've seen these quite a bit and haven't noticed anything other than Frank walking in and, a short time later, leaving with the bag."

"Well I ran the tapes back and started running them from 22:00 hours on the 22nd of June until 10:30 on the 23rd, long after Frank leaves the terminal. TT showed me how to run this in spilt screen," Francine said manipulating some of the controls, "so I'll put the gate camera tapes and the main terminal tapes up on the screen and run them simultaneously," Francine looked at the display to make sure she had it right before continuing. "OK, that looks good like that."

Jessica smiled a little. She was getting a little bit of a kick out of watching her colleague using her newly acquired technical skills and the play by play she provided along with it.

"I'm going to move right to 00:00 on the 23rd because there was nothing of interest prior to that time. Now take a look at the gate camera tape—you see these people here getting off the bus," Francine said, freezing the tape. "Now watch what happens as I enhance the picture and move forward in slow motion. There, see him, the guy in the Army uniform, Notice how the people who just got there, they turn to look over their shoulder and down the bus toward the back."

"OK," Jessica said, "I give up."

"This guy was never on the bus with them, he's trying to force his way into line to make it appear he's getting off the bus. Let me run it again, first at normal speed then in slow motion."

Jessica watched the presentation again, this time focusing on the arriving passengers and sure enough, the man in the Army uniform was forcing his way into the stream of passengers getting off the bus and walking into the main terminal.

"I see it Francine and I agree with you but what exactly does it mean?" Jessica asked.

"Well, by itself it doesn't really mean all that much. Maybe he just wanted to have a cigarette and happened to pick that route as his way back in. But when you look at this," Francine said, fast forwarding until she had the spilt screens showing 01:03, "now it's 3 minutes past one in the morning on the 23rd and our soldier walks outside for a much needed nicotine fix. There he is now on the gate camera view, now watch him, he walks over into a darker area, lights his cigarette and pulls out a cell phone. We know Frank got call a little after one in the morning right?" Francine asked, reconfirming her time line.

"Yes, a little after one," Jessica confirmed still glued to the surveillance tape with her interest peaked, "but that's still a decent stretch, Francine."

"That's just what I thought," Francine admitted, "but let's watch some more," Francine said, fast forwarding until she saw Frank entering the terminal.

"Here's Mr. Whickers entering the terminal. He goes into the bathroom to retrieve the locker key, as we have all seen a million times before, he gets the bag and leaves. Now, watch when I put the other terminal camera footage up, this is from the camera pointing at the opposite end of the terminal from where Frank entered. When I put them in split screen, we can now get almost 100% coverage of the terminal area. Our solider is lying on these chairs over here somewhat out of Frank's view," Francine pointed out using the mouse cursor, "apparently catching some sleep while waiting for a connecting bus.

"Now watch him as Frank leaves the terminal, his head turns ever so slightly so he can watch him leave the terminal, then his fatigue miraculously leaves him and he gets up and heads back toward the departure gates." Francine was having fun as she switched video feeds once again. "Notice how he goes to the same location as he did at 1:03 a.m. and tries to make a call. I say tried to because we can see when we enhance it a bit that he bangs the phone a few times and shakes it. I think his phone has run out of juice, at least that's my typical reaction. So he comes back into the terminal and uses the pay phone, and as you can see, he pulls out a calling card to do it. After he makes his call, he waits a little while and actually boards the next bus."

"I can see it now," Jessica said with evident admiration for Francine in her voice.

"Yes, what clinched it for me was that our solider didn't have a suitcase, a duffel bag or even a change of clothes. I've never seen a military guy taking a bus without at least a duffle bag, have you?" Francine asked.

"I can't say I have, Francine, and if I don't have a duffle bag, I have at least one piece of luggage," Jessica answered. "That's an excellent piece of detective work!"

"Thanks, Jessica, coming from you that means a lot. I'm going to call our Chicago office and get the phone records for that pay phone sent over here along with the destination of the bus that he got on. He made the call at 2:55 a.m. and the phone wasn't used a half hour on either side so the number should be an easy find. This guy here," Francine said as the face of the soldier grew larger on the screen, "is the middle man, and when we find out who he called we should have a pretty good idea of who hired him."

"I think I'd like to ask Trevor to do some facial enhancements on that shot right there," Jessica said, "It's not the greatest picture but maybe we'll get a few matches using our facial recognition system. At best, it's a long shot but worth a try nevertheless. What about prints?"

"No good," Francine replied. "The cleaning crew wipes everything down including the phones every morning. Unfortunately, it's one of those rare companies that actually fulfills its contractual obligations down to the minutest detail. I'll be sending someone over to see if we can get a description but it's pretty doubtful. Also, the bag must have been put in the locker on the 22nd. The system was down for twenty minutes that day while the security company performed some preventative maintenance. All the tapes prior to that time are clear. So whoever put the bag in the locker must have known when the cameras were going to be off. We'll be checking into that also."

Jessica had a genuine need to compliment Francine and did so. "I've got to tell you something, Francine," Jessica began, "Elias definitely made the right choice when he promoted you. You've done some pretty outstanding work today, very intuitive and thorough, just what we need on a tough case."

Francine didn't say anything. She just looked at Jessica and thanked her with a smile.

Brian Miller reached over to pick up the phone, still feeling the steam escaping from under his collar, the remnants of his less than pleasant visit with Agent Flynn.

Detective O'Hara was on the other line calling from Lexington. O'Hara was Brian's detective of choice to go up there; not only did Ryan grow up there, he also had a great relationship with the people on the local police force.

"L.T., its O'Hara. I'm afraid we've got some bad news. This girl you wanted me to talk with hasn't been heard from since Saturday. We stopped by the bank and she didn't show up for work today so we swung by the house and she wasn't there either. According to a Ms. Wells, a co-worker that spoke to her Saturday, they were supposed to meet on Sunday and do some antiquing. When Ms. Wells arrived at her house, no one was home. Wells guessed that something must have come up in a hurry otherwise she would have gotten a call to cancel. She also said that the Petrova woman hadn't missed a day of work in about three years."

"Well, here's some more bad news," Brian said. "I just had a visit from one of those government agent types and I think this case is a heck of a lot bigger than I had originally thought. We really need to find her Ryan; she may be a key witness in that murder case. I want you to stay up there until we find this girl and get some answers. We don't have a whole lot of time so if you think we need more folks up there to supplement their manpower, let me know."

"Why are the Feds interested in this?" Ryan asked.

"It's not the FBI, it's the Justice Department," Brian clarified.

"Same thing," Ryan answered back with indifference.

"Yeah, you're right," Brian said, having to agree. "I'm not real sure; we ran a set of prints and got some government web site telling us we couldn't have them without some special authorization and then, poof, this government agent's in my office telling me I need to cooperate with him. It all happened just a little bit too fast for my liking. It was like they were outside the station just waiting. I'm guessing one of their stars went the other way and now they've got to grab him before he exposes something they're up to."

"Is this the guy we're after, the one the kid got the prints on earlier today?" Ryan asked.

"Yes, that's the guy alright. As I said, we've got to stay frosty on this one, not waste time, and not miss a trick, otherwise I think we'll end up with one very dead young man," Brian reiterated.

"I wish we had something on this guy. Do we have anything from Connecticut on their piece of this?" Ryan asked hoping for some good news.

"I haven't talked with Hank Beard yet. He's going to be our guest for a few days and coordinate the Connecticut effort from here. Hopefully, by pooling our resources, we come up with something quick."

"Alright, Lieutenant, until I hear differently, I'm camping out in Lexington. I'll get us some answers!" Ryan said with conviction.

Becky had retreated to Brett's bedroom having taken two extra strength pain relievers to help take the edge off her headache in hope of maybe sleeping it off. Brett knew she had been drained of all her strength and thought if she rested, maybe getting one of her twenty wink naps it would help. He must have been right because shortly after stretching out she was sound asleep.

Brett hurried over to the phone hoping the ring volume wouldn't wake Becky up. He picked it up quickly and found Detective Miller on the other end.

"Mr. Allen, this is Detective Miller, how are you holding up?"

"*Becky* and I are fine," Brett said pointedly to remind him that his girlfriend was also pretty heavily involved in the situation, "and please, Detective, call me Brett."

"I'm glad to hear that you're *both* doing OK considering all you've been through. We ran the prints that we found on the glass and we are still waiting for some answers," Miller said stretching the truth about as far as he could.

Brett was really frustrated that their efforts hadn't, as of yet, resulted in anything helpful. "Can you tell me how long *still waiting for some answers* really means?"

"Could be anytime now, Brett," he replied. "Look, it's really important that you go about your normal routine. We've come up with a couple of ideas that will allow us to stay one step ahead of this guy."

"I'm listening, Lieutenant," Brett said anxious to hear the *one step ahead of this guy* solution Brian Miller had come up with.

"We'd like to drop by your apartment tonight and deliver a couple of gifts, courtesy of the Boston Police Department. A tracking device and a hands-free communication system. The tracking device let's us keep track of where you are and the communication system allows you twenty-four seven contact with us. The communication system comes with an earpiece, so unless you're wearing it, it will be pretty much just be you talking to us. The activation switch will be in your pants pocket so when you want or need to talk with us, reach in and activate the switch. Both devices have an effective range of about five miles."

"I'll never get past security with any of that stuff," Brett reminded him, "so unless it's easy enough to set up from inside my car I can't do it."

"No problem, it's all state of the art, very small, and easily concealed. It's some of the latest gear our narcotics folks are using and they really like it. So assuming you're on board with this, we'll have some folks nearby just in case you need to make contact. Not so close that they'll arouse any suspicion, but close enough to move in quickly if necessary. Our guy will show up in a cable truck, give you the gear along with guidelines on how to setup and use the equipment."

"Alright, let me make sure I fully understand what we're doing. You're sending someone over under the guise of a cable problem I'm having. This person will give me the equipment and explain how it works. Then I have to use this stuff so you can keep some officers close enough to help and far enough away so they don't get noticed. I have this switch thing hidden in my pockets so if I need to communicate with anyone, I activate the switch in my pants pocket," Bret said, completing his characterization. "It sounds like an emergency response unit to me."

"Right in all cases," Miller responded, "so what do you say, Brett, are we on?"

"Yup, were on. When can I expect my visitor?" Brett asked.

"I'll have someone at your place within an hour," Miller replied. "After you get everything, call me on my cell phone so we can over a few things and if you have any questions, we can over them then. I'll talk to you later, Brett."

"OK, Detective," Brett said, hanging up.

Brett checked on Becky once more before he went into the living room. Sitting down, the enormity of the situation began to overwhelm him. Massaging his forehead for some semblance of relief, he began to reflect on his young life.

As with most people, there were times in his past that he wished he could go back to. Times where he felt safe and secure and not overrun with the burden of adult worries and responsibilities. A carefree time when his biggest worry was making sure he took the garbage to the curb on the right day.

Those days were long behind him and now his mortality was staring him right in the face. Brett thought about a last will and testament and quickly pushed it aside. He was going to come out of this, that's how he had to think. It would take almost every ounce of hope he had to convince himself that this was a survivable situation, but this was a time when hope was all he really had.

Despite Brett's hopeful outlook, he knew it was time to see his father and tell him what was going on. He was also going to tell his father some things he hadn't said in a long time. Things like how much he appreciated having him as a dad. How grateful he was that his father not only helped him grow up but grew up with him, never thinking he was too old for catch, or a game of whiffle ball with he and his little league buddies. How much fun he was to be with, how much his advice and opinions were welcomed and to tell him, maybe for the last time, just how much he truly loved him. As Brett thought more about it he just couldn't imagine his father being left totally alone. Just the thought of it made his heart heavy with sorrow. Struggling to rescue his thoughts and keep them hopeful, he wiped a single tear from his cheek, picked up the phone, and called his father.

"Agent Kelly, we've got some preliminary analysis on those addresses you wanted!" the operations technician informed her.

Francine was anxious to hear what he came up with and hurried over to his workstation. "OK, Trevor, let's have it!"

Trevor had been an operations technician for quite some time. It didn't matter what assignment he was given, he always got excited and talked a little fast after uncovering big chunks of information on a difficult project. It also made him feel important because suddenly he was the focus of attention and everyone listened to what he had to say.

"First of all, it's important to understand that we could only take a reasonably educated guess at the locations he marked. There are several variables, the biggest one being how careful he was on placing those dots near the actual location. At any rate, here is what we have so far. First we have the Dug Out, no need to elaborate on that just yet. The second address we checked out turned out to be a professional building that is being used by some private practice physicians, real estate agents, and other small businesses. We cross checked the business owners in that building with the other addresses that Mr.

Whickers had indicated and came up with a match at the Norwood address. A Doctor Joyce Davenport, a fairly well known psychiatrist that has done an ample amount of work with both the state and local police."

Francine started thinking out loud. "It's possible that someone she helped put away might be trying to get some revenge. Make a note Trevor to check on all the cases she has worked on with any law enforcement agency with special emphasis on anyone that might have been considered high profile."

Jotting down a few notes, the technician acknowledged Agent Kelly's request with a nod of his head and continued, "The Lincoln Street address is an apartment building and matches the address of one of the Dug Out employees from the list Unit 5 was able to get from the owner. The young lady's name is Rebecca Williams; she has been waitressing at the Dug Out for a while. Preliminary indications reveal a rather unremarkable history. But we're looking a little deeper into that."

"Good," Francine said encouraging Trevor's analytical mind to continue its quest for answers. "I want to know if she has a vendor's license. Maybe she sells the Nelson crowd coffee and doughnuts in the morning from the back of a truck. It's a stretch given the distance but worth checking out. I want some information on the parents and siblings as well. I want to know if any of them have been in any kind of trouble. We're also going to need a list of current tenants and information about the owner."

Trevor replied quickly as he scribbled down her instructions, "Got it. We're still checking out the Prudential Building but so far nothing corresponding with the case we're working on. I'll have all data printouts and an overlay summary ready for your 7:00 a.m. briefing."

Francine thanked Trevor and started across the operations center to Andy's make shift office with an impressed Jessica Pierce at her side to request some field support. As good as computer information was, it couldn't replace having feet on the street and that's what Francine needed right now.

The entire group had been on the go since 5:00 a.m. and after a grueling twelve and a half hours on the job, it was time to turn over the operations center to the second shift. Elias had total confidence in the night crew that consisted of one agent and a handful of technicians. All were capable, well trained, and knew if something came up that Elias was only a cell phone away.

Everyone was hungry and Elias had decided to treat everyone to dinner. He chose a secluded hole in the wall place suggested by one of the local agents. Normally they would dine at an establishment that was considered a little more on the fancy side but Elias didn't want to have Jessica at a marquee restaurant and take the chance of Frank Whickers walking in. Even though they knew his whereabouts almost every minute of the day, Elias always erred on the side of caution.

Brett guessed that Becky was somewhere in the ten to fifteen wink range of her twenty wink nap when the doorbell rang. He hurried to the door and looked through the peephole. Standing outside, rather nonchalantly was a young man from the local cable company. "That was quick," he thought. Brett was more suspicious now than ever and decided to get some verbal confirmation before opening the door.

"Who is it?" Brett said through the door.

"Cable Company, Mr. Allen, we're here to provide you with some new equipment and go over your new package to make sure you understand how to use all the features." The young man standing on the other side of door answered back, "Mr. Miller scheduled the appointment and told me to be here between six and six thirty so I'm a little early, I hope that's OK."

"It sure is," Brett said opening the door to let him in.

"Thanks, I'm Officer Salazar, are you alone?" he asked taking a quick look around.

"No, my girlfriend is sleeping in the bedroom but it's OK."

Salazar shook his head in agreement. "I was told she might be here, anyone else?"

"No one else," Brett said.

Salazar lifted his toolbox and put it on the small table in the kitchen. "OK, let's see what we have in here." The toolbox reveled exactly what Brett had suspected to see, tools. *Nothing spectacular yet,* Brett thought.

Salazar reached in and grabbed a small gray plastic utility box, the kind that typically holds small drill bits and opened it up presenting the contents to their new owner. There were two small devices about the size of a quarter and one piece of thin rubber coated wire perhaps two inches long with one side holding what looked like a bronze teardrop.

"One tracking and one communication device," Salazar said describing the objects as he removed them from the box and put them on the table, "this here," he said reaching back into the box, "is our microphone"

"Pretty tiny," Brett commented. "They look like really thick quarters. Do these things really have a five mile range?"

Salazar displayed a sideways sort of smile. "Actually, the operational range is closer to ten."

"You're kidding right?" Brett asked in disbelief.

Salazar kept his smile and shook his head from shoulder to shoulder. "Tested this set yesterday and its working fine. I could give you a rundown of the technology but I was told to keep it simple. What I will tell you is that this is the best nark gear money can buy and our guys swear by it. Now let me explain how this stuff works. The tracking device is pretty simple; it's either on or off." Salazar picked it up to demonstrate. "Here on the side, you can see the rough edge. Move it upwards and you're on—the small green light in the center confirms your transmitting. To turn the thing off, you need to pinch and maintain pressure on the top and the bottom of the device—right here over the LED in the center then with your other hand, move the switch to the off position. This prevents accidental shut-offs. So go ahead and give me a demo," Salazar instructed, handing Brett the tracking device.

Brett turned it on OK but had a little trouble shutting it off. It required a little more pressure in the center than he had thought. On his third attempt, Brett was finally able to shut it off. He repeated the process a few more times until both he and Officer Salazar were comfortable with his performance.

"OK, now that we have that down, it's important to remember the operational life of the battery is almost 48 hours and they're not rechargeable. I brought you two extras so if the LED ever turns red, it means you have about an hour of battery life left so change it out just as soon as you can."

Salazar grabbed the other device and microphone from the table and continued, "Here is our communications switch and microphone. The only major difference between this and the tracking mechanism is the color, bronze for tracking and gray for communications. They operate in exactly the same way. Once it's on, you'll get the same dark green light letting you know you're operational then you can communicate using the voice-activated microphone. Now don't let the size of it fool you, it's extremely sensitive. It's so sensitive that we have special filters on the receiving gear to cut out erroneous background noise. You could almost put it in your shoe and we'd still be able to hear you."

Brett looked at the microphone curiously, "How do you put it on, there's no clip?"

"You can put it here," Salazar showed him as he wrapped the thin flexible cord around a button on his shirt. "Once it's on, you can tuck the head right under the seam, like this, and now it's invisible, same thing with a collared shirt. If you wear a hat you can put it inside the headband. There are lots of options with this little beauty," he said digging in the bottom of his toolbox. "If you wear a collarless shirt or one without any buttons, you can always use this," Salazar

DON PERRY

said holding up duck tape, "it works every time and sticks like glue. I've found the skin on the top of the shoulder to work best. Go ahead and put on the mike and fire up the gear, I've got a guy in the van waiting to make sure everything is working on both ends."

Brett did as Salazar had instructed and turned on the tracking and communications mechanisms and placed one in each front pants pocket then twisted the microphone wire around the bottom button of a three-button short sleeve shirt and hid it like he was shown.

Salazar had to encourage him a little bit. "Go ahead and say something."

Brett was a little embarrassed when all he could say was "Testing, one, two, three, testing."

Salazar put his hand to his ear hoping to hear a little better and for the first time, Brett saw he had an earpiece. Shaking his head and smiling, Salazar said, "I'll tell him," in response to something his invisible partner had said. Brett looked strangely at Salazar, who turned up his collar revealing a microphone of his own.

"Everything's working just fine," Salazar said, the smile still on his face "If you could do us one favor, please get the microphone in place before switching the communication unit on, it sends a pretty strong feedback signal the other way. George is worried about losing his hearing so he's a little touchy lately. Ever since his daughter turned fourteen and found out what the bass and treble adjustments do, he claims to lose at least a decibel a week."

The undercover officer got a quick response in his earpiece. "Very funny, Sal!"

"Sorry, I won't do that again," Brett said. "Tell George I'm sorry."

"I heard that, Sal. Let's not string this kid along too much, I want to get home sometime before my kids go to bed OK?" his partner in the van replied.

"He heard you, Mr. Allen, no apology necessary. We're going to leave now, unless you have any questions or would like me to go over any of the equipment again."

"No questions, thanks for bringing this over."

"You're welcome. One last thing," Salazar said shutting the toolbox unbuttoning his shirt. "Take this," he said, removing his Kevlar vest and putting in on the table. "Don't forget to call Lieutenant Miller," he reminded Brett as he was putting his shirt back on. "You have the number, right?"

"Yes officer, I've got the number. Thanks again."

"Good luck, kid," Salazar said, picking up the tool box on his way to the door.

Brett's conversation with Miller was short a sweet. With the exception of being at the research facility, his tracking device would remain with him and on at all times. Undercover officers would be on round the clock duty and only minutes away from his location starting immediately. Miller also recommended that the microphone be left on unless he was in a personal scenario that required a greater level of privacy. Brett reached a compromise with regards to the voice system. He would keep the microphone equipped for use in an inconspicuous fashion and activate the switch on an as needed basis rather than use the voice-activated feature.

Now that Brett had settled his business with the detective, he went to the bedroom and found Becky still lost in a deep sleep. Brett really admired her courage during this whole thing. A lot of people would have folded under the stress but not her. She was a real trooper and played her part flawlessly. He hoped that this time next week they would be able to look back and put all this stuff behind them. Brett left the bedroom and closed the door.

Sitting at the computer, Brett opened up his address program and typed in Harvard. He got several names back and selected Dr. Jeff Dalton to call.

"Jeff, it's Brett Allen," he said, announcing himself.

Mr. Dalton just had to tease his fellow alumnus. "Brett Allen, the man who decided to pursue gainful employment outside the confines of his alma mater? The very same man we're still trying to convince that university research work is the more honorable occupation despite the economic downside?"

"Yes, Jeff, the very one," Brett admitted, anxious to get to the point. "Look, Jeff, I don't have a lot of time. I meant to stop by the university today and drop something off but just couldn't make it. I was hoping I could get your email address so I could send it to you right now."

Jeff was curious now. "Sure, Brett, it's JDalton@harvard.edu. Do you mind telling me what it is you'll be stuffing in my inbox?"

"Something that will put your research ten years ahead of schedule," Brett answered attaching the formulas to the email. "OK, I just sent it."

"Yup, it's coming in now," Jeff confirmed. "Let me open the attachment and have a look see."

The silence over the phone lasted so long Brett had to ask if Jeff was still there.

"Yes, I'm here" was the hesitant reply. "This is, without question, the most revolutionary work I've ever seen."

The line went silent again, the information drawing more and more of Jeff's attention as he continued to review the information. Brett had no intention of sitting on the phone while Jeff went over every aspect of the formulas he had just sent.

"Jeff, you've got to take this to the University tomorrow and verify as much of this information as soon as you can. I'll try and give you a call in a few days to see how you're doing."

Doctor Dalton couldn't hide his astonishment with what he was looking at. "I just can't believe what I'm looking at. How long did it take you to come up these genetic reconfiguration schemes, Brett?"

"It's not my work. A friend of mine got it started and a few days ago I was asked in a roundabout way to help get his worked finished. I'll explain later, Jeff, but right now I've really got to go. Can you do it? Can you take it with you tomorrow?" Brett repeated the request to drive home the point.

"Are you kidding, I don't think I'll be able to get much sleep tonight. When I get off the phone with you, I'm calling the research department heads. With your permission, I'd like to send them each a copy and coordinate an early morning meeting to go over this and come up with an aggressive plan so we can get underway."

Brett could almost feel Jeff's excitement through the phone. It was this level of excitement and enthusiasm that guided Brett's decision to share Russell Craft's work with him. Brett knew it would spread like wildfire and Jeff was just the right match to get it started.

"Share it with everyone, Jeff, in fact the more the better. I hope you're able to get some sleep tonight."

"I'll try but it's going to be hard. Even if I manage to get anywhere near a bed I doubt my brain will slow down enough to let me nod off, let alone sleep. Call me when you can to explain. I've got to go now and get busy myself" Jeff said, now with an urgent need of his own to satisfy.

25.

Hank Beard walked into Brian Miller's office having returned from Connecticut with a warm handshake and a bit of bad news.

"Welcome back, Hank. Come on in and have a seat," Brian said, pointing to the chair in front of his desk. "You just missed the fireworks!"

Hank titled his head slight and raised an inquiring eyebrow. "Fireworks?"

Miller shared the entire story explaining everything that had transpired. Detective Beard leaned forward listening intently until his counterpart wrapped things up.

"Well, well, well," Beard said as if he had just uncovered some deep dark secret, "The boys from D.C. are in town, how interesting. I guess we might as well toss in my bad news. Richard Nelson is out of town until tomorrow afternoon, so my detectives won't be able to talk with him until then, and Bob MacReynolds, the former CFO, apparently moved to Tampa after he retired about a year and a half ago. We've been in touch with the Hillsborough County Sheriff's Office and they've agreed to help in any way possible. One of my detectives is on his way down there and should be landing in a few hours. We've also managed to get the names of all the board members of the company at the time the partial memo was written. I'm afraid I won't be able to add anything of value to the case until later tonight or maybe even tomorrow morning."

Miller shook his head. "Tomorrow will just have to do. I can't think of anything else we can do here so why don't you follow me home and we'll have

233

some supper. I know we agreed about not tailing this guy that's after Mr. Allen, but I thought it was a good idea to put someone on him so I went ahead and did it anyway."

"I think that was a wise choice, Brian. We've got to keep some sort of tabs on the guy or we might as well be blind," Hank said standing to leave. "Oh by the way," Hank said, pausing, "before I forget, remind me to be extra early tomorrow I'd like to help run interference."

"What do you mean interference?" Brian asked, caught off guard.

All Hank could do was smile. "You know, from your new D.C. buddies."

Brian smiled. "Sure, but you might have to get behind Sergeant Johansson. He had a pretty good run in with Agent Flynn. Seems like this guy Flynn has been around the block a time or two. I just hope the department doesn't cave and let them take over."

"I hear that," Beard said assuredly. "The Feds have been known to really mess things up. Who's on our side?"

"I really won't know that until the dust settles tomorrow," Miller answered honestly, "so let's get going. If we're too late, the food will get cold, my wife and kids will be upset, and you'll have an unexpected overnight guest in your hotel room."

Beard chuckled slightly. "I can almost have you arrested for making threats like that. So what do you say we both avoid the embarrassment and get over to your place, like now?"

"When you put it that way, Detective, the alternative doesn't sound that appealing to me either. After you!" Brian said extending his arm toward the elevator.

As the two detectives left police headquarters, hopeful that the food would be warm when they arrived, Becky was stirring to consciousness. She could have kept right on sleeping but she knew she had to get up. Not accustomed to napping during the day, she was fairly disoriented when she finally managed to sit up.

Blinking hard a few times to help her see through the sleepiness that settled in her eyes Becky looked slowly around the room and realized she was at Brett's apartment. She could hear his muffled voice from another room. From the solitary stop and go talking pattern, she guessed he was talking on the phone.

Feeling a rush of dizziness from getting up a little too fast, she quickly sat back down to collect herself. After a few deep breathes she decided to try standing again; this time she was OK and headed to the bathroom. Substituting her fingers for the teeth of a large comb Becky moved her hands through her hair and made some necessary adjustments. A closer examination of her reflection confirmed that she looked pretty good despite the difficulty of the day.

"I really need to bring a toothbrush over here," she said, using her finger once again to get some toothpaste across her teeth.

Brett heard the water come on in the bathroom and headed in to see how Becky was.

Brett stopped in the doorway and saw her trying to brush her teeth and noticed right away that she was a little embarrassed to be caught in the act.

"Hi there, is the headache gone?" he asked, getting a nodded yes in return.

Brett left the doorway for just a moment and returned holding a new toothbrush in his hand and put in on the sink next to her. "Here, use this. Medium bristles so don't scrub too hard," he added with a wink. Becky looked over, her index finger trying to work some toothpaste to her back teeth and shot him a playful scowl in return.

As soon as Becky finished up in the bathroom, she joined Brett at the kitchen table. He was pointing at his chest when Becky sat down and she couldn't figure out why. Brett didn't say anything and went about unbuttoning the bottom button until he knew she could see it.

"How do you like my new secret agent communication set?" he asked her.

"What is that?" Becky asked.

Brett began to empty his pockets. "It's a microphone and these things here," he continued placing two circular objects on the table, "this one is a tracking device and this is the on/off switch for the microphone."

"Are they listening to us talk right now?" she asked curiously.

"No I don't have it turned on. I'm not going to use the microphone all that much. If it's an emergency and I really need it, all I have to do is reach in my pocket and turn it on. "The tracking device is on and I've agreed to carry that with me all the time. The batteries will last a couple of days before I have to change them. Our new police friends want to keep close tabs on me."

Becky looked across the table at Brett with genuine admiration. He was worried and tired but not beaten. He was playing the cards he was dealt like he always did and he had gotten some pretty rotten hands in the course of his lifetime yet always managed to come out of it OK. Becky hoped for both of their sakes that this wasn't the last hand he was going to play.

A sudden knock on the door startled them both. Unsure of exactly what to do, Brett whispered to Becky to go into his bedroom. It was the room farthest back in the apartment, had a phone, and if necessary, you could escape through one of the windows. Becky got right up and complied with Brett's request as he switched the microphone on and put the devices back in his pocket.

Brett could hear his heart pounding in his ears as he stood up and could feel goose bumps rise on the skin of his arms. Fear added what seemed like a thousand pounds of weight to his shoes as he labored his way slowly to the door. Glancing back and being satisfied that Becky was as safe as she could be, Brett got his body as close to the wall of the short foyer as possible and edged himself to within a slight leans distance. Brett noticed his throat was very dry but still managed a hard swallow. Leaning over, he took a look through the peephole, and saw nothing. Pushing himself and his eye closer to the peephole he took a better look and still saw nothing. The concave lens gave a distorted appearance of the world outside his door and captivated him for a moment as he tiried to figure out the indistinct shapes.

Then, out of nowhere, a face appeared, it happened so fast and scared him so much that he almost let out a shout.

"Brett, it's me, Dad, open up!" Michael Allen yelled through the door.

"Dad," Brett whispered under his breath as he turned off the microphone. Reaching for the deadbolt and unlocking the door. Brett gladly let him in.

"Hey, Brett. After we got off the phone, things just didn't seem quite right so I decided to drop by. I hope that was OK."

"Of course it's OK Dad, come on in. It's OK, Becky," Brett yelled toward the back of his apartment, "it's my father."

Becky emerged from Brett's bedroom, not knowing exactly what to expect or how the whole "girl coming from my son's bedroom" thing would be received. She liked Brett so very much that she couldn't bear the thought of making a bad first impression with his Dad. Knowing there wasn't much she could do about it Becky decided to do what she did best—be herself. Coming around the corner with a slightly embarrassed smile, Becky said hello and stopped at Brett's side, grabbing his hand for comfort in an obviously uncomfortable situation.

Brett took care of the introductions and everyone sat down in the living room. The initial awkwardness that often accompanies people meeting one another for the first time quickly evaporated. Both Michael Allen and Rebecca Williams got along really well and seemed to genuinely like one another after only spending a short time together.

Brett started to explain everything that had been going on while his father sat and listened intently. As hard as it was, Michael Allen sat both motionless and speechless until Brett had finished telling the entire story.

"The reason I didn't share this with you before was that I didn't want you worrying too much about me," Brett said, finishing.

"I worry about you all the time, Brett," his father admitted. "I know it's probably hard to understand that but after you become a parent you'll know the feeling. Look, from the sounds of things, you and, I guess you'd call them, the team have got this pretty well thought out. I was thinking that maybe you should come and stay with me until this thing is over, or maybe I should come over here and stay with you."

"That's a great idea, Dad," Brett said grateful that his father was there to listen, "but if this guy suspects something, he might disappear for a month or two then try and nail me when we're not so prepared. If we can't get him now than the rest of my life will be spent looking over my shoulder and being afraid to answer my door. That's not much of a life. I've really got to go through with this, Dad. I don't see another choice."

Michael Allen looked at his son with pride and marveled at just how courageous he was being.

Here is a young man that has had more than his share of adversity in his twenty-five years existence than most people experience in a lifetime and he's facing it head on just like his mother always did, Michael Allen thought.

Michael was holding himself together but just barely. The thought of losing his son tugged away at the last ounce of his emotional stability but Michael tugged right back. Thinking about a stranger roaming the quiet countryside waiting to pounce on his son made his blood boil with anger. Determination to prevent it and the anger he felt would be the glue that he would use to hold himself together through this ordeal.

"I suppose you're right when you put it that way. There has to be something I can do to help," Michael said, pausing to think for a minute.

His father continued his thought and after a brief pause, he continued wanting to make sure his son was OK with it, "Brian Miller and I went to school together and were pretty good friends, still are as far as I know. I've seen him at all the class reunions. Maybe he would have some ideas on how I could help. Do you mind if I call him, Brett?"

"No, Dad, not at all. In fact, I've got all his contact numbers right here," Brett said, moving to his computer desk to retrieve them.

Brett copied them down on a yellow sticky and gave them to his father with a grateful smile. He doubted there was anything his father could do to help but wanted to give him every opportunity. Who knew, maybe detective Miller would have some suggestions after all.

The three of them talked for another hour. Michael Allen was careful to keep the conversation general so Brett's girlfriend could be included and not just have to sit there and listen to the two of them talk. Deciding it was time for him to go, he stood up and hugged his son. A tear formed in the corner of his eye as the thought of losing Brett passed through his mind. As he fought back the tears, he knew he needed to be strong for his son's sake. He wouldn't be of much help to anyone if was an emotional wreck.

"We're going to get through this, son!" Michael said pulling back from his son's embrace.

Brett smiled reassuringly at his father. "We're going to get through this alright. We've got to remember to think," he said, reciting something his Dad always told him before a ball game. "The ball's going to be hit right to us and we're going to need to know what we're going to do with it when it is."

That drew a strained smile from his father as he said his goodbyes. Brett walked him to the door and hugged his Dad one more time.

"Try not to worry, Dad; everyone is doing their very best, and I know deep down in my heart that we're going to get him!"

"You're asking a lot, Brett, and all I can say is that I'll try my best. Call me later tonight OK?" Michael asked.

"Sure thing, Dad, I'll call just before I hit the sack. Be careful on your way home."

"I will," his father replied, getting into his truck.

Michael waved goodbye as he headed out of the complex and hooked up his hands-free unit. Looking down at the cell phone in his right hand he used his thumb to dial hoping that a call to Brian Miller might shed some additional light on Brett's story and help settle his nerves a bit.

Looking at his ringing cell phone, Detective Miller debated answering it. Dinner was just getting ready to be served and everyone had finally settled down. From across the table he could see his wife's eyes saying *not again.* All he could do was shrug his shoulders.

"You guys go ahead and start without me, I'll be right back," he said rising from his roast beef and mashed potato dinner. As he walked out of the dinning room and into the living room he answered.

"Miller"

"Brian Miller, this is Michael Allen, how are you?"

There was a somewhat long period of silence before he answered "Hi, Michael, sorry about that, you caught me off guard. I'm doing OK, what can I do for you?"

Maintaining a close friendship and seeing someone to share memories with at a class reunion were two totally different things. Michael and Brian fell into the latter category, so the chance of his call being received with overwhelming joy wasn't good to begin with and judging from the tone in Brian's voice his call more than likely had come at a bad time.

Not wanting to pretend their relationship was more than it actually was, Michael got right to the point. "I understand you met my son this morning in Joyce Davenport's office and are working with him on a case."

"That's your boy!" Brian exclaimed, truly surprised. "I had no idea."

"He's told me everything that's gone on so far. At first I thought he was having some sort of disjointed hallucination but as I listened and understood more I knew the situation was real. I was wondering and hopeful to be quite frank, that I could somehow help," Michael said, tossing out the suggestion to see if Brian had any ideas.

"It's the strangest thing I've ever been a part of but everything your son has told us checks out, I mean everything," Brian said emphatically. After a brief pause he continued, "I'm thinking there is something that you might be able to do. Did your son mention whether or not any government people had questioned him?"

Michael answered right back "No he didn't mention anything like that at all. What does the government have to do with this?" he asked with his curiosity now on full alert.

"I'm not really sure yet, but I don't think the people from the Justice Department know about your son, at least not yet, or they would have spoken with him, and that's just the way we have to keep it," Brian answered. "We probably know just as much as you do at this point but I'm convinced Agent Flynn knows a lot more. He was in my office a few hours ago demanding cooperation and I'll bet come morning we'll have to transfer investigative control to him and his crew. Just the thought of them bullying their way in really scares me."

"What do you mean scares you?" Michael asked, his tone demanding an answer.

Brian's answer was quick to follow. "I've seen them or their types anyway, really mess up some investigations. I'm not saying that's what would happen in this case but I can't rule it out either. Messing up on this one is just not an option. It appears we are going to get one shot at this guy so we've got to make it count."

"Why can't you just arrest him to protect my son?" Michael pleaded.

Having kids of his own, Brian totally understood the desperation he found in Michael's tone and wished there was something more he could do or say that would comfort him, but there just wasn't and the last thing he wanted to do was paint a rosy picture.

"I'd love to pick him up, Michael, but we just don't have anything on the guy. Other than your son's story, which I wholeheartedly believe, and a set of fingerprints…we have absolutely zero. If I picked him up, he'd be out on the street a half hour later. Not only would he be free to walk the streets, he'd know we were on to him. He could go into hiding for a week, a month, maybe even as long as a year, then pop up wherever and whenever he wanted, finish his business and disappear again. We've got to get this one right the first time and I can't stress enough how important it is that the Feds don't know who Brett Allen is."

"Yeah, you're right" Michael said, realizing the logic in Miller's explanation. "Is that what's got you worried about this Justice Department guy, Flynn, I think you said. That he'll make a mistake and you'll lose the chance to nail this guy?"

"Yes, that's it alright. Look," Brian went on getting ready to drop his very pointed hint, "I can't tell you what you to do but if I had a father in the United States Senate I'd call him and see if he could put a little pressure on the Feds to work with us on this instead of the other way around."

"I know exactly what you mean, Brian. Thanks," Michael said, hanging up the phone feeling like there was actually something he could do to help his son. Pushing one and holding it down activated the speed dial on Michael's cell phone and automatically called Senator George Allen in Washington.

As Michael told Brett's grandfather the bizarre story that led to the phone call, George Allen could hardly believe it. If it had been April, he would have called it one of the worst April fool's pranks he had ever heard. But it wasn't April and his son wasn't kidding. After asking how everyone was holding up under the circumstances, Senator Allen started to express his feelings about the whole thing.

"Michael, if this wasn't coming from you and I didn't know some of the people involved in this thing, I'd have hung the phone up ten minutes ago," the senator admitted. "I'm having a hard time with this but I'll call Todd over at Justice and get him to quietly adjust some things. You said it was a guy named Flynn, right, and you're sure I should stay put?"

"That's right, Dad, Agent Flynn, and for now everyone needs to stay put and keep things as normal as possible, and please don't mention Brett's name. They'll find out soon enough," Michael reminded his father.

"I'll take care of it, son, and don't worry, I'm not going to let anything happen to my grandson. In the morning these Justice Department agents will be working for the Boston P.D., and if necessary, I'll have someone from my office up there to act as a liaison. I want you to give that detective the number to my office and tell him if he gets any flack whatsoever to call right away. I'll leave instructions for my staff on what to do. I've got to go if I have any hope of reaching Todd. I love you, son, and tell my grandson I love him too."

"Same here, Dad, and thanks," Michael said, hanging up.

Brett closed the door behind Becky as she got in the passenger seat of his Mustang. He had to be at work early in the morning so it was essential for him to get some rest tonight. They toyed briefly with the idea of Becky staying the night and both readily agreed that it wasn't a good idea. Brett's gas tank was below empty and he knew he was operating strictly on battery power at this point.

Not having had the benefit of being able to rest, his fatigue, which had been building all day, finally caught up with him. For the first time in his life, Brett actually believed he could fall asleep standing up. Yawning deeply, Brett got the Mustang pointed in the direction of the Dug Out and headed that way.

Their ride over was quiet, each lost in their own thoughts as they reflected on the events of the day and wondered what tomorrow would bring. Looking out her window, Becky saw that the long rays of the sun had grabbed the horizon and began pulling itself closer toward evening. The wonderful, almost light raspberry sherbert color of the sunset reminded her of the *red sky at night sailors' delight* saying. She hoped with all her heart that she could somehow frame that old proverb and all it implied around Brett's day tomorrow.

As she pulled into the Dug Out, it was pretty obvious that it was the beginning of the week. The sparse crowd would have been considered good patronage at most places but not here. Brian Jones had tried every gimmick in the book to get people in but the first day of the week proved to be a tougher opponent than he expected. Brian wasn't concerned about the Dug Out's business; it was great and made him a millionaire a few times over. It was simply the challenge that he loved, but his time for finding a solution was running out. In a few months, Monday Night Football would have them here in droves and the cars would be squeezed into the parking lot tighter than sardines in a can. But the Red Sox weren't playing, so Brett had no trouble in finding a place to park that was close to Becky's car. Turning in his seat to face Becky, Brett shut the down the Mustang.

"I want you to know, before this whole situation gets any crazier than it already is, that these past few days have been some of the best in my life. Despite all the ups and downs, the uncertainty and fear, you've managed to somehow make each moment of our time together special. I don't know how you do it or even think I could begin to understand it. I just know I wouldn't trade in those moments with you for anything."

"You're scaring me, Brett," she said through her tears. "This sounds like a so-long speech, like you know that awful guy is going to take you away."

"I have no intention of saying so long or letting this guy succeed," he said, reaching over to take her hand. "It seems that all this craziness has managed to take over and it's hard sometimes for me to think straight. I just wanted to make sure that you know how deeply I care for you and how hopeful I am for our future."

"I know, Brett," she said sliding across the car and hugging him, "I know. Until you came along," she said, fighting the sniffles, "I'd forgotten what it was to really feel alive and have something to look forward to. There's a big difference between living and existing and for me, Brett—that difference is you."

Each could feel the other's pre-sobbing, uneven gasps for air as they struggled to keep their emotions under control. All Brett could do was hold on to her as he grappled with the stark reality of the situation he was in. Looking for anything he could find that would help restore his sense of optimism and determination, his thoughts settled on his mother. It wasn't the good memories that came flooding back. What his mind rested on instead was the memory of being in his mother's hospital room and the conversation they had just before she died. He was amazed that his mother, with the last ounces of strength she had, tried to comfort him as the sickness in her body moved to complete its morbid task.

Pondering his thoughts, Brett remembered there was someone he could legitimately hold responsible for his mother's death and his anger returned. Not only was his current employer guilty but so was the guy that was following him. Like flipping on a light switch, a new focus point appeared in his mind, avenging the death of his mother. That alone propelled him past his current feelings of hopelessness and helplessness to his more determined, action oriented, and now anger driven frame of mind.

"Hey," Brett said pulling away from their embrace so he could look at her face "I'm not going to let these people win. A lot of people are dead because of them and they're not going to get away with it, not this time. Besides," Brett went on trying to inject a little humor, "I owe you a trip to the stables and I know how upset you'll be if I don't pay up."

That statement took Becky totally by surprise. "What?" Becky asked, looking at him through watery eyes as if he just rambled off a totally incomprehensible scientific equation.

"Horse back riding. I owe you an afternoon of horseback riding" he answered with a tired smile.

"I'm going to hold you to that. Take a look at this parking lot and you'll see why the beginning of the week is a good time for me to make plans, so I'll be expecting an invitation soon," she said as positive as she could, "You're right you know."

"Right about what?" Brett asked.

"That they're not going to get away with it. I don't know how I know it, I just do," Becky said with conviction. "I'd better get going," she said, leaning over to give him a kiss.

"OK," Brett replied returning her affection. "I've got an appointment with Dr. Davenport after work tomorrow so can I call you after I finish up with her?"

"If you didn't, I'd be really upset," she answered. "How about this instead?" she asked, prepared to give her counter offer. "Why don't I meet you tomorrow at lunch time at the research center? I'll grab the key to your place, do some shopping and have a nice dinner waiting for you when you get home. What do you say, Brett?" and without waiting for an answer, she softly added with a hopeful look, "I know I would really enjoy it."

"You know what," Brett said after thinking about it for a second, "I'd like that too! Why don't you meet me at the security guard building at noon or so? When you get there just tell one of the guards to call me at the lab, or you can call me yourself from your cell, and I'll come out to meet you."

"I'll look forward to it. Listen, if you have any trouble sleeping or have another one of those dreams or just want to talk call me, it doesn't matter what time. OK?"

"OK," Brett repeated reassuringly. "Thanks, I will."

As Becky got into her car to go home, Frank was leaving the Triad. He had enjoyed a nice quiet dinner and no matter how many times he looked down at the ring Veronica had given him, it made him feel good. She hadn't been gone that long but Frank missed her just the same.

Everyone at the table heard the beginning of Yankee Doodle playing from the cell phone buried somewhere inside Jessica's handbag. Not everyone at the table knew exactly what that meant, but Elias sure did and casually looked over at Jessica with a raised eyebrow of concern.

"Excuse me," Jessica said grabbing her bag with a smile. "This will only take a minute and if he comes back before I do, I'd love a cup of black coffee."

Jessica headed straight for the ladies room, answering her phone on the way. "Frank, what a nice surprise, I guess you really do miss me."

"Yes, Veronica, I've got to confess, I really do. Are you working tonight?" Frank asked from his parked car despite knowing he shouldn't have.

"Frank, you know we agreed not to talk about my work," she said in a perturbed tone entering the bathroom, "but just so you know, I've decided not to work until after we talk. Tonight I'm just out with a couple of friends. You'll still be home at the end of the week right?"

"Yes everything is still on schedule. I should be home by Friday afternoon. I was thinking maybe we could start our talk Friday night," he suggested.

"That sounds good, Frank. I'll look forward to that. I know this is wishful thinking but is there any chance you'll be home earlier?" she asked, looking for a more definitive answer.

"There's a slight chance but it's not very likely. I just wanted to call and say hello and I don't want to keep you from your friends, so how about you give me a call sometime tomorrow or Wednesday, OK?" Frank asked.

"I will, Frank, probably sometime tomorrow night if you're not working late," she said, moving aside so a young lady could use the lone mirror to freshen up.

"Call me anytime after seven and that should be fine," Frank informed her. "I'll talk with you tomorrow."

"OK, tomorrow, good night, Frank, miss you," Jessica said, and hearing Frank's goodnight, she hung up.

Trying to maneuver her way back between the tables was a little frustrating. Why did people always have their chairs sitting farther from the table than they needed to be? It almost seemed liked the long stretch to get the food on their plate was something to be enjoyed. Or maybe it was some sort of wager amongst the people dining at a table. See who could eat the most from the greatest distance and spill the least while trying to get food in their mouth. Whatever it was, the backs of the chairs served as obstacles and the people sitting in them always seemed reluctant to slide in and give you room to pass. It was that reluctance to be helpful that really irritated Jessica but she pressed on squeezing between chairs keeping her disdain silent as she negotiated the maze. Arriving at the table to a fresh cup of coffee and an inquisitive Francine Jessica put a somewhat transparent smile on her face and sat down.

"What happened. Did the waiter get here as soon as I left?" Jessica said as more of a statement than a question.

"Elias, I told you that my sister and I had planned an Alaskan cruise in a few weeks didn't I?" Jessica asked.

"Yes you did. Is that still on schedule?" Elias wondered.

"Sure is, everything is on schedule so as long as we're wrapped up here, do I still have a green light?"

"Of course, take a few weeks. Three if you need them," Elias said, trying to decide which side of the cheesecake to take the first bite out of. Jessica had just told him that Frank had called her and his timetable hadn't changed. It was also very good to know that he wasn't suspicious about anything.

"Are you the oldest?" Francine asked trying to strike up a conversation.

Jessica knew that Francine was a nice person and was genuinely trying to establish some sort of relationship with her but she just didn't have the energy to put into it. Wanting to remain polite and avoid a remorseful situation like the one that transpired between them earlier, she gave her an answer. It was a total lie but an answer nonetheless.

"Yes, I'm the oldest. My little sister Connie and I grew up Maine. A few years after I went off to college she married the man of her dreams. Turned out he was a monster that nightmares are made from. I warned her about him, that he'd hurt her, but she went ahead and married him anyway. I think she knew but thought she could change him. I guess several years of trying finally got to be too much. Her divorce was finalized just a few weeks ago, so I thought it would be nice if the two of us spent some relaxing time together. She won't admit it but she's still hurting."

"That's such a sweet thing to do, Jessica. I hope the two of you have a great time. I've heard the Alaskan cruises are wonderful!" Francine said emphatically.

"I've heard that too," Andy Campbell chimed in. "I wouldn't mind doing that myself if I could find someone to share it with and wouldn't have to go alone."

"Come on, Andy," Francine cut in. "When are you going to learn that finding someone to share those kinds of things requires effort on your part beyond the typical Neanderthal behavior patterns?" she asked jokingly while subtly referring to their failed attempt at a relationship.

Elias was in the middle of a sip of water when he uncharacteristically burst out into laughter sending a shower of water from between his lips onto the table. That got everyone laughing, including Andy. Between his giggling, Elias managed to get a napkin and wipe his mouth and apologize for his bad imitation of the human squirt gun. Once everyone settled down, Elias grabbed the check and got the group up and ready to go.

Back in Washington, Senator Allen wasn't wasting any time; as soon as he hung up from his son, he called the Justice Department. It was a little past normal business hours but when people wanted to find you, especially powerful ones, there was no place to hide.

Todd Abraham and his wife Deidre were attending a very formal, D.C. style retirement party complete with black tuxes, elegant evening gowns, a string quartet, and a lot of political maneuvering.

Todd's wife of fifteen years was still amazed at how things worked. People were strategically seated at tables based largely in part on the greatest department need at the time. This was a retirement party but the Attorney General was looking to get his budget numbers to get through in October so he had invited several key congressional members to the party he was hosting.

There was nothing like a high roller's party to get things done. Several of the local media outlets had always maintained that more work gets done at these types of functions than anywhere else regardless if the politicians were in or out of session.

Deidre had been left alone with a couple of congressmen's wives while her husband was busy entertaining their congressman husbands. Todd had done very well for himself in Washington and had ascended the political ladder rather quickly. He was cunning, shrewd, and used his power carefully. Deidre wasn't much for playing in the political arena but absolutely loved the power and prestige she had found there. Being the wife of someone important had its drawbacks and these functions, at least in her mind, were a big one.

The large ballroom chosen for the event reeked of elegance. Every table was adorned with its own hand-sewn linen white table cloth providing an atmosphere of sophistication that was well suited to the fine china and crystal. Near the center of the room soft dinner music played from a small dais that sat atop the highly polished white marble floor. Waiters and waitresses dressed to the T armed with trays of drinks and hors d'oeuvres scurried about making sure no one was in need of anything.

Deidre looked on as a man in a grey suit approached Todd and the group of congressmen he was with. Excusing himself, the messenger leaned in and whispered into Todd's ear that Senator Allen was on phone. Todd excused himself and followed the man who delivered the message to what could be best described as a courtesy phone tucked away in a relatively remote and somewhat quieter area of the ballroom.

"Good evening, Senator Allen," he said picking up the white phone.

"Evening, Todd, sounds like your party is very much underway, so I'll be brief," Senator Allen said with his trademark directness. "I need your help with a situation up in Boston.

"One of your men, an agent Flynn is up there and has caused quite a commotion over an investigation being run by the Boston Police Department. I would consider it an enormous favor if you could make sure that the local law enforcement gets to keep this one."

Todd was surprised by the senator's request and didn't try to conceal it. "That's a pretty strange request, Senator. I'm not sure I've ever been asked that by anyone. Can I ask why you're involved?"

"You can ask, Todd," the senator replied making it clear by his tone that no answer would be forthcoming.

"OK, Senator, I'll take care of it for you. Flynn you said," Todd asked restating the agents' name and writing it down on the small pad next to the phone.

"Yes, Todd, that's right," the senator confirmed, "Flynn. Thanks and please give my regards to Congressmen Williams and Marsh."

"OK, Senator, I'll be sure and do just that. Good night."

Things in Washington usually happened at the speed of your influence. Unfortunately for Senator George Allen, he wasn't very well liked by Todd Abraham. It wasn't as if someone had done something awful to the other; Todd didn't like him from the first moment he met him. Putting that aside, he knew he had to play ball and doing an enormous favor for George Allen meant he would be owed one in return. Just the prospect of having that kind of leverage, an ace in the hole if you will, made it a lot easier for Todd to get past his personal feelings.

Todd walked into a small back room and turned on his cell phone. "Marty, it's Todd. I want you to do me a favor. We have an op in Boston, Mass, that's being run by an Agent Flynn, make sure he cooperates with the locals and let them run the investigation, or at least *think* they are, if you know what I mean. Also, I'm not very familiar with what we've got going on up there and I think I need to be. Please see to it that I get briefed on that in the morning, let's say 9:30 in my office. Oh and one more thing, I need this to be done pretty quickly so get right on it for me."

"I understand, sir. I'll see you at 9:30 tomorrow," Todd heard Marty say and hang up.

Todd started walking back to the group of congressmen he had just left a few minutes ago. Intercepting a waiter along the way, he removed a glass of champagne from the tray and smiled inwardly. He wasn't sure how much mileage he could get from this favor but Todd was going to get every single one he could because it was IOU's that ran Washington. The more you had in your back pocket, the more powerful you became and that's what got things done in this town. He had been tucking little things away in his IOU drawer for a good number of years and adding this one from a prestigious senator like George Allen would put him over the top.

Dinner at the Miller's had just concluded and the two detectives had moved to the living room coffee table and were pouring over Brett's journals looking for more clues.

"Reads almost like a book of short stories," Hank commented, scratching his chin as he continued to read.

"No kidding," Brian replied his gaze still fixed on the journal, "Wish I took one of those speed reading courses a few years back when that was the *in thing* to do. It would come in awfully handy right about now."

Hank agreed "I know what you mean. I'll finish" he said stopping mid sentence so Brian could answer his cell phone. Seeing Detective Ryan O'Hara's number, Brian eagerly answered.

"Hey, Ryan, what's going on in Lexington?" Brian asked skipping all the pleasantries.

"Not good, L.T. Our girl Nadia is dead. They found her body in a cheap motel room only a few miles away from her house. Looks like a suicide…overdose of a pain killer that goes by the name Oxycodone. The ME has already taken the body and is going to start an autopsy right away. From what we can gather, she showed up alone on Saturday afternoon and paid cash up front for a three-day stay. I guess some time late in the afternoon today, the chamber maid was concerned after seeing the do not disturb sign up for so long and knocked on the door. When she didn't get an answer, she opened the door and found Nadia face down on the bed. That's when she ran across the parking lot to the main office and called 911. We're tracking down the pharmacy to see what we can find out there and pretty soon we'll be looking at the VHS tapes of the parking lot that shows her door to see if she's had any visitors since checking in. Oh and just so you know, Bernie is here from the State Police."

"OK, Ryan. Call me right away with any news, I mean anything!" Brian said as if he couldn't stress it enough. "Nothing is too trivial, understand? And stay close to your pals up there. We don't want Bernie making this an exclusive State Police matter and cutting us off at the knees if you know what I mean."

"Yeah, I know what you mean, L.T. Don't worry, I'm all over this one," he reassured his boss was they walked back to the crime scene. "The coroner was contacted and agreed to start on this right away. It would be nice if we could get that kind of response from our coroner. I'll be heading over there pretty soon and hopefully I'll be able to call you with some preliminary information.

"Thanks, Ryan," Brian said hanging up the phone and turning to Hank. "Well, my friend, the plot thickens. Nadia is dead, apparently an overdose of pain killers but that's much too coincidental for my liking."

"No kidding," Hank said emphatically concurring, "and in this line of work, I've never met a coincidence that I've liked."

Brian answered with a slight touch of amazement, "O'Hara thinks he can give us a preliminary coroner's report in a few hours. I guess they move faster up there than most. Maybe we'll be able to get some answers. Oh and the Mass State Police just jumped in the sand box with the rest of us."

Hank shook his head and smiled. "I hope the box is big enough for all us to play nice in, otherwise we're going to get buried in those sand heaps full of bureaucratic red tape and jurisdictional bickering."

Brian just couldn't contain the sarcasm. "And that's something we *really* need to have more of around here! I'm anxious to see if this kid's grandfather can get some string pulled for us," he continued. "From what I understand, he carries a lot of weight down there; just how much I don't really know, and I suspect we'll find out in the morning just how much."

"My biggest concern," Hank added contemplatively, "is that we can get to the bottom of this before Brett runs out of time."

All Brian could do was to shake his head in agreement. Both the detectives had children and in the privacy of their own thoughts were deeply sympathetic with the entire Allen family and more determined than ever to stop whoever this guy was from completing his mission.

26.

Frank Whickers was leaving the Triad after a late dinner feeling better than he had in a very long time. It was amazing to him how that one phone call could affect him so much. *Did she really say that she had stopped working and was going to wait until after we talked?* he thought, still struggling to believe it. *Could she really quit her work and settle down? Could I really put her past behind me or would it rear its ugly head as time went on and cause huge problems?*

Just the thought that she had stopped working out of respect for him and the outcome of the conversation they were going to have was more than he ever expected. That action alone gave him some pretty good insight as to the direction she wanted the conversation to go and gave him some time to think and prepare for it.

Frank's mind stayed on Veronica as he began to run down his pros and cons list on whether to develop a deeper, more personal relationship with her. Reminding himself once again that his past, which would also include these next few days, was far from pristine seemed to help him over some rough spots but only a little. There was just something about spending the rest of his life with a professional escort that didn't sit right with him and perhaps at the end of the week, Veronica could help him get past that.

As it often happened when Frank was working, he was a little bored. Despite having to be up early in the morning to finalize his ambush position in Bedford, he decided to find a cinema house and take in a movie. He was clueless as to what was playing and decided that once he got there, he'd pick something from the marquee that sounded good and give it a try.

Seeing a large cinema complex just up ahead, Frank pulled in and parked near the front entrance. It was obvious that Monday wasn't the evening of choice for most movie goers. There were maybe fifty or so vehicles in the parking lot all huddled up near the entrance and a few scattered a pretty good distance away. These were probably people that had newer vehicles and were willing to walk those few extra steps to try and keep their newly acquired mode of transportation scratch and dent free for as long as possible.

Those are the ones that get keyed in Chicago, Frank thought as he glanced at them through the last slivers of daylight before he turned and walked in.

While Frank was watching his movie, the coroner had been methodically examining Nadia's body. Ryan O'Hara stood in the examination room with his friend and Lexington PD Detective Peter Townsend and listened intently to the coroner give them her preliminary findings. It only took a few minutes with her before Ryan had the information he needed and excused himself.

"L.T., it's O'Hara" he said. Not that Ryan had to say it was him calling; he was the only one that addressed Brian Miller with an abbreviated version of lieutenant.

"What did you get, Ryan?" he asked, noticing the clock had just passed 9:30 p.m.

"The coroner confirmed the cause of death. It was an overdose of Oxycodone alright that on the surface appears to be a suicide, but it wasn't. There was a lethal amount of the drug in her system but the amount was inconsistent with two tablet fragments found in the stomach. Her lower colon is completely clean, which indicates in all likelihood that the lethal amount was administered using some sort of enema. There were trace amounts of ether in her system also, just enough to put her out. A look at the security tapes showed she had a visitor at about 11:30 Saturday evening. Apparently, what happened is her visitor must have given her a towel or something like it soaked in the stuff to put her under then pumped her full of the stuff. I thought something else was interesting; her prescription read 'take one tablet every twelve hours for pain as needed,' so whoever killed her must have known quite a bit about her. Discussing Oxycodone over coffee just isn't something people do, if you know what I mean. The tape isn't going to help us much either as the system in use is old and outdated and the tape is of poor quality and really dark. What we *can* see is that there was no forced entry, whoever it was just

251

walked right up to her door, knocked and was let in. Then about twenty minutes later they walked back out. Not much to go on, I'm afraid. They're looking for next of kin and going to start, if they haven't already, going through her house for clues. The crime lab folks up here are going to be busy."

"Nice work, Ryan. I'm going to rustle up the gang and head downtown, so in about half an hour or so, you'll be able to reach me on my department line. You're my eyes and ears up there so stay frosty; we can't afford to let anything get by us on this one."

"Got it, L.T." O'Hara answered.

"Looks like were in for a long night, Hank," Brian's concerned voice alerted Detective Beard. "Nadia was a homicide, so I think it's time we head back downtown and set up shop there for the immediate future. I'll fill you in on the details along the way."

"Like I said, Brian, I never met a coincidence I've liked…never!" Hank said, collecting the journals from the table.

As soon as Brian had finished saying goodbye to his family, they got in his car and headed to Police Headquarters. Brian called Detective McCoy from the car and told him to get his team pronto and meet him at the station in an hour and then he started to fill Hank in on the information he'd gotten from Lexington.

Both men knew the entire situation was reaching critical mass and the funnel of the hourglass had gotten wider, allowing the sand to empty into the bottom even faster. Hank's comment about bureaucratic red tape and jurisdictional bickering kept running through Miller's mind and he realized he was just as guilty of wanting to keep things "in house" and under his control as the other players involved in this case.

"It's time to lay the cards on the table," Miller said, breaking the silence that filled his car.

Detective Beard responded as Miller thought he might. "I couldn't agree with you more, Brian. If were going to nail this guy everyone has to be on the same page. Once we explain the situation, as unbelievable as it sounds, and show our willingness to cooperate, everyone, including this guy Flynn, should be more than anxious to come around. I'm convinced from everything that's happened today that this guy needs to be stopped at all costs. I hate to say this but the thought had crossed my mind of planting some evidence so we can pick this guy up."

"I've thought about it too, Hank," Miller confessed, "and I haven't ruled that out. Flynn said something when he left my office that still has me wondering.

He said that I had no idea what we were up against so I've got to assume that they do and have a plan of their own. If we don't get some answers from him tomorrow, I think picking this guy up is going to be our only option. I just can't stand by and take a chance on this kid getting killed. When we get to the office let's check in with the team that's tailing this guy and see what they can tell us and start planning how we're going to go about picking him up."

"Agreed, I don't know how I'd feel if we let this guy succeed based on all that we know. Seems to me if we stand by and do nothing, we'd be accomplices. Hopefully after we get some of the other players interviewed tomorrow, we'll have a better of idea of just who the *real* accomplices are. I just have a really bad feeling about this whole thing."

Miller frustratingly echoed his passenger's sentiment "Me too!" as he pushed down of the gas pedal, now more anxious than ever to get into his office.

Back at the restaurant, Elias and his team had finished paying and were getting into the company leased SUV when his cell phone started ringing. "Special Agent Flynn," Elias answered as he settled in behind the wheel.

"Agent Flynn, it's Trevor," the excited voice said. "We ran a check on the phone calls made from the pay phone at the bus station in Chicago. The call was made to a Nadia Petrova, who, get this, lives in Lexington, Mass. We've already sent someone over there to check it out. We should have some info anytime now. The call from the pay phone was made using a calling card from one of those pre-paid calling cards so we're not going to have much luck on that end."

"OK. Good work," Elias said acknowledging the efforts of the evening crew. "We're on our way back and should be there in about thirty—" Elias stopped for a second, interrupted by his call waiting feature announcing another call was coming in. "—minutes. I've got another call," he told Trevor signifying the conversation was over and took the other call. Elias wasn't on his second call very long and everyone in the SUV could visibly see he was upset.

Their lingering jovial mood of just a few minutes ago, largely at Andy Campbell's expense, disappeared with the snap of a finger and was replaced with tension that hung thickly inside the vehicle.

Francine called up from the back seat with a hint of trepidation in her voice, "What's going on, Elias?"

"Washington, that's what!" Elias answered his voice quivering with anger. "Apparently, someone outside of our department has an interest in what were doing. We're supposed to let the locals lead on this and share all of our information with them. I don't know who got this pushed through or how but I don't like it one bit."

Jessica couldn't believe her ears. All that she had done and all that she had sacrificed now seemed meaningless. She was already having major difficulty coming to terms emotionally with what she had personally done for the good of humanity in order to make a case against this guy, and this latest news pushed the dagger deeper into her heart. Jessica turned her head to look out the window so no one could see the tears glistening in her eyes.

"I'm not turning anything over. As soon as we get back to the ops center, I'm going to put a stop to this!" Elias said, knowing full well that he had little chance of doing anything about it. He knew if this went through, it would ruin Jessica. Not only did he admire and respect her work as an agent but he liked her personally and he was going to do everything he could to honor what she had done and let her know that it wasn't done in vain.

"I really hope you can talk some sense into them. We don't need anyone blowing this for us!" Agent Campbell piped in from the passenger seat. "What on earth are they thinking!" Campbell's statement resonated in everyone's mind as they drove back, everyone except Jessica's. Her thoughts drifted back to the first time she met Elias and had eagerly agreed to work for him. Now she wondered if that wasn't the worst mistake of her life.

The rest of the ride was silent which was just fine for Jessica. Somewhere in the twenty-minute time span from the restaurant to the operations center, her enthusiasm for getting Frank Whickers had turned into remorse over the things she had done. Unfortunately, there was no magic potion she could drink or eraser big enough to wipe her memory clean. When she agreed to the whole thing, she knew it was going to be tough to live with her actions and now that the investigation was being turned over, it was like all that she had done and put herself through was being thrown away as easily as someone taking out the trash.

No one saw her tears that flowed freely in the middle of the night, no one could understand just how dirty and cheap she felt when she had to be with Frank. She had given away her dignity and self respect to get this guy and now after it was all said and done, no one really cared. That was the straw that broke the camel's back, and she decided that it was time for her to take matters into her own hands and do something about it.

Getting out of the SUV, Elias told agents Campbell and Kelly to go on ahead. Standing next to Jessica, Elias could see that she had been crying. He felt so bad for her and did his best to console her and assure her that he would call in all his markers to get this case back. Wiping her eyes clear, she looked at him and asked to be relieved from the case.

They talked for a few minutes in the parking lot and Elias agreed to let her go. He didn't try to talk her out of it, as that would have just deepened an already cavernous wound.

"Take as much time as you need, Jessica, you more than deserve it," Elias said in a comforting tone. "You've done so much and now I know it seems it was all for nothing, but I can tell you, it wasn't. We're going to nail this guy and without you, we couldn't have done it. I know you need to do this and I'll support whatever it is you need or want to do. If you need anything, and I mean anything, call me."

"Thanks, Elias, and I will call you. I just can't promise you when. I guess the one thing you can do for me now is to have someone take me to the airport," she said. "I don't know where I'm going or for how long. I just know I need to get away from here. You can take my stuff from the hotel and throw them away or burn them for all I care. I don't want anything around me that's even touched this investigation."

"Done," Elias responded right away. "When do you want to leave?"

"I'd like to go right now," she said, "You know what, never mind about the ride. I'll call a cab. I just want to get out of here.

"Please, Elias, just let me go. This is hard enough on me. I'm going to be OK I just really need to do this and I need to do it my way."

"OK, Jessica, if that's what you really want. Remember, anything you need is only a phone call away. This is see you later, right? Not goodbye?"

"Yes, see you later, Elias, and thanks for letting me do this," she responded.

Standing next to the SUV, she watched Elias walk into the operations center and pulled out her cell phone to call a cab. Jessica didn't waste time and started to think about her next move. Fifteen minutes had passed before the cab turned the corner and approached its new fare. When your mind is busy, time really does pass quickly and those fifteen minutes passed in the blink of an eye.

"Hell hath no furry like a woman's scorn," she said confidently reaching for the door to get in.

Inside the operations center, Elias watched with mixed emotions as Jessica got into the cab. Watching the taillights disappear into the darkness, he wondered if this entire turn of events had just shattered Jessica's entire life. From what just transpired, he was pretty sure that even her astonishing inner fortitude was damaged beyond repair. In the solitude of that moment, he hoped for two things; that he didn't destroy the rest of her life and that she somehow and in some way could find it in her heart to forgive him.

Leaving the little side office, Elias headed for the briefing room where Francine had just gotten the bad news that the facial recognition program that was run for the man who had placed the call from the bus station had yielded no results so far but was continuing.

Elias entered the room and greeted Randy Brink who was, for a lack of better terms, the operational shift supervisor and Trevor. "So, Randy, what do we have so far?" he asked, taking his customary seat at the head of the table.

"We just heard from Agent Masi; the Lexington address is crawling with state and local police. We kept a very low profile but were able to find out that the woman in question, Nadia Petrova," he said looking at his notes for confirmation, "committed suicide sometime over the weekend. The body was discovered this afternoon and is currently undergoing an autopsy."

"Send Masi to the coroner's office NOW!" Elias demanded. "I want to know those results just as soon as they're available. Lose the low profile approach. If we have to kick in some doors to get what we need then that's what we're going to do. I'm sick and tired of having to walk on egg shells around here."

Randy stood there for a just a second before Elias laid into him "Well, what are you waiting for?" his voice now loud and angry.

Everyone was startled by the volume and anger contained in his order. Both Andy and Francine knew it was prompted by the call he gotten and they wondered how successful he would be when he called them back if his demeanor remained as it was.

Elias sat there stunned, his disapproving gaze locked on Randy Brink as he left. The events of the day were running through his mind. He couldn't figure out why they kept bumping into local enforcement. Did they know something that he and his team didn't? This was a highly sensitive and secretive operation he was running yet everyone and their brother always seemed to be a step ahead of him. The Boston P.D. had already tried to run prints on Frank Whickers. Now the Nadia link to the case had state and local police involvement before Trevor and the team had even established that a link existed. He couldn't figure out what was going on and he didn't like it one bit and now wondered if the call he had gotten to turn things over was related.

Everyone sat quietly until Randy Brink returned. Randy informed everyone that the agent on scene was en route to get the autopsy results and that he had dispatched another.

"I thought it would be a good idea to have a team there. Having a team of two will make a greater impression" he said justifying his decision.

Elias shook his head in agreement and apologized to the group for his outburst.

"Sorry, everyone, as you can probably tell, I'm pretty frustrated. It just seems like this is getting out of our control. The state and local police always seem to be a step ahead of us and I need to try and find out why. Tomorrow I'm going back to talk with the Boston P.D. to see what I can get from them, if anything. Just so everyone in this room is aware, I got a call not long ago from our boss to turn over jurisdiction, but I haven't even started to fight that battle yet. And before the questions start coming in," Elias said now ready to outline his cover story for Jessica. "I've sent agent Pierce to get the next flight down there. I think both her presence and direct knowledge of the case will help us hold on to this."

Satisfied that his explanation was well received by the group Elias turned his attention to Trevor.

"How is your research coming with the items that Francine had you check out?" he asked of the technician.

"We've started to check out the cases Dr. Davenport had worked on and so far nothing that fits the profile of the case we're working on. Granted, we don't have all the data in yet, but most of the people she seems to have testified against would not be able to employ the services of Mr. Whickers. We're also running a check on all insurance claims of the people she has seen over last twelve months," Trevor explained. "Once that information has been collected we'll cross reference the insurance carrier information with the companies they provide services for to see if we can establish a tie in with the pharmaceutical company that way."

"That's an outstanding idea" Francine said, interrupting him.

"I agree," Elias confirmed. "I want to talk with you later about a promotion," he added with a smile.

Trevor returned Elias's smile with one of his own and eagerly continued his briefing.

"Our waitress, Rebecca Williams, shows nothing mysterious. Her mother filed for divorce on the grounds of abandonment a long time ago. Based on that document, we've also found out that she is an only child. There is no significant history with Rebecca or any family member and she has no vendor's license. The company that owns the building is putting together a list of current tenants and one of our people will be able to pick it up in the morning. Just a footnote, there doesn't seem to be any connection with her and Dr. Davenport. So far, nothing on the Prudential Building or a place called the Triad, where he went his evening for dinner. Right now, believe it or not, we think he's sitting in a cinema watching a movie."

"We've gotten the list of everyone that's working at the bus station."

Not wanting to be outdone, Randy chimed in cutting Trevor off, "— including the people who run the surveillance and security system and the company that has the cleaning contract. The guy who was working the late shift that night left for vacation the next morning and isn't due back until this Friday. According to his girlfriend, he's in on one of those South Carolina golf getaway deals. She gave us the name and location of his hotel and some phone numbers. I've contacted some of our people down there and they'll track him down for us."

"Another thing," Trevor jumped back in, "the bus that our solider boarded was headed for Pittsburgh. We're sending someone over to collect the security tapes, ask around etc. Maybe we can find out if he stayed in Pittsburgh or continued on. Eventually the trail will end and I think it's a good assumption that when it does, we'll have a general idea of where this guy lives."

"We've got people running around all over the country and a lot of information that has yet to come in that we'll need to organize and assimilate almost immediately," Elias commented, "Do we need additional support resources here?"

The question wasn't directed at any one person but more of an open question directed at all of them. Trevor was the only one that responded.

"I think I could use an extra hand, Elias. I have a friend that works on the international side; you might know her, Kimberly Radcliff. She's excellent and I know she would be a tremendous addition to the team."

"I don't know her," Elias responded writing her name down on, "but if you need her I'll make it happen. Is there anything else?" he asked polling the occupants of the briefing room and everyone remained silent.

"OK. Thanks for all your hard work. You've gotten a lot more information than I think anyone expected in a short amount of time and I want to commend everyone. I also want a priority put on the Pittsburgh angle…so make it happen, and make it happen *tonight*," Elias said, giving some final instructions before leaving to call his boss. "Have them convert the stuff so they can send the video to us through our computer system and call me as soon as it comes in. I don't care what time. We're going to get started tomorrow at o-five hundred ,so I suggest, Andy, that you and Francine should get some sleep. I'll see you back here then."

Collecting the briefing material in front of him, Elias left and went back to his office to use his direct line to the Justice Department. "Maybe," he said, "I can talk some sense into these people!"

Despite his best efforts, the call went pretty much as Elias had suspected it would. He was told in no uncertain terms to *work with it* and was given no solid answer when he asked who was behind it. It certainly raised some questions in his mind. Perhaps someone from the CIA had a deeper interest in this case than he thought. It just didn't make sense that they would hand over their messy situation for him to *quietly* clean up then make a public declaration by dropping some information in the laps of the Boston P.D.

If that were true, they would have to know a lot more about Frank Whickers than they had ever intended to share with him. The more he thought about the entire situation, the whole CIA possibility made less and less sense. He couldn't dismiss the fact that the locals were ahead of him each step of the way so it had to be something else.

Elias was in a somber mood as he watched what he perceived was the evaporation of his case with little or nothing he could do to stop it. All the work and all the sacrifices started to seem, even to him, like a big waste of resources and an outrageous disregard for Jessica's huge personal sacrifice. Picking up a collection of information from his desk, he started to leave for the night and quietly hoped Brian Miller, his favorite police detective, would be able to shed some light on it in the morning.

Jessica got out of the cab and gave the cabbie a one hundred dollar bill and asked him to wait for her to return. Getting out of the cab, she entered a late night department store. She thought the evolution of these stores was quite something. They were transformed to meet the public's demand for one-stop shopping. Not only could you buy a pair of jeans and a sweatshirt you could also do your grocery shopping, banking, and even grab something to eat in the food court.

Walking quickly down the aisles she collected some much needed articles of clothing, bras, panties, a pair of shorts, two pairs of jeans and a few summer shirts. Then she headed to the shoe department for some sneakers and white socks, never once thinking about trying anything on.

Whizzing by the luggage section, she picked up a small, carry-on type suitcase and made her way to the toiletries section for a hair brush, dental floss, toothbrush and the like. The one last item she needed was a greeting card. After a few quick reads, she found one she liked and went to the check out.

She was grateful that the lines were very short and quickly went through the check out, paying cash just in case someone might have an interest in keeping track of her credit card purchases. Her bill was much cheaper than she thought it was going to be.

"Is it OK if I just put everything in this bag?" Jessica asked hading the cashier money.

"Sure can," the cashier replied, careful to demagnetize the protective strip on the bag. "There you go, you should be all set now," she said satisfied her work was complete.

"Great," Jessica replied, stuffing things inside while she waited for her change.

Hurrying out of the store, she jumped back into the cab and instructed the driver to take her to the nearest hotel. When they arrived, she grabbed her bag, collected her change and got herself a room.

Back at Brett's apartment, the police provided electronic gadgetry sat huddled together on his night stand as he prepared himself for what he hoped would be a decent night's rest. He knew it was probably wishful thinking. Brett was drained emotionally and physically from all that had transpired but his mind was racing, and unless he could shut it off, any kind of rest would prove to be elusive.

Walking in the bathroom he swung open the medicine chest knowing full well there was nothing in there to help him sleep. Picking up the box of a nighttime cold remedy, he read the label and thought about taking some. Somewhat reluctantly, he put it back, closed the door and went to the bedroom to lie down.

Fully clothed, he stared up at the ceiling. In the middle of his thought about calling Joyce Davenport to see if her offer for sleeping pills was still on the table, his body, desperate for the rest that only sleep could provide, did something that Brett couldn't do on his own—it shut everything down and he drifted off to sleep.

Detective Miller watched the last member of his team arrive and wasn't really all that surprised to see that she looked pretty upset about having to come in.

"If she's upset now," Brian said, moving his head to draw Hank's attention to the last arrival, "what I'm going to tell her will send her over the top."

"Shall we?" Brian asked Hank.

"There's no time like the present," Hank replied as both men stood up.

Brian introduced Hank and began to outline the situation to the four detectives. It was a little tough at first for his team to swallow the whole ESP/psychic thing, but by the time Brian was done everyone was a believer.

260

"Do we know anyone in the D.A.'s office that would be able to help us?" Brian asked, soliciting their input.

The consensus was unamimous and not surprising. The evidence, if you could call it that, wouldn't stand a chance in court. There wasn't even a chance to get this in front of a judge. Even if they could, the most junior public defender would be able to waltz his way to a dismissal with what they had.

"OK, Smoltz and Fredrickson are tailing this guy right now and from what I understand he's taking in a movie at the Brockton theater complex. We should be able to set up some perimeter surveillance by the time the movie is over and he leaves. Remember, no team tails him any longer than twenty minutes. If you even feel like you're being made, drop off, and call in another team. I want to remind everyone this is confidential and stays within our team."

Brian's last statement wasn't something he said very often and reserved for only the most delicate of situations. They knew Brian was one of them and wouldn't have asked them to give up their evening unless it was something very serious and time sensitive. Based on Brian's briefing, they knew someone's life was at stake and the initial disappointment about having to work through the night disappeared as they left for their cars.

27.

Frank's four a.m. wake-up call had him wishing that he had come straight back to the hotel instead of seeing a movie. The quality of the movie he saw wasn't worth the tiredness he tried to shake from his body as he slowly moved back the covers, sat up and put his feet on the floor.

Coffee was the first coherent thought that came to his mind. Wiping the sleep from his eyes, he yawned deeply, flipping on the cable news channel. Walking from the bed to a small coffee pot, a sliver of white paper stuck in his door caught the corner of his eye.

The questions as to what it was were quickly answered when he bent over to pick it up. Opening the envelope, he found a card that said "I'm So Sorry" on the front. Opening the card, he read the note that was folded inside.

Frank,

I can't tell you just how sorry I am. We are both in a lot of trouble. We have a mutual friend, Billy Smothers, that turned me in for my recreational cocaine habit and I guess told them a whole lot more. Some guys from the government picked me up about a month ago and told me you were a very dangerous man and unless I helped them, they were going to lock me up and throw away the key. I was so scared, Frank. I didn't know what to do. They made me give you the ring, Frank, and I need to tell you, it has some kind of tracking thing in it so they can watch you. I snuck away late last night and got the first flight back to Boston.

I don't think anyone followed me. I was scared to call you because I know they can listen.

Please forgive me, Frank. I know you probably hate me but I want to go away with you; it doesn't matter where. Please take me with you, Frank. I'm throwing my heart into your hands because I love you. I didn't realize it until this weekend so I had to do something to try and help you and hopefully help us.

I'll be at the Duck Boat launch at noon and I'll tell you everything I know. If I don't see you, I'll understand.

Forgive me, Frank...I DO love you!

Veronica

Anger grabbed on to every fiber of Frank's being and tugged away at him as hard as it could as he glanced at the ring on his finger. A rampage of emotions raced through his mind until his anger settled on Veronica. Having done it himself on a multitude of occasions, Frank knew all too well how his former colleagues could pinch people to get information and influence both their actions and behavior patterns.

His anger slowly shifted to whom he perceived the source of his troubles were. Slowly, his anger turned to outrage, outrage to hatred, and hatred to a need for revenge.

"Billy, you're going to go slow and painful if it's the last thing I do," he said. "In fact," his mind continued refusing to let it end there, "you will be my last job and the one I'll look forward to and enjoy the most!"

"I'm not sure what's in store for you, young lady," he mumbled as he read the note again trying to get himself under control.

Frank walked over to the bed and moved his hand under the covers like he was looking for something, casually slipped off the ring and left it there as he dressed. His mind drifted back to his agency days as he reran the entire Billy Smothers and Veronica scenario through his mind to try to determine what they wanted from him. It was pretty obvious, they didn't want to bring him in or that would have already happened. "They've got to know why I'm here, they're not stupid," he reminded himself, "So why all the hocus pocus to keep an eye on me?"

After a quick analysis, Frank categorized his current situation as something that would have been called in old agency terms "loose surveillance mode." You keep an eye on someone but from a pretty good distance, establish traffic patterns, behaviors and the like. Very similar in fact to Frank's map of Brett Allen's activities but on a much more sophisticated scale.

He could feel the birth pangs of panic begin to swell inside and walked back to the bed. "The room's probably been compromised," he told himself as he retrieved the ring and slid it back on his finger. "You've got to go through your normal routine and stay calm!" his mind told him.

Nonchalantly examining his room for any evidence of surveillance apparatus, he came up empty. Frank knew that just because there no visible indications, it didn't mean they weren't there. His hunt was after all exceptionally cursory so as not to alarm any possible on-lookers. Assuming the worst, Frank went into the bathroom, tossed his clothes on the floor, turned on the hot water and took a shower.

It didn't take very long for Frank to wash up and one good look at the bathroom told him there was enough moisture in the air for him to get started. Moving to the small vanity that sat next to the toilet and removing the drawer, Frank found the envelope he had duck taped to the underneath. Retrieving it, he examined the back and found the minute piece of transparent tape he had strategically placed on the very edge of the folding flap still intact.

Using the thick steam to provide a shroud of privacy, he closed the door and sat down on the toilet. He opened the envelope and took a quick inventory of his self-made emergency kit. A heavy sigh escaped as he started removing his French Passport, French and international driver's licenses, twenty crisp one hundred dollar bills, and a credit card—all carried the name of Francois Bedeau.

They went to a lot of trouble to put a tail on me, he thought, impressed by the obvious sophistication of the operation. *How could I have been so careless? One thing's for sure, I'll be visiting you, Billy, when I get out of this mess, you can count on it!*

Safely tucking the cash and credit card in his wallet, Frank gave the documents one last glance. Placing the passport and driver's licenses in his front pocket, Frank opened the door, dried off and got dressed. It was time to leave and he had no intention of ever returning.

So this is what it's like being hunted, Frank thought entering the hallway. A feeling of paranoia and panic started to rear its ugly head again and not without good reason.

This was totally new territory for him; usually he was the one doing the watching and planning, not the other way around. Panic could be a formidable enemy to clear thinking and Frank needed all of his wits right now. "Get this under control," he whispered, passing the ice and vending machines on his way to the elevators.

Pressing the call button summoned one of the two elevators that had parked themselves on the main floor. The familiar ding announced that his transportation had competed half of its trip and was now ready to accept him as a passenger. Frank was relieved when the door slid open, revealing an empty elevator car. Stepping inside, he reached over and punched the button for the main lobby. The doors quickly closed in response to his request and the elevator car started heading back to where it had just come from.

Feeling a little claustrophobic, he tugged at the already loose collar of his shirt, trying to somehow increase the size of his airway making it easier to breathe.

Relax, Frank, just relax, he thought, *everything will be fine if you don't lose your head.* Taking a few deep, deliberate breaths while the elevator moved downward helped him to clear his head and refocus on what he really needed to do, come up with a plan.

Moving coolly past the reservation desk, sure that surveillance cameras were covering the lobby, he noticed Janice sitting there passing the time with a book. Frank offered a wave on his way to the parking garage that caught Janice's eye. She looked up for just a moment, gave him a wave and smile in return and dove back into the book she was reading.

The hollow echo of footsteps accompanied Frank through the parking garage. With each step, Frank's desire to analyze the past twelve months grew stronger. Knowing that if he had the time to actually do it, he would uncover some mistakes that were made that ultimately resulted in this current dilemma. For now, that look into the past would have to wait.

Frank started the Audi and drove out of the garage. His first destination was the Nelson research facility. Keeping a watchful eye in his mirror, he noticed a set of very distant headlights come on and the vehicle pull out from its curbside parking space.

"Looks like I have a few new friends," Frank said to an empty passenger seat with just a touch of surprise and sarcasm. He couldn't imagine them putting a tail on him since he was obviously broadcasting his whereabouts. "I'll let you follow along…for now!"

The trip to Bedford was quiet and went by much faster than Frank anticipated. His mind was busy going through escape and evasion planning. Frank kept his eye on the vehicle behind him and noticed the switch in tail cars. "What a bunch of juveniles," he muttered under his breath as he closed in on his destination.

He had also been on the look out for a phone, a pay phone. Taking the round about way to Bedford brought him through several rural communities and afforded him the opportunity to scan gas stations, strip malls and such, looking for one. He could have used his cell phone but didn't want to risk a bad connection or possible disconnection.

It always seems to be feast or famine. Regardless of what you were looking for, when you want to find something you never can and when you aren't really looking, it's available in seemingly over abundance. This item on his mental to do list fell under the *never around when you need one* category. As soon as cell phones became affordable, pay phones went on the endangered species list. It seemed to that everywhere there should have been one, there wasn't and that really irritated him.

"There you are!" Frank exclaimed, pulling into large, all-purpose gas station where you could buy oil, magazine, milk, etc. Frank parked, walked over to the pay phone and removed the calling card from his wallet. His new friends pulled in and parked right in front. He watched them go into the store, probably to buy some coffee and kill some time until he was back on the road.

Quickly punching in the necessary numbers, he started to count the number of rings. After the tenth ring, he heard his answering machine pick up and started punching a sequence of eight numbers.

The answering machine served as a microphone and sent the touch tones traveling through his empty apartment while the transmitter/receiver sitting next to phone kept an attentive electronic ear. It was carefully listening and comparing the tones from the answering machine to the ones stored on its memory chip. Hesitating briefly before pushing the last digit, Frank thought about hanging up but it was too late to turn back now. There was nothing he could do at this point but finish what he had started and reluctantly pushed the last number.

A pulsating green light on the homemade device indicated it had a sequence match and was now functional. Almost as soon as the sequence was confirmed, a signal was sent across the room. In the guestroom closet, a very thin, almost hair-like wire, carried the signal from the receiver to a small explosive device it was attached to inside the safe. The small blast broke open three beaker shaped bottles that contained an acid that was just concentrated enough to destroy all the paper inside without burning through the safe itself.

Hanging up the phone, Frank said so long to the contents of the safe and found himself feeling somewhat relieved with the knowledge that everything in there that could even be remotely considered incriminating was now destroyed. The only other thing he had to do was to take care of his computer, but that would have to wait, although not very long.

Frank wasn't the only one who just finished a phone call. Brian Miller had just had an early morning conversation with Elias Flynn and based on their 5-minute conversation, Brian had called the team that was following who he know knew to be Frank Whickers, and told them to abort the mission immediately and return to police headquarters. Brian was more than wide awake and was hurrying to get ready for another day on the job. As the warm water from the shower washed over Brian he could only hope that he had not made a terrible mistake by having Frank followed. Brian agreed to meet Elias in an hour for a more in depth and detailed discussion about what was going on. Both men were very eager to get all the information on the table and begin to work together. "You might not know this, Michael, but calling you father may have just saved your son's life," he said, shutting off the water so he could dry off, get dressed and get to the station.

Frank stood next to the pole that held the pay phone and watched as the two men walked out of the store and much to his amazement drove off. *Hmmm,* he thought, *could I have been wrong about this? I've left my guard down for way too long, big mistake but no more!*

Getting back in his car, he surveyed the vehicles in the parking lot, all three of them, made a mental note of each one and continued his trip to the research facility.

Elias was upset that he hadn't received the tapes from the Pittsburgh bus station but was assured by the local office that they would have them by nine o'clock. Turning the corner, he parked right in front of police headquarters and grabbed his Frank Whickers dossier and made his way straight for Brian Miller's office.

Elias was greeted graciously this time by Brian and asked to take the seat next to Hank. As a good faith offering, Elias shared the information from Frank's file with both detectives while explaining the sophisticated resources they were using to keep an eye on him and their hope to reach the person or persons responsible for mobilizing Frank and his funding his current contract.

Brian in turn explained the entire situation, as he understood it, outlining the call from Joyce Davenport, the meeting with Brett and the entire hypnosis scenario. Elias listened intently with a touch of amazement and a lot of skepticism as Brian told the story and how it led to the fingerprint operation that brought them together yesterday. When Brain showed the composite sketch from the information Brett Allen had provided after his hypnotic session his skepticism was replaced with awe.

"I've got to tell you, Detective Miller, and you, Detective Beard, that when you started filling me in, I thought you were both a little over the edge. Now, I believe your story and welcome any way that we can help each other on this." Elias sat thoughtfully then outlined his opinion and request. "The organ transplant theory is fascinating and I was wondering if we could arrange a meeting with Mr. Allen and the doctors that formulated it and performed the hypnosis. I'd really like to ask them some questions."

"I think I can arrange that for *us*," Brian said, wanting to make sure Elias got the message that they were going to stay involved.

"Great," Elias said opening his cell phone. Using the radio feature of his cell phone so that everyone present could hear and too demonstrate his good faith, he punched in Trevor's radio code. "Trevor, what's Frank Whickers current location?"

"He's nosing around the research center right now as we expected. Everything appears, at least at this point to be normal," Trevor answered back.

"Great!" Elias answered back and turned to the detectives. "Apparently he either didn't make your surveillance team or you called them off just in time for him to question if he was actually being tailed."

"Just an FYI," they all heard as Trevor chimed in again "We think he should be stopping for breakfast soon, just like he did his last trip, then head back toward the hotel. If all that happens, I think we can breathe a little easier."

"Understood," Elias said, confirming Trevor's radio message.

"I think it would be a good idea," Elias said, "if you and your detectives joined us at our operations center at let's say 9:30 so we can fully brief one another and put a plan together that will protect Mr. Allen and lead us the financier."

"Alright, Agent Flynn, consider us there!" Brian said.

Elias gave them the location, shook their hands and paused at the door of Brian's office before he left. "It's going to be good working with you on this. I think we can really help each other!"

"Sounded sincere to me," Hank said to Brian as he watched Elias disappear around the corner.

Brian agreed, "Me too, sounds like they've got a really sophisticated setup. This is one bad apple were after. I've got to agree with him, we need to get the person at the top. If we don't, whoever it is will just send somebody else after Brett. I'm thinking that for the next twenty-four hours, we can break the rules and bring this guy in."

Brain looked over at Hank picking up the phone "The law is supposed to protect the innocent, not put them in danger."

After finishing his breakfast, Frank made his way toward the city. It was a little after nine a.m. so he knew they would be open when he got there. Turning the corner he spotted the library and quickly pulled in. Walking in the front entrance, Frank could almost feel the silence and he welcomed the calming effect it had on him. It was a good-sized library with more than its fair share of large oak study tables that stood amidst the rows upon rows of books.

Frank imagined that when the local universities were in session, this place would be bursting at the seams with young adults from all walks of life cramming for tests, completing research to finish a thesis, and the like. This was the middle of the summer however, and aside from the librarian and a few people looking for an obscure book, the place was empty.

Frank walked over to the young librarian seated at the desk placing the cards in the recently returned books and asked here where the internet capable computers were. Responding to his question, she simply pointed down toward the stairway that apparently led to a basement level and the computers.

Going down the stairs, he saw a mirror image of the floor he had just left. The only exception was a different librarian and a glass walled room that comfortably housed four computers.

Frank sat down at the terminal facing away from the librarian. She probably wouldn't understand what he was about to do but he wasn't taking any chances especially now. Frank typed in www.franks911.com and went to his self-constructed web site. The site loaded quickly and the under construction announcement scrolled across the screen. The web site hadn't changed since he built it a few years ago.

There were several large icons placed symmetrically on the page and one very small button located inconspicuously in the bottom left hand corner of the monitor. Frank clicked it and waited for a response. Entering his password at the prompt, he hit enter and waited again. A second dialogue popped up and asked for another password that he quickly entered. "Third time's the charm," he whispered as he was asked again to enter a password. Leaning around the monitor, he shot a quick glance at the librarian and found her still sitting at the desk engrossed in whatever it was she was doing. He entered the last password and prepared for the final question which asked for his favorite animal—typing in the word *cherry pie* he hit the enter button.

"Come on," Frank said anxiously, watching the words *establishing link* continuing to flash on the monitor as the software he had written accessed the computer in his Chicago apartment.

It took about ten seconds for, *Link Established—System Validated—*

Commence 911 Procedure?, to pop up on the monitor. Frank hit the letter Y and entered his final password. The entire process was now irreversible and would run on its own. Frank closed the website and erased his internet trail from the computer he was using. Once that procedure was finished the computer would reformat the hard drive and install a totally different operating system.

Frank headed for downtown with the initial steps of his evasion plan completed. He kept wondering what they wanted with him and why they hadn't moved in on him yet. If they wanted him dead, he was sure it would have happened already so it had to be something else. "They had Veronica keeping an eye on me for some time," Frank said, starting to think it through a little more "What was it they wanted and why were they waiting?" He wished he had time to think more about it but there were more important things that required his immediate attention to take care of so he pushed that question and its entire accompanying mind set to the back of his mind.

Walking had always been his remedy of choice for stress and a good brisk walk was just what the doctor ordered. Approaching the outskirts of the city, Frank began looking for a place to pull over and park, take a quick walk to clear his head then move on with the next step of his plan. He started thinking about Veronica again. She had alerted him that he was being followed, that was true, but the magnitude of deception she had been a part of really concerned him.

Replaying moments in his mind of times they had spent together with the knowledge it was all big lie, including the past weekend, was like lighting a match and tossing it into a gasoline-soaked wood pile. Anger quickly ignited and spread to ever fiber of his being. Even he was surprised by the swiftness and intensity of his fury and how easily it overpowered him. "Never make important decisions when you're angry," he said checking his rearview mirror for potential tails. "I can grill her when I pick her up!" Pretty certain he was, at least for the moment, not dragging someone behind him, he pulled into an open parking spot on the passenger side of the street.

The car rocked back and forth a little as Frank brought the Audi to an abrupt stop. Neglecting to check his side mirror, he hastily swung the door open to get out and was greeted by the screeching of tires and the wail of someone's horn. A car swerved by barely avoiding a collision and taking the driver side door off. "Whew," he said aloud, trying to swallow his heart and send it back where it came from, "that was close!"

Looking at the car that had almost hit him, he could see the driver tilting his head to get a good a view from his mirror. A hand went quickly up in the air and although Frank was too far away to see fine detail, he had a real good idea of the intended message.

"I don't blame you one bit," Frank said, checking his side mirror. "That was a pretty stupid thing for me to do!"

Carefully checking his mirror and finding no oncoming cars, he opened the door and stepped out. Closing the door, still feeling a little nervous from narrowly avoiding an accident, Frank took another look down the street just to double check and make sure no one was coming. Seeing just a few parked cars, he made his way toward the back of the car and onto the sidewalk. The tall buildings on the somewhat distant horizon marked Boston's core, and that was the direction Frank started to walk.

I've really got to be careful, he thought as he edged closer to the city one step at a time. *If I don't watch it the biggest enemy I'll face will end up being myself. I've got the advantage here and not only am I going to slip away from under their noses I'm going to finish what I came here to do. That ought to leave them with a lot of questions to answer when this is all over.*

Frank's inner voice reared its ugly head once again telling him not to mess around with Veronica or finishing the job. It told him to get out of Dodge just as soon as he possibly could. Frank's ample amount of pride had been bruised, however, and the only way to show them he was still the best was to do the job right in front of them and then just disappear into thin air and that's exactly what he intended to do.

Standing on the street corner still, he glanced at the ring on his finger and wondered how many people were involved in keeping an eye on him and how long it would take to realize they had fallen for the ruse he had planned from them.

It was time to put the third step of his plan into action, deciding what to do with his now unwanted piece of jewelry. At first, he considered dropping it on a young mover and shaker type. The kind of person whose personal philosophy closely mirrored the old adage *a rolling stone gathers no moss.* Someone that didn't stay in one place too long and always had places to go, people to meet, and things to do.

The only potential problem was what the person would do when they found a ring in their pocket that didn't belong to them. Worse yet, what if they didn't find it and it got left in a set of clothes hanging in someone's closet. The tracking device would become stationary for way too long. It was of the utmost importance that the ring be mobile for quite awhile, the longer the better. If he could get the feds looking the other way long enough, he could perhaps lose them, slip silently into obscurity, get the job done and be gone before they knew what happened. Frank continued on his way toward the city and had gone about a quarter of a mile when it finally came to him.

He started down the street with one purpose in mind, finding a homeless person. Giving the ring to a homeless person would almost be an act of charity. Veronica's so-called gift would be traded for money to obtain alcohol, food, drugs or a combination of the three. It was sad even for a guy like Frank to think about it but he knew there were plenty of people willing to take advantage of just about anyone for personal gain, even a homeless person. Frank was far from a saint and knew he would also be taking advantage of the situation, and his survival instinct quickly erased any momentary compassion.

It would take an hour maybe two for the jewelry to exchange hands. If the person receiving it had half a brain they would take it somewhere and get it appraised. That could happen within hours but more likely would take place tomorrow. He was hoping that the new ring bearer would want to show it off a little and keep their newly acquired treasure handy to corroborate the embellished story that would undoubtedly accompany it. That was the scenario Frank hoped for but wouldn't count on. What he really hoped for was a minimum of a three-hour distraction to throw off what he guessed were some of his former colleagues.

Continuing to walk, he kept a wary eye out for potential candidates and noticed that his pace had quickened, probably from the adrenalin. Frank didn't want to give anything away to prying eyes and consciously shortened his stride to slow down some. Apparently finding a homeless person wasn't going to be as easy as he thought so he stopped dead in is tracks and waited for someone to walk by.

Stopping the next person he saw, Frank explained that he was trying to find the nearest homeless shelter was so he could see about volunteering some of his time there and was hopeful he could get directions. Finally, on about the fifth passerby, he was able to find someone that could tell him he was about eight blocks away.

Eight blocks wasn't that far away but he needed the car nearby so he could somehow pull off a switch. That meant he had to walk four blocks south to get in his car, negotiate Boston's one way streets, and end up at the soup kitchen. Even for a Boston native, that task could prove to be pretty challenging.

Frank thanked the young man who gave him directions and started walking over to the car. He really needed this whole thing to go smooth and quick if he hoped to put some distance between himself and the people following him. When he got to the car he took a quick glance at his surroundings looking for anything that might be different than when he parked there not to long ago. He opened the door and stood for a minute to let the heat escape before getting in. Reaching into his pocket, he grabbed his notebook to write down the address of the soup kitchen and some of the landmarks he should look for along the way.

Walking back, he got into the car and pulled out, paying special attention to the rear view mirror and looking for anything that even remotely resembled a tail. Frank assumed since he was still transmitting his location to someone and that the investigative direction as it pertained to him called for a loose surveillance mode and he wouldn't have anyone too close. He was also pretty hopeful his assumption was correct. It might be his only chance to dump the ring and get a new vehicle

Just the same he wasn't going to take any chances and decided to make the trip an adventurous one. If there was anyone trying to follow him they'd stick out like a sore thumb. He turned around and headed back to a gas station that he had passed earlier to see if he could get a detailed city map. The one he had in the car wasn't a street map of the city and he wanted more detail if he could get it. When he got back to the station, he wasn't disappointed.

After buying the map he hoped would unlock the secrets of Boston's one way streets, he sat in his air-conditioned Audi and began to figure out his route. His finger would move over the thin lines that represented roads and one way streets until it reached an intersection. His finger stopped moving and he wrote down the street names and the direction he should turn in his notebook. Frank repeated the process until it was all written down on paper that way he wouldn't have to try and carefully examine the map while driving.

Frank's route analysis led him to a design that resembled a rough outline of a horseshoe. It wasn't the most direct way nor was it designed to be. If anyone was tailing him, this route would make it obvious. The limited directional access to the streets he would be traveling eliminated the possibility of any tag team followers and would result in one of two outcomes, the person following would be discovered or in order to avoid detection, they would have to give up.

Comfortable with the trail his finger had blazed across the map, it was time to get to the soup kitchen, shelter, and food pantry. Hopefully, he would able to find someone quickly, dump the ring and begin the disappearing act. Frank was getting closer to his destination and started to feel a lot more comfortable.

"What do you know?" Frank mumbled to himself checking his mirrors again and seeing nothing suspicious. "Looks like I finally caught a break!"

If someone was following him, they weren't following close enough to worry him and making his charitable donation should go undetected until it was too late.

Frank's mind drifted across the Atlantic to the house he had in Southern France and now regretted ever coming back to the United States. It wasn't that he liked France all that much, it was just plain easier to hide in their society. Being fluent in the language and the way he dressed while there helped him blend in. Even the French people he met didn't know he was an American so they treated him with dignity and respect.

"I'm going back there when this is over," Frank told himself, negotiating the last intersection of his trip, "I'll spend rest of my life eating crepe suzettes and drinking wine as Frank Bedeau. There *are* worse lots in life."

Still a block away, Frank took his foot off the gas and started scanning the street for a place to park. He would park a ways away from the shelter and walk over; if he was lucky he'd find someone on the way over and get the ball rolling. Seeing a break between two cars, Frank started to pull in and suddenly saw a motorcycle parked in what he thought was an empty spot.

"That should be illegal!" he said, continuing down the street. "There's no way they should be allowed to park there and take up an entire space!"

Just getting the car back up to a reasonable driving speed he noticed another potential parking spot and halfheartedly approached fully prepared to see another motorcycle. Pleasantly surprised to find it was really empty, he started the parallel parking ordeal. Frank was really good at this as he pulled up even with car that would be parked in front of him when this was over. Frank didn't need the typical back and forth final adjustments used by novices to complete a good parking job. He simply turned the wheel hard right then left as he backed in.

"Perfect," Frank said, surveying the distance between the car in front of and behind him. Not bothering to straighten out the steering wheel, he shut off the car, checked his side mirror twice and got out.

Frank slid the ring off is finger and put it in his pants pocket, his eyes scanning the surroundings for potential recipients. Not familiar with the shelters schedule Frank concluded, and correctly so, that the type of person he was looking for would be lingering around the area even after the breakfast meal had been served.

As Frank neared the shelter, he could start to see smattering of just what he was looking for. Now the trick was to try and pick the healthiest person. The thought being that the better shape the person was in, the more likely they would be to take the ring a greater distance and increase the value of the sale or trade. He wanted someone who could physically do it and was also smart enough to know that walking to more affluent part of town would be well worth it. This would increase the likelihood of the keeping the device moving and not raising any suspicions.

Frank examined a few people that were hanging around a newspaper box across the street and decided that the taller of the two gentlemen would be his preferred choice. Frank whistled over to get their attention and both men looked over, a little startled.

Pointing to the taller man, Frank waved for him to come over. The man on the other side of the street pointed to his chest questioning if he was the one being summoned and got nodded confirmation. Before crossing the street he mumbled something to his buddy who leaned over the newspaper box as if he let Frank now he was keeping an eye on him.

As the man crossing the street got closer, the smell coming from his body got stronger. It was like every pore on his body was trying to eradicate layers of the pungent odor that came from weeks if not months of neglect. Frank was surprised that even being outside he could smell the approaching individual well before he made it all the way across the street.

"What do you want?" asked the homeless man, looking slightly down at Frank.

Frank looked directly at the man and could tell despite his homeless situation that there was an active and aware mind just behind the clear blue eyes looking down at him.

"I want to give you something. I have a ring," Frank explained pulling it out of his pocket so the man could see it, "that was given to me by someone I thought was a very special person in my life. As it turns out she was just using me," he continued, noticing his roadside companion looking at the ring in his hand.

"At first, I was so mad I almost threw it away, then I was going to take it to a pawn shop and get some cash for it but I thought I might as well try and do something good at least once in my life so here I am," Frank said finishing his hard luck story.

"Look, man, that looks like a pretty expensive ring. Why not pawn it yourself? Is it stolen or something?" he asked suspiciously.

Frank couldn't believe he had to play twenty questions with this guy. "No, it's not stolen and I don't need the money. I was just trying to help someone, that's all, and that someone just turned out to be you. If you don't want it, I'll walk over to the shelter. I was on my way there anyway and I'll give it to them or someone else who might want it, either way I don't really care."

"No, I'll take it. I just don't want to get in trouble. Just look at me," he said. "I'm in enough trouble right now. It would really help me out," he said thankfully, extending his hand.

Frank put the ring gently into the palm of his outstretched hand and closed the stranger's fingers around it. "OK it's yours. By the way, when do they serve lunch at the shelter?"

"Oh, they start serving lunch right after the twelve o'clock whistle goes off," the stranger answered. "Today, we're having pea soup with ham and cheese sandwiches but I'm going to miss it. I'm taking this ring into town. There's a place I know that'll give me a good price for this. How can I ever thank you?"

"No need to thank *me*?" Frank replied. "Is the place you know far from here, can I get you a cab or something?"

"It's not far," the stranger answered back, "maybe take an hour to get there and it gives me something to do other than sit around here all day. I better get started, thanks again, mister."

Frank watched the guy make his way back to his friend standing guard at the newspaper box. They started talking and both looked over at Frank, who could only imagine what they were saying. He could tell they were examining the ring and talking with amazement about the good fortune that had came their way. Suddenly both men looked up again, offering a quick wave as they turned and headed off together toward the center of the city to trade in the ring for some cash at *the place he knew*. Frank was also grateful for the time line he had gotten from the man now carrying Veronica's ring.

"Hi, this is Jason Galloway," he declared, using his cell phone. "I'm over near the homeless shelter on the west end of town. I think it's called the Boston Outreach Center. Can you send a cab right away? I'm in a hurry."

"Are you at the Outreach Center now?" the emotionless voice asked.

"No, but I can see it so I'll start walking towards it," Frank said feeling into his back pocket to make sure he still had his notebook.

"Well I have a cab that's almost there; maybe five minutes."

"Just tell him to wait if he gets there before me" Frank told the dispatcher as his paced quickened. "Jason Galloway, tell him to wait for Jason Galloway."

"OK, OK Jason Galloway don't worry, I'll have him wait," the dispatcher said seemingly a touch annoyed as he abruptly hung up the phone.

Frank walked back to car and drove it over to the shelter and pulled around

276

back, parking in a spot labeled volunteer. Taking a glance to his left he saw the proud new owner of an almost brand new gentleman's ring/tracking device and his friend turn the corner and disappear behind a building.

Good timing, Frank thought feeling a little more comfortable with things. Walking to the front of the building, he watched the cab slowly come to a stop.

"I'm Jason Galloway!" he said as the window came down.

"That's nice," the cabbie replied, "were you the one that called for a cab?"

"Yes I did," Frank said not all that surprised the dispatcher didn't give the driver any instructions, "I need to rent a car."

"Hop in," the cabbie said.

"You've basically got two choices. I can take you to the airport if you want a name brand company or you can go to a local company about a half a mile from here called Rent a Clunker. Their cars are fine; they just use the name to draw attention to their low prices."

"I'd prefer whatever is closest and will take the least amount of time," Frank answered, anxious to put some distance between himself and the transmitter he just got rid of.

"OK," the cabbie said, making a U turn "Rent a Clunker here we come."

Rent a Clunker looked just like any of the other car rental companies. A relatively small square building that sat in the middle of a decent sized parking lot. A few attendants were stationed behind the rental counter waiting for a customer to break the monotony of their day, and when Frank walked in both attendants looked at him hopeful that the new customer would come to their name plate that sat atop the counter.

Frank recognized what was going on and went to the person farthest from the front door, figuring that the attendant whose work area was closest probably got all the business.

"Good morning," Frank said with an obvious sense of urgency in his voice, "I need a rental."

"Good morning" the young attendant responded, "What type of vehicle did you have in mind?"

"Nothing in particular as long as it's not a big car," Frank responded.

"We have two and four door economy sedans that were renting for twenty dollars a day, with unlimited mileage," the young man offered.

Frank started pulling the driver's license and credit card of Jason Galloway from his wallet. He had stolen the identity of this person about six months ago just for an occasion such as this. "That would be good," Frank said putting his Jason Galloway's driver's license and credit card on the counter.

"Let me see, I need this," the attendant said, looking over and taking the driver's license.

"All right, Mr. Galloway. Would you like the weekly rental I mentioned for twenty dollars a day with unlimited mileage," the attendant asked. "Oh and before I forget, I would you like full insurance coverage?"

Frank just wanted to hurry up, get the car and get out of there. "Yes the one week special and full insurance," he said not wanting to waste the time it would take for the sales person to go over all the details.

The attendant had finished filling in the empty spaces on the rental contract and started to explain some the areas he would have to read an initial. Frank waved his hand telling the young man he was all set and initialed by each "x" and signed the agreement. Frank exchanged the signed contract for his documents and complimentary map of Boston.

"Shall I bring the car to the front for you?" the attendant offered.

"No thank you. If you point it out to me, I'll go over and get it," Frank said politely refusing the offer and taking the keys.

The young man pointed to a car through the showcase style window. "It's the forest green sedan parked right over there."

"Ah yes. Thank you," Frank said as he walked away to get in his new car.

Frank could tell as soon as he got behind the wheel that this wasn't a luxury model. The seats were a little on the uncomfortable side with no way to adjust them for back support and the like. Closing the door, he didn't get that familiar solid well built car feeling nor was the interior anything to marvel over but was grateful just the same that he hadn't wasted too much time.

Frank headed back the way along the same route the cab had used to deliver him the rental center. Driving just past the shelter, he turned down the driveway leading to the large parking lot in the back. The exit would have been considered inconvenient for most but suited Frank's purpose nicely. The exit led to a small one way street that apparently fed into a larger artery somewhere to the east of the building.

"This is a good thing here," Frank said continuing to survey the parking lot as pulled in next to the Audi. He couldn't help glancing over at the barely visible news box where his homeless friend had been standing not that long ago wondering how far along he was on his journey and more importantly how his new merchandise would end up when it got there.

Completing a quick visual survey and seeing nothing suspicious, Frank opened the trunk of both cars and quickly transferred his equipment into the trunk of the rental. Taking one last look around the parking lot, he closed the trunks of both cars, hopped into the forest green four-door sedan and drove out.

Like a snake shedding its old skin, Frank was feeling like he had a new life. Driving out of the shelter parking lot, he knew he had successfully scraped away the suffocating blanket of surveillance that had been wrapped around him.

"Now for the final touch," Frank said. Hooking up his hands free unit, he punched in 411 on his cell phone.

28.

The morning had been full of surprises for a lot of people and Brett quickly found out he had a few of his own to deal with. He had a solid, dreamless night of sleep that he was very grateful for and was anxious to get into work so he could start pulling his research material from Nelson's computer system. Brett had thought about several ways to get the information past security before settling on the method that Russell Craft had used.

Looking at the picture of his mother he had on his desk he reached into the drawer, grabbed a legal pad and headed over to check the Petri dishes marked Cytanepax 23. This time the notes he recorded would be leaving with him.

He had almost forgotten that Becky was supposed to me meet him and get his key at lunch time. He called her apartment, not surprised to get the answering machine at his hour of the morning and left a message that he wasn't going be able to meet her and he'd call later in afternoon.

Making his way through the lab, he struggled to focus on his work. Despite his best efforts to remain strong and positive, the events of the past week were starting to take its toll. Doubts about seeing his 26th birthday that he had so successfully avoided started swirling around in his head like vultures in the desert.

"Stop feeling sorry for yourself and don't give up," the voice inside his head said in a firm scolding manner. "You've got a lot to look to look forward too so don't lie down now. There are 27 outs in a baseball game and the game's never over until the last out is made. No forfeits! So pull yourself together and let's get on with it."

"Easy for you to say!" he replied audibly, half expecting the conversation to continue.

Brett pulled one his Cytanepax 23 dishes from the incubator, extracted some material and put it ever so carefully on a slide. With the stage clips holding the specimen firmly in place, Brett peered into the ocular. A smile broke out on his face as he peered down at the molecular world below. The white blood cell activity was normal, in fact everything appeared normal. The two different organ and tissue types were coexisting in perfect harmony.

Jumping up and down like a little boy who'd just gotten the birthday present he had always wanted, Brett forced himself away from the table. Moving slowly back to take another look, hoping what he had seen wasn't an apparition, he confirmed it—Cytanepax 23 had worked.

Brett quickly began recording information trying his best not to write so fast the he wouldn't be able to read it. This was a monumental breakthrough. His excitement and optimism were running at full speed which was the perfect medicine to extricate those vultures, at least temporarily.

"Wow!" he exclaimed with a touch of disbelief. "I did it, I actually did it!"

Knowing full well that lab results were often different than those obtained using living specimens, he was extremely excited and anxious to move into that phase. He thought about Russell Crafts' experiments and was certain that he could incorporate that work into his own.

"I should be able to fast track this," he said, walking back to his desk.

He picked up the phone and peeked at the clock, 9:15 a.m. As he was sure that Jeff Dalton would be there he punched in his number.

"Good morning, Jeff, it's Brett."

"Hi, Brett, what time is it?" Jeff asked.

"It's quarter after nine. Did you spend the night there?" Brett asked to confirm his suspicion.

"Sure did," Jeff confessed, "I was so excited that I couldn't sleep, so why not. I've already started the validation process and what little I've been able to get through looks good, better than good in fact. In about an hour, the department heads will be here for a meeting. Looks like were going to suspend some of the other projects were working on and focus on this."

"Great!" Brett replied enthusiastically.

"We're going to move as fast as we can without sacrificing thoroughness. Can I arrange a time when you can stop over?" Jeff asked. "Everyone wants to talk with you about this."

"Now is just not the right time," Brett responded. "Hopefully sometime early next week. I'll call you near the end of the week and maybe we can coordinate something then, would that be OK?"

"OK, Brett, I'll wait to hear from you and fill you in on our meeting when I do," Jeff Dalton said, the excitement in his voice still very evident.

Brett turned to his computer terminal as he hung up the phone, punching in his username and password to access his data. Maneuvering the arrow with the mouse, he clicked on the file C22 to access the information from his previous experiment. What he got back was a bunch of machine code that had transformed his meticulous documentation into a series of incomprehensible numbers and symbols.

A worried "Uh oh" escaped from Brett's lips as he recalled that Russell Craft had lost access to his work shortly before his execution.

"We're working on it, Dr. Allen. Some sort of virus managed its way through our firewall protection. It's attacking our network and file servers. We can't even access our stored data, that's how serious this is. Our disaster recovery and security people are doing their best. I can't tell you any more than that right now and we have no idea of when we'll be back to 100%," the voice from the company's help desk department explained.

That wasn't what Brett wanted to hear and he knew this couldn't be explained away as coincidence. Turning back to his desk, he started to record from memory everything he could. When lunch time rolled around, he would try and get his research information past security and into the hands of Jeff Dalton. *I might be seeing you sooner than we both expected,* he thought as his pencil feverishly made its way across the paper.

Brian Miller, Hank Beard and detective Salazar got out of the car and started walking to the operations center entrance, each one carrying a leather portfolio.

"Amazing what can happen when you get politicians involved," Hank commented.

"Yeah, I'll bet Agent Flynn has a lot more riding on this now than just brining this guy in. If he succeeds he's a hero, if he fails and the senator's grandson isn't protected, his career is over, maybe ours too! I'm very interested to see what he has in mind," Brian said in response.

Reaching the door, they were greeted by a gentleman that must have walked right out of a recruiting poster. "Follow me please," was all he said and led them to the briefing room.

Much in the same way a tourist examines the surroundings of a new place, so were the three police detectives. It seemed like their heads were on swivels as they looked around with awe. Each of them stopped dead in their tracks when they saw the large display screen.

"Gentleman, please follow me!" their escort said firmly. "Special Agent Flynn will take you through the center once your meeting is over."

Brian and his group obliged him and were seated in the empty briefing room. As they were waiting for Elias Flynn, special agents Andrew Campbell and Francine Kelly joined them and sat down. After exchanging a few social pleasantries, an uncomfortable silence hung in the air until Elias walked into the room.

"Good morning, Detective, sorry I'm late," Elias said noticing it was 9:45. "I assume that we've all met each other and that you're eager to get started. I just got off the phone with Todd Abraham and we've been ordered to pick up Frank Whickers."

Glancing over at Andy and Francine, he could see the concern written all over their faces and continued to explain the sudden shift in direction. "It's important for everyone in this room to know that the target is a scientist by the name of Brett Allen, who just so happens to be the grandson of Senator George Allen. We now believe that we have sufficient evidence to bring him in on drug trafficking charges."

Francine glanced over at Andy from the corner of her eye knowing full well they didn't *really* have sufficient evidence to support that charge and the big boys from DC had just given their blessing for Elias to be *creative*.

"We have in our custody a man by the name of Billy Smothers," Elias said, continuing his explanation, "who is prepared to testify that Frank has purchased large quantities of heroin and cocaine. We'll be working with the US Attorney's office in Boston on this and I'm told we already have their full support."

"Excuse me, Agent Flynn. Can I talk you with you for a minute?" he heard Trevor's voice behind him.

"Excuse me," Elias said to group and followed Trevor to his console, "What is it, TT?"

"We have a behavioral abnormality. Let me give you the last twenty minutes," he said moving his fingers across the keyboard. "Looks like he's been walking for quite awhile."

"And?" Elias asked looking for a better explanation.

"He hasn't spent more than ten minutes walking anywhere. I didn't notice until the computer alerted me either," Trevor said, slightly disappointed with his performance.

"Get Tack 2 in the air right away and I want Tack 1 on tarmac alert! How long until our ground units are at his location?" Elias asked anxiously looking at the agent overlay.

"Two minutes," Trevor replied. "Tack 2, this is operations. This is an emergency scramble, I repeat an emergency scramble. Coordinates are being sent to your onboard systems now. Scramble, Scramble, Scramble! Tack 1, this is operations. Your status is now tarmac alert, I repeat tarmac alert."

As the pilot and copilot ran to the chopper, Trevor punched in the necessary information to provide Tack 2 with a direct feed so they could have real time target information. Just as Trevor finished punching in the codes, two more alerts popped up. The pilot of Tack 1 walked to his airplane where he would sit ready to take off until he heard otherwise.

"What is going on?" Elias urgently demanded to know.

"Two more alerts," Trevor quickly answered, moving to the alert console. "Credit card activity, he just booked a flight from Logan to O'Hare that leaves in twenty minutes; he also chartered a small plane from an airport in Framingham to Seattle with a scheduled departure of 10:30."

Elias's heart sunk to the bottom of his shoes. "Bait," he said.

"What?" Trevor asked. "What do you mean bait?"

"We've lost him, Trevor, he's gone! He's sending us in opposite directions, spreading our resources thin so he can slip away."

Elias watched the events unfold on the agent overlay as his units closed in on Frank's signal. *I hope I'm wrong about this,* Elias thought watching his three units tighten the noose.

Three vehicles came to a screeching halt as they surrounded the two homeless men. Jumping out their cars, and they drew their guns using the open doors as protective shields.

"Freeze!" one of the agents yelled.

Stopping at once, they looked at each other with fear as the agents approached. They were pushed up against the closest building and frisked. Finding no weapons, the agents backed up a bit and told the two men to empty their pockets. Everyone heard the ting when the ring bounced off the pavement.

"When did you get this?" one of the agents asked, moving in to pick up the ring.

"I don't know exactly. Maybe an hour ago maybe less, I don't have a watch and neither does my friend. This guy in an Audi just pulls up near the shelter and gives it to me. He told me he wanted to do something nice. He gives me the ring and tells me to pawn it because the girl that gave it him broke his heart. I knew I shouldn't have believed him. He told me it wasn't stolen, honest!"

"Relax, you're not in any trouble!" the agent said, grabbing a radio. "Operations, this is unit 2…. he's gone, we've been decoyed. He dropped the ring on a couple of homeless people and told them to take it to a pawn shop. They were on their way there when we stopped them. Looks like he might have as much as an hour head start on us."

"Roger 2… Stand by," Elias said to his field unit. "Trevor, go into the briefing room and bring them some coffee or something, apologize for my absence and tell them I'll be there as soon as I can."

"OK," Trevor said unable to hide his disappointment at being outsmarted by Frank Whickers, he went to deliver Elias's message.

"Operations, this is 2…I'm afraid that's all the information we're going to be able to get; they didn't see him leave."

"Roger, 2. Let those guys go. I want *you* back here. Send one in your group over to Logan and have the other get started on their way to Framingham. I'll have Trevor contact everyone with details in a few minutes."

"Copy."

Brian met Trevor at the door to the briefing room. He had had one cup of coffee too many and it was time for a bathroom break. He couldn't see completely around the corner but what he saw told him something pretty substantial was underway. The number of different voices and tones he heard reminded him of a large cocktail party.

"What's going on?" Brian asked "Seems like someone turned on the light switch in there!"

"Yeah…we're a little busy right now," Trevor said, admitting the obvious. "Agent Flynn will be in just as soon as he can and brief the group so if you would kindly go back and have a seat, I'd be happy to bring you and the members of your team some coffee or tea."

"I actually need a bathroom," Brian said.

"Right over there," Trevor said, pointing to a door not far away.

He must have made the tail Miller had on him and then tied in the ring, which also means he knows about Veronica and most likely has connected her to us. Those are the assumptions I'd make, he thought, trying to put the pieces of his broken operation together.

"All set, boss!" Trevor said, returning from the briefing room.

"Thanks. I want to know the name of every car rental outfit within a thirty-mile radius of the drop point. He's probably changed vehicles once if not twice already. I've got unit 2 headed back here. Check in with 1 and 3 and give them the applicable details about Framingham and Logan. I'm going to see if we can mobilize some local support."

"I'll have the information you need in a flash," Trevor said, trying to show some enthusiasm.

"I know you will, Trevor, but I really need it quicker than that. And where are my Pittsburgh tapes?" Elias asked getting up to go back to the briefing room.

"We should have had the Pittsburgh tapes already. I'll turn the heat on over there!" Trevor assured him.

"All the way up, Trevor," Elias said as emphatically as he walked away. "Turn it all the way up!"

Elias entered the briefing room and was annoyed that Miller wasn't there. Just as he was getting ready to start, Brian reappeared and took his seat.

"I have some bad news," Elias said in an even, composed tone. "We've lost him." Careful not to implicate Brian Miller or his team, he continued cautiously. "I'm not sure what went wrong but earlier this morning he handed over our clever tracking device to a couple of vagrants and gave us the slip.

"He has about an hour's head start on us so we believe that he has changed vehicles once, maybe even twice by now. We're compiling a list of every car rental company within a thirty-mile radius. Detective Miller, would it be possible to get some manpower support from your department?"

"Absolutely," Brian answered without hesitation. "I'd like to suggest that we call them all first to see if anyone has rented vehicles between the hours of nine and ten. If we get a few hits we can try and get a description over the phone. It hasn't been that long ago and people aren't in the habit of renting cars at this hour so we should be able to cover a lot of territory without ever leaving the precinct."

Elias concurred with Miller's assessment and action plan. "Excellent idea, as soon as Trevor gets me my list, I'll turn it over to you so you can disseminate it to your people. Now would be a good time for us to start sharing information so we can determine the investigative direction we should take from this point going forward. I'll go ahead and begin then answer any questions. After that, we'll let the detectives have the floor."

"Before you get started Agent Flynn," Brian said temporarily interrupting him, "I've gone ahead and coordinated the meeting you asked about this morning. We have to be at Joyce Davenport's office at 4:00."

Andy and Francine exchanged a quick glance when they heard that name and it spiked their curiosity. Just the fact that Elias had them at the operations center told the two agents that they knew some pretty important information.

Elias shook his head in thanks and acknowledgment. "Are they any questions before I get started?"

"Since we are assuming that Frank Whickers knows we're here," Andy said framing his question, "do you think it would be a good idea to let him know in very tangible ways that we intend to take every measure possible to protect Mr. Allen?"

"I'm not sure I understand exactly what you mean," Elias said, perplexed by Andy's question.

"Things like putting police tape in the wooded area around Bedford or placing his picture on local television to mobilize the public. Maybe we should consider placing Brett in protective custody."

"Those are some good thoughts," Elias replied, "and do warrant further consideration. Let's get through this briefing first to see what we have as a group. Then I think we should revisit your suggestions and decide on an appropriate course of action once we have a better look at the big picture. Is there anything else?"

Everyone was sitting quietly in their places with pens and pencils ready. Taking their silence as a no to his question, Elias started filling in the group. For Andy and Francine this was mostly review but for the police this was all new and extremely informative territory.

29.

Brett had just finished recording the results from the C23 experiment and was troubled by the fact that he couldn't get to his data. He had a few formulas in his C22 folder that he really needed and despite several additional attempts at the computer, the results were the same, more machine code.

He thought about memorizing the information but there was just too much, so he'd have to get this paper out of the building. Looking at his mother's picture, he came up with another idea. He would simply fold the papers, put them in the bottom of shoes and just walk it out. This eliminated the need for him to take anything with him when he scooted out for lunch and certainly would make his trip through security a lot less suspicious.

He took his four pages of notes, broke them into pairs and folded them as best he could to conform to the shape of his shoes. Taking off his right shoe, he laid the folded papers in the bottom, put the shoe back on and stood up. The tight fit turned out to be a good thing. *Excellent,* he thought, taking a few steps around his small office, *no sound of wrinkling paper when I walk.* Satisfied with the results, he took off the other shoe and repeated the process.

It was closing in on 11:45, and it was time for Brett to go. Closing the door to the lab, Brett headed down the hallway toward the main entrance.

"They're back, Dr. Allen" he heard Elaine say to him.

Brett looked out and saw that the animal rights folks were once again protesting. He thought the crowd looked a little larger than it was last week.

"Looks like they brought some reinforcements with them this time," Brett said in response. "I'm going out for lunch, Elaine, and should be back in a few hours."

"Can't say as I blame you!" Elaine said. "The cafeteria menu doesn't look very appealing to me either."

Brett gave her a wave and started walking to the gate keeping an eye on the crowd. He knew they were throwing some pretty choice words his way but he was still too far away to make out exactly what they were. Closing in on the security gate, his cell phone started ringing.

"Hi, Dad," Brett said, stopping to put his finger in the opposite ear so he could hear a little better.

"Hi, Brett, where are you? I hear a lot of commotion in the background," his father asked.

"I'm just shy of the research center security gate. The animal rights protestors are here again and as you can hear they're a pretty vocal bunch," Brett answered.

"Brett, can I meet you for lunch today? I would really like to see you."

"Can you meet me at Harvard, the main campus building?" Brett asked. "I'm leaving now so depending on where you are it shouldn't be too long of a wait."

"Main campus building it is. I'll be waiting out front."

"OK, Dad, see you in a little while," Brett said, hanging up.

"Hey, Dr. Allen," one of the security guards said as Brett approached.

"Hi, Paul, looks like you've got your hands full out there," Brett said casually, referring to the crowd of protestors.

"You're not kidding. No briefcase today?" Paul asked, noticing right away the change in Brett's usual pattern.

"Just going out to grab some lunch," he replied calmly. "Looks like they want to serve meatloaf as the main course today, and I don't need to be sick if you know what I mean!"

Paul laughed as Brett stepped through the metal detector "I do indeed. Don't pay any attention to them, Dr. Allen," Paul said, looking at the protestors "They yell a lot and wave their signs but they seem to be a peaceful group just the same."

"I won't, Paul. Thanks," Brett said, leaving the security gate.

That was a lot easier than I ever thought it would be, he thought as he made a bee line to his Mustang. "I guess all the commotion with the protestors has them a little off their game. They're usually more thorough than that." For the very first time he was grateful to the animal rights people for being there.

Closing his car door he opened the glove compartment and got hooked up with the gear that detective Salazar had given him. Putting in the earpiece he grabbed the small microphone and held it close to his mouth.

"Hello, this is Brett Allen is anyone there?" he asked.

"We're right here," Brett heard immediately in response.

"I was just testing this out again to make sure I knew what I was doing," Brett said almost apologetically.

"That's good practice, Mr. Allen. Just so know, the microphone you have is very sensitive so you don't have to put it so close to your mouth. It gives us a little bit of feedback when you do that."

"Sorry," Brett said apologetically.

"Don't be, we know this is new territory for you," the voice replied.

"Just so you know," Brett said moving the microphone away from his lips, "I'm on my way to Harvard. I'm going to sign off now."

"OK, thanks for the heads up, Mr. Allen."

As Brett wiggled his way out of the parking lot, Jessica Pierce was standing at the Duck Boat Tour entrance wondering if Frank would show up.

She was certain that her preparation and trip to the airport last night would add some validity to her story. With the help of her badge, she was able to have a boarding ticket printed that showed an 8:00 p.m. departure time from Chicago and a 12:00 a.m. arrival time at Logan. She had also emptied the bottle of hairspray and tube of toothpaste until both were about half full.

She was startled when she heard Frank's voice from behind her.

"Don't move," he said patting her down. "I want you to bend down and slide your bag back to me."

Jessica stood still and heard the zipper on her bag. The boarding ticket was lying right on top and although she couldn't see him, Jessica knew he was looking at it. After a few seconds of silence, she could hear him digging around in the bag looking for anything suspicious. It seemed like an eternity before she heard him zipper the bag shut.

"Let me have your purse," she heard him say.

"Frank," she said, managing a few tears for effect, "I'm SO sorry!"

"I want you to turn around now and walk to the parking lot," Frank said calmly. "You'll see a silver Mitsubishi, go to the passenger side door and get in. I'll follow you."

Frank stayed behind her during their short walk to the car; the silence was maddening but Jessica knew she had once again infiltrated his inner defenses. She heard the door locks move to the open position.

"Throw your bag in the back seat," he instructed her.

When she turned to grab the door handle, Jessica got a look at Frank for the first time since seeing him Sunday when they parted ways at the airport. She was surprised that he looked so calm.

After Frank sat down in the driver's seat, she produced her cell phone and handed it to him as he requested. Looking into her directory, he noticed only two numbers stored there, his and an entry he recognized as the escort service's main number. Starting the car, Frank pulled out and maneuvered to the highway. Jessica didn't want to say anything until Frank started the conversation. Once on the highway, Frank used Jessica's cell phone to call the escort agency.

"Professional Escorts. This is Amanda, may I help you?"

"Yes you can," Frank replied. "Last week a good friend of mine referred your services to me and suggested I ask for a young lady named Veronica Taylor."

"I'm sorry, sir, Ms. Taylor resigned last Friday and no longer works here. Could I interest you in—"

Frank hung up not giving Amanda the chance to finish and tossed the cell phone out of the window. Checking the rearview mirror, Frank saw the cell phone breaking apart as it bounced along the highway behind him.

"Tell me what you know, Veronica, and I mean everything," Frank said, finally breaking the silence between them.

"It started with Billy Smothers. I used to see him once in a while for a little coke. I was working the streets back then and Billy said I was pretty enough to be a professional escort," she said as she laid out her story, hoping her intermittent sobs would add just the right touch. "He told me I could turn high class tricks, get a lot more money and get off the streets for good. So I went and checked it out. They gave me some blood test to make sure I was clean and then an advance of ten thousand dollars up front to get cleaned up, find a decent apartment and some nice clothes. I was on cloud nine.

"One morning about a month ago, I was walking down the street one afternoon and some guys in suits tossed me into their car and brought me down to the docks. They told me they had been talking with Billy and that he told them about our relationship. Then they said if I didn't follow their instructions to the letter, I'd never see the sun rise again. I was so scared, Frank." Pausing for a second to wipe the tears from her eyes, she pressed on.

"They told me you were dangerous and they were afraid to use their normal methods, whatever those are, to find out what you were up to. They were afraid you'd find out and disappear."

"Exactly what did they tell you to do?" Frank asked.

"They told me to get you to fall in love with me and to tell them all I could about you. I told them I didn't know anything about you except that you were always good to me. One of them said they'd be watching me all the time, and if I messed up I'd go straight to federal prison."

Federal prison, Frank thought. *So it is my ex employer.*

"In the process of trying to get you to fall in love with me the opposite happened. I fell in love with you, Frank, and now my whole world is crumbling down around me. Please forgive me, Frank. Please!" she pleaded through her heavy sobs.

"They must have something in my apartment because right after I got off the phone with you about coming to Boston, they visited me again and told me to give you the ring when I saw you."

"Hmmm," Frank mumbled. "So the string you used to get my ring size was their idea. When did you get that for them?"

"I don't remember exactly, Frank," she said, wiping her cheek, "And it wasn't their idea, Frank. They gave me string because I guess they knew you'd ask. Who are they, Frank, and how do they know all these things?"

"They're my former employers," Frank said evenly.

"I didn't know you were cop" Jessica said with just the right amount of surprise.

"I wasn't a cop. I did some work for the government when I was younger," he said to straighten her out, "Now tell me how you got here!"

"After they gave me the ring, I went in to work as I usually do. My best friend Alicia was there and I told her I was in trouble. She's really smart. We worked out a plan, or I guess I should say she did so that when I got back to Chicago, I'd be able to slip away from those people and get back here."

"Tell me about the plan, Veronica," Frank said in a tone that she had never heard before and couldn't really describe. What she did know is that she had to really careful here.

"Alicia and I are the same size in almost everything. We worked out a plan where we would go out to dinner and pull a switch. When you called me yesterday, we were kind of in the middle of it. After dinner was paid for, we went into the bathroom to freshen up. When we were in there, we got undressed and exchanged clothes and keys. Alicia always carried a big bag and inside she had two wigs, one for me and one for her. After we were ready, Alicia went out the back exit of the restaurant and took my car. I watched when she drove past and they followed her just like she said they would. I went out the back and got in her car and went straight to the airport. After I parked, I grabbed her travel bag, she had put a few things in there for me to wear, and ran into the airport just in time to pay for a ticket and get on the plane."

"Pretty intricate plan for a couple of escorts," Frank said skeptically, pulling into a rest area and stopping the car. "Reach in the back, Veronica, and give me the bag."

Frank took the bag from her hands and put it in his lap and unsnapped the small leather cover from the identity label people filled out in case their bags got lost and read it aloud.

"Alicia Kontreras, 4239 N. Hermitage, Chicago." Frank grabbed his cell phone to get connected with information. Jessica's heart was racing as she listened to him ask for the phone number. "This could be it" she thought as Frank glanced over at her waiting for the operator to give him the number.

"I'm sorry, sir, I'm not showing a listing under that name," the voice replied to Frank's request.

"Nothing for Kontreras, K-O-N-T-R-E-R-A-S?" he asked again. Frank's glance turned into a glare. Jessica could feel her nerve endings unravel as she braced for the worst.

"I apologize, sir. I did the lookup using C not K, let me check again....Alicia Kontreras on Hermitage. I'm connecting you with 773-555-1212. Have a nice day."

Frank listened as the call was connected and heard the answer machine pick up, telling would-be callers that she was not home and to leave a message. Tossing the bag in the back seat, he got the car moving toward the entrance ramp and slowly got the car up to speed.

I knew you'd do that! Jessica thought, very relieved. *He just confirmed the location our safe house and cover ID on the north side. So far so good! Either he's very predictable or I'm just a great cop!*

Frank decided to ask one last question. "How did you get the card up to my room?"

"The plane landed about twenty minutes early which worked out well. I left the airport and took a cab to a pharmacy and bought the card. The cabbie knew a little hole in the wall bar just a few blocks away from your hotel so I had him take me there. It was close to closing when I walked in and I just asked if anyone wanted to make fifty bucks for twenty minutes' work. I told the guy that I gave the card to that I had a fight with you. I was trying to avoid a scene and asked if he would slide the card under the door of your hotel room so you'd have it when you woke up. When the guy came back and told me he had done it, I gave him the fifty bucks and went to a dingy hotel and got some sleep."

Frank stared at the highway as they headed for Rhode Island, not saying anything, and Jessica followed suit. She had planned her reintroduction to Frank carefully, and from what she could tell, it had worked. Now it was up to Frank to make the next move.

* * *

Brett could see the main campus of Harvard from the driver's side window and noticed his Dad's truck sitting in the parking lot. These new pickup trucks were big and it sat well above all the other vehicles parked there.

Brett placed the microphone and earpiece in the glove compartment as he wheeled the Mustang in next to the truck. His father stepped out, using the sideboard to get to ground level, and left the door open.

"Come over here, Brett!" his father said. "I want you to have this." Reaching behind the drivers' side seat, he removed a small pistol from under the *Boston Globe* and put it in Brett's hand.

Brett was surprised. "Where did you get this?" he asked.

"It doesn't matter. If you ask questions in enough of the dark corners in this city you can get almost anything you want. Now listen, son, and listen good! There are all kinds of government people after this guy too, not just the police. I'm not real sure the police or these government agents are going to be able to protect you, so I want you to carry this with you at all times!"

Looking into his fathers eyes, he saw fear and desperation. Brett knew if he didn't make it out of this, it would literally kill him.

"It's a small 22 caliber pistol," Michael Allen began to explain to his son, "with hollow point ammunition. The hollow points flatten out easier and giving the gun better stopping power, so I'm told. Safety on," his father said, switching the small lever next to trigger to show him. "Safety off" he went on moving the metal lever in the opposite direction. "It only holds three shells to keep it small, one in the chamber and two in this specially modified clip."

"OK," Brett replied letting his dad know he understood. "Put it down for a second, OK?" Brett asked, slipping off his shoes to remove the pieces of folded yellow paper from his shoes.

Brett started to unfold the paper. "I'll take the gun, Dad," he said obligingly, "but I need for you to do me a favor. Take these to the research department find Jeff Dalton and give them to him."

Michael Allen glanced down at the papers his son had just handed him and thought he was looking at a foreign language.

"He'll know what they are," Brett said, noticing his father's puzzled look. "I'd do it myself but I wouldn't be able to get away from him. Better yet, just go into the main building here and have him paged. I can assure you that you won't be waiting very long."

"Alright, Brett," his father said. "I guess were not going to have lunch are we?"

"I can't, Dad. I wish I could, but I just can't. Even this is far from my normal routine, and I was told I have to stick as close to it as possible."

"I just feel so helpless, Brett, like there's nothing I can do to help," his father confessed remorsefully as he handed him the gun. "Promise me, Brett, that you'll carry this with you all the time."

"I will, Dad," Brett said, taking the small pistol and putting it in his front pocket. "I can't even notice it's there," he said, a little surprised.

"What do you see?" he asked his father as he stood there.

"Looks like you've got a lot of keys in your pocket!" Michael said, confirming just what Brett had thought. "Just to let you know, son, I've taken a leave of absence from work so I'm going to be around. I'm also going to ask Detective Miller if I can help in any way. I just can't sit around when there's a madman out there somewhere," he continued, looking toward the city, "just itching to get his hands on you!"

"I think that's a good idea, Dad," Brett replied.

"I know you've got to get going so let me get these papers in there. Jeff Dalton right?" he asked turning away.

"Yes, Jeff Dalton and, Dad," Brett paused, fighting back tears, "I want you to know that I love you!"

"I love you too, son," his father said, also doing his best not to cry. Turning away from his son, he started walking for the entrance and wiped his cheek.

* * *

"Are there any questions you'd like me to answer?" Brian Miller said, expecting a salvo of questions as he wrapped up his portion of the briefing. The two agents that were sitting across from him reviewing several pages of notes they had taken.

"Let me make sure I have this straight, and I don't want to repeat a lot of what you've just told us but I'm having some difficulty here," Andy said immediately after Brian opened the meeting up for questions, "you're telling us that Brett Allen received a heart transplant from Russell Craft and as a result, he not only inherited his heart but his memories, and as a result of hypnosis, you've gotten all this information!"

"Yes, Agent Campbell," Brian said, responding to his question, "in a nutshell that's precisely what we're saying. I know it's hard to believe but everything he has told us, including the information about Nadia Petrova and Frank Whickers, substantiates it as factual."

Francine didn't seem to have as much trouble accepting the detective's summary as her colleague and was more interested in making sure she had the investigate facts recorded properly. Looking over at Brian, she saw Trevor whisper into Elias's ear and watched them leave the briefing room together.

"I'd like to do a quick review to make sure I have everything," Francine stated, flipping back a page in her notes.

"First of all, I want to make sure I'm clear about the assets we have at our disposal. I'll start with those we have and leave out the technical staff. There are currently six field agents engaged in this operation with two additional resources we'll move out of the hotel which will bring our total to eight. We have units 1 and 2 both of which are currently airborne.

"On the investigative side, we are waiting for information from Pittsburgh in hopes of getting a lead on the apparent middle man. We are also interviewing employees, security personnel, and the cleaning company associated with the bus station in Chicago. Our goal it to isolate the person responsible for leaking the surveillance system maintenance schedule allowing the drop to take place unrecorded. We're also going to be speaking with, if we haven't done so already, the man on vacation in South Carolina who was working the night shift the evening Frank made the pick up.

"On your side, Detective Salazar has the *shadow van* linked to Mr. Allen with your tracking and communicative equipment. Detective Beard from the Connecticut State Police has investigative responsibility for Nelson's corporate office. Specifically your team is looking for missing information to fill in the holes from the partial document," Francine continued picking up a copy, "provided by Mr. Allen. You've also acquired the list of board members and plan on interviewing them."

"Yes, that's right," Hank Beard interjected to provide a few more details. "We're interested in finding and interviewing all the people who attended the board meeting of 5/91 and of course speaking with both Richard Nelson I and his son Richard Nelson II, respectively the former and current and CEO of that company."

"Thank you," Francine said jotting down some additional information.

"Detective Miller, in addition to the shadow van, you can provide six additional detectives and three undercover officers. It's also my understanding that you will act as liaison between our collective team, the Massachusetts State Police and the Lexington Police Department. You also have a detective in Florida that's working with the Hillsborough County Sheriff's Office to question the former CFO Bob McReynolds."

"Actually, Agent Kelly, it's one of *my* men down there," Hank beard said, correcting her error.

"And finally," Francine said making the change to her notes, "we have Nadia Petrova, who, based on the coroner's report, was administered a lethal dose of Oxycodone. We're working together up there with detective O'Hara who is going through her house and pulling phone records looking for any possible leads. Have I missed anything?"

"No, Agent Kelly I think that's everything," Brian said, assuming power of attorney over the detectives with him.

"So," Agent Campbell, said sarcastically, "despite Frank disappearing for reasons *unknown,* we still have two solid links to this case that I hope we don't screw up!"

Hank looked over at Brian Miller and thought he saw the hair on the back of his neck stand on end. The implication Andy Campbell made was direct and to the point.

Brian could feel his face turning red with anger and couldn't contain himself. "If you were more interested in saving a life than keeping *your little secrets*, we'd never be in this situation Agent Campbell!"

"That's enough!" Elias yelled ,walking back into the room, his anger directed at Andy Campbell for his unprofessional outburst. "We're all to blame, so let's stop pointing fingers and get back on task!"

Elias stood at the doorway for a few seconds making sure everyone's temper was under control before he started.

"I'm going to share something with all of you that I've been keeping to myself. Once I explain it, you'll understand why. Operation Escort, as you know, involved one of my best deep cover agents. What you don't know and must now be told is that the agent's name is Special Agent Jessica Pierce."

Francine's heart dropped to the floor.

"A few minutes ago, a call came in to our people running the Escort cover from a man looking for Veronica Taylor. Veronica Taylor was Jessica's code name for this operation. The call came in from her cell phone. A few minutes after the phonecall, our North Chicago safe house rang. This time the call came from Frank's cell phone number."

Elias waited a minute to let that sink in.

"What this means is that Jessica has somehow managed to get back with Frank. I can only surmise that the calls he's made were to check out whatever elaborate cover story she managed to come up with. When she left yesterday she said something to me that's just now starting to make sense. She said she had to do this on her own."

"She wouldn't take things into her own hands would she?" Francine asked, still trying to digest the new information.

"Apparently she already has!" Campbell jumped in.

"If you mean, will she take the law into her own hands, I don't know," Elias said honestly. "What I do know is that she felt betrayed and her tremendous emotional sacrifice and personal dignity were being cast aside as easily as you and I throw away a gum wrapper."

"So Agent Pierce has just become the wild card to this operation," Brian said, void of emotion. "Is it possible we can get a picture of her so I can pass it along to our folks on this investigation?"

"Yes," Elias said, "I'll have one of the technicians take care of that as soon as were done here. I've also arranged to get 3 secure radios for each of the detectives and one for the shadow van crew so we can stay in constant contact and share information just as soon as either of us get some in. These radios have a direct frequency link to me, that way we'll keep the tactical channels clear. I'll disseminate the information to the proper unit as soon as I receive it and when I pass along information, the detectives can get it to their people. If there's nothing else, I'd like to suggest that we break for lunch. If you have no objections, Detective Miller, I'd like to meet you back at your office at 2:00 p.m."

"No problem, Agent Flynn," Brian said as he and his group started to leave. "We'll see you then."

"One last thing," Elias said, delaying the detective's departure, "I think it's wise we don't announce to the fact that we're on to him. Frank doesn't need to know we've fallen for the decoy. The longer we can keep him from knowing for certain, the better chance we'll have of actually sealing things off. His Logan and Framingham plans were made just as any of us would have done— by the book and precautionary. He doesn't know for sure that we're on to him yet, so let's it keep it that way, at least for now."

"Sounds reasonable to us, Agent Flynn," Brian said standing up. "Who do we see for the radios and Agent Pierce's picture?"

"Trevor will see that you get them; he's the one that showed you where the bathrooms were," Elias said as the detectives moved past him and out the door.

Elias stood next to the door and waited until he was sure the detectives had gotten their radios, photograph and left the center. He had a few things left to say to his team of agents and closed the briefing room door and sat down."

"I don't have to tell you just what an incredible risk Agent Pierce has taken nor remind you of how much danger she is in right now. Although I agree in part that the locals blew our cover, I feel that we're responsible for where Jessica is right now. So let's do our best to bring her home safe. Now listen carefully," Elias said firmly. When he saw he had his detectives' undivided attention, he continued. "We've been authorized from Washington to take any and all necessary action to ensure the safety of the senator's grandson. That means the gloves come off, shoot on sight and shoot to kill."

"What about the Billy Smother's story?" Francine asked.

"That was a story for the detectives. As it turns out were going to need their help to find him," Elias replied.

"What if they apprehend him?" Andy asked.

"There's absolutely no chance of that happening, so let's not worry about the impossible. It's going to be up to us. The price of failure for you and everyone in this operations center is extremely high so let's get it done and get it done right." Elias stood up and looked at agents Kelly and Campbell. "Understood?"

A harmonious yes was the answer he was looking for and it was the one he got.

"Good, now get the word out and do it quickly and quietly!"

30.

"Listen," Frank said, finally ready to say something, "I want to say thanks for warning me and coming back, that took a lot of guts. I'm not happy with what happened but I've pinched people before and gotten them to do some pretty shocking things, so don't be too hard on yourself."

"Then you forgive me, Frank, you really honestly and truly forgive me?" Jessica asked.

"I'm not real sure about that yet," Frank said, his eyes fixed on the road, "I'm grateful yes, but it might take me sometime to get over what you've done to me. What I'm saying is I understand how they operate and how it could happen to just about anyone. I don't like the fact that it happened to me."

"Who are they, Frank, and why are they after us?" Jessica asked.

Frank liked the fact that she used the word *us*; it made him a little more relaxed about the whole situation. *In her mind, we're a team now,* he thought before giving her an answer.

"THEY are government agents, CIA mostly. They got their hooks into me when I was a senior in college. They waved the flag, sold patriotism, and painted a picture of travel and excitement. I bought it all, Veronica, I bought it all!

"After I got all my clearances, I went to Virginia for evaluation and training. Turns out I had a knack for sharp shooting. So they made me an instrument of foreign policy."

"Foreign Policy, what does that mean?" Jessica asked, playing her role perfectly.

"Let me give you an example. During the past few years you hear a lot

300

about the Columbian Drug Cartel and all the high ranking officials being killed. A lot of those killings are being done by people just like me. I was a messenger."

"I'm sorry, Frank, I don't understand what you mean."

"When we're having difficulty persuading a foreign government to see things our way, especially the smaller ones with less global influence, we send them a message. Now do you understand?" Frank said a little irked by her lack of understanding.

"I think so," Jessica said.

"When we, the United States, encounter resistance to some of our demands, someone like me would go into that country and kill a lower ranking member of the ruling government. The message is play ball or next time it might be you. That's the kind of messenger I was!" Frank said still annoyed at how naïve she was.

"I thought that was just stuff they put out on TV to get people to watch the shows I had no idea it really happened. So if you were doing your job, why are they after you?" Jessica asked now with a genuine interest to find out why he went underground.

"As I said, I *used* to work with them. I had a very good friend that used to work with me on most of our operations. They killed him and I was next. Eventually, you know too many secrets and you're considered more of a liability than you're worth. So to make sure they cover their backs, they just make people disappear. I wasn't going to be a side show in one of their magic acts, so I cut and ran."

"Well if they wanted to make you disappear like your friend, why didn't they just do it? Why did they force me to do what I did?"

"I went freelance when I dropped out of sight. I've done both private and commercial work; by commercial work, I mean foreign government work. All I can figure is that they want to know who I've been working for, details of the assignments that I've been on for foreign governments, things like that," Frank said thoughtfully, explaining things. "They can't get that information if I'm dead. They can't pull me away in the middle of the night and try and force it out of me. They're the ones that trained me how not to give information when captured, so that wouldn't do them any good. They can't arrest me for anything substantial. Well, maybe buying a few ounces of this and few of that from Billy Smothers.

"So if I were running the show," Frank continued, "I'd be trying to get someone like me right in the middle of executing an operation, maybe with the help of the local police to add some validity to the arrest. Once I had the person

301

in custody, there would be two options, information exchange, which equates to counter intelligence, and get a deal or go to jail for a long, long time. For most people in my profession, jail is a death sentence anyway so a long time is usually a year, two tops! Eventually they slip something into your food; you have a mysterious accident, something like that. The real kicker is, you never know when it's coming. So you sit there in your 4 by 4 cell, trying to figure out the day and if it's a former client or former colleague that makes sure your present gets delivered."

All Jessica could do was think about everything Frank had just said. She knew it was all true and actually could begin to understand how and why Frank turned out the way he was. If he wasn't this way, the spooks would have killed him, so for personal survival he did what he had to do. That still didn't give him the right to knock off innocent Americans. She could have cared less if he was blowing the heads off of drug dealers in Columbia but killing fellow citizens went way over the line.

"So you're here to do *that* kind of work?" Jessica asked.

"Yes, Veronica, I'm here to do that kind of work," Frank answered her without a trace of emotion.

"Where are we going to go to drop out of sight, Frank?"

"I'm afraid it's not that simple, Veronica. You see, I'm here on a commercial contract and I have to finish it. If I don't there's a very good chance the small hole my client has arranged for me to make my get away will disappear. If that happens, I'll be able to hide for a while but eventually I'll end up in a big rubber bag."

"Commercial contract, didn't you say a commercial contract was for the government?" she asked, genuinely surprised.

"Yes, that's what I said, and if you look out your passenger side window, you'll see who my latest and last commercial customer is," Frank said.

Not knowing what to expect, Jessica looked out her window she saw a large American Flag waving proudly from a flag pole in someone's back yard. Jessica had all she could do to keep her composure as a slew of thoughts and emotions raced through her heart. She tried as hard as she could not to believe it, to convince herself that Frank was lying but it didn't work. Jessica knew he was telling the truth and now she knew beyond any doubt that just like Frank, her own government played her for a fool.

"You…you don't mean the American government do you?" Jessica asked, hoping he would say no.

"Yes, the very one. Ironic isn't it. I'm here to a job for the government, and the same government is trying to stop me."

"I don't get it, Frank. How can that be?" Jessica asked, truly a little surprised by his statement.

"There are a lot of secret agencies running around and within each of them are smaller more dangerous ones," Frank said, scanning his mirrors for potential trouble. "You just never know who you can trust. Too many people are playing both sides of the fence."

"I'm really scared, Frank, what are we going to do?" Jessica asked, not totally sure she didn't mean it.

"Well, tonight we're camping in Rhode Island. I need some more time to think. Hopefully by morning, I'll have come up with a few good ideas."

Jessica was certain now that Frank had fully accepted her and had managed to take her under his wing. What she didn't like were all the questions that were dancing around in her head. *I know whose after you, Frank, and they're closer than you think, but who's on the other side of this equation?* she asked herself as they cruised down the highway.

Jessica stared out of her window in silence, trying to make heads from tails. Suddenly she remembered what Elias had said a few days ago when he outlined the operation, it was something like *The CIA is being surprisingly helpful. Hmmm...I wonder how helpful,* she thought looking past the guardrails. Jessica watched the houses they passed by noticing that a lot of people had American Flags displayed on or near their houses. With each one that passed by, another question was plugged into her head.

* * *

Much to Brian and Hank's pleasure, Salazar had volunteered to drive back to the station.

"Well I can see why Agent Pierce was selected for the assignment," Brian said, handing the 8x10 black and white to Hank sitting in the back.

"Wow!" Hank said "Where on earth did they find her?"

"It makes me wonder what they do to brainwash a beautiful girl like this. I mean she is absolutely stunning. On a scale from one to ten."

"Eleven," Hank said loudly from the back seat, finishing Brian's sentence for him.

"Exactly," Brian said. "I guess you could say that the phrase, for the love of country, just got redefined."

Brian stopped the discussion momentarily to answer the call his ID told him was detective O'Hara. Miller didn't get a call from him unless it was something pretty significant so his curiosity level was very high.

"What is it, Ryan?"

"Hey L.T., we found a shoebox in the victim's house that she was apparently used to store important papers. It wasn't sitting on a shelf in the closet or anything like that. She had it tucked away in the basement hidden in a garment bag. Not a great hiding place, but it's obvious she didn't want it just lying around. Anyway, we've got her birth certificate, a copy of her adoption papers showing she was adopted a week after she was born which changed her birth name from Nadia Kingston to Nadia Wilson and still another court document changing her name from Wilson to Petrova. "

"So, she never liked her name," Miller sarcastically interrupted. "What are you getting at, Ryan?"

"Her phone records show that she made two calls on Saturday. One to an antique store here in town and another to a Beatrice Kingston in Bedford. Bea Kingston is the name listed as the mother on the birth certificate. I'm thinking when Allen came up to see here it really shook her up, so she called Mom for some advice," Ryan said.

"What's the father's name?" Brian asked.

"No name listed for the father, L.T. She also has an unusual amount of books and magazines about Russia; I mean a highly unusual amount. I could probably fill my kids' school library with them and have a few left over."

"Get on it! Find the mother, Ryan, and take your government side kick with you. I want her in the station for questioning just as soon as you see her. Don't sit around and wait for her to get home either, this is urgent. You find her pronto! Do I make myself clear?"

"Crystal clear, Lieutenant, I'll call you when we have her and are en route," O'Hara said, hanging up.

"Salazar, drop Hank and I off right in front. I've got to check something out," Brian said, seeing police headquarters just up ahead.

"You got it," Salazar said, whipping around the corner into the entrance.

Brian hurried his way up to his office with Hank in tow. "What's going on, Brian? I know we've got to stay fit and all that but this is a little extreme."

"Let me see the list of board members from the 5/11 meeting," Brian said whipping around his desk. With one hand extended to grab the paper Hank was giving him, he used the other to power up his computer.

"Nadia is somehow involved in this whole Nelson ordeal, right?" Brian said methodically using the one finger on the keyboard method. "Ryan told me the father's name was left off her birth certificate. She was adopted and had her name changed three times. She went from her birth name to her adopted name and then had it legally changed to Petrova. She also had a library of Russian books and magazines. I'm thinking she found out who her father was and I'll bet we're going to find him on your list."

"We don't have any Petrova's on our list," Hank said.

"I know, I know—just give me second," Brian said, asking Hank to bear with him.

He typed Russian names into the search box and opened the first web site that was offered.

Petrova—Daughter of Petrova is the ending for a woman's last name.

"Take a look at this, Hank," Brian said, turning the monitor so he could see it a little better.

Hank looked at the monitor for a second and wasn't getting whatever it was Brian was trying to point out.

"What am I missing here, Brian?" Hank asked, trying not to feel like something had just went flying over his head.

"Here, take a look at the list," Brian said, tossing the paper across his desk. "There is only one person listed with the first name of Peter, Peter Ivanov."

"You know," Hank said taking a hard look at his list for the first time "Now that I'm looking a little closer, it seems that a third of the board members have Russian names. Do you find that as peculiar as I do?"

"I hadn't really thought about it," Brain replied. "I'll tell you one thing though; I can't wait to talk with Beatrice Kingston."

"Isn't that a bit of a stretch?" Hank asked trying to make the connection. "Why wouldn't she have changed her name to Ivanov?"

"There's no father's name on the birth certificate," Brian said in an attempt to show that a bit of a stretch, as Hank called it, wasn't a stretch at all. "We can take a pretty good guess that her father wanted nothing to do with her and Mommy too, for that matter, since the adoption was effective a week after she was born."

"So Beatrice Kingston finds out she's pregnant," Hank said, beginning to understand, "gets the adoption process started so she can get rid of her daughter right after birth. Nadia decides to find out who her real parents are, does some research and bingo. She finds her mother and through her, finds her father."

"Once Nadia finds out," Brian said, jumping back in, "she learns the language and as much as she can about her heritage in an attempt to win the affections of her real father. That would explain all the Russian literature in her house. And the way this investigation is starting to play out, I'll bet *Daddy* wasn't real happy with the reunion!"

"I don't think I'm going to sit on this," Hank told Brian on his way out the office to use a land line. "If I find out this guy still lives in Greenwich, I'm going to talk with him myself."

"We might want to consider bringing Mr. Ivanov in now, assuming we can pull it off. I'd hate to let them have an opportunity to compare notes," Brian suggested, following him to an empty desk.

"Point well taken," Hank said, picking up the phone. "Do I have to dial 9 to get out?"

Brian shook his head and Hank placed a call to Connecticut telling the person on the other line to send someone out to pick up Peter Ivanov for questioning.

"Will you take care of the hotel thing for me, Brian? As it is, it's going to take me a few hours to get back and I'd like to get back as soon as possible."

"Consider it done, Hank!" Brain said "With any luck maybe our Russian friend will be waiting for you when you get there."

"Yeah and let's not forget his lawyer," Hank reminded him. "These fat cats rarely go anywhere without them. I'll call you just as soon as I get back."

Brian went back to his office so he could try out his new radio and brief Elias on what he found.

Elias was sitting at his desk reviewing the information they had just gotten from the man on his South Carolina Golf trip. He wasn't surprised at all that the interview proved fruitless. The young kids that worked at these stations during the midnight shift were more concerned about playing their portable video games than noticing what was going on around them. Suddenly his radio came alive.

"Flynn, this is Miller," Elias heard.

"What is it, Miller?" Elias asked not removing his eyes from the report.

A snotty little attitude Brian thought. "I heard from O'Hara in Lexington. He's found some interesting documents up there."

"Yes, Agent Masi just checked in a few minutes ago and filled me in. What do you think?" Elias asked, controlling his growing frustration.

Miller explained what he had done on the internet and the connection he had established between Nadia and Peter Ivanov. Elias listened, somewhat impressed that he was able to make the connection.

"We're going to bring her birth mother in for questioning sometime today, and Hank," Miller said pausing, "I mean Detective Beard, has just left for Connecticut. He's going to handle the questioning of Ivanov personally."

Elias exchanged the interview summary he was looking at for the report Trevor had given him nearly twenty minutes ago. Trevor had arrived at the same conclusion and established the same links as the ones Miller had just finished describing. A smile came to his face as leaned back in chair.

"Very impressive, Detective, and thanks for filling us in," Elias said sincerely. "Funny that we didn't see that. I can see already that this joint effort is going to be very beneficial. Thanks for the information. By the way, have you had any success finding out about the car rentals?"

"As a matter of fact we have. He picked up a car not far from the drop point at a place called Rent a Clunker. The clerk gave us a positive ID on his picture. He used the name Jason Galloway. We've got the description and are looking for the vehicle now."

"OK, Detective. Nice work! Don't bother trying to find the vehicle as I can tell you with the utmost certainty that he has switched vehicles again and he won't be using the same name," Elias said, finishing his conversation.

Well, Elias thought, *It's nice to know our latest team members are willing to cooperate. It also looks like I get an unexpected bonus; I won't have to spoon feed ideas to get them going in the right direction.*

Trevor walked out his office and saw Francine and Andy huddled over one of the display consoles, trying to figure out just exactly what they were looking at. Elias approached and answered their question before they even had a chance to ask.

"I hadn't been told this was functional yet," Elias' irritated voice rang out, startling the two agents. "What you're looking at is another fine piece of technical work put together by Trevor and his team. I can almost guarantee that Frank will make his move within a few days and now that we can keep an eye on, Mr. Allen, we'll have a pretty good idea of where we'll be able to find him."

Trevor's voice carried across the room "Special Agent Flynn, I've got Pittsburgh on line 3!"

"OK, Trevor!" Elias said, his voiced raise just enough for Trevor to hear him. "I'll take it in my office."

Andy looked at Francine after Elias had gone into his office. "It seems like we're watching everybody these days. I guess that make us what the public calls *big brother.*"

"I know what you mean. I've never seen Elias quite like this. I'll bet if he fails and the senator's grandson ends up dead, he's going to take a big fall!" Francine responded with concern.

Andy threw a smirk Francine's way, "And all the kings' horses and all the kings' men wouldn't be able to put Elias together again."

"This is Special Agent Flynn," Elias said picking up the phone.

Elias started writing things down as fast as he could until finally the voice on the other end stopped.

"I am really concerned as to why we didn't get the surveillance tapes. I'll be looking into that personally as soon as this is over. I guess we won't need them now!" Elias said into the phone and hung up.

Walking quickly out of his office, he snapped his fingers a few times. Getting the attention of Francine and Andy, he motioned for them to go into the briefing room. "Trevor! Join us in the briefing room, will you?"

Once everyone was assembled, Elias began to share the information he gotten from the Pittsburgh office.

"Here's the latest," Elias began "The man that were looking for, the one in the soldier's uniform, got off the bus just as it crossed into Pennsylvania. The driver of the bus said they were only a few miles from an intermediate stop but the guy demanded to get off before the bus got there."

"Yesterday, in a small wooded area very close to where the bus driver said he got off, the police found a man in a soldier's uniform with a bullet in his head. The time of death is also consistent with the timeline we've established with our traveler, so we're pretty sure it's the same guy. They found no identification but were able to get a fingerprint match. The middle man we've been looking for is Justin Fortis, who is an employee of the Food and Drug Administration."

"Wow!" Trevor exclaimed unable to hide the shock.

"That's one way to put it," Andy said, seeming to grow more sarcastic as time went on.

"So this guy was the bag man for someone at the pharmaceutical company. We'll need to find out all we can about this guy. I doubt he was dumb enough to leave a very visible trail, so we've got to find out everything we can about him. Maybe he made a mistake," Francine said across the table.

"That's the conclusion I came to as well," Elias said patting Francine on the back in a round about way, "and since this operation has turned into a new animal, I've made a decision," Elias stated capturing everyone's attention. "Andy, as of this moment I want you to run operations from here. Francine, I'm going to arrange for you to be a part of the shadow van crew since it looks like that may end up being our closest ground asset."

Elias turned to Trevor, "I want Agent Kelly to carry a standard A4 tracking device so we can keep the van and Mr. Allen on our overlay system. I think this will give us a better real time tactical assessment of the situation. I also want an M27 installed in my vehicle."

Trevor wasn't sure heard Elias' highly unusual request correctly "You mean an M27 portable overlay unit?"

"That's right, Trevor. How long will that take?" Elias asked already knowing the answer.

"About ten minutes. If you want real time feed, about twenty." Trevor responded.

"Alright, you've got twenty minutes so you better get started," Elias told him, implying that he did in fact want real time overlay information pumped into his vehicle.

Agents Campbell and Kelly couldn't believe what they were hearing and it showed on their faces.

"That's right," he said, now facing his two agents. "I'm going out into the field. Don't look so surprised, you two! I still consider myself to be one of the department's best field operatives. I've studied Frank Whickers so much that I almost know how he thinks!"

One of Trevor's technicians appeared in the door with a Kevlar vest and handed it to Elias. Oblivious to the minor interruption, he continued.

"If I'm right and I happen to believe that I am, I can be much more effective out there than running things from in here. I'll make just one suggestion, Andy, before I have to leave for meeting with Detective Miller, it might be a good idea to have your air assets return to base, refuel and keep them on tarmac alert."

"Yes, sir," Andy responded.

"I'll continue to provide the information I get from local police directly to you, Andy, for evaluation, assessment and action. Francine, you and I will be leaving; if Trevor is a good as I think he is, in about twenty minutes. You'll follow me in a separate vehicle. Your presence there will help solidify getting you in as part of the shadow van team. Make sure you wear a vest and bring along the A4."

Francine was disappointed that Elias had selected Andy to run the operation and put her in the field. It just didn't make sense. It was obvious to everyone that she was much more astute and capable of making major tactical and investigative decisions than Andy could ever hope to be. Her conversation with Jessica about wanting to be back out there came to the forefront of her mind.

"Be careful what you wish for," she mumbled under breath before confirming everything Elias had asked of her putting any unfounded concerns he might have to rest.

"I'm sure you're aware of just how delicate this has become now that there seems to be a government connection to our case. All the information we have on Justin Fortis and any new information regarding him or his involvement is to be kept strictly confidential and on a need-to-know basis. As far as I'm concerned, the only people that have and need to know already do!" Elias stated firmly. "Francine, why don't you go and get the things you need and meet me in my office in twenty minutes. Andy, just as soon as I'm finished meeting with Trevor, I'm turning the operations center over to you." With that, Elias left the briefing room and grabbed Trevor, who was busy making some initial adjustments on the equipment he'd requested. Trevor put the portable overlay down and followed Elias to the office.

"Take a seat, Trevor," Elias said closing the door. "I know I don't have to tell you this but I'm going to anyway. All the information and any new information about Justin Fortis is considered highly confidential."

Trevor responded with a nod. "Of course!"

"I'm turning over operational control to Andy. Francine and I are going out in the field."

Noticing Trevor's eyebrows raise with obvious concern, Elias felt he owed him a little more of an explanation.

"I know Francine is the far better choice and if I didn't desperately need her things would be different, but I've got to save this senator's grandson, and I need my best people where they can do the most good. Officially, Andy will be running things; unofficially, I'm still running the show. I want all information, especially that pertaining to this new development, sent directly to me so I can decide what to do with it."

"You mean bypass Agent Campbell?" Trevor asked.

"Yes, bypass him until I have a chance to evaluate it and get back to you. We can communicate with each other through the M27, correct?"

"We sure can, and we can do it without degradation to the real time transfer of overlay information," Trevor said with a tinge of pride and relief that Elias had only turned things over to Agent Campbell on a lame duck sort of arrangement.

"Terrific!" Elias said, truly grateful to have such a competent and loyal person on his team. "Before you go," he added with gratitude, "I'm putting you in for a two-step increase when this over."

"Thanks, Agent Flynn, I really appreciate it. I'd better get back to my little configuration project," he said, looking at his watch and added jokingly, "near as I can tell I only have about ten minutes left!"

* * *

Brett pulled into his apartment complex after leaving his father to do an errand for him. To say he wasn't feeling right would have been an understatement. He took a look at the gun sitting alone in the passenger seat.

He shut the engine off and reached over to grab the tiny weapon. As soon as he had it in his hand he experienced what Dr. Joseph Kaufman had warned might happen. He experienced his first crossover vision.

Brett gasped quickly and deeply for air, exactly the way someone would when jumping into a pool of ice cold water. Although he was frozen and couldn't move, his senses were very much alive. At first he wondered if he was going to have an out of body experience. He could see in the distance the white puffy clouds slowly moving together, joining forces against a deep blue sky. It started as a cool gentle breeze, the perfect form of relief for a muggy summer night. Then someone or something hit the time-lapse photography switch.

The clouds quickly rolled together forming large cotton like towers in the sky, their peaks eerily reflecting the late afternoon sun as they surged toward him. Then with the speed of a falcon diving on its prey, the sky turned from blue to a deep menacing purple. The once cool breeze was now a stiff wet wind as the rain began pouring down, falling so heavily and hard that it hurt.

He watched helplessly, consciously trying to move as he saw himself and Becky, blinded by the intensity of the rain, scurry for the shelter of his car. The passage of time returned to normal just as quickly as the rain had descended upon them. Brett could barely make out sound but thought he heard an ambulance or police car passing and looked out of his window to see what was going on. He noticed right away that their surroundings had somehow changed despite the fact he never started the car. Brett recognized that they were parked on the side of the video store he always came to when he wanted to rent movies.

Then as unexpectedly as his crossover vision started it ended and reality came crashing back. Brett coughed and quickly opened the door of his Mustang and threw up. After spitting a few times to try and clear his mouth, he sat up shaken and bewildered.

The entire crossover experience lasted about five seconds but for Brett it seemed like an eternity. Fear and anxiety once again grabbed hold of him, his head was swirling, trying to figure out what just happened. With the images seared into his mind he tried to discount them but just couldn't.

Getting out of the car, he placed the gun in his pocket and meandered unsteadily to his door. Once inside, he went right to the bathroom so he could brush his teeth and get rid of the foul aftertaste in his mouth. Spitting out the last of the toothpaste, he leaned down, cupped his hand just under the faucet directing the water in into his mouth and rinsed.

Still feeling a little nauseous, Brett hoped a couple of crackers would help settle his stomach. Going into the kitchen, he grabbed a couple and gingerly began to eat them. Standing in the kitchen, he waited a few seconds for the verdict, hoping his stomach wouldn't reject them and send him running for the bathroom.

"So far so good," he thought turning the faucet on to let the water run. When he reached into the cabinet to get himself a glass, he noticed his hand. The blotchiness from the day before that had started to fade was once again a bright pink. Brett did the math putting two and two together and quickly came to the conclusion that Russell Craft had just paid him an unexpected visit. Steadying his hand, which was now shaking uncontrollably, he managed to get some water in the glass and drink it.

Brett found the nearby chair and, not paying close attention, nearly missed it as he sat down. Massaging his forehead hoping that it would help to clear his mind, he decided not to go back to work knowing his return would be pointless. He had already gotten as much information as he could from his most recent experiment and knew the mysterious computer virus would prevent him from retrieving the enormous amount of data he had stored there over the years. "Besides, as soon as this thing is over I'm resigning," he said further justifying his decision not to return.

Amidst the turmoil whizzing through his mind, he remembered that he had left Becky a message that he was going to call her. Fearing he would forget if he didn't do it now, he went to the phone and dialed her number.

Becky was delighted to hear from him. He explained that he couldn't stay on long and she totally understood given the recent circumstances. Not wanting her to worry, Brett didn't mention his latest episode and did a decent job at staying jovial and positive. Becky agreed to Brett's suggestion to have dinner at the apartment with his father. Brett hadn't asked his father yet but he was sure his invitation would be readily accepted. Becky was looking forward to seeing Brett's father again. She considered it a chance to put her best foot forward and get to know him a little bit better. After agreeing to a 6:00 o'clock show time, Becky told him she would do a little shopping and enjoy the opportunity to make dinner. Brett thought that was a great idea and told her so before they hung up.

31.

As Elias and Francine were headed over to Brian Miller's office for their 2:00 p.m. meeting, Connecticut State Police Detectives Garvey and Hawkins were just being escorted into Richard Nelson's office. They were both seasoned detectives and had seen just everything under the sun but nothing could have prepared them for their first class welcome and the regal appearance of the office they had just entered.

When the detectives entered the office, they saw three men sitting comfortably in large plush chairs. The oldest of the three stood up and invited the detectives to seat themselves in the two remaining chairs.

"I'm Richard Nelson," the oldest said directing their attention with his hand "this is my son Richard the second, and last but certainly not least, I'd like to introduce Brandon Ohliger, our long standing President of Operations."

Detective Garvey took care of introducing himself and his partner. Both immediately saw the resemblance between the Richard Nelson and his son. The years had whitened and thinned Richard Nelson's hair. He was very thin and it made the wrinkles in his face more prominent making him look older than what Garvey would guess to be a man in his early seventies. Sitting to his right was Richard Nelson II. Despite his full head of hair and a little more meat on his bones, there was no mistaking that they were father and son.

Detective Hawkins wondered if his partner was feeling the same air of conceit that filled the room as he was. Hawkins wasn't a big fan of arrogance and if wanted to be honest with himself, it was a quality he absolutely detested.

Hawkins began, wanting to set the tone, "As you may already know, Detective Garvey and I are here to ask some questions surrounding a former employee, Dr. Russell Craft. We were wondering what you could tell us about a project your company labeled Research Project C2765."

Hawkins was well prepared for this meeting and very pleased to see that his introduction had caught everyone off guard.

Richard Nelson Sr. took center stage.

"What happened to Dr. Craft and his research assistant was the biggest tragedy our company has ever known, the effects of which were felt globally. I say this because he was an honorable man and a brilliant scientist that would have made enormous contributions to humanity if his life was not brutally and tragically cut short."

Richard Nelson paused for just a second to take a small sip from the brandy snifter sitting next to him before continuing.

"Research project C2765 that you referred was the company's project that Dr. Craft was leading. I'll keep this extremely simple," he said with the obvious implication that what he was about to say was beyond the detectives' comprehension.

"C2765 was our painstaking effort to find a cure for cancer. The research focused around genetic reconfiguration schemes, the theory being that we would be able to detect cancer triggers and then alter their make up rendering them harmless. Our loss of Dr. Craft and his assistant was, as I said, devastating to us but the loss to humanity was far greater."

"Yes you said that," Detective Garvey replied. "So who took the project over after Dr. Craft's death?'

"No one," Nelson Sr. answered. "In addition to losing Russell Craft, we also lost of his research material."

"You LOST his research material!" Hawkins said suspiciously. "How could something so important turn up missing?"

It was obvious that Nelson Sr. still commanded a great deal of respect and was running the show from the company side of side of things.

"Brandon, would you be kind enough to enlighten our guests?" Nelson Sr. said in a manner that made Hawkins's blood boil.

Brandon Ohliger jumped right in "I'd be delighted to, Richard. I'm sure you're both aware that Nelson Pharmaceuticals is the country's leading company in research and development. We achieved that distinction in large part by hiring only the very best and brightest. In order for us to protect our investments, we also employ the most rigorous security measures to protect our assets from industrial espionage.

"In the early nineties, computer security would be considered barbaric at best compared to the technology we have today. Although our network security measures and data storage capabilities were considered state of the art for their time, we were unknowingly vulnerable to what we today call cyber attacks."

"So the best and the brightest applied only to your scientists and not your computer people," Hawkins said cynically.

Nelson Sr. was visibly irritated and jumped back into the conversation. "I'm sure that even in an unappreciated profession such as police work, you have officers you consider to be very talented. Take yourself for example, Detective Hawkins. I'm convinced, and please correct any part of this you feel is inaccurate, that you think of yourself as an outstanding police officer despite your brazen attitude and lack of respect. Better perhaps than your partner, Officer Garvey. I'm equally convinced that someone just out of the police academy, someone with fresh ideas and keen eye for detective work would give you a run for your money. My point is that no matter how good you are, how good you think you are, there is *always* someone better."

Hawkins was really hot now but managed to maintain his composure due in large part to his partner.

"I think you've made your point. You know we're probably not the smartest people in the world but neither my partner nor I have ever lost something of such monumental importance," Garvey said returning the insult.

"May I continue with my explanation, Detective?" Ohliger asked surprisingly politely.

"Be my guest," Garvey said extending his hand to signify he was turning over the floor to him.

"As I was saying before being so rudely interrupted, the computer attack that infiltrated our system had a level of sophistication that far exceeded our defensive capabilities. It sat dormant within our network and migrated to each workstation and server in the company. It was so advanced that as backup systems were activated, the virus would see them and migrate into their operating system. It was a super virus with an intelligence all its own. Once it recognized that all primary and redundancy systems were infected, it somehow activated itself and destroyed everything. It started with documents and maneuvered its way to all the hard drives causing critical system errors and outages."

"Didn't you keep hard copies?" Garvey asked suspiciously.

"Oh no," Ohliger replied. "That was considered too great of a risk. If one of our competitors managed to get someone in here, we'd have lost everything to them. Even today you won't find one printed page with any of our research material on it. And as an added precaution we now do extensive background investigations on everyone we hire so we can further lower our risk."

Garvey was curious and asked a follow up question. "How do know so much about this whole computer thing, Mr. Ohliger, and how did you finally find out you had this super virus?"

"I've been the President of Operations for twenty-five years," Ohliger proudly responded "It's my business to know everything that affects the smooth operation of this company. As far as finding the super virus goes we hired several of the best known system security professionals in the country. It still took them two months to find it."

"I assume that Mr. Nelson didn't have any hard feelings," Garvey said, looking at Nelson Sr.

"Of course not, Detective," Nelson Sr. replied. "No one could have foreseen those events and circumstances"

"Nice!" Hawkins said. "So because of your greed, millions of cancer patients have probably died needless deaths."

The room went dead silent. Hawkins had definitely struck a nerve and no one in the room could argue with the logic of his well-honed statement.

Hawkins was ecstatic with himself. He had led the overly educated and overly wealthy group of executives right down the trough he had prepared before he and his partner arrived.

"Now," Hawkins went for the knock out punch, "I'm just going to think out loud here for a minute, so please bear with me. If memory serves, I think I remember seeing that if this research made it into the medical community, Nelson Pharmaceuticals stood to lose almost 2 ½ billion dollars. Do I have those figure correct?"

Garvey noticed the three men had a look of surprise that he had never seen before. He assumed, and rightfully so, that the documents Hank Beard had faxed over were internal memo's meant only for the higher-ranking company officials.

"I highly resent the implication you just made, Detective, but you're figures are correct," Nelson Sr. said almost without emotion. "Can I ask how you've managed to obtain your information?"

Hawkins was glad to respond. "As you were kind enough to point out just a few minutes ago, some detectives are just better than others!"

Speaking for the first time, Richard Nelson II stood up "I think we're done here!"

"Good enough," Hawkins said as he and Garvey stood up to leave.

"By the way, Detective," Nelson II said, "What I don't think you know despite your good investigative work is that we convened a board meeting shortly after the financial impact study and decided to move forward and fully support Dr. Craft's research and potential discoveries. So next time you want to present your cogent innuendos, try to make sure you have all your facts in order!"

Richard Nelson II closed the door as the detectives left and returned to his chair. "I thought we were done with this whole Craft/Dobson investigation. It's not like it happened yesterday! I also want to know how they managed to get their information. They certainly weren't asking those kinds of questions when they spoke with us after our employees were killed, so it's fair to say that they probably just recently got more information."

"I'll look into it, Richard," Brandon said, getting up to leave.

"You do that, Brandon," he said firmly in response Brandon's remark.

Richard Nelson II was very agitated but you'd never know it to look at him. He stood in the middle of the room, CEO of the largest and most profitable pharmaceutical company in the entire United States, and he wasn't going to let a couple of cops try to implicate him in any sort of wrong doing.

"Sit down, son. Relax and have a brandy with me," Nelson Sr. said to his son. "We've done nothing wrong. I'd also like to suggest that after our drink, it might be a good idea to call the members of the board and let them know what just happened."

"OK, Dad," he said, sitting down to accept his father's offer, not all sure if what his father had said was the right thing to do.

Richard Nelson's assistant Elizabeth led the detectives back to the main entrance. On their way both detectives noticed the memorial placards for Russell Craft and Cynthia Dobson. Not breaking stride the detectives glanced at one another and were thinking the same thing. There was a 2 ½ billion dollar motive behind the deaths of those two people.

The interview in Florida with Bob MacReynolds was also finishing up. The retired chief financial officer of the pharmaceutical giant had little to offer. He was equally surprised that the interviewing detective had somehow gotten his hands on company confidential information. MacReynolds expressed his genuine sadness over the events that occurred in 1991. He also explained in quite a bit of detail the financial impact study process and informed them that it was standard procedure to outline the financial impact the company would experience whenever a new discovery was on the verge of being released.

Despite the detective's professionally persistent line of questioning, it was very clear that Bob MacReyonlds knew little else. Before the detective left, MacReynolds provided his cell phone number and graciously offered to answer any additional questions that may arise as the investigation moved forward.

Elias and Francine had both parked in the visitor's parking lot and made the short walk into the building. They were a little early for their meeting but were escorted directly to Miller's office.

Brian was surprised to see Francine tagging along. He wondered if there was a new development or a shift in the operation.

Seeing Miller's expression, Elias took the lead. "Detective Miller, we've made some changes to our ops plan. Before we can go forward, I'd like to know what you think."

Brian was equally surprised with Elias's statement, not because there was a change in plans but that he was soliciting his opinion. "Shoot!" Brian said, indicating to everyone to grab a chair.

Elias laid his cards on the table as succinctly as he could. "Shortly after you left, we had a little brainstorming session. I've decided to go back out into the field until this operation is over. I believe that I can be of more value there than sitting at the operations center. I'd also like to suggest that Francine be added to the van crew. If things get busy around here, as I suspect they will, your crew will be busy getting information out to your team. Francine's presence will allow for a quicker exchange of information with my team and allow us to deploy resources more efficiently."

Brian took Elias's cue. "I think both ideas are good ones. When this thing goes down, it's going to happen fast. I also think we should have Brett radio in his itinerary. He's been doing so on most occasions but I want to make sure he knows how important it is. As far as the van goes, Francine, we're running two crews each on a twelve-hour shift. The shifts run from 8 a.m. to 8 p.m. and I'm guessing you'll want to be part of the day shift."

"Yes," Francine said. "From my vantage point, I think those are the peak times for activity."

Miller confirmed her thoughts. "I agree. If you'd like, I can arrange a technical briefing for you to bring you up to speed on the equipment we're using. I'm not sure it's as sophisticated as the stuff you guys have, but I think you'll find it interesting and informative."

"I'd like that very much, Detective Miller," Francine replied more out of politeness than actual interest.

"I'll set it up for you. By the way, Beatrice Kingston is on her way in. She should be here in about twenty minutes. It might be a good idea if you listened in."

"Are you taking her into an interrogation room?" Francine asked suggesting in her tone that she didn't think it was a good idea.

"We are," Miller responded. "It's not a traditional room. "There's a nice mahogany conference table, several high back chairs and it's actually decorated with some plants and on the walls there are a few nice paintings. It's actually pretty relaxing."

Elias liked the idea. "Have you found that type of atmosphere more conducive to questioning?" Elias asked.

"Depends on the person we're questioning and the style of questioning we plan on using. In this case, we want to be gentle; we're not sure if Ms. Kingston knows anything at all, including the fact that her daughter is dead."

Elias was nodding his head in approval. Removing a small pad from his lapel pocket, he jotted down a reminder to bring this modified interrogation room to the attention of his boss at the next budget meeting.

Brian Miller offered her a chair and then took one himself. "Thanks for coming down to talk with us, Mr. Kingston."

"The officer that brought me here told me it was important." Her voice cracking with the nervousness he could see in her eyes. "He said someone I knew was involved in a murder investigation, and I might be able to give you some information that might help."

Brian's speech was non confrontational and deliberate. "Yes, we're hopeful that you can. During the course of our investigation, we've uncovered several leads that we're looking into. A young lady by the name of Petrova surfaced a few days ago and we're hoping you could give some information about her."

"If I can help you, Detective, I will. Who is this Petrova woman, and what possibly could she have to do with me?" she asked anxiously.

Miller couldn't believe it. She was hiding the fact that she was her mother. "That's what we're trying to find out. Excuse me for just a second," he said, walking toward the door. "I need to get something from my office. I'll be back before you know it," he said calmly, adding a warm smile.

Miller joined Elias, Francine and Ryan O'Hara in the small observation room wanting to get the documents his detective brought back. He also wanted to give Ms. Kingston a few minutes alone to ponder what may be coming next.

"She's one nervous Nelly," Elias said, looking through the two-way mirror.

Miller reached over to Ryan taking the documents into his hand "Is this everything?"

"Sure is, L.T.," Ryan replied, handing him the manila folder.

"Let's see how she reacts when I show her these," Miller said on his way back.

"Sorry," he said reentering the room.

Miller sat down and placed the folder between them and noticed that her eyes had not left the folder since he came back in.

"Can you tell me where you were last Saturday, Ms. Kingston?"

"I was home most of the day. Saturday has always been the day I clean. Why, Detective?"

"Did you happen to talk with anyone?"

"No, I didn't. I live alone and I didn't go anywhere. I wish you would just tell me what's going on," she said pleading with him.

Realizing he needed to be precise, he repeated his question. "Did anyone call you on the phone?"

"Yes, I spoke with my daughter and someone trying to sell me a magazine subscription," she answered, trying to understand what he was getting at.

"What did you and your daughter talk about?"

"We weren't on the phone very long. We were supposed to meet for dinner Saturday night. She said she had something important she had to do and wanted to reschedule. So, we're going to go out this Friday instead. How did you know she called me?"

She doesn't know it's her daughter we're talking about! Miller thought. *This is really bizarre.* "What's your daughters name, Ms. Kingston?" he asked to see if his suspicions were right.

"Nadia Wilson. Why?" she asked fearfully. "Is she involved? Has something happened to her?"

Brian had no choice now and had to tell her that her daughter was dead. She rejected it at first until he showed her the documents. With her mouth ajar, the tears began to trickle from the corners of her eyes. The realization of her daughter's death brought the weight of the world down on her shoulders. Putting her head down on the table, she wept hysterically as he did his best to comfort her. She took tissues from the box he had given her and struggled to put herself back together.

"I told her not to. I told her it wasn't good for her!" she said, clutching tightly to a tissue.

"What, what wasn't good for her?" Miller asked.

Beatrice Kingston had to start from the beginning and Miller let her talk until she was finished.

"It tore my heart apart to have to put her up for adoption but I had no choice. She found me when she was a teenager. Said she wanted to get to know her real parents, but I wouldn't tell her who her father was. One night about twelve years ago, my daughter tracked me down at the company Christmas party."

"I was secretly dating one of the company presidents, Brandon Ohliger. A secretary doesn't date an executive, that's taboo. We're at the pavilion and my daughter comes in. Brandon was really drunk. When he spotted her, he pulled her aside. They talked for a few minutes and my daughter kisses him on the check and waved goodbye to me. She never even stopped to say hello to me. I don't know how he knew but when he walked over to me, he told me that my daughter just found out the name of her father."

"Who's her father Ms. Kingston?"

"Peter Ivanov. When he found out I was pregnant, he told me to have an abortion. I pleaded with him until he finally agreed to adoption. He wanted nothing to do with her and suggested that I shouldn't either."

"Why would he say something like that?" Brian wondered.

"He said his associates wouldn't approve, something about an oath."

"You've got a pretty good memory," Brian said surprised at the details she seemed to able to remember.

Beatrice caught the implication. "If someone said you had to give up your unborn child, you'd remember too!"

"How did you meet this Brian Ohliger?" he asked.

"Peter offered to give me a job and a nice sum of money to help ease my pain. So I worked at his company, Nelson Pharmaceuticals. I was Brandon's secretary."

Elias and Francine listened as she continued to tell her tale. As far as he was concerned, he had enough information to a make the connection and wanted to see if Miller concurred.

After Ms. Kingston left for the coroner's office to see her daughter for the last time, Brian led Elias and Francine back to his office. Brian agreed when Elias asked if he could share the conclusions he'd arrived at watching the interview unfolded from the observation room.

"I think we can all agree," Elias began, "that even though Ms. Kingston worked at the company for twenty years, she has nothing whatsoever to do with this case. That having been said, I think we need to find Brandon Ohliger. It appears, at least on the surface, that he might have some things to tell us that we'll find useful."

Brian started rifling through the documents on his desk, looking for the list of board members while Elias continued outlining his conclusions.

"The course of events is also pretty amazing and in my judgment goes far beyond coincidence. About twelve years ago, a number of things happened. Nadia makes a surprise appearance at a company Christmas party and finds out from a drunken executive that her father is Peter Ivanov, a member of the board. She changed her name in Jan. of '91 obviously to get her father's approval and attention. What we don't know is if Nadia attempted to contact him, so let's just assume that she did since the odds are heavily in our favor."

"I'd make that assumption," Miller said in agreement.

Francine knew that Elias didn't like being interrupted when outlining his ideas but when she looked at him, he didn't seem to mind one bit.

"In May or June of that year," Elias said, plowing through Miller's statement, "Russell Craft and Cynthia Dobson are both killed; they also just happen to work for the same company as everyone else we've tied into this mess. And then we have the documents that in my opinion more than establish motive."

Elias could tell that Miller was on board with his analysis, and since he had an ally, it was time to put a wrap on it.

"I'm not sure if everyone caught this so let me throw it out there just in case. Ms. Kingston said Mr. Ivanov's associates wouldn't approve and something about a code. Based on my past experience in federal law enforcement, the things Ms. Kingston has told us that fact that five of the board members are to be of Russian descent, I think we're dealing with the Mafia, the Russian Mafia."

Miller wasn't sure he heard him correctly. "The Russian Mafia?"

"Yes, the *Russian Mafia*" Elias said wanting to drive home the point. "They're very tightly knit, and not unlike our homegrown organized crime syndicate, they take any family impropriety very seriously, oftentimes dealing out harsh consequences. So Mr. Ivanov has an affair that results in Ms. Kingston getting pregnant. Then he has to cover his tracks."

"I agree," Francine said, "There are just too many coincidences after Ms. Petrova discovers the identity of her father."

Brian sat there and suddenly remembered what he had told Hank before he left. *Daddy wasn't real happy with the reunion.*

"Yes. I think I see it now," Miller said. "I'll need you to bear with me on this. Ivanov meets with his unwanted daughter. She is desperate for his approval and agrees to help keep tabs on Craft. She may or may not have known the reason but agrees just the same hoping that through her actions she can gain his acceptance. Ultimately, Craft is eliminated to keep company profits soaring. Twelve years later, a young man, no more than kid really, shows up at her door talking about Russell Craft. Allen tells her he needs some mysterious disk. At first, she thinks he's a nut until it surfaces exactly where he told her it was. She panics and needs to contact her father so she can tell him, but first she clears her schedule and cancels dinner with Mom, then leaves the house and contacts him. After sharing the story about the strange visitor and mysterious disk, she becomes a liability he can no longer carry, especially since the next person on the hit list was the very person that had just paid her a visit. He agrees to meet her at that dingy hotel or maybe he sends someone to meet her. We know the rest!"

Elias' pleasure with Miller's reasoning was reflected in his tone. "Detective Miller, I think we've got a case against the company that we can tie in very nicely with Frank Whickers. After we're done meeting with Mr. Allen this afternoon, let's head over the US Attorney's office. I think we have enough to present our information and get some federal warrants issued."

"Excuse me, Lieutenant," one of his police officers said, standing at Miller's door, "you've got a call from Detective Beard on line 2."

Brian excused himself and picked up the phone. Hank filled him in on the results of his detective's interview with the trio at the pharmaceutical company as Brian jotted down some of the highlights. Brian reciprocated by sharing the results of the Kingston interview, their theory about the Russian connection and their plans to visit the US Attorney.

Brian hung up the phone and scanned his notes before looking up at the two federal agents. "I know you'll find this interesting," Miller said. "You'll remember that in Russell Craft's note he mentioned he couldn't find his material on the company computer system. As it turns out, Brandon Ohliger was and still is in charge of those computer systems. He claims a super virus ran through the entire place and they lost all of the research data on Craft's project."

"Hmmm," Elias said. "It would seem that our theory gets more and more credence with every turn. They didn't lose the data to some virus, they destroyed it!"

"I'd like to make a recommendation," Elias said, preparing Miller for his suggestion, "I think it would be a good idea if we postpone the interview with Ivanov. Once we have the warrants in our hand, a coordinated arrest may give us an edge."

"Yes," Francine chimed in, "if we can bring everyone in together, none of them will know who's saying what. The more nervous we can make them, the better chance we'll have of getting someone to make a deal."

"Leniency in exchange for testimony?" Miller asked.

"Precisely. Getting testimony would have a large impact on our heavily circumstantial case," Francine said adding, the punctuation mark.

"Then, we'll be able to unravel this whole thing and get *everyone* that's involved," Elias said, adding his footnote.

Miller picked up the phone "I'll let Hank know and get him turned around!"

32.

At Elias' suggestion, Francine followed them over to Dr. Davenport's office skipping the technical briefing so she could also meet Brett Allen and perhaps bring some insight to the situation with her bright mind.

Miller was riding with Elias and was impressed with the M27 unit mounted on the dash board. Elias was careful to only have the agent overlay displayed as he didn't want Miller knowing that Trevor had tapped into the police frequency so he could also keep an eye on Brett Allen.

"This is some terrific stuff," Miller exclaimed seeing the real time position of all the federal agents. "So you could still run the show from here if you had to?"

"That's right and since I'm responsible for the mission's outcome, I need to know as much information as I can," he replied. "This is tied right into the operations center so I can see what they see."

Miller was staring at the screen for a few minutes and decided to ask "Where is our position on the display?"

"I'm glad Francine's not riding with us because I'm a little embarrassed to tell you that in my haste to get everything coordinated, I forgot to bring a tracking device for myself."

Brian started laughing. "Nowhere near as bad as forgetting to pick up a gallon of milk on the way home." With that, Brian watched Elias burst into laughter.

Standing outside the door of Dr. Davenport's office, Elias wanted to make one final suggestion before meeting the cast of characters on the other side of the door.

"Let's keep our information and plans about the Nelson side of this confidential for the moment. Since we've concluded that we can have officers in place at 4:30 p.m. tomorrow to bring these people in, we shouldn't tell anyone outside of our channels until they're in custody. Besides, we don't want Mr. Allen to get the wrong impression and think he's out of the woods. False hope can be a very bad thing."

Everyone agreed and went into Dr. Davenport's office. The cast of characters was already assembled and were waiting for them in her office. Miller introduced Elias and Kelly; Dr. Davenport introduced Joe Kaufman and Brett.

Once everyone was seated comfortably, Brett began answering Dr. Kaufman's question regarding his hypnotic session from the day before. Elias and Francine sat dumbfounded, listening to Brett tell it was far different than Miller's version. Brett retold his story, detouring along the way to answer some specific questions that Dr. Kaufman had.

"Brett," Joyce Davenport said, getting his attention. "When we spoke yesterday about your sudden illness at the Dug Out just before seeing Frank Whickers, Dr. Kaufman and I had a long conversation. We've concluded that you had, what we call, a crossover experience."

"I'm not sure I know what that means, but it doesn't sound good!" Brett replied.

"We think that you've established a like between two realms of consciousness," Joe Kaufman said ready to finish the explanation. One here, the other one, well let's just say, with Russell Craft. Based on our session yesterday and what happened at the Dug Out we think Russell Craft is somehow giving you advanced warning of potentially dangerous situations. What we don't know is if these apply exclusively to Frank or if there may be other occurrences that trigger the crossover experience."

"I completely understand what you said and can't deny the fact that it happened or that it may happen again. I suppose it's a good thing to have an early warning system, but I'm still having trouble letting this entire thing sink in! It's like my life doesn't belong to *me* anymore!"

"I can't pretend to know how scary and frustrating this has been for you," Joyce said with every ounce of sympathy in her body. "I think that when this is over, maybe we should think about one more session. Somehow try and close the door on this bridge that's been built so you can have your life back."

"When *will* this be over?" Brett asked, directing his question to Brian Miller.

"We're getting closer all the time, Brett. Every hour that passes means we're an hour closer. We want you to do something for us that you've already started to do. Before you go anywhere, use your communications gear and let us know. This way we can have our undercover people there before you arrive. I think it's an added layer of protection that will greatly enhance our efforts to nail this guy."

"I can use all the protection I can get, and I'm grateful for what everyone is trying to do, but I'm starting to lose my stomach for this," Brett confessed, "and I don't want to give up but I don't like the idea of being used as bait."

"Mr. Allen" Elias said breaking into the conversation "I can assure you that every possible resource at our disposal is being brought to bear on this. You mentioned that your life isn't your own. The only way to reclaim it is for us to catch him and without your help we won't be able to do that."

"I know...I know," Brett replied sadly. "There's something else I think should be brought to your attention. All of my research material is inaccessible. I guess some sort of virus. I can't help remembering that Russell Craft couldn't access his data a few days before he was killed."

Everyone sat silent, not knowing what to say. Elias and Brian exchanged a quick glance knowing for certain that not only was Brett right but their theory had just turned into fact.

Brett stood up. He was all done with the meeting and just wanted to go home. If he could have found a rock to crawl under and hide, he would have done so. For the rest of the night at least, that rock would be his apartment.

"Thanks, everyone, for all your help. I really mean that. I'm going home now!" And with that Brett walked right out of the room.

Joyce wanted desperately to reach out to him but knew that from this point on, he would have to see this thing through to the end, and he'd have to do it alone.

Francine decided to go back to the operation's center. She would drive back to the police station in the morning for her 7:00 a.m. pickup and join the relief crew in the shadow van.

Elias and Miller went to the US Attorney's office and presented the information they had and were rewarded with the arrest warrants they requested. On their way back to the station, Brian agreed to double check with Hank and make sure the timing of the arrests were coordinated with the federal agents in Connecticut so everyone would be ready to go on time.

Brian extended Elias a dinner invitation as they pulled into the police station. Elias was hungry but declined. He had to be in Brighton and start getting familiar with the territory out there. As they were saying goodbye, Elias got a call on his radio.

"This is Flynn," Elias said waiting for a response.

"Brian Ohliger was killed in an automobile accident just a short while ago. I thought you'd need to know."

Elias looked over at Brian Miller. "It's game time!"

There was little more they could say or do and both men knew that the time was drawing near. In a day or two, Brett's involvement in this case would be ending; they just hoped the outcome would be a good one.

* * *

Dinner at Brett's house was for the most part a silent affair. Brett poked around at Becky's wonderful dinner, wishing he had an appetite. Everyone at the table was lost in their own world of uncertainty. There wasn't much anyone could say and the conversation bordered on shallow.

Brett's father wanted to stay the night with his son but he had to get a full construction crew up to Bedford and be in place at five in the morning. Detective Miller had suggested and gotten the governor's approval to replace all the guard rails near the entrance of the research center. This would eliminate the research center as one of Frank's engagement zones. Elias didn't think it was a concern but Miller wanted to give Brett's father something to do so he would feel helpful and to keep his mind off of things.

Michael knew Becky was going to stay and that's probably what Brett would prefer anyway. He was, after all, a man now. Despite Brett's age, he would always be his father's little boy and Michael was thankful Brett didn't mind.

As Michael said goodbye to his son, he wasn't sure if he would ever see him again. They hugged each other with all their hearts hoping to get enough to last a lifetime. Tears fell from their faces as they were reminded of the last hug they had given to Brett's mother.

"Son," he said through teary eyes, "I want you to know how proud I am of you! Ever since you were born, it's been an honor to be your father. Whatever happens," he said sobbing heavily, "nothing will be able to separate you from my love!"

"Me too, Dad," Brett said, weeping deeply. "I've always wanted to make you proud. If this doesn't go the way we hope, I'll tell mom when I see her just how much you love and miss her. You always told me not to give up and I won't, Dad."

"I know, Brett," his father said wiping his eyes. "I'd better be going now. Try and get some rest son. This isn't goodbye, it's see you later!"

"See you later, Dad!" Brett said, wiping his eyes. "I'll see you tomorrow!"

33.

As Michael was driving home from his son's apartment looking for answers, Frank was on a Rhode Island highway looking for something else. Frank was in the market for some much needed clothing and when he saw the large department store he got off the highway so he and his companion could do a little shopping. Jessica noticed that Frank's method of shopping was almost identical to what she had done just the night before. He moved quickly through the aisles, not trying anything on, obviously anxious to pick up what he needed and get out the store as fast as possible.

Frank had selected a well-known, middle-of-the-road hotel and parked as close to the front as he could. Frank walked into the lobby doing his very best to avoid showing too much of his face to the video cameras covering the main desk.

He pulled out the same credit card he used when he switched from the green sedan to the silver Mitsubishi and checked them in as Mr. and Mrs. Francois Bedeau. The doors to the rooms were outside and Frank parked near the end of the building in the space which indicated the number that corresponded to the room number.

Frank carried their bags up the outside stairway and opened the door. It smelled a little musty but it was bearable. Pushing the button that cranked the air-conditioning unit to full blast, they heard it whine its way into service. Below the thin orange bed spread, Jessica noticed an uncharacteristically large dip in the mattress.

"That doesn't look very comfortable," Jessica said, getting Frank's attention.

"No, it sure doesn't," Frank agreed. "I expected the accommodation to be nicer than this. We'll be getting up tomorrow morning at 4:00 a.m. so I think it would be a real good idea if you lay down and tried to get some sleep."

"I haven't been in bed at 9:00 p.m. since I was in grammar school," she responded, "but I don't think I can ever remember getting up that early. I'm not even sure that I'm all that tired."

Jessica didn't want any physical contact with Frank so she walked over to the bed took off her shoes and laid on top of the bedspread. She hoped that since she was still fully dressed, Frank would get the hint. She was obviously much more tired than she thought and drifted off into a deep sleep.

Frank turned the T.V. on and kept the volume low. After an hour or so, he got up from the small wooden table he was sitting at and walked over to the bed. He wanted to be sure she was really asleep. He shook her a little and got no response. Walking to the end of the bed, he ran his finger gently across the bottom of her foot knowing this was one of her tickle spots. Seeing no reaction Frank went back to the table. Opening the drawer, he pulled out a pad of paper and envelope both of which carried the hotel chain's logo and sat down to write her a short note.

After looking it over for a few minutes to make sure he was satisfied, he folded the paper in half, put it in the envelope, and sealed it. *Now it's time for a little clean up work,* he thought.

Grabbing a towel, he turned off the television, left the room, walked back down the stairs and over to the car. There were only a few lights in the parking lot which was just fine for Frank. He would have just enough light to see and as long as he could finish what he was about to do, he'd be a happy man.

Opening the trunk, he dialed 7622 into the lock so he could get at the weapons in the case. He gently lifted the rifle up just enough to be able to get the towel around it and moved as fast as he could to get all the prints off, pausing every so often to make sure no one was around. Finished with the rifle, Frank removed the 9mm pistol, put the silencer on and inserted a full clip. Setting the pistol down in the bottom of the trunk, he went ahead and removed his prints from the case itself.

Frank picked up the pistol and placed in beneath his belt then pulled his shirt over so it couldn't be seen. Taking one last look around and finding that the coast was clear, he locked the case with the rifle inside and picked it up with the towel around the handle.

Moving quickly around the corner and behind the building, Frank hurled the case over the six foot stockade fence that ran the length of the hotel. *Looks like I won't need you after all,* he thought listening to the case crash down the steep bank on the other side.

With that done, Frank walked back to the car and placed the envelope containing the note for Veronica in the glove compartment and locked it, closed the truck and then locked the doors. He could feel just how tired he was both physically and mentally and couldn't wait to go up to the room and get sleep.

When he got back in the room, Veronica was just as he left her. Removing the pistol from beneath his belt, he placed it in his large gym bag beneath his new clothes. Rising slowly, he stood at the side of the bed for a few minutes and just admired her beauty. To him, everything about her was just perfect. A big yawn told him he better get into bed, so he took off his shoes and laid down next her, wondering before he fell asleep if he was really going to make it through this assignment and be able to escape.

Frank had woken up, showered, and dressed about a half an hour before the alarm was to go off and started to think over his makeshift plan. It was bold and dangerous but he had very little choice. He would drive to Bedford tomorrow and try to pick up Brett's trail either at lunch or when he left for work. If he got there and saw he wasn't at work, he'd try his apartment. Either way, he had to try and get this done sometime today then immediately head for Canada. From there, he could make his way back to France and resume some sort life as Mr. Bedeau.

Looking at Veronica, he knew there was no way she'd be coming with him. *Too bad,* Frank thought feeling somewhat sorry for himself. He had grown very fond of her the past twelve months and wished things had worked out differently between them. Then maybe he would have tried to persuade her to come along. But given the recent history, he knew that was totally out of the question. *Besides,* he thought, *she's 100% committed.*

"I'm sorry," Frank whispered through the drone of the air conditioner, "I'll let you free just as soon as this is over but not before." He didn't relish the idea of holding a hostage and hoped it wouldn't come to that but if it went bad, that's exactly what he'd have to do.

Jessica slowly started to wake up. She had slept so deeply that she was a little disoriented when her eyes finally opened. Slowly making her way to a sitting position, she rubbed her eyes a little and almost screamed when she saw Frank sitting at the table.

"You scared me, Frank!" Jessica said with a sleepy voice. "What time is it?"

Frank got up and walked over to the alarm clock and turned it off. "It's almost four."

"Do we really have to be up so early?" was her second groggy question of the day. "I feel like I could sleep until noon."

"I'm afraid you do have to get up. I want to leave as soon as you're ready to go" he said, walking over and helping her up.

"Follow me," he said, leading her into the shower. "I'll go down the road and grab us a cup of coffee and a pot luck breakfast; you take a shower and get ready to go. I'll be back in twenty-five minutes. I know that's not a lot of time to get ready but please do the best you can." With that, Frank closed the door and left the room.

Wow, Jessica thought, *I'm so happy he didn't try anything last night or this morning for that matter. I'd better be dressed and ready when he gets back. I don't want him to get any ideas.* With a renewed purpose for getting ready, she took one of the fastest showers of her life.

When Frank came back he found Veronica sitting on the bed watching a cable news channel, ready to go. He was definitely impressed with how fast she had gotten herself ready and that even at 4:30 in the morning she was still a beautiful and stunning woman.

"I've got to tell you, Veronica," he said, standing at the door with a refreshment tray with two cups of coffee in one hand and a brown paper bag in the other, "you're one amazing woman."

Coming into the room, he grabbed the bottom of the door with his foot and swung it closed. It was obvious by the way the door slammed shut, he had swung it a little too hard. The normal stillness at that time of the morning made it sound even louder.

"This should hold us until we get into Massachusetts," he said, putting the coffee on the table and emptying the contents of the bag.

"Massachusetts! You mean were going back there?" Jessica said looking at the breakfast buffet.

"Yes. As I told you yesterday, I don't have much of a choice. Now you better get something in your stomach. I know it's not the greatest selection," he said, "but it's going to have to do."

Jessica knew that today was going to be the day and hopefully soon she would be able to get his targets information from him. Once she had that, she'd have to find a way to somehow get away from Frank for just five minutes so she could call Elias and let him know. She knew she had to play her role to perfection now. If she slipped up even the slightest bit, Frank would send her to meet her maker!

"Let me see," Jessica said examining the items on the table a little more closely, "You have two ham egg and cheese sandwiches wrapped in that *keep it warm forever* foil, and a box of assorted doughnuts. That's not bad, Frank, for this time of day!" she said, smiling for the first time since they had gotten reacquainted yesterday afternoon.

"Let's eat!" Frank said grabbing a sandwich and opening his coffee. "We've got to get going in a few minutes."

After they finished breakfast, Frank checked out of the room and returned to the running car. Reaching into the map pouch, he took out a map and gave it to her.

"You're the navigator," he said, "I've outlined the route and I'd like you to make sure I don't miss a turn, OK?"

Jessica opened the map, turned on the small map light and took a look at it as they got onto I-295 North. She saw the dark lines Frank had drawn over the route he wanted to take. *What's he doing going to Bedford?* she thought, noticing the dark traced lines ended there.

"I'll keep you on the right track, Frank, don't worry," Jessica said trying to fold the large map into a more manageable size. "These things are impossible!" she said struggling with the folds.

All Frank could do was chuckle. "They sure are!"

"I'm really scared, Frank," Jessica said, having spent the last fifteen minutes in silence coming up with a plan of her own. "Look at my hands, they're shaking! Please, Frank, can't we just go away and forget about this whole thing," she pleaded with him. "We can go somewhere that they can't find us, start a life together."

"You just don't get it, Veronica. If I don't finish this, there is *no place to hide!*" Frank said. "They always know how to find you,"

Jessica had to sit and think about that and started a dialogue in her mind. *Elias had said from the beginning of Operation Escort that Frank had gone into hiding and surfaced in Chicago. We needed to set up this sophisticated operation and hopefully get someone close so we could keep an eye on him and find out what he's doing back in the country. That was my part. If what Frank had said was true, then the CIA knew all along exactly what Frank was here for so why didn't they fess up? Was this one of those secret highly classified agency's within an agency that Frank had mentioned yesterday?*

Hmmm, she thought continuing her analysis, *If the CIA knew where he was all along why didn't they just pick him up?* Then it came to her that Frank must be working for one of those secret little agencies that are embedded in the CIA and although the clean part of the agency knows it exists, they don't know who they are or what they're doing. *They certainly can't investigate it without alerting the clandestine group so they call us in on the QT to do it for them.*

"We're getting close aren't we?" Frank asked.

Jessica didn't answer at first as her entire mind was focusing on trying to figure out just what was going on based on the information she had.

"We're getting close aren't we?" Frank asked again in a stern tone.

"I'm sorry," she said, bringing her mind back. "Close?"

"Yes, close to switching highways!" Frank said, a little perturbed by her lack of concentration.

"You're right, Frank, we are," she said looking out the window to get a mile marker for reference. "You'll have to turn in about fifteen minutes."

Jessica unhooked her visor and moved it as close to the window as possible hoping to cut down on the glare. The dashboard clock showed it was 6:00 a.m. and she knew that any time now the traffic would start to build. She needed all the time she could get to figure out how she was going to get Frank to tell her who the target is and then somehow find a way to inform Elias.

34.

As the wonderful aroma of Becky's cooking spread out through his apartment, Brett had realized that he once again managed to wake up with a sore neck. When he fell asleep on the couch, Becky had moved him around to what she thought was a comfortable position and tossed a light blanket over him. Unlike Brett, she didn't know the well-deserved reputation his couch had for unsuspecting sleepers. Despite his sore neck, he had slept pretty well. Rubbing his neck and moving his head in from shoulder to shoulder provided some relief, but he was going to once again need help from inside his medicine cabinet.

Rising up from the unforgiving sofa, Brett went into the bathroom, swallowed down two pain relievers, got cleaned up and walked to the kitchen. Becky was flipping eggs on the stove and had not seen him come in. Brett walked up slowly and quietly behind her.

"Good morning," he said noticing her flinch a little bit.

"Don't do that!" Becky said playfully. "It's not nice to scare the chef in the middle of her work!"

Brett knew she was trying to stay up beat and jovial to keep his spirits up but his somber mood, at least for the moment, couldn't be overcome.

Becky turned around and gave him a warm hug. "Mmmm," she sighed, "This feels so nice, I don't think I want to let go!" With her head still buried in his shoulder, she made a suggestion. "I've got to pick up my check this afternoon from work. What do you say we go to the video store and rent a couple of DVD's and stay put in your apartment?"

"OK, Becky," he replied softly, "I'm starting to think that following the normal routine isn't that great of an idea. Look at all that stuff," Brett said looking at the corner table. "Bullet proof vest, special police equipment and a gun. How safe can it really be for me running around town or sitting at the Dug Out watching a game?"

"I don't care what that government agent said yesterday," Brett said, moving Becky's head back so he could see her face. "They want this guy to get close enough to take a shot at me and I'm starting to get *real* uncomfortable with the whole thing. I'm not sure how I was able to manage it in the beginning but I just don't think I can do it anymore," he confessed, the weight of his burden forcing him to sit down.

Becky turned off the burner on the stove and sat down to join him. Not only did she fear for him, she feared for herself and she wished there was something she could do, someway she could protect him. She had found a man that she knew she loved and couldn't bear the thought of losing him. If something were to happen to him, her life would return to the emptiness she had known as a child, a hollow existence, void of meaning, direction and love. She loved her mother deeply, but the love of a daughter for her mother was far different than the love shared between a man and a woman taking on the challenges of life as a couple, and now that she had found it, she didn't want to let go.

"Ever since your father left," she said, reaching her hands across the table to grab his, "I was thinking that maybe we should just leave town for a few weeks, kind of like a vacation. Maybe this guy will lose heart and give up if he can't find you."

"I can't go on with life, our life," he said including her as part of his future, "always having to look over my shoulder. Always wondering if the next time I cross the street could be my last. Believe me, if I thought that would work, we'd have left a few days ago.

"I think staying in today might be good for me," Brett confessed. "Maybe I can find the courage I need to step out there and put an end to this thing, one way or another."

Becky wanted desperately to change the subject, "Why don't we eat before it gets cold?"

Brett agreed. He wanted to change the subject as well and hoped that the change in conversation would work its way into his mind and change the way he was thinking.

Francine wasn't having breakfast; she had finished eating over an hour ago and was waiting patiently at police headquarters for the shadow van crew to pick her up so they could relieve the night shift. She wasn't enjoying the wait nor was she looking forward to sitting in a van all day long. The more she thought about her role as a special agent supervisor, the more she disliked the thought of being demoted to field agent and the humdrum life that went along with it. Francine had crossed paths a few times with local police and each experience was a bad one. The prospect of having to endure it yet again added to her displeasure.

Francine watched from the main doors as a maroon Lincoln Continental slowed to a stop in front of the building. *Here we go,* she thought recognizing, just like most people do, the traditional unmarked car. A man slowly got out and started walking toward her. Francine was sizing him up as he approached "At least he looks like a reasonable and friendly guy. I hope there isn't a brick wall he plans on throwing up between us or it's going to be a very long day!"

"Agent Kelly I presume?" he said, stretching out his hand immediately offering both a greeting and a truce before they walked over to the car. "I'm Detective Dykstra and my partner in the car is Detective Otten."

Wanting to get off on the right foot and set an amicable working relationship Francine's reply was cordial and sincere "Good morning, Detective."

"We're looking forward to working with you," Dykstra continued. "It's my understanding from Detective Miller that you've been fully briefed but I'm going to guess you still have a few questions. The shadow van is in Brighton. We'll be driving over there to meet so we can talk on the way."

When they got to the car, Dykstra was a gentleman and opened the back door for her to get in. Francine was pleasantly surprised to see that his partner was a female.

As Dykstra was filling her in on the way over, she was surprised to learn that Elias and Miller had decided to keep the mobile units two blocks from Brett's indicated position.

"At that distance, will the response units be able to get there quickly enough?" Francine asked fully letting her astonishment be known.

"I know," Dykstra responded with some astonishment of his own. "We have a bunch of our best undercover people in or near the places he frequents on a regular basis. We have several of yours out there as well. Mr. Allen doesn't move around a whole lot so maybe the thought is that we have all the bases covered. I guess this guy Whickers is pretty slick. I think they, your boss and mine, are afraid of overkill and raising his suspicions."

"Actually, the more I think about it, it may not be a bad idea," Francine commented, remembering that Jessica was their ace in hole. Apparently, she thought, that information hadn't been given out.

"Here we are," Detective Otten announced, putting on her blinker.

Pulling into the large car dealership, Otten drove back towards the maintenance bays. Off to the right, she noticed several vans parked together. *Must be one of those,* she thought.

Letting herself out the car, Francine started to walk toward the oldest and boxiest looking van she saw, certain that it was the shadow van until she heard detective Otten call out to her.

"Over this way please, Agent Pierce," she said, pointing her finger to a luxury model with a smile, "This one belongs to us....Surprised?"

What could Francine say other than yes? What she had envisioned was jaded by her previous stake out experience a few years ago. Then, she worked out of what could only be described as old plumber's van.

"I am!" was the only answer Francine could give.

"You guys want to open the door?" Dykstra said over the radio as they got closer.

The back door of the van opened slowly. Francine watched a tired-looking police detective get out, close the door and walk toward them. It was common practice on these late night surveillance details for detectives to work in shifts. One sleeps while the other works. Judging from the disheveled appearance of the man coming their way, Francine wondered if he had slept the whole night through. She wanted to tell him not to bother with the finger comb. His attempts to straighten out his hair were futile and he wasn't working on the big piece that was sticking up from the back.

"Good morning, Tonto" Detective Otten said, trying to hold her laughter.

"Tonto?" the tired detective asked.

"We're admiring your Indian feather," Dykstra said, bursting into laughter.

Francine was giggling too even though she felt a little sorry for the poor guy for getting picked on and was wondering how he would respond. Her answer wasn't long in coming.

The sleepy detective wasn't fazed in the least. Lightly touching the back of his head he knew what he had to do. Moistening his fingers with his tongue he matted it down. "Tonto ready now for tee-pee, Kimosabe. Tribal iron horse ready. Tonto also make warm drink for you and party of braves!" With that, a roar of laughter broke out.

Once everyone calmed down and caught their breath, they got the shift change briefing. Basically, Brett had been in his apartment since late yesterday afternoon. Francine got in first and was again surprised by what she saw. Three plush captains' chairs were smartly placed between the equipment that took up all the remaining space. Sitting down, she found the chairs to be very comfortable with ample room to move around. Dykstra was the last one in. As he was closing the door, Francine looked in her purse to double check that she had brought her paperback book which she wondered if she would have time to finish.

35.

Frank pulled over at a gas station to let Veronica use the bathroom and walked in with her to get the key. He didn't want to take *any* chances at this point. Although he knew her pretty well, he was still slightly suspicious. Once she was in and the door closed, he took the opportunity to remove the pistol from his bag and stick it under belt near his left hip. This way she wouldn't be able to see it unless she could somehow see through his body. He adjusted his loose-fitting shirt until he was satisfied it was hidden as well as it could be.

Jessica opened the bathroom door and Frank waved her over to the car. She couldn't understand why.

"Come on, get in!" Frank said sternly through the passenger side window.

"What about the key?" she asked.

"Toss it over near the front door and get in…please, we're running out of time," he said again in a more persuasive and less demanding tone.

Jessica did as Frank asked and got in the car. She wondered what had happened when she was in the bathroom to make him act this way. *Hmm, maybe he doesn't trust me and that is definitely not good!* she said to herself hoping she was wrong.

Frank drove just as fast as the speed limit would allow and was happy when the sign telling him he was entering Brighton appeared. It wouldn't be long now before Frank would find out if he was going to pick up Brett's trail. Frank negotiated the intersection masterfully. Jessica knew he had been here before and when they pulled into the Spruce Tree Apartment complex, she knew what he was looking for.

Driving slowly through the entire complex just as he had done in the huge parking lot in Bedford, Jessica hoped he would fixate on the vehicle he was looking for but he never did. Adding to her frustration, Frank drove through the entire complex and never once moved his head.

"OK," Frank said pulling out, "Now we're going over to that strip mall on the corner there and we wait."

After they had been sitting there for over an hour, Jessica thought it was a good time for a question. "Why have we been sitting here for so long, Frank?"

"I'm waiting for my special friend so I can finish this and we can get out of here!"

"I don't feel so good about this, Frank. I mean, I'm really nervous and scared!" she said convincingly.

Frank sat unresponsive, constantly scanning the surroundings for any sign of trouble. Jessica found his silence and lack of response unsettling.

I'm so glad this operation is almost over, she thought, *Looks like I'll have to take you down myself, Frank.*

* * *

"Mr. Allen, this is Brian Miller," Brett heard when he answered the phone. "Are you sitting down?"

"Good afternoon, Detective," he said apprehensively. "I'm not sitting down. Do I need to be?"

"That all depends on how you want to prepare yourself for the news," Miller said.

Brett was almost afraid to ask. "What do you mean by news?"

"We've just issued arrest warrants for a few of your employers. We've got some pretty solid evidence that they're behind this and had a hand in the death of Russell Craft and his assistant. That's part one," Miller said pausing, "Part two is equally as good." Again Miller paused.

Brett's was starting to get cautiously excited and wanted to get Miller to spit it out.

"OK. I'm sitting down," Brett said, "Let me hear it!"

"Agent Flynn had told me that one of his deep cover agents is with Frank Whickers!"

"Does that mean you're going to arrest him?" Brett asked hopefully.

"Yes, that's exactly what it means," Miller confirmed. "The case is pretty solid now and the US Attorney's office is very comfortable with it. He feels that with your testimony and that of your psychiatrist the case will tie together nicely."

"Just tell me when and where," Brett said. "I can't wait testify and get this monkey off my back."

"It's not quite that simple and a pretty long story, so I'll give you the abbreviated version. One of Agent Flynn's deep cover operatives is with Frank right now and apparently Frank has no idea. The problem we have is that we don't know exactly where they are nor does she know that we've issued the warrants. So as far as she knows, everyone is still operating under old guidelines."

Brett didn't like the sound of that.

"Since Agent Flynn hasn't actually heard from her, we're assuming Frank is still on the move. The good news is their agent being in such close proximity will be able to provide a level of protection that we could have only dreamed about."

Brett wasn't real sure this was as good of news as the detective portrayed it to be and asked a very good question. "How do you know Frank didn't find out about this agent and kill her?"

"Maybe I better give you some of the details that Agent Flynn shared with me," Miller said, and proceeded to outline the entire course of events. The phone call lasted longer than either of them had expected and when Brett hung up, he was feeling a lot better than he had.

Becky burst into tears of joy as Brett retold the story Brian Miller had just shared with them. It was hard to hide the relief they were both feeling. Becky was acting like a little school girl playing hop scotch at recess bouncing around the apartment with a grin that spread from ear to ear.

"Finally," Brett said, "I feel like they can really protect me."

"Let's go pick up my check, get a movie, a bottle of wine and celebrate. This is *my* treat!" Becky said feeling the weight of the world lifted off of her shoulders.

"Alright, but I'll get the movies, you can pick up the wine!" Brett counter offered.

"You have yourself a deal, but on one condition!" she said.

Becky saw a careful and inquisitive smile break out on Brett's face.

"Do I want to ask?" Brett asked with the same caution reflected in his smile.

"I don't know so why don't I just tell you," Becky said, walking over close to him. "I get to stay here tonight and since I don't want you to have another neck ache you don't have to sleep on couch."

Brett felt a combination of excitement and embarrassment as his cheeks turned red.

Becky picked up on it right away and decided to close the deal on her own "I'll take that as a yes, so let's get going and get what we need. For some *strange reason,* I'm very anxious to get back!"

As soon as Brett grabbed his keys, Becky grabbed his hand and led him out the door.

"I forgot something," Brett said after letting Becky into the car. "Wait here, I'll be back before you know it."

Becky sat in the car and watched him run up the stairs and go back inside. Closing her eyes, she whispered a thank you. Brett came back down the stairs and got in the car.

"What did you forget?" she asked.

Brett showed her the little tracking device "Just for giggles!" he said slipping it into his pocket and starting the car. "I used the transmitter from the apartment to let them know our itinerary, just to be on the safe side."

"We're off!" he said, backing out.

"I'm a little anxious to get back myself. I can't wait to call my dad and share the good news with him," Brett's added wink drew a smile.

"There we go," Frank said, looking at the apartment complex exit, seeing Brett's car behind one getting ready to pull out.

Jessica wondered which one Frank was going to follow and made mental notes of both makes and models as the two vehicles pulled out almost together, heading in the same direction. It didn't take long for Frank to stop once again. Jessica had a big problem as both cars pulled into a place called the Dug Out so she couldn't be sure who he was after and she knew any further questions would be way too risky.

Frank watched to see what Brett and his girlfriend were up too. He watched Becky get out of the car and thought it peculiar that Brett didn't get out and go with her.

Sitting in the car, Brett noticed his friend Mark, the one who had the comical strike three routine, waving him over to his outdoor table. Brett considered just waving him off. "I'll only be there for a minute or two and a dose of his humor is always a treat." Getting out and cautiously walking over to Mark's table, Brett could see his wide, contagious grin and readily reciprocated.

Mark had gotten an early start. Standing next to a full bottle of beer, Brett saw two empty bottles and a full glass.

"Brettster, long time no see!" he yelled out. "What's going on my man? No work today?"

"Hey, Mark. There's not a whole lot going on. I took today off."

"I hear you're making time with Becky…NICE!" Mark said, moving his head up and down. "Good catch, don't let her get away!"

"You could say that," Brett replied looking for Becky to come back out, "I just gave her a ride to pick up her check then we're going to get a couple of movies and lay in the weeds."

"Good idea, my friend," Mark said, looking at the sky, collecting his glass and full bottle of beer. "Looks like a big storm coming in. Matter of fact, we might want to head inside."

Brett looked up and saw nothing but blue sky. When he turned to look behind him that's when he saw what Mark was referring too. The joy and confidence he was feeling from his phone call with Miller was replaced with fear. *Oh no,* he thought, gazing into the fast approaching storm. *This is just what I saw in my vision.*

The cold stiff wind kicked up bringing with it a hard driving rain and deep rumbles of thunder. Becky came out of the Dug Out, running for the car with Brett close behind her. She had managed to somewhat protect her check from getting wet by putting it under her shirt.

They both arrived at the same time and got in as fast as they could quickly, closing the doors to keep as much rain out as possible.

"Whew," she said getting into car, "where did that come from?"

Brett's uneasiness was reflected in the way he was moving and in his tone of voice.

"Yeah," he said loudly so he could be heard above the sound of the rain that was just pelting the car. "This is a bad one!"

Becky knew something was wrong and had noticed that he had been talking with Mark.

"Is Mark alright? You seem a little down all of a sudden."

"Mark's fine, I'm just feeling a little uneasy all of a sudden," Brett admitted, not wanting to mention the vision he had. "Let's go get those videos and that bottle of wine you wanted."

Jessica watched the two cars, trying as best as she could to see while trying not to be too obvious. *This is like trying to look through a glass shower door,* she thought. Then she noticed one of the cars near the exit preparing to make a right turn.

"This is no good," Frank said pulling out into traffic, which really surprised Jessica.

Jessica was really confused. *Apparently, he's not following anyone now,* she thought.

They had traveled maybe a mile and Jessica was straining to see.

"Clear now, Frank," she said over the sound of rain beating the top of the car and Frank responded immediately.

Frank knew his opportunities to finish this assignment were running out. Based on his surveillance of Brett, he made an educated guess on where he was going when he left the Dug Out and he wanted to get there first, hoping he would show.

"I need to pull over here, Veronica," Frank said struggling to see the road. "Maybe the storm will blow over in a few minutes."

"I hope so, it's awful out there. It sure doesn't look like anyone is going anywhere fast," Jessica said, glad to be off the road.

"Veronica, can you look at the map and figure out our best route to Buffalo?" Frank asked leaning over to turn on the map light.

"Sure I can," Jessica replied, wondering why he was interested in Buffalo.

Frank's eyes kept shifting from the rear view mirror to Veronica. He wanted to make sure she wasn't paying attention to what he was doing. Using the marker Frank had given her, she started to trace out a route heading north and east.

Frank shifted his eyes again and saw what he was looking for. He watched Brett pull on the other side of the big box truck. *Time to get to work,* he thought.

"Hey, Veronica, I've got a sugar craving and I'm pretty sure they sell candy in these places, do you want any?"

"You're going out in this for a piece of candy?" Jessica asked, honestly surprised.

"I'm hungry, what can I say? So, do you want something or not?" he asked once again with his hand poised at the door handle.

Jessica was hungry herself. "How about a candy bar, doesn't matter what kind."

"I'll be right back," Frank said getting out the car.

Brett parked and just sat there for a minute trying to overcome the uneasiness he was feeling. Jumping out the car, he figured he could literally run in and grab something real quick and run right back out.

As soon as he slammed the car door shut, the awful nauseousness returned. Though he desperately tried to get back in the car, he was frozen in the heavy downpour waiting for the inevitable as the contents of his stomach swiftly moved upward. Hunching over, he wondered why it was always so hard to breathe when you got sick to your stomach. Almost before he could finish the thought, he gagged and his now mouth opened spewing mucus and small portions of undigested food onto the rain-soaked parking lot.

Jessica saw that Frank had just walked right past the front door. Jessica knew this wasn't good and quickly got out of the car and started calling his name and running toward him. As she got close to the front door, she saw a man come out holding a gun. She couldn't believe her eyes, it was Elias.

Elias quickly got himself in shooting position and tried to get his voice to carry above the rain "Drop the gun, Frank!"

Jessica couldn't comprehend what she was seeing. Things were moving too fast and there was too much information for her to process. Looking over toward Frank, she saw that he must have heard the warning.

Thankfully, he heard the warning and stopped. Brett's rain-soaked hair acted like a vinyl awning sending streams of water in front of his face. Wiping his eyes and pushing his hair back, he stood up. Through the heavy rain, he saw someone walking slowly toward him and wiped the rain from his face to get a better look.

Whoever it was wasn't real concerned with the weather. They just kept walking slowly toward him. Then he suddenly stopped. Squinting and wiping his eyes again, Brett saw that it was Frank Whickers and knew his moment of truth was at hand. Before Brett could move, he saw Frank raise his gun and heard a loud bang.

The impact of the bullet threw Brett back into the car, and he dropped to the pavement like a bag of cement. Becky was frantic and tried to get out the car so fast she fumbled with the handle a few times, opening the door.

She was crying uncontrollably as she moved as fast as she could toward Brett's limp body, the rain beating down with relentless perseverance. Sitting down next him she put his head in her lap and cried uncontrollably while rocking slightly back and forth screaming "Help me… please, somebody help me!"

Responding to Becky's cries for help, Elias left Jessica and told her to see about Frank and ran toward her. Squatting down next to her, he pulled out his radio and told someone to immediately send an ambulance. Elias put his fingers up against his neck, looking for a pulse.

Jessica knelt down next to Frank and tried as best she could to comfort him. She had seen this before and knew he didn't have much time left. "Hold on, Frank—stay with me, the ambulance is on the way."

Frank moved his lips and Jessica bent down putting her ear close to his mouth. It was hard to hear now with the sounds of distant sirens and the commotion this incident caused.

"I left something for you, Agent Pierce" he said as loudly as he could. Mentioning her real name nearly made her faint. "It's in the glove compartment. Don't tell anyone else that I know who you are." Frank coughed weakly as blood started to run form the corners of his mouth. "Don't let anyone see the note." He tried to smile but it was quickly replaced with a grimace of pain. "You're a good cop, and I wanted you to know…" and Frank went silent. He was dead.

"Rebecca…Rebecca!" Elias said shaking her to get her attention. "He's going to be OK!"

"You're a smart kid!" Elias said to Brett.

"What?" she cried in disbelief "What did you say?"

Elias smiled and lifted Brett's wet shirt revealing the Kevlar vest. "He's unconscious but OK!"

"Oh my gosh! I can't believe it," she said starting to regain her composure, "before we left the apartment, he told me he had forgotten something in the apartment. I know he wasn't wearing it when we got in the car, so he must have put it on when he went back inside."

Jessica was still kneeling down next to Frank's dead body. The water in the parking lot around him was turning pink and the blood drained from the wound in the middle of his back and mixed with the rain.

Jessica saw Elias walking back toward her. Two undercover police cars came to a screeching halt in the video store parking lot and Elias put down his gun and raised his hands.

"Special Agent Flynn!" he yelled hands high in the air. "It's over!"

Seeing the detectives respond by putting their guns away, Elias walked over to Jessica.

She rose to meet him and they hugged each other. Still holding her in a comforting embrace, he asked her if she was OK. Elias didn't get his answer in words but knew she wasn't as she broke down and sobbed on his shoulder.

"It's going to be OK. Everything is going to be OK!" he said, reassuring her. "That was a pretty risky stunt you pulled. I am SO glad you're safe.

"I've got to go over and talk with Detective Miller for a minute and tell him what happened," he said, seeing his car pull up. "I'll be right back, OK?"

"Go ahead, Elias, I'll be OK," she said wiping her eyes. "I'm going back to Frank's car to get my bag. I'll catch up with you in just a second."

Walking slowly back to the car, Jessica started to collect herself as best she could given the circumstances. Her legs were weak with fatigue. She was drained emotionally and wasn't really sure what she was going to do now. The one thing she *was* certain about was resigning. After debriefing, she would hand in her resignation and find another line of work in a state she had never lived in before. Her excruciating assignment was over now and so was her career as a special agent. It was the right time for a fresh start.

She still had a lot of questions that were unanswered and wasn't really sure if she cared to get the answers. She was still astonished that Frank knew who she was and wondered how long he had been dragging her along.

She remembered Frank's last few words; *don't let anyone see the note*, and *I wanted you to know*. She took a look around to ensure she was alone, then opened the glove compartment, removed the envelope, folded it in half and put it in her front pocket.

Reaching over the seat, she grabbed her bag from the back and walked over to Elias.

Miller recognized Jessica right away. "Special Agent Pierce, I'm Brian Miller. I'd like to shake the hand of one of the bravest people I've ever had the privilege to meet," he said, extending his hand toward her.

"How do you do, Detective?" she said, shaking his hand.

"Jessica," Flynn barged in, "Detective Miller tells me that the governor and mayor need me down at the Capitol building. I guess they want a debriefing."

Grabbing his radio, he went out on all channels. "This is Special Agent Flynn to all federal units. We've got Agent Pierce back and she's safe. The operation is over. I repeat, the operation is over. All agents are directed to report to the Operation Center immediately for debriefing. Nice work, everybody."

"Do you feel up to debriefing?" Elias asked, looking at Jessica.

"The sooner we can close the books on this, the better for me," she replied.

"Francine will be here in just a few minutes and I'll have her drive you over. Detective Miller has offered to give me a ride in so you two can take my car," he said, handing her the keys. "I know you have a lot of questions and I'll answer them just as soon as I get back from the Capitol building. In the meantime, I'm confident that she'll be able to fill you in and take care of at least some of them."

"Alright, Elias, I'll see you when we get back," Jessica said.

"You did a superb job, Jessica, and I know a thank you isn't nearly enough. When I get back, I'd like to talk about that too."

As Jessica watched a smiling Agent Flynn and Detective Miller get in the car and leave the scene, she saw Francine come tearing around the corner looking for her.

As soon as she saw Jessica, Francine ran over to her and gave her a big hug.

"I'm so glad you're back safe Jessica, so glad!" Francine said.

"So you know?" Jessica asked.

"Yes and so does Andy, but no one else. When I joined this circus, I always wanted to meet someone I could admire, and now I have!" Francine said with every ounce of genuineness her heart contained.

"That's the sweetest thing anyone has ever said to me, Francine. Thank you. Elias said we could take his car back to the operations center for debriefing. Would you mind doing the honors?" she asked, dangling the keys.

"Not at all," she said, grabbing the keys, "Are you ready to get out of here?"

"I'm so ready, you wouldn't believe it," Jessica said picking up her bag, "Let's go!"

As Francine and Becky were on their way to the car, they had to stop to let the ambulance carrying Brett Allen get started toward the hospital.

"Who is he?" Jessica asked curiously.

"Brett Allen, grandson of Senator George Allen," Francine said.

"Senator Allen's grandson?" she asked, making sure she heard it right.

"The very one," Francine said with a smile. "Come on, I'll fill you in on the way."

Brett's eyes opened slowly to the sounds of a siren and not so unfamiliar surroundings.

"Where am I?" he said, coming around to consciousness.

"You're on your way to the hospital," he heard Becky's voice say, "Your father's on his way to meet you there."

"What happened?" Brett asked groggily. "I feel like someone hit me in the chest with a sledge hammer!"

Becky's voice was comforting. "We'll talk about all that later, you just rest for now!" she said. Taking his hand, she watched him slowly close his eyes.

36.

"I guess I should start from the time you left and bring you right up to the present," Francine said pulling out of the parking lot.

Now Jessica knew that Francine was a fast talker but never imagined she could go as fast as she was right now. Each word was almost blended together and Jessica was having trouble following along. Jessica didn't know if it was because she was tired or had just become accustomed to hearing Frank speak slowly and clearly. It didn't really matter either way, so she politely asked Francine to slow down.

Francine touched lightly on the panic it caused when Frank ditched the tracking device while Jessica sat quietly listening not wanting to reveal just yet that she was responsible for that. Jessica was fascinated as Francine told the story of George Allen's grandson Brett. The entire heart transplant piece of the briefing and the theory that he had acquired the skills of the donor was something she never heard of and it really caught her interest.

Francine continued with her briefing and was over two thirds of the way finished when they pulled into the operation's center.

"Welcome home," Francine said light heartedly. "Why don't you go into the bathroom and get out of those wet clothes? I'll get us both a nice fresh cup of coffee and we'll pick up the story again later."

"That does sound good. I am feeling a little clammy but I have to ask you one question before we go in?"

Francine turned so she could face Jessica "Of course you can, anything!"

"I'm still a little puzzled. How did Elias end up being at the rental store before we even got there?"

"Sure. I was going to get there eventually but now is a good time as any. As I said, Elias and I were back out in the field. He had Trevor install an M27 real time unit in his car so he could monitor the tactical situation. I was sitting in the van when Brett Allen called in using his com gear and gave us his itinerary for the afternoon. First stop was the Dug Out, then the rental store, and finally the liquor store. Once that information was relayed, we passed it along. The locals already had an undercover officer at the Dug Out. I guess the guy frequented the place so we only needed coverage for the rental store and liquor stores. Elias immediately got on the radio and told us he was the closest field asset and since the rental store and liquor store were so close to one another, he could cover them both."

"OK, that makes a lot more sense now! I was really going crazy trying to figure that out!"

"I think Elias wanted to be there because he knew you were with Frank and wanted to make sure the job got done right. He was really scared for you, and if you don't know it, let me tell you that you mean the world to him!"

"Thanks, Francine, for everything you did. If it wasn't for such an outstanding professional group, a few more people would have ended up dead tonight!" Jessica reached back to get her bag. "I'm going to head in and change, then I'll look you up for a cup of coffee."

"I'm looking forward to it," Francine said watching Jessica run into the operations center.

Jessica didn't like to complain but the bathrooms were barely big enough to serve their designed purpose and certainly not made for people to change their clothes in. When you added the fact that wet clothes are always hard to get off, it made the bathrooms seem even smaller than they actually were.

After bumping the walls a few times with her elbows and knees, Jessica had finally got some dry clothes on, and boy did it feel good. Reaching down, she grabbed her wet jeans and folded them in half. Noticing the corner of the envelope sticking out just enough to see, she thought this was a good time to read Frank's note. The dampness of her jeans had soaked into the paper so she had to be extra careful removing it, otherwise she would have no more than paper pulp in her hand.

Working slowly and diligently, she eased the envelope out of her wet pocket and moved her finger nail carefully along the fold in the back, freeing its contents. The paper was wet too but came out of the envelope with no difficulty.

Sitting on the toilet, she unfolded the piece of paper and began to read.

Special Agent Pierce,
Something has gone wrong if you're reading this...
First of all, let me say that I'm sorry for stringing you along. I'm sure you're wondering how I knew your real identity, and unfortunately there isn't enough time for me to go into that now.
I want you to think about this. I know you're an excellent officer of the law and have a very bright mind, and if you use it, you'll find out who sent me here.
"One never knows how high the mountain truly is until they take the first step and see for the first time that there are hundreds, perhaps thousands of steps reaching even higher."
To take your first step, find the laundry man. Break the code and see where it leads you!
Be very careful. I can assure you that it's dangerous! One last reminder, don't show this to anyone.
Good luck, Jessica.
—Frank

Jessica read it over three times, almost memorizing it. She had no idea what it all meant but knew she wanted to find out. She crumpled up the letter and put it in the front pocket of her relaxed fit jeans and walked out of the bathroom.

"If he knew who I was, he must have had some idea of why I was there," she said, holding a conversation with herself. "Why did he take the ring I gave him, and more importantly why did he meet me at the boat launch and play the game?" Jessica knew the answer to the why did he play along for an entire year question, and it made her stomach turn.

"First step...laundry man...crack the code, crack the code," she repeated it in her mind, walking back towards the briefing room. Turning to go in, she was greeted by a resounding, "SURPRISE!" Almost everyone in the operation's center was there and it nearly floored her. After saying hello to everyone and thanking them for the nice surprise, she managed to get Trevor off to side.

"Trevor, we can access agent files here, right?" Jessica asked.

"Off course we can," Trevor replied, a little puzzled by the question.

"Does that access allow us to retrieve code names?"

"I can't do that, but I think you can." Trevor said.

Jessica instantly rejected that idea. "What do you mean? I'm a novice when it comes to computers."

"What I mean is *your* access code might be high enough to let you in. Where are you going with all this, Agent Pierce?" Trevor asked, becoming more puzzled as the conversation progressed.

"I know we're getting ready to wrap up here, but I need a favor from you," Jessica said, looking him squarely in the eye.

Trevor really liked Jessica and would do just about anything for her as long as it wasn't breaking any rules. "I don't mind hanging around a little longer Agent Pierce, what do you need?"

"Oh, Trevor, you're a sweetheart, and please call me Jessica. I'd like to run a search of code names. The name I want you to run, if we can do it, is Laundry Man. Let me have your pen and a piece of paper."

Trevor handed the pen from his shirt pocket and a yellow sticky sitting next to his console. After scribbling for a few seconds she handed them back to him. On the sticky note Trevor saw Laundry Man and Code: 34D23.

"Do you mind if I stand here and watch you work?" Jessica asked.

Trevor knew he'd feel funny, but used her first name just the same. "Not at all, Jessica," he said smiling as he turned toward his console.

Trevor started hammering away at the keyboard, the information on the screen changing almost as quickly as he could type. Finally, he stopped. Sitting in front of them was the portal for the highly secure code name database.

"Hey, you guys," Francine said walking by, "Elias will be here in about a half an hour. I guess they're calling him a hero now. Come on, you two! Stop playing computer games and let's start shutting this place down. I want to go home!"

"OK, Francine, we'll be right there," Jessica replied, hoping she wouldn't come over.

"I can't promise anything," Trevor said to spare her any ill will she might feel if her access level was too low. "You've also got to know up front that once I put your code in, someone is going to know you're nosing around whether you get access or not."

"Let's go. I'm not concerned about that," Jessica said, worried that when Elias got back he'd make them shut down and close up shop. "Stick my code in there and let's see what happens."

Trevor typed in 34D23 and hit the enter key. "Let's see what happens."

A few seconds went by before big red letters came back on the screen. "ACCESS DENIED."

"Oh well, Trevor, thanks for trying," Jessica said a little disappointed and turned to walk away.

"Wait, Jessica, come back, quick!" Trevor said almost in a whisper. "Someone from the outside is accessing the system in Washington and linking us in. Entering your access code must have been the trigger. It's not supposed to be possible, but it's happening right before my eyes," Trevor said staring at the screen. "I'll try to trace the origin."

"No! No! No! Leave it alone, Trevor, and let's just see what happens."

Suddenly there was a message on the screen.

I'm sorry to say that I've been expecting you, Ms. Pierce. I know you probably don't have much time. I'm the old friend Frank told you about, and as you can see, I am still very much alive. I will miss Frank.

Just to satisfy your curiosity, Frank contacted me after he found your apologetic card under his door and asked me for a favor—to find out who you really were.

Despite his past and what you think of him, he was a good man. Funny how each of us, no matter who we are, has a slightly checkered past, isn't it?

If you want to find the Laundry Man, you'll need to hit shift+F1. This will give you about sixty seconds of access time to retrieve some very sensitive files. One day in the near future our paths will cross, of that I have no doubt. Good luck with the decision you will have to make!

"What is this, Jessica?" Trevor asked, totally flabbergasted.

Reaching over his shoulder, Jessica hit the shift and F1 key and a series of files came popping up on the screen.

"What are you guys looking at?" Francine asked, stepping a little to Trevor's right so she could see.

The three of them were huddled around the monitor, silent and deep in thought. "What do we do?" Francine asked.

Jessica knew what to do. "Can you put those files on a disk, Trevor? I'd like Elias to have a look at them just as soon as he gets in."

Elias arrived at the operation's center right on time, riding high on cloud nine. He had saved the senator's grandson and eliminated the assassin. He didn't care what happened to the people at the pharmaceutical company, as far as he was concerned, his part was finished. Elias had spoken to Senator George Allen directly and was going to be his very special guest at a dinner tomorrow night that the senator was hosting in his honor. It was awesome to be riding on top.

Walking into the operations center, he was surprised that it was so quite. *Folks are shutting things down,* Elias thought. *I don't blame them I want to get home myself.*

Elias loosened his tie and walked into his office and sat down. On the screen he saw what Jessica had told him she wanted him to see.

Elias Flynn—Code name: Laundry Man
First assignment—Undercover drug fraud/bribery investigation—May '76
Associate Agency—FDA
Associate Agency Contact—Justin Fortis
Company investigated: Nelson Pharmaceutical Company—Groton, CT
Company contact: Brandon Ohliger
Investigative results: Insufficient evidence—Case Closed Jun '76.

Elias sat in his chair, staring at his computer, shaking his head from side to side. Out of the corner of his eye, he saw someone standing in his doorway, but he didn't know who it was nor did he want to turn his head to find out.

"There's more! Why'd you do it Elias? All those innocent people not to mention what you did to me!" he heard Jessica's voice ask and responded without looking at her.

"I knew you were a good cop, Jessica. I had no idea you were this good. This was going to be my last one. I was going to retire in Spain next year. Do you like Spain, Jessica?" Elias asked, not really expecting an answer. "The southern shore is magnificent."

"This was set up perfectly. I hired Frank last year and brought him back just for this assignment. Frank, he tends to get lonely, so I took care of him."

"By setting up your bogus operation and using me!" she said disgustedly.

"Calm down, Jessica. The operation wasn't bogus. It just happened to belong to me. I guess you could say more on a personal level than departmental one. It satisfied my need to have someone close just in case Frank tried to give me the slip."

Jessica's anger was on the verge of being out of control. All she had to do was squeeze the trigger but decided that would be too good for him. She wanted him in jail, waiting for his day, his accident, or his special plate of food.

I've got to be careful, Jessica thought, *not to let him draw me in.*

"Once I had everything arranged with Frank, Brandon calls and finally tells me who he needs bumped off. Brandon, you see, had been at that company forever and watched the egotistical jerk Richard Nelson the SECOND, a marginal worker at best, steal the executive office. Brandon and I worked hard on setting up that whole Russian mafia rabbit trail, and everyone, I mean everyone, bought it."

"When I found out this young man was a relative of a very powerful, senator I had to change plans. Allen had to get knocked off; there was no question about that. Frank would eventually find out and when he did, he'd have tried to get even. He has this thing about patriotism that sometimes gets in the way. I couldn't have that you see. It would totally spoil my retirement plans. My plan, and it would have worked if that kid didn't get those wacky visitations, was to finish off Frank right after he did his job. So I had to bring everybody out here to make that happen. I couldn't just let Frank complete the mission, find out about the senator then come after me. Besides, his usefulness had run out and he would be a loose end I just wouldn't need."

"Just like Justin Fortis and Brandon Ohliger," Jessica commented.

"Yup, just like Fortis and Ohliger. It's a shame too as they were both pretty decent guys but we all know what money can do. In *every* company, there is always someone that you can turn. The trick is finding out who that person is. Once you do that, it's easy to manipulate and control the circumstances that get them working for you," he said without a shred of remorse.

"When I found out you were with Frank, I was delighted. I knew Frank would try to finish the job no matter what and figured you'd find a way to get him. I was disappointed quite frankly that you weren't able to do so. Good thing the kid had that communications gear so I knew where he was going. I watched Frank walk by the front door, and when I didn't see you right behind him, I knew I had to get out there. It's that whole, if you want a job done right thing. Anyway, I yell for him to stop then wait a second or two so he has time to pull the trigger. I saw the kid hit the car so I shot Frank right through the middle of his upper back. I thought it was perfect. With both Allen and Frank dead, all my loose ends disappear."

"You run over to Mr. Allen and are very disappointed that he's still alive," Jessica said, helping him along. "If I wasn't there, you would have shot Allen *and* the girl?"

"No question about it!" Elias said. "The one thing that still bothers us is that we don't know just exactly what Brett Allen knows. He might still be a danger."

"Who's us?!" she demanded to know.

Elias just sat in his chair smiling at her.

Jessica was truly bewildered. She had never met anyone more heartless than Elias. "What kind of a man are you?"

"Just a guy doing his job," Elias said, hunching his shoulders and smiling.

"I know Frank did the Craft and Dobson murders but why did you have them killed?"

"Ah yes. They were easy to eliminate. Why? As I said, I'm just a guy doing my job. I'll give you a hint, something to chew on before we end our conversation. Global economics and power," Elias said continuing to smile.

"Who are you working for, Elias?" Jessica asked.

"Tisk tisk tisk," Elias said standing up, "Sorry, Jessica, I can't give you that information."

"Easy, Elias! Stay where you are!" Jessica said, raising her gun to the firing position.

"You've somehow managed to get files that only a very few have ever seen. This whole thing," he said, pointing to his monitor, "is so much bigger than you'll ever realize or be able to do anything about. If it isn't you who kills me, someone else surely will. My life is over now," he said, reaching inside his coat and slowly taking out his sidearm.

"Don't, Elias, don't do it!"

Two shots rang out causing Francine and Andy to run to Elias' office. Jessica was sitting on the floor staring off into space.

"Jessica, are you OK?" Francine asked.

"Oh yeah, just tired and really confused, that's all. Is he alive?" Jessica asked.

"Barely," Andy said, "I'll call an ambulance!"

"Is Trevor still here?" Jessica asked.

"He sure is," Francine said, her heart going out to Jessica. "Want me to get him for you?"

"No," Jessica said, making it to her feet, "I'll find him."

Jessica had to look harder than she expected to find Trevor and didn't see him until she went outside. He was just standing there looking into sky.

"Did you get into the records?" Jessica asked, walking over to stand beside him.

"I did. When they access his medical records, it will be there," Trevor confirmed. "Do you think it will work?"

"I don't know, Trevor; if it happened once, it's possible that it can again."

Jessica said. "We just have to keep our eyes on this and see where it goes. There's a chance that Elias could pull through," she continued, over the wail of the approaching ambulance siren, "but it doesn't look very good."

Trevor did what he thought was right and wanted Jessica to know. "I went ahead and listed them all. I never understood why people would just donate one organ, so after I entered that he was a heart donor, I plugged in all the rest."

"That was the right thing to do, Trevor," Jessica said, as they watched the ambulance come to a stop in front of the building.

Francine came running out of the building towards them yelling. "They're taking Elias to the hospital. I'm going to ride in with him. I'll let you know as soon as I hear, but the paramedics aren't very hopeful." With her information delivered, she turned around without breaking stride and got into the ambulance.

"Is it over, Jessica?" Trevor asked.

Jessica had to think about that for a minute before answering.

"I don't know. I just don't know!"

37.

Brett tried to open his eyes and see through his blurry vision. "Dad?"

"Right here, son," Michael Allen said, grabbing his son's hand, "I'm right here!"

The sedative the doctors had given Brett to help him rest also slurred his speech slightly.

"Everything's going to be OK now. I saw Russell Craft. He opened a door for me and I emerged from the darkness into something very bright. He told me that I was out of the dark now and everything would be OK. He had a key in his hand. After I walked out of dark, he closed the door behind me, and I heard him lock it. I'm free!" he said, drifting back to sleep.

"It's nothing to worry about," the doctor standing behind Michael Allen said, "probably just the medication. He should sleep through the night now. We're going to keep him here until morning so if you want, you can pick him at eight o'clock."

"We're not going anywhere," Becky said, which drew a big smile from Michael Allen.

"With the exception of me taking this young lady to get a bite to eat, we'll be staying here tonight," Michael told the young doctor.

"Don't blame you a bit," the doctor said and left.

"Come on, Becky, let's get something to eat. For the first time in a long time, I have an appetite."

"Me too, Mr. Allen. I mean Mike. For what it's worth, that doctor doesn't have a clue. Probably the medication...yeah right!"

Jessica was sitting in Elias' old office and had just finished calling everyone to have the people that were brought in released when Francine's radio broke the eerie silence.

She reached across the desk to get what used to be Elias' radio.

"It's Jessica, go ahead, Francine."

"Elias just died and they're taking him to surgery!"

"Listen to me, Francine...make sure we find out the name of the organ recipient that gets his heart!"

"I understand, Jessica. I'll let you know just as soon as I can," Francine replied.

Sitting alone at the desk, she looked at the file Trevor had put on Elias' screen. Her mind kept replaying her conversation with Trevor. "Is it over, Jessica? I don't know. I just don't know."